"Jane Po... ...'s heart."
...ling author
in the City

"Porter writes with genuine warmth and quiet grace about the everyday problems all women face."
—*Chicago Tribune*

"She understands the passion of grown-up love. . . . Smart, satisfying."
—Robyn Carr, #1 *New York Times* bestselling author of *Return to Virgin River*

"[Porter's] musings on balancing work, life, and love ring true."
—*Entertainment Weekly*

"Once more Porter is able to write about painful life situations with dignity, grace, and authenticity. What might be heavy and depressing in other writers' hands is gentle and cathartic in Porter's."
—*Library Journal*

"Two stories of heartbreak and loss wrap into one, demonstrating the depth of emotion humans are capable of and how extensive the healing process can sometimes be."
—*RT Book Reviews*

"An extremely well written, emotional, and resonating story of grief and with an ending that isn't traditionally happy and neat . . . For fans of Porter's Brennan Sisters trilogy, you'll be delighted with a number of guest appearances."
—Chicklitplus.com

"An introspective, sometimes heartbreaking, piece of women's fiction by the exceptionally talented Jane Porter . . . From tragic loss of loved ones to newfound friendships, and from the end of a love story to the beginning of a young romance, *It's You* will be sure to bring out your compassionate side."
—Harlequin Junkie

FLIRTING
with the
BEAST

JANE PORTER

BERKLEY ROMANCE
New York

BERKLEY ROMANCE
Published by Berkley
An imprint of Penguin Random House LLC
penguinrandomhouse.com

ISBN: 9780593438404

First Edition: November 2022

Printed in the United States of America
1   3   5   7   9   10   8   6   4   2

Book design by George Towne

For William Hunter Gurney Jr.,
the father of my beast.
I love you.

Chapter 1

RAIN SPLATTERED THE KITCHEN WINDOW, WHILE INSIDE the house smelled of roast turkey and cinnamon and cloves from the simmering mulled wine. Andi McDermott peeked into the second oven, where the stuffing, potatoes, and various side dishes were keeping warm. It was December twenty-second and Andi was celebrating Christmas early, hosting her stepson, Luke, and his fiancée for dinner. She'd spent days cooking, decorating the house, even putting up a big tree—a first since her husband, Kevin, died five years ago.

It was the first Christmas since Kevin died that she felt festive. Maybe it was the cooking and baking that put her in a good mood. Or maybe she'd finally accepted that Christmas would be different, and she couldn't compare the holiday now to what it had been when Kevin was alive.

But it'd be lovely to see Luke, to have him here. Her stepson was a busy doctor living in McLean, Virginia, just outside DC, and when he returned to Southern California, there were so many people for him to see that it was hard for him to squeeze her in, but this year he'd accepted her Christmas invitation, and he and Kelsey were to arrive any moment.

Andi glanced from the rain-streaked window to the small TV. The local evening news was wrapping up with a feel-good story set at Lake Arrowhead's Santa's Village. It was snowing in the mountains and the pretty reporter kept batting away fluffy flakes as she laughingly asked Mr. and Mrs. Claus if the snow would hamper the delivery of gifts. Santa Claus gave a jolly chuckle, saying that the reindeer were experts, and Rudolph always led the way. The cameraman panned over the charming snow-dusted village and the reporter concluded with the reminder that Santa's Village would be open through five o'clock on Christmas Eve, inviting all to come enjoy the live entertainment, the scheduled light shows, and of course, meet Saint Nick himself.

Andi flashed back to the year she and Kevin had taken Luke to Santa's Village. It hadn't been a successful trip. California had been in the middle of a drought. There was no snow and the pine trees looked parched. The park hadn't yet been refurbished and nine-year-old Luke wasn't impressed, announcing to a line of children that Santa wasn't real, even babies knew that.

Andi smiled, remembering the horrified looks of the other parents. Luke had never been like the other kids. He'd known from kindergarten he wanted to be a doctor, and he'd done just that.

After brushing a crumb from the counter, she turned off the double ovens and tried to remember the last time she'd been to the cabin in Blue Jay. It had been years, two or three at least, and she'd only driven up because she'd been notified by her intimidating neighbor, Wolf Enders, that one of the big sugar pines on her lot had fallen. While it had missed her cabin, the tree had crushed the old shed and was blocking her driveway.

She hadn't been able to go to the cabin immediately due

to work but drove up one Saturday morning to meet the tree removal service, paying them a fortune to cut up the huge tree and carry away the massive logs. Any moment she'd expected Wolf Enders and his German shepherd to appear, but thankfully, neither did. She'd escaped back to San Juan Capistrano without any uncomfortable scenes. To be fair, she'd never quarreled with Wolf herself, but Kevin had, and once Kevin sued Wolf for defamation of character, claiming Wolf was slandering Kevin in their mountain community; the animosity between Kevin and Wolf made trips to the cabin unbearable.

Andi had hated how Kevin obsessed about their "trashy neighbor," hated how prickly and uncomfortable she felt whenever Wolf Enders looked at her. Wolf made her feel naked and she didn't like it. She wouldn't call him trashy—she wouldn't call anyone trashy—but they definitely moved in different social circles.

The evening news ended. Andi glanced at her watch. Six thirty.

Luke said he and Kelsey should arrive sometime between five thirty and six, depending on traffic. They were coming from Newport Beach, where Luke's mom and grandparents lived, and traffic could be a bear, especially this time of year. The drizzle of rain just made it worse.

Andi drew a short breath, anxious, excited. The house looked wonderful. The brandied cranberries and green salad were already on the table. A bottle of red and white wine had both been opened just in case Luke and Kelsey didn't want the mulled wine.

Muting the TV, Andi wandered into the formal living room to fluff a couch pillow. The tree glowed with lights and shimmering ornaments. Candles glimmered on the stone mantel. A fire crackled brightly in the hearth. She'd forgotten how pretty the house looked decorated for the holidays.

Back in the kitchen she adjusted the cake stand on the

marble island, then smoothed her dark green beaded sweater over her hips. She felt a little too solid—thick in the middle—but the beaded sweater had been one of her last gifts from Kevin and she'd never had a chance to wear it before he died, so she was wearing it tonight. Tonight was a celebration. Luke would be here, and they'd be a family, and being ten or fifteen pounds overweight wasn't the end of the world. Being twenty pounds overweight wasn't the end of the world. Her weight wasn't important.

Family was.

Christmas.

Miracles.

Suddenly Andi's phone rang. It was Luke. She quickly picked up. "Hi," she said, breathlessly, leaning against the island. "Where are you? Have you hit some traffic?"

"We haven't left Mom's yet." Luke's deep voice was so very much like his dad's that it gave her a pang. "We got to talking and the time slipped away from us."

She pushed a loose tendril from her warm cheek. "That's okay. I've got everything in the oven. Just give me a buzz when you're a few minutes from the house and I'll dish up. That way we can sit down straightaway—"

"Something has come up," he said in a rush. "We're not going to be able to make it. I'm sorry. I know it's last-minute to cancel."

Her heart fell. For a moment she couldn't speak. "Kelsey's not sick, is she?" Andi asked, grateful her voice didn't quaver.

"No, she's good. We're all good. Mom surprised us with tickets to Segerstrom for the Holiday Organ Spectacular tonight. She forgot we were supposed to be going to your house for dinner, and Kelsey is an organist, she played all through school, music being her minor at Johns Hopkins, and . . ." He stopped talking, waited a split second before adding, "You don't mind, do you?"

Andi blinked hard. Her throat thickened with emotion. She minded. Oh, how she minded.

But she'd never tell him. She was his stepmom, not his mom. She couldn't afford to make a misstep.

Luke filled the silence. "I hate doing this last-minute. It's hard keeping everyone happy—"

She wasn't going to cry. She wouldn't be difficult. "I understand."

"Kelsey does want to meet you."

"Drop by tomorrow." She glanced to her double ovens, filled with turkey and casseroles. "I'll have plenty of food."

"Maybe. That could work," he said.

Her heart fell again. A maybe from Luke was never a positive thing.

He cleared his throat. "Next time we're home, we'll get together. I promise. You'll meet Kelsey before the wedding. Maybe at the bridal shower in February?"

Andi heard the maybe again. Maybe meant nada. Nothing. She hated the ridiculous pain making her chest burn. She'd always been the stepmother, never mother, never mom, never needed or wanted; at least, not by him. "Maybe," she echoed, brushing a tear from her lashes before it could fall. "Give your family my best."

"I will. Merry Christmas, Andi."

"Merry Christmas, Luke."

Hanging up, Andi set the phone down on the island and rested her hand on the cold marble, throat aching, chest tight. *Don't think, don't feel, don't get emotional. Things happen. Life happens. Roll with the punches. You're good at that.*

But her chest was on fire and she wished she were anywhere but here, in this big empty house, with a big tree that no one but her would see.

This wasn't how Christmas was supposed to be.

This wasn't how she wanted to spend the holidays anymore.

The house was too big for her. She'd been widowed too young. The memories were hard. She missed Kevin and knew he wasn't coming back. She'd even begun dating, but if she was brutally honest with herself, it wasn't going well.

Friends had invited her to join them for Christmas, but being a plus-one at Thanksgiving was a different thing from being a plus-one at Christmas. Christmas was about family, intimacy. It wasn't a party like Halloween or New Year's Eve. It was quiet, personal, *sacred*.

Heart aching, Andi turned and looked at the three-layer Christmas White Cake on the pale pink cake stand—an heirloom in the McDermott family. The Christmas White Cake could have been plucked from Santa's Village with its dusting of sparkling sugar and miniature forest of edible pine trees. It was an old *Southern Living* recipe, something Andi's mother had made when Andi was growing up, and when Andi made it the first time as a newlywed, Kevin asked that she make it every Christmas, and she did. The three-layer cake was a labor of love, and she regretted the afternoon spent making all the delicate sugar decorations.

Why had she gone to so much trouble? Why didn't she learn? Why hadn't she just bought a cake? Why had she thought Luke would show?

Luke had tolerated her, but never loved her.

He was the only child she'd ever have, and she'd tried and tried, not because she had to, but because she wanted to. And now she was fifty-seven, almost fifty-eight, with no children of her own, no husband, and another Christmas alone.

She couldn't do it. Not here. Not like this.

But the cake wouldn't be wasted. Knocking away tears, Andi reached into a drawer for a knife, cut a huge slice from the cake, and fed herself a humongous bite. The cream cheese frosting clung to her lip. The cake was moist. She cried stupid tears as she chewed. She took another bite, and then another.

The cake was perfect.

The house looked perfect.

Dinner would have been perfect.

The tears fell harder. Cake eaten, she tore off a strip of paper towel, wiped her mouth, dried her eyes, blew her nose. She couldn't do this. Couldn't fall apart just because Luke had bailed on her.

She needed to rethink the holiday, come up with a new plan, one that didn't require her rattling around this huge house on her own.

Maybe she should drive up to Lake Arrowhead and open the cabin, have Christmas there. With all the fresh snow, it'd be a white Christmas. She'd always loved the cabin. It'd be magical once she was there.

Of course there was Wolf Enders, but maybe he'd be gone. And if he was home, so what? She wouldn't be intimidated. She was tired of being stepped on. Tired of accommodating everyone else.

She was going to create new memories. Start new traditions. She'd drive to Lake Arrowhead early in the morning and have a memorable Christmas all on her own.

THE DISTANT, RHYTHMIC THUDDING WOULDN'T STOP, the dull sound irritating, interrupting Wolf's focus.

Wolf set his drafting pencil down and listened. There was a pause and then the thudding resumed. Someone was chopping something, and very close by.

But there were no neighbors close to him. He lived high on the mountain in a gated community. He was one of the few people who lived here year-round. Wolf had a small house in San Juan Capistrano in the historic Los Rios District, but he rented it on Vrbo, and thanks to its proximity to the mission, the ocean, and Disneyland, it was booked most of the time, providing steady income.

When Wolf had bought the cabin ten years ago, it was a wreck, having been on the market for over a year, the asking price—as well as the condition—discouraging other offers. But Wolf wasn't discouraged, and he'd made a low offer, aware of all the work he'd need to do, and ready to do it, as he'd just retired from defense contracting work after a long career in the Marine Corps and had time on his hands and a burning need to stay busy.

The owner rejected Wolf's offer, but when five months passed, and no other offers came in, he reached out to Wolf's real estate agent and indicated he was open to a decent offer. Wolf followed up with an offer even lower than his initial price. The owner countered. Wolf countered again, and this time his offer was reluctantly accepted. The bank wouldn't approve the loan after the home inspection report came in. Between termites and wood rot, the inspector said the 1927 cabin should just be scrapped. Tear it down, clear the lot, build again. But Wolf liked the big old logs, the vaulted ceiling, the scarred hardwood floor, and he was able to get a VA loan, allowing him to purchase the place and do the work himself. Over the next three years he fixed the foundation, replaced logs, reroofed, scraped peeling paint from original windows, put in a new furnace and water heater, and replaced the chinking. His cabin might have been rustic on the outside, but it was comfortable inside. It was Wolf's haven, and with Jax for company, he was rarely lonely.

The chopping sound stopped, but Wolf was now curious. He rose from his drafting table and stepped outside. His dog, Jax, followed, always close to his side. Wolf had only two real neighbors—the McDermotts and the Olsens—and neither had been up to Blue Jay for years. The Olsens were in their eighties and lived in a retirement community in Palos Verdes, and after self-righteous Kevin McDermott died five years ago from a heart attack, his widow didn't visit anymore. Who would be cutting what? And where?

Jax whined and Wolf touched the top of Jax's head. "Should we go check it out?" he asked.

The dog nudged his hand.

Wolf went inside, put his heavy boots on, and grabbed

his winter coat from the hook by the door before heading back out. The chopping sound echoed through the trees. Wolf crossed the shoveled walkway to stand at the top of his property. He could see a faint light glowing from one of the McDermott cabin's upstairs rooms. Someone was there.

The slope between his place and the McDermotts' was fairly steep and thickly wooded. Wolf had been adding cedars and dogwoods each autumn for the past several years, wanting more privacy, enjoying his seclusion.

Jax took off, bounding in front of him. Wolf followed, boots crunching snow. It was a cold, clear morning. The sun was shining brightly in the blue sky, casting long gold rays through the tall trees. There would be no more snow for days, maybe weeks, but this high on the mountain, beneath the shade of the big trees, the white stuff would linger.

Wolf heard a shriek and, quickening his pace, reached a clearing where Jax was staring down Andi McDermott. He snapped his fingers and Jax sat, his German shepherd's intent gold gaze locked on the neighbor's face.

He didn't blame his dog. Andi McDermott had a very pretty face.

Her head jerked up, long dark curls falling over her shoulders, wide brown eyes meeting his. "So, Axel is still terrorizing the neighborhood," she said tautly, heat blazing in her eyes.

Wolf's dog Axel had been the source of complaints that led to the lawsuit. "Axel died," Wolf said bluntly. "This is Jax. He's just eighteen months. Still a pup."

She glanced down at the black and gold dog and then up at him, expression incredulous. "A pup?"

"He is a big shepherd," Wolf agreed. He snapped his fingers again and Jax retreated, coming to stand at Wolf's side.

"He shouldn't be off leash," she said, shifting the hatchet from one hand to the other. Her gloves lay at her feet. Her hands were dark pink with cold.

"He's on my property," Wolf answered. "And so are you,"

he added, looking past her to the tree she'd savaged. "What are you doing?"

Her chin lifted. She arched an imperious brow. "Cutting down a Christmas tree."

He matched her arched eyebrow with one of his. "You don't have any trees of your own? You had to take one of mine?"

"One of yours? What do you mean?"

He pointed to a yard stake with pink tape over in the distant corner, and then to another stake on the opposite side. "That is your property, south of the stake. Everything north, including where we are standing, is mine."

"I don't know where those sticks came from, but you have it wrong. This is the McDermott property. It's always been our backyard. It's where we used to have a treehouse for Luke. This is where he always played."

"Yes, on *my* property. I never pushed it with your husband, as it seemed pointless with all the other garbage going on, but after your husband died, I had a surveyor come, mark boundaries. Just in case you chose to sell your place."

"Sell? Why would we sell? This property has belonged to the McDermotts for generations. *Generations*," she repeated. "You bought your cabin just a few years ago—"

"Ten," he corrected. "I've been here for ten years now, and I wanted to make sure we were both clear on our property lines." Wolf gestured to the stakes again. "This is all mine. That," he said, pointing to a narrow strip of land below the stakes, "is yours, plus whatever land is in front of your cabin."

"Why am I only learning about this now?"

"You haven't been here in years." Wolf caressed Jax's head. "But now that you are, you can see the stakes, and let the rest of your family know. My land versus your land."

"And this tree?" she said, two splotches of color in her cheeks, a fiery contrast to the paleness of her skin.

"Mine," he answered.

"Yes, but what do we do now? Do I leave it? Can I have it?"

"You can buy it from me."

She swallowed. "How much?"

"Two hundred dollars."

"What?"

"These are not seedlings that sprang up in this corner. I planted each of these trees over the past few years. They came in twenty-five-gallon containers—the five in this corner alone were over twelve hundred dollars."

"You're bluffing."

"You want to see a receipt?"

"Yes. No." Andi McDermott reached up and touched a line of red on her jawbone. She'd either scratched or cut herself. She turned away from him, staring at the little thicket of trees, and then the snow-covered slope. "There are so many trees here already. Why plant more?"

"For privacy. I don't want to see your cabin from my place."

She gave him a quick look before glancing away. "I would have never taken one of your trees if I'd known."

He said nothing.

"Nor would I have trespassed," she added fiercely. "You should have sent a letter, or called me, told me about the survey. You were able to let me know about the tree on the shed. Not sure why you couldn't let me know about the property lines."

"It's not a big deal."

"But it is. I've just killed one of your trees and spent money I didn't intend to spend—" She broke off, pressed her lips together. "Will you accept a check? I don't have that much cash on me right now."

"You can pay me before you head back down the mountain."

"Thank you," she said stiffly.

He held his hand out for the hatchet. She frowned, not

understanding. "I'll finish the job for you," he said. "Might as well take advantage of me since I'm here."

Wordlessly she handed him the hatchet. It took him just two whacks to fell the tree. He then made a few more cuts, cleaning up the base, making it more level, and removing a few of the lower branches so she'd be able to get it in the stand.

He returned the hatchet to her and lifted the tree, swinging it easily onto his shoulder. "Lead the way."

"You make it look so easy." She picked up her gloves and started walking. "I've been out here forever."

"It would have been easier to just buy a tree already in a stand," he answered, following her. "The tree lots are full of them."

"I thought this would be more fun. Kind of like *Little House in the Big Woods.*"

She sounded a little forlorn and looked like a marshmallow in her big white puffy coat, the tail of her red flannel shirt sticking out beneath. "Next time use an ax," he said. "It's bigger. Even a handsaw would have been better."

"Isn't this an ax?" she asked, lifting the tool.

"It's a hatchet. Axes are bigger. They usually need two hands."

"There aren't many tools anymore, not after the shed came down."

"You never replaced it," he said.

"I didn't see the point. It was mostly storage for summer months, and no one was coming here anymore."

But she was here now, he thought, climbing the stairs to her porch and placing the tree upright against the cabin.

"Thank you for the help," Andi said, facing him, her breath clouding in the air. She looked at the tree, and then reached out to touch one green springy branch.

From this angle, the tree was big. Eight feet, at least. "Do you need help getting it into the stand?"

"I'm fine. I can manage."

"If something goes wrong . . ." He didn't finish the thought. She did. "I know where to find you, but I won't."

Because they weren't friends, and her husband had hated him. Wolf nearly smiled. It was time he left, but there was something he needed to say. He hesitated. "If I hadn't said so before, I'm sorry about your husband."

"You sent a card after he died."

"Did I?"

She nodded. "It was kind of you, considering . . . the friction."

He admired the way she glossed over a five-year feud. "I'm sure it hasn't been easy, though."

"No," she agreed. "But I'm learning to stand on my own two feet, and it's been good for me. I never had to be independent before." And then, as if she'd said too much, she reached for the tree. "I promise to get you the money before I leave."

"Don't worry about it."

"No, I will. I don't want to owe you anything. It's better this way."

"Fine, then. Merry Christmas, Mrs. McDermott."

Color flooded her cheeks. Her head jerked up and her eyes, brown with those flecks of gold, locked with his, her jaw jutting, before she looked away. "Merry Christmas."

Wolf headed down the steps, crossed her driveway, and walked to the street to his driveway.

He'd never seen Andi McDermott in jeans before. Or hiking boots. Or in a puffy coat with a flannel shirt hanging out.

He'd never seen her with her dark curls down, or without her pearls, because Andi McDermott always wore pearls—pearls with cardigan sweaters, pearls with tailored blouses, pearls with a perfectly done face, even in the mountains. She dressed like the women who had been his mother's friends in New Orleans. Polished. Sophisticated. Sinless.

He liked women who sinned. Women who loved sex.

And he doubted proper Mrs. McDermott loved sex, much less hot, dirty sex. He imagined everything was tame in the McDermott bedroom, and if Kevin wanted something non-vanilla, he went elsewhere.

Although beautiful, the married Andi McDermott hadn't been his type, but the widowed Andi struggling to chop down one of his trees intrigued him.

It wasn't just the jeans and flannel shirt. It wasn't just her dark hair falling down her back in long ringlets. It was the emotion in her eyes, the red flush of exertion, the cut across her jawbone, the press of her full lips. She had the most extraordinary mouth. A mouth made for kissing. And other things.

As she'd talked, he'd let her words slide past and he focused on her lips, and the gold speckles in her eyes.

He imagined his hands on her waist and sliding them down to cup her butt. She'd be warm, soft. He hadn't been with anyone in months, too busy with project deadlines, but suddenly he felt the ache of desire.

Of need.

But they weren't friends. They weren't even neighborly. When Kevin died, they'd been in the middle of a lawsuit. Wolf had laughed when he'd read that Kevin McDermott was suing him for defamation of character, but the cost of hiring an attorney to handle the lawsuit hadn't been funny.

Andi withdrew the lawsuit three months after her husband's funeral.

Wolf had received a letter in the mail from his lawyer, letting him know it was over, done. Mrs. McDermott had paid the legal fees for his attorney, too, and after two years of bitterness, everyone was free to move on. Let bygones be bygones.

He should have thanked her today for dismissing the suit. He should have said something about it, but she'd caught him by surprise, chopping down one of his trees with a ridiculously small hatchet.

At his door, he knocked the snow from the soles of his boots and then eased them off once inside. Closing the door behind Jax, Wolf hung up his coat, straightened the boots so they were neatly lined up, and poured a fresh cup of coffee. Returning to his drafting table, he reached for his pencil and stared down at the drawings. He was behind on his deadlines, having accepted too many projects. But when you worked for yourself, you didn't like turning work away.

Yet as the minutes passed, and his coffee cooled, Wolf made little progress. He liked the addition he'd been commissioned to do. He was invested in the remodel, historic cottages being his specialty, but he kept thinking of Andi McDermott dragging that tree into her cabin and getting it into a stand. It wasn't going to be easy for her.

But she hadn't asked for his help.

She'd made it clear she could handle it.

And to be honest, he didn't want to put up her tree. He wanted to handle her.

ANDI WATCHED WOLF AND HIS DOG WALK AWAY.

She hadn't seen Wolf in years, and she'd forgotten that he wasn't just tall but big. Huge. He still carried a lot of muscle, and muscle coupled with broad shoulders and long legs made him incredibly imposing. Barefoot he was probably six foot four. In his hiking boots he was an inch taller. He'd towered over her, a barely civilized mountain man with thick salt-and-pepper hair and a matching beard.

She'd forgotten other things about him, too.

She'd forgotten the slash of cheekbones, the strong brow, firm mouth, and light gray eyes that looked like mist. He had very straight, white teeth, which she rarely saw since he wasn't inclined to smile, or speak often.

He'd spoken to her today.

Seeing him up close had been daunting. His dog—even if a new one—still terrified her. No dog should come flying down a mountain at you. No dog should stare at you as if it wanted to eat you.

Years ago, Andi had heard that Wolf used to be part of the military, and did lots of dangerous secret operations. She'd always wanted to know more, but Kevin hadn't liked her questions, unhappy that his wife was curious about someone so completely opposite himself.

Kevin *hated* Wolf. Everything about Wolf—his attitude, his motorcycles, his beard, his tattoos—set Kevin off. She'd never thought Wolf was as bad as Kevin made him out to be, but marriage was about loyalty, and the lines were drawn. She knew she had to have Kevin's back. It wasn't an option.

Taking a deep breath, Andi lifted the tree and half carried, half dragged it through the front door, into the living room. The tree was tall, but slender, and after some wrestling, and wrenching of screws, she got the trunk into the stand, and the screws into the trunk. She was not going to ask for help, and certainly not from Wolf.

It took a good ten minutes, but Andi finally had the tree in an upright position, secure in the old metal stand. She quickly wrapped strings of lights around the tree and plugged them in. The white lights shone between soft green branches.

Andi gave a little cheer, her battered self-esteem restored. She'd done it, by herself.

Everything suddenly seemed brighter.

Chapter 2

ANDI WAS IN THE MIDDLE OF HANGING ORNAMENTS ON the tree when her phone rang. It was her friend Margot, whom she'd met a year ago. Margot might have been a new friend, but she'd become a good friend. Andi and Margot talked a couple times a week.

"So how did it go with Luke?" Margot asked. "What's Kelsey like?"

Andi dug through the bottom of the box looking for extra hangers. "They couldn't make it."

"You're joking."

"No." Andi found one and hooked a glossy red glass ball, hanging it near the bottom of the tree. "They ended up having something else to do."

"But I thought you were making dinner."

"I did."

"No."

Andi found another hook, hung another red ball. "It's fine. I should have expected it."

"How could he do that to you?"

"It's fine," Andi repeated and then added, "Okay, it wasn't fine. I was pretty upset."

"I'd be livid."

"I was hurt, but I'm better." Andi straightened, glanced around her cabin with the simple tree and glowing fire. She'd even hung her red and white knit stocking from the fireplace mantel. "I've come up to the cabin. I decided I'd have Christmas here." She hesitated. "I don't suppose you'd want to come up? Join me for a few days? I have a guest bedroom and there's snow everywhere. It's gorgeous right now."

"Where is your cabin?"

"Near Lake Arrowhead in the San Bernardino Mountains." Andi hesitated. "I'm not sure how long a drive it would be from Paso Robles, though."

"Give me a sec. I'll check," Margot said. Silence stretched across the line and then Margot asked, "You said your cabin's near Lake Arrowhead?"

"Yes, just a mile from it, in the little town of Blue Jay."

"Well, I'm looking on Google Maps now, and it says from Paso, if I go through Lancaster–Palmdale, I can be in Blue Jay in less than five hours. Four and a half if there's no traffic. I think it's too late to try today, but if I leave early in the morning, I could be there by noon."

"Oh, I'd love that! How long can you stay?"

"I just need to be back by New Year's Eve. I promised Dad we'd spend the evening together. He made a reservation at his favorite restaurant."

"Margot, that would give us almost a week. Please come, and bring some books, we'll do some puzzles, drink some wine—"

"And talk."

"And talk," Andi agreed happily. "Text me when you're on the road tomorrow, and please drive safely."

After hanging up, Andi added the rest of the red balls to the tree, and then the last of the wooden toy soldiers, ornaments bought for Luke when he was a boy. While Andi added each of the soldiers, she thought about Margot. They had met last Thanksgiving at her friend Elizabeth's house.

From the first, Margot had fascinated Andi. Andi had never known a professional actress before, and if Kevin was alive, she and Margot wouldn't have become friends because all of her friends during her marriage were friends of Kevin's. He'd set the tone for their marriage, gravitating to people, and couples, like him. Like *them*. Andi's new friends—Elizabeth, Paige, Margot—were nothing like her, but they cared about her, and included her, making sure she knew she was important. Valuable.

Andi had met Paige first, as Paige was a new professor in the math department where Andi worked as the executive assistant to Dr. Nair, the department chair. Paige had introduced Andi to Elizabeth, Paige's best friend since high school and an English professor at Orange, a small, private university in Mission Viejo. Like Paige and Elizabeth, Margot was also from Paso Robles, and had attended the same high school, but was six years younger.

Paige never knew Margot, but Elizabeth did, as Elizabeth's mom had been the high school English and drama teacher, and Margot had been one of Mrs. Ortiz's favorite students, as well as the most talented drama student to graduate from Paso Robles High maybe ever.

Margot had introduced herself as Mrs. Ortiz's chauffeur, but Mrs. Ortiz indignantly replied that Margot was a gifted Broadway actress, having spent eighteen months playing Mary in the *Jesus Christ Superstar* tour, as well as Elphaba in a US tour of *Wicked*. "I could name all the shows she's been in, but I don't want to embarrass her. Margot is an outstanding actress, singer, and dancer. She can do it all."

While Mrs. Ortiz sang Margot's praises, Margot caught Andi's eye and smiled faintly even as she gave her head a small shake.

Andi decided then and there she liked Margot and they found chairs together at the Thanksgiving table, and then later, after helping with dishes, carried glasses of wine outside and talked as Margot smoked.

"I need to give it up," Margot had said, smashing the cigarette butt into a small tray. "No one in California smokes, not unless you're hanging out with actors."

Andi wondered what Kevin would think of Margot—young, slim, blond, beautiful, and still very single. Margot had never married or had kids, too focused on her career. "Why do actors smoke?" Andi had asked.

"It kills your appetite. Everyone has to stay thin." Margot grinned, flipped her straight smooth hair back. "And it gives us something to do with our hands."

Margot was the opposite of Andi in every way. While Margot was blond, Andi had thick, unruly curls, curls that would be gray if she didn't keep her roots touched up. Andi had rather boring brown eyes while Margot's were jade green. Andi looked her age—creases and lines, a soft jawline—while Margot's skin was flawless. She claimed to be midforties but looked a decade younger.

"Botox and fillers," Margot explained, when Andi commented on her amazing skin. "And sunscreen, as well as good skin care. At one point I did a lot of commercials and great skin was important with high-def TV."

"You've had the most interesting life," Andi said.

"It was, until it wasn't." Margot's smile faded, and she reached for another cigarette before stopping herself. "I was lucky. I could find work, and I worked a lot. I never got that Tony nomination, but I was in a lot of shows, and then in a half dozen touring productions. I taught acting classes, and movement classes, and did workshops and went for whatever audition my agent thought I should go to. But I never made it big, not the way you imagine when you first move to New York."

"Are you married?" Andi asked, not seeing a ring on Margot's finger, though that didn't necessarily mean anything anymore.

"I was engaged. For ten years." Margot smiled mockingly. "Patiently, and then impatiently, waiting for a wedding to take place, and then suddenly, after ten years he left me for a producer twenty years his senior. Miranda could do things for his career that I couldn't—like finance his shows. They're married now, with five-year-old twins, carried by a surrogate." Margot grabbed the cigarette box, tapped out a cigarette, and lit it. "Sorry. I need to cut back, I know."

Andi wasn't fond of cigarette smoke, but she didn't mind Margot smoking. She liked Margot, and liked her stories. Andi's life hadn't been half as interesting. Until recently, she'd never worked full-time, she'd never supported anyone financially, nor had she ever lived anywhere on her own.

"I'm boring myself," Margot said, tipping her head, exhaling a fine stream of smoke. Her blond hair spilled down her back and Andi could see a hint of dark roots. "Tell me about you. You're Southern. I'm trying to place the accent."

"My good old Tennessee twang. After twenty years in California I thought it was gone."

"It's soft, but it's pretty. Let me guess, Nashville?"

"Knoxville. Well, just outside."

"Was your husband from Tennessee, too?"

"No, but I met him at Clemson. He was a SoCal guy. Newport Beach." Andi lifted her wineglass. "That's how we ended up here."

Andi shook her head, not wanting to dwell on the past, and focused on her decorating. She stepped back from the tree and examined her efforts, trying to see if there were any branches that needed something.

But it was hard to let the past go. The past was always with her. Maybe that's why she felt stuck, trapped in her life with Kevin, even though he was no longer here.

Kevin had had a heart attack, shocking everyone, as he had been fit, athletic, a member of the Dana Outrigger Canoe Club. He was rowing when the heart attack happened.

It had been a practice run, not a race. His friends had tried to save him.

His death had knocked her sideways. For the first year she was just numb. She went through the motions. As she approached the anniversary of his death, she knew she needed a job. She needed a purpose. She couldn't just grieve. Andi put together her resume and, on advice from a friend, highlighted her skills gained from years of volunteering and fundraising. She was hired as a temp at Orange University, filling in for a secretary in the administration building, and then covering for an assistant in the math department out on maternity leave. When Dr. Nair's assistant said she wasn't going to return after all, he asked Andi to stay. She liked her job, loved working with the kids and staff. It was good to be needed.

Andi collected the ornament boxes, stacked them in the plastic tub, and carried it upstairs to the attic, glad she'd decided to come up to the cabin.

Everyone needed change. Just like marriage, not all traditions lasted forever.

THERE WERE PLENTY OF LEFTOVERS THAT WOULD HAVE worked for a nice lunch when Margot arrived, but Andi was feeling restless and wanted to head out. "Up for a walk?" she asked Margot after greeting her with a hug and helping carry her bags in.

"Yes. I'd love to stretch my legs. But I warn you, I am hungry."

"Good. We're walking to a favorite restaurant of mine. It's just a hole-in-the-wall place in the shopping center on Highway 189, but they make the best soup and sandwiches; all the bread is homemade—everything is homemade."

"Let me change into warmer clothes and my hiking boots and I'll be ready to go."

The walk downhill was easy. The road had been plowed

and it was a long, relaxed descent. Returning would be more challenging, as it would be all uphill, but they didn't have to worry about that yet.

"So how is it going?" Margot asked, adjusting her knit cap over her shoulder-length hair, their soles crunching snow and ice. "You okay?"

Andi buried her hands in her coat pockets and nodded. "I am. I'm happy. And with you here now, it feels like I'm on vacation."

"Good. The drive was pretty easy. I'm glad I didn't do it last night, though. Wouldn't have liked those turns in the dark."

"Or in the fog," Andi said. "I've done that once and didn't like it at all."

The sound of a vehicle had them stepping to the side of the road. A khaki-colored Land Rover on huge snow tires passed. Andi glanced at the driver, and her chest tightened, air bottling in her lungs. Wolf. He was wearing polarized sunglasses, but it was him.

He raised a hand. Andi's heart raced. Margot waved back.

"Do you know him?" Margot asked her, as Wolf's Land Rover continued down the road.

"He's my neighbor." She glanced at Margot, adding, "He's not my favorite person."

"Why?"

"He and Kevin didn't get along, and—" Andi broke off, feeling petty. Was that really it? Wolf and Kevin didn't get along, and she'd been drawn into it? Or was there more to it? Did she dislike him because he made her uneasy? Like yesterday, she'd felt . . . weird. Uncomfortable. Almost hostile. "We're just not on good terms, and yet because of the way our properties are, he can't reach his cabin without passing mine."

Margot seemed fascinated. "You don't speak?"

"We try not to speak. But we did yesterday." Andi touched her tongue to her upper lip. "My Christmas tree came from his yard. I thought it was growing on my property." She looked at Margot, wrinkled her nose. "Worse, it was a tree he'd planted and he wasn't happy. He said I'd have to pay him back."

Margot's jaw dropped. "How much?"

"Two hundred dollars."

"Wow."

"That's what I said." Andi pictured the tree in her living room and felt a stab of guilt, because it was a beautiful tree, and she'd killed it. Not that she wanted to think of it that way, but to be fair, until she took her hatchet to it, the tree had been alive, and then, well, it wasn't. "I hadn't expected him to be up here now. I thought he was like us, and just came in the summer."

"Is he married?"

"I doubt it. I've never seen a woman up here. He's usually alone, but if he has guests they're his biker friends, and sometimes, rarely, his sons. He has two."

"Interesting," Margot said, sounding thoughtful.

Andi glanced at her, feeling a little annoyed. "What's interesting?"

But Margot just shook her head and gave her a smile. "Nothing. It's just great to be here. I love all this cold, fresh mountain air."

They reached the highway ten minutes later and after a short walk into town wrote their name down on the list of folks waiting for a table.

"Girls, there are some open seats at the counter," one of the waiters said. "You're welcome to those, or wait for a table."

Margot looked at her. "I don't mind the counter."

Andi didn't, either, but when she glanced at the counter her insides fell. He was here. Well, there.

"Let's go somewhere else," she said, turning to Margot. "It might be a long wait."

Margot frowned, baffled. "But you said the food is amazing and it can't be more than a ten-minute wait." And then she spotted Wolf at the counter, and she elbowed Andi. "Isn't that him? Your neighbor?"

Wolf was so big his long legs took up tons of space. He filled three barstools. "Yes."

"He's *tall*," Margot said in a hushed voice, her tone almost reverent.

Andi gave her a look.

"But yes, I can see why the counter is out," she said briskly. "But we can wait for a table. I saw they have beef barley soup on the chalkboard menu. I love beef barley soup."

"There's a taco place across the street."

"We'll have to do that after Christmas."

They stepped back outside into the sunlight. Cars and trucks filled the parking lot, many of them with chains on the tires.

"I have a feeling I know why your husband didn't like your neighbor, but why don't you?" Margot asked, rubbing her gloved hands together.

"He's just . . . blunt. Rude. I don't care about his friends or tattoos, but he doesn't try to be nice, doesn't try to get along. And when he talks to me, Wolf gives me this look—"

"*Wolf*?" Margot's eyes lit. "Is that really his name, or is that what you call him?"

"No, that's really his name. Wolf Enders." Andi's stomach knotted just talking about him. "I'm not sure if Wolf is short for Wolfgang, or just wild animal, but he suits his name. His dogs are wild, too." She bent over, picked up a wet penny, dried it on her thigh, and then slipped it into her pocket. "His dog Axel apparently attacked a little dog in the community. The dog almost died. Wolf said it wasn't his dog. But Kevin said it was."

"Did Kevin see the attack?"

"No, but Axel was never leashed. We don't have fenced yards, and the dog ran wild. I was scared to death of him, so Kevin reported Wolf and his dog to the association, but it didn't change things. Even here, in a private community, people can pretty much do what they want. And Wolf Enders does."

The restaurant door opened and a waiter appeared, gestured to Andi and Margot. "I have a table for you, ladies."

They followed him to a small booth and thanked him as he placed menus on the table. "Drinks?" he asked.

"Black coffee for me," Margot said.

"Iced tea," Andi said.

"Iced tea?" Margot repeated as the waiter walked away. "It's freezing outside."

"I like iced tea with a sandwich, preferably sweet tea."

"I guess you can't take the girl out of the South."

Andi smiled, amused. "Kevin sure tried. He thought I was charming in South Carolina, still cute in Houston, but once we were in California, I didn't quite measure up anymore."

"Why?" Margot asked.

But the waiter returned just then with a steaming black coffee and a glass of iced tea. He made a little chitchat, asking about their Christmas Eve plans, before inviting them to his church's service that evening and giving them the address. When Margot answered they already had plans, he looked deflated as he took their order.

"I thought he was flirting with us," Margot said as he moved on to another table. "Turns out he was just trying to save our souls."

"Could be both," Andi said, adding a Sweet'N Low packet to her tea and giving it a stir. "Last summer I dated a man whose idea of a good time was church on Sunday, Bible study on Wednesday, and dinner fellowship with good Christians every Saturday. When I ended it, he said I wasn't listening to God's will. I asked him how he knew God's will for me. Surely, God would want to include me when He made plans for me?"

Margot grinned. "You're exaggerating."

"I wish I was." Andi removed her spoon from the iced tea, set it on the table. "Now I'm dating someone who is very nice, and very smart, as well as financially secure, and I'm miserable. I'm trying to figure out how to end it without hurting his feelings."

"Just say it's not working."

"He thinks we need to give our relationship more time." Andi grimaced. "I thought dating would be a little more fun."

"It can be, if he's fun. But if he's not fun . . ." Margot shook her head. "It's not worth it. Life is too short."

"That's how I've been feeling." Andi shifted, feeling a cool tingly sensation at her nape, and another shivery tingle down her back. She glanced up, confused, her gaze sweeping the restaurant, and then her eyes met Wolf's. She exhaled in a rush.

So that was it.

It was him.

She didn't know how long he'd been watching her, but she blushed, heat rushing through her, making her feel prickly and out of sorts. She forced her attention back to Margot. "What were we talking about?"

"How dating isn't always fun."

"Right." Andi swallowed, still warm, still shaken. There was no way that Wolf could hear them, and yet she felt caught, exposed. Maybe that's what she objected to—his intensity. The way he looked at her. The way he spoke to her. The way he seemed to dominate everything around him. She didn't like it. He made her self-conscious, aware of herself in a way that no one else did—or had, in years.

"What's going on?" Margot asked, glancing over her shoulder before looking at Andi with a knowing smile. "Oh, I see. I should have known. You have a thing for him."

"I *don't*." Andi was adamant on this point. There were men she found attractive, and men she'd like to date, but Wolf Enders wasn't one of them. She was drawn to educated men, men who liked good food and good wine, men who were cultured and were as comfortable at the opera as they were at a football game. Well, Kevin didn't like opera, but he'd take her to musicals and plays, as well as serious movies. She couldn't imagine Wolf enjoying *Moulin Rouge!* or *Hadestown*. "He's not my type."

"What's your type?"

"Kevin was my type, and Bruce could have been my type if we'd clicked more—"

"You can't count Bruce if you didn't click."

"Maybe if we keep trying."

"Ugh. Sounds miserable."

Andi privately agreed. It should be over. Maybe it was over. She hadn't heard from Bruce in a week. Admittedly, they were taking a break, so maybe he was just honoring that.

Andi didn't realize she'd even glanced in Wolf's direction again until she found herself studying his muscular back, taking in the width of his shoulders, his gray hair brushing the top of his black collared shirt. It seemed strange to see him here, out in public. She'd never seen him around Blue Jay before, and she'd come to think of him as this reclusive mountain man who rarely left the community. For that matter, she'd never seen him without a dog, and she wondered if his "pup" liked being left on his own at the cabin.

Lunch appeared, and while they ate, she and Margot discussed menus and what they wanted to eat tonight, tomorrow, and the day after. Both Margot and Andi had brought some food with them, but there were plenty of things they wanted to pick up. Margot wanted to make Christmas brunch, and Andi said she'd do Christmas dinner and tonight they'd do a big appetizer tray and nibble on things as they watched a Christmas movie.

When Andi next glanced toward the counter, she discovered Wolf had left.

She told herself she wasn't disappointed, but the counter definitely looked empty. Wolf knew how to fill a room.

After lunch and shopping, they began the trek back to the cabin. Even in good weather, it was a hike, and laden with shopping bags filled with wine, champagne, eggs, milk, and more, the walk was fatiguing, requiring Andi to stop and catch her breath, and switch hands on shopping bags. "I'm so out of shape," Andi huffed as they began walking again. "It doesn't help that I've put on fifteen pounds since Kevin died and I can't get them off."

"I think you look great," Margot said, marching up the hill without undue signs of exertion. But then, she was twelve years younger. And slim.

Andi was just about to ask to take another break when a white Mercedes approached, and they stepped onto the shoulder with its slush of dirt and snow. The car passed. The driver waved. Andi smiled. They continued on for another few steps and had to step to the shoulder again when a car pulled up next to them. It was the khaki Land Rover. Wolf.

He braked next to them, lowered his window. "Can I give you a ride up?"

Andi shook her head even as Margot said yes. "That would be wonderful," Margot added warmly. "I'm beat."

Andi gave Margot a look of displeasure. "You can't be serious," she said under her breath.

"It's thirty-one degrees, I'm freezing, and we have at least a half mile still to go," Margot answered. "All uphill."

"I thought you were doing fine."

"I wasn't going to make you feel bad, but if I can get a ride? Heck yeah." She turned to Wolf and gave him a smile. "I'm Margot Hughes, a friend of Andi's."

"Wolf Enders," he answered. "Hop in."

Margot glanced at Andi, expression clear. Andi needed to get in the vehicle, and not make a fuss.

Andi knew she had a choice. She could accept a ride,

make her guest happy, *and* avoid a scene, or she could be an ass and trudge along with her heavy bags and blistered hands.

A ride it would be.

Margot took the passenger seat and Andi climbed in the back. The Land Rover was lifted, and a high step up, made trickier by the narrow opening of the back door and Andi's hips, and the clinking wine bottles. But eventually she got settled and tried to buckle in, but the seat belt didn't work.

She almost said something but didn't. What was the point? Sighing in exasperation, she looked up. Wolf's gaze met hers in the rearview mirror, locking with hers. There was something in his eyes that always made her feel warm. She didn't understand it and today it was doubly confusing. For a moment she couldn't focus, thoughts scattering, and then Wolf looked away, shifted into drive, and the spell was broken.

It felt like he was playing a game with her. He enjoyed this, whatever it was, which just made her fume.

She didn't like feeling beholden to Wolf. It was one thing to drop the lawsuit, but that didn't mean she'd forgotten the years of animosity between Kevin and Wolf. Wolf was no angel. She knew he'd gone out of his way to antagonize her husband. Both men had been childish.

Margot chattered as Wolf drove, telling him she'd just arrived from Paso Robles, where she'd been raised, and was staying with Andi through New Year's Eve day. Wolf told her he liked the Central Coast, and used to go pig hunting on a ranch not far from there, the ranch close to the little town of Parkfield.

Margot knew of Parkfield and asked if he'd ever been to the Memorial Day rodeo there. Wolf said he hadn't. Margot confessed she'd never been to it, either. They talked until Wolf reached Andi's driveway, and shifted into park.

Andi quickly climbed out of the back, bumping her hip on the door and landing on a patch of ice, which nearly sent her flying. She grabbed the side of the car, righted herself, and prayed no one had seen. But Wolf did. Of course he'd been watching her with that narrowed silver gaze that made her feel like a bug under a microscope.

She met his eyes, feeling fierce. She'd had enough of him, and his ridiculous macho, alpha energy. "Thanks," she said crisply, closing the door. "Appreciate the ride."

And then as Andi headed for the door she heard Margot echo her thanks, and then invite Wolf to join them later for a glass of wine and some appetizers. "We're making a charcuterie board," she told him. "We thought it'd be fun to have little plates instead of a big dinner. Drop by if you have nothing else to do—"

"No," Andi said, turning quickly and cutting Margot off. "What I mean is that I doubt a charcuterie board would appeal to Mr. Enders. Men like hearty dinners. Roasted pig and things like that." Andi gave Wolf a significant look. "And I'm sure he has plans, something far more interesting than watching an old musical with us."

The corner of Wolf's lips lifted, his silver gaze rested on her face, a glint in his eyes. "I don't think I've ever had a charcuterie board before—"

"We're watching *Meet Me in St. Louis*," Andi said.

"And I'm opening wine at six. Come anytime," Margot continued as if Andi hadn't interrupted. "Thanks again for the ride." She flashed Wolf a last smile before walking up the path to the cabin.

It baffled Andi that Margot would do that. Her temper surged before she checked it, reminding herself that anger never helped anything. She shifted and briefly glanced at Wolf. "You're not going to come tonight, are you?"

"Kevin would disapprove?" he asked mockingly.

"No, because I'd disapprove." She straightened her shoulders, lifted her chin. "We're not friends. We've never been friends."

"True. But surely we don't have to disillusion Margot.

She seems to think we'd get along, given the opportunity." He shrugged. "We might. Stranger things have happened."

Her chest tightened. Something inside of her heart ached. There were times she felt Kevin's death keenly. Now was one of them. Andi changed hands on her shopping bags. "Except for sharing a property line, I don't think we have anything in common."

"I'm sure there's something."

"It wasn't a challenge, Mr. Enders."

"I wasn't making it one, Mrs. McDermott." His cool silver gaze heated. "Not unless you're interested in some fun and games?"

A shiver raced through her. Not fear, but something else, something she didn't want to identify. "No," she said shortly, walking away from him.

"Judy Garland," he called to her retreating back.

"What?" she asked, pausing at the top of her porch stairs.

"She stars in *Meet Me in St. Louis.* It's a good choice for tonight, but I would have thought you'd go with a Bing Crosby movie, maybe *White Christmas* or *Holiday Inn.* Maybe *Holiday Inn*, as it was filmed first. They used the same set, you know. Just a little Christmas trivia."

She looked at him, really looked at him, emotion rising. She missed a past she no longer had and was overwhelmed by a future she'd never expected. She didn't want to be unkind to Wolf Enders, but he was unsettling . . . unnerving, and not at all good for her peace of mind. "You're not going to drop by tonight, are you?"

"No."

Andi nodded, grateful, and disappeared into her cabin.

ANDI COULD TELL THAT MARGOT WAS HOPING WOLF would show. She'd cleared off the coffee table, set the charcuterie board in the middle, added small plates, and fanned the package of festive cocktail napkins she'd picked up that afternoon at the grocery store. She opened the wine, placed three glasses on the table.

"He might not come," Andi said to Margot.

"I think he might."

"You don't know him like I do."

"He seemed like he wanted to come by," Margot said, taking a seat on the couch and covering her legs with one of the soft red plaid blankets Andi had brought out of the linen closet. "What else does he have to do?"

"I don't know, but he's a loner. He prefers his own company."

Margot gave Andi a teasing smile as she reached for her glass of red wine. "You apparently have a great deal of insight into this neighbor you don't like." She took a sip of the wine. "Mmm, good."

"Is it another of your Paso Robles reds?"

"It is."

Andi sat down and took the glass Margot had poured for her and picked up the remote, doing a search for *Meet Me in St. Louis*. It didn't pop up on any of their streaming options. *White Christmas* did, as well as *Miracle on 34th Street* and *It's a Wonderful Life*. "What do you think?" Andi asked.

"I've seen those so many times. Let me look up classic Christmas movies on my phone. Maybe we could find something else we could watch." She spent a few minutes scrolling through websites and then found one. "What about *Christmas in Connecticut*? They call it an early rom-com. Have you seen it lately? I haven't watched it in years."

"I've never seen that one," Andi admitted, but she was able to find it, and as she pressed play, she turned to Margot and lifted her wineglass. "Thank you for joining me in Blue Jay for Christmas."

Margot smiled. "Thank you for inviting me."

They clinked glasses.

"So you're not still mad I invited Wolf to come by?" Margot asked, settling into the couch cushions.

"I wasn't mad," Andi said, taking an olive and popping it into her mouth.

"You were. I kept waiting for you to say something."

"I was rattled. I'm not comfortable around him, but I wasn't going to have a tantrum."

"You don't need to be BFFs with him, but being friendly might be useful. You're awfully isolated here."

"I'm not at the cabin that often."

"Even more reason to have a friendly face next door."

"Have you seen Wolf's face? It's not friendly."

Margot laughed, the sound warm, husky. "I have seen his face, and I like it."

"You do?"

Margot nodded. "I think he's really good-looking. He's all man."

"So you'd go out with him?"

"No, I'd stay in with him. I bet he's great in bed."

Andi blushed, unable to imagine it. "Now, this is where you can tell we're different generations. I never look at a man and think about sex, and whether he's good at it."

"Oh, come on."

"I don't. In fact, I almost never think about sex."

Margot tossed a pillow at Andi. "You're not that old."

"You're still in your forties, you have mojo. I don't—"

"The right man will give you mojo. You haven't met the right man yet. Unless Bruce ticks that box?"

Andi would never admit it, but she and Bruce *had* slept together twice, and it was something she'd rather forget. He'd struggled to maintain an erection the first time. The second time he took something and he was hard, but she just didn't feel anything, and she couldn't climax, which seemed to frustrate him. After it was over, he asked questions about her sex life with Kevin—specifically, could she orgasm? Did she have difficulty in bed?

The answer to both was yes, and no.

Kevin could always make her climax, and making love with her husband hadn't been a chore. But the conversation with Bruce had felt like an accusation and she'd been turned off ever since.

She'd never felt so fat and unattractive in her entire life. Bruce had been clueless, though. He wanted to spend the night while she'd wanted him gone. It took every bit of her patience to get him dressed and out the door. She avoided his calls for a few days, which was admittedly immature, but she needed time to figure out what she wanted. Her silence frustrated Bruce, and he got mad. His show of temper alienated her even more. They agreed to take a step back, reevaluate their relationship after the holidays.

As if reading her mind, Margot pressed, "How are you and Bruce in the bedroom?"

"Not great," Andi admitted. "But it's probably a me thing, not a him thing. Sex is just one way of communicating, but there are other ways to feel close. Talking. Cuddling. Spending time together. I don't feel a need to take my clothes off."

"You liked cuddling with Bruce, then?"

Bruce was really intelligent, and very successful. She did enjoy talking to him, and liked going to dinner and movies with him. It had been nice holding his hand, and sitting together on the couch had been pleasant. But after actually sleeping with him? No. She didn't want to do it again. She just felt better about herself when she kept her clothes on. "It's hard moving on from Kevin. He was my first, and I loved being with him. I felt safe with him, and making love was satisfying. It's not the same now." Her voice cracked and her eyes stung. Chilled, she got off the couch, went to stand in front of the fire, hands hovering over the flames. "I'd rather never have sex again than do it and feel nothing."

"Have you enjoyed it with anyone else . . . besides Kevin?"

"I don't just hop in men's beds, Margot."

Margot spluttered on a laugh. "I never said you did. But it's okay to enjoy sex. Sex is healthy. It's good for you—"

"And for thirty-five years of my life, I only had it with one person." Andi turned to face Margot. "Wasn't it hard for you to move on after your engagement ended? You and Sam were together for over ten years."

"Twelve," Margot said briskly, and she picked up the remote, pushed pause on the movie since they'd just talked all the way through opening credits, and hit rewind. "And once he ended our engagement, I dated like a madwoman. I spent my entire thirties locked down, so I played the field and caught up on lost time. It got serious a couple of times, but never so serious it progressed to marriage."

"And you wanted to marry."

"Only if it was the right person. But Prince Charming never came along."

"Do you believe in soul mates?"

"No, and I don't think there's only one person for each of us. I think there are hundreds of possibilities. It's just a matter of being in the right place at the right time when the right person appears. That's the tricky part." Margot pulled another blanket from the arm of the couch and draped it over herself. "Now, let's watch the movie. We're supposed to be having a double feature tonight."

Andi returned to the couch, covered herself with a blanket, and sipped wine and nibbled on appetizers while watching *Christmas in Connecticut* and then *The Holiday*, starring Kate Winslet and Cameron Diaz. By the time the movies were over, it was past eleven, and Andi was sleepy, a tiny bit tipsy, and ready for bed. Margot was ready to call it a night, too, and washed the wineglasses as Andi packaged up the food.

After locking doors and turning out lights, they headed upstairs.

"Does your power ever go out?" Margot asked from her bedroom doorway. She had the room that used to be Luke's, but the bunk beds had been replaced with a queen bed.

"More often than it should," Andi said, smothering her yawn. "It's even worse after a heavy snowfall. But if we lose power, we have the fireplace for heat. It's gas. The stove is gas, too. We won't freeze and we won't go hungry."

"And coffee?"

"I have a drip carafe as a backup. I learned that one year the hard way."

"You think of everything." Margot crossed the hall and gave Andi a quick hug. "Merry Christmas. Thanks for being such a good friend, even when I'm a pushy broad."

Andi laughed. "You're not a pushy broad, you're my friend, and I value your opinion. I love having you here. Sleep well."

"You, too."

But tucked into bed, Andi couldn't fall asleep, despite the late hour and the wine humming in her veins, because every time she closed her eyes she pictured Wolf, and the way he looked at her, his gaze focused, intent.

He was as different from Kevin as a man could be. She still didn't know who actually started the fight, but Kevin couldn't even pretend to get along with Wolf, not even for her sake. There was one time, a year before Kevin's death, when they'd packed to head home but their car wouldn't start, and she'd gone up and down the road, knocking on cabin doors, hoping someone would be home, and that someone could help them jump-start their car, because of course the jumper cables were back in San Juan Capistrano in the other car.

But no one answered the door, and then, desperate, and after discussing it with Kevin, who was still waiting by their car, she'd gone up to Wolf's cabin, walking up that long,

long driveway in the dappled shade of ancient trees. She'd forced herself to knock on his door, and forced herself to stand on his front porch, waiting patiently. He'd finally opened the door and she politely asked for help, explaining the situation, and he'd had the nerve to smirk at her.

Smirk.

Silver gaze hot. Lips curved. Expression taunting.

"Not prepared?" he said, leaning against the door frame, his black corduroy shirt halfway unbuttoned, revealing a scar on his broad, tan, tattooed chest. Many tattoos. He had a muscular chest, too, but she didn't care about that, and she wasn't going to study the tattoos, either, even though there was one with wings, and maybe a gun.

"Can you help us or not?" she said tautly, chin jerking up, trying to meet his eyes but failing, and so she studied his collarbone, and the scar running below. It was the palest pink, an old wound, disappearing into a tattoo. "If you can't, just tell me."

"You ask so nicely," he said.

His sarcasm stung. Flushing, she looked up at him then. Kevin was tall, but Wolf towered over her. He had a hard face, high angled cheekbones, a firm mouth. This close she could see the small white line beneath his lower lip, and another scar that intersected his dark eyebrow. His eyes were the shade of steel, but his lashes were thick and dark, like his shaggy hair.

It was the closest she'd ever been to him, and she sucked in a deep breath, feeling raw and bruised. He was overwhelmingly male, overwhelmingly physical. She felt naked, and uncomfortable, so uncomfortable it was painful. "Do I need to ask more nicely?" she said through gritted teeth, trying to keep her wits about her. She'd heard about men like this but had never met one until now.

"Maybe." He smiled at her, the smile of a big, dangerous, confident animal.

"In that case, maybe I won't."

He laughed lowly, and his gaze slowly skimmed her, lazily sweeping over her face, spending time on her mouth, and then dropping to her chest, and below. "I have cables in the car. I'll drive over to your place." The corner of his mouth tilted. "If you wait a moment, I can give you a ride."

Heat rushed through her in unrelenting waves. Could he tell she was blushing? Did he know the effect he had on her? "I'll walk, thank you."

"Coward."

Her eyebrow shot up. Her lips parted. Did he really just say that? But before she could speak, he disappeared into his cabin and she went flying down the front steps and then dashed down his long, steep driveway, jogging back to where Kevin waited with the car.

"Not home?" Kevin asked.

Her heart was racing. She felt tingly and breathless, hot and exposed, as if she'd just done something illicit. "No, he's on his way."

Andi had stayed in the cabin while Wolf jumped the McDermotts' car, and then he disappeared and she and Kevin drove home.

Andi turned over in bed, curling on her side. Okay, so she had reasons to be uncomfortable around Wolf. She wasn't just being unkind. Wolf liked the tension between them. He enjoyed rattling her. He enjoyed being wicked.

Chapter 3

THE NIGHT WAS SILENT AND COLD. WOLF'S BOOTS crunched ice as he and Jax walked up the road to the top of the mountain. Years ago there had been a pair of cabins at the ridge, but they'd burned down in a forest fire, and the association had bought the land, turning it into common property, shared for everyone to use and enjoy.

The ridge was a good twenty-minute walk from Wolf's cabin, uphill, and a welcome exertion after hours spent at a desk.

Wolf wasn't a Christmas person. He didn't have any holiday traditions. For him, it was just another day. He couldn't remember the last time he'd celebrated Christmas. Had to have been when the boys were young, and still believed in Santa and were sleepless on Christmas Eve, excited for the morning.

His boys weren't young anymore, though. Stone, his oldest, was gone. The other two were in their twenties. Lincoln lived on the East Coast. Maverick was back at Camp Pendleton. He hadn't seen either one in months, but there were no hard feelings between them. His sons had careers, and when they did get some time off, they usually headed to New Orleans to see their mom. He preferred it that way, too.

Reaching the mountaintop, Wolf looked up at the sky, the stars bright against the dark purple backdrop. He could see the Big Dipper, the Little Dipper. It always reassured him that the constellations were the same. Life on earth brought change, but the stars provided continuity. Reassurance. Even after all he loved was gone, some form of life would go on.

Wolf headed back to his cabin, Jax at his side, ears pricked, listening to the hoot of an owl and sporadic rustling from within the woods.

As he neared the turnoff of his driveway he could see a glow of light from the upstairs of the McDermott cabin, and then the light went out, and the cabin was dark.

Andi shouldn't interest him.

There was no reason to have her on his mind.

He wasn't going to let himself think about her. There was no point. She wasn't for him. She was off-limits, Andi with the full soft lips, and curious brown eyes.

WOLF WOKE TO JAX GROWLING. HE THREW THE COVERS back when he heard a door downstairs open and close.

Barking, Jax was off the bed, lunging at the bedroom door. Wolf pulled on a hooded sweatshirt and glanced out the upstairs window, spotting a big matte black truck parked in his driveway.

Maverick's truck.

"Enough," Wolf said to Jax. Jax stopped barking, but his gaze was locked on the door. "Stay," Wolf added, pointing to the floor as he opened the door.

Jax did.

Footsteps sounded on the stairs. "Wake up, old man,"

Maverick called, his big frame filling the stairwell. "You've got company."

Wolf met his youngest halfway down the stairs and gave him a bear hug. "Watch yourself. I can still take you."

"Ha. I'd like to see that."

Wolf grabbed Maverick's shoulder, squeezed. Maverick was solid, tanned, a little weathered. He looked happy, healthy. Some of the tightness inside Wolf eased. "What are you doing here?"

"Got some time off. Thought I'd come see you."

"What about your mom?"

"She's got Linc, she's fine." Maverick shivered. "Can I turn up the heater? It's freezing in here."

"Sure. You can make coffee, too. I'm going to get dressed."

Jax had appeared in the doorway behind Wolf, and the dog followed Wolf back into the bedroom. Wolf gave the Jax a firm pat. "He's one of the good guys. You can relax."

Downstairs, Maverick had coffee brewing and was unpacking a bag of groceries. He'd brought a cream cheese danish for breakfast, plus a wedge of ham, as well as steaks for dinner and crab and shrimp he'd picked up the day before at the fresh seafood market at the San Diego Harbor.

They watched a football game for part of the afternoon and then Maverick said he was hungry, and Wolf joined his youngest in the kitchen, thinking he'd lend a hand, but Maverick had a plan, and after turning on the oven for the sweet potatoes, he mixed ketchup, grated horseradish, Worcestershire sauce, and juice from half a lemon into a cocktail sauce for the shrimp.

"Why didn't you tell me you were coming up?" Wolf asked, leaning against the log wall.

Maverick sprinkled hot sauce into the mixture. "I wasn't sure I could make it, and didn't want to get your hopes up." He used a small spoon, tasted the sauce before adding more hot sauce. "Mom wanted me to come see her. I think I told you Linc is there. But I didn't feel like getting on another plane." He added pepper, another squeeze of lemon, tasted it again. "You still like heat?"

"I do."

"Me, too." Maverick stirred, tried it once more, nodded. "Good." He looked at his dad. "What's happening with the house in San Juan? Is it still rented?"

"Through the first week of January. I've got a couple weeks open, and then February until fall is booked pretty solid."

"It's been a good investment."

Wolf nodded. "Why aren't you at your mom's?"

"I already told you."

"She takes it hard when you don't come home."

"She's got a full house. She's okay." Of Wolf's three sons, Maverick most closely resembled him, at least before Wolf went gray. Dark hair. Light eyes. Big frame. Two-day growth of a beard on his strong jaw. "You're the one I worry about. You're the one who pushes everyone away."

"I don't."

Maverick sliced up a baguette, scooped it up from the cutting board, and put it on a plate with the crab, shrimp, and sauce. "No one's heard from you for a while."

Wolf shrugged. "I took on too much work and got behind after the surgery. I'm still playing catch-up."

"Are you having pain still?"

"It's better than before the surgery. But there's no way to replace everything that hurts. I just have to tough it out."

"Is that what we have to do, too? Tough it out?"

"What do you mean?"

"You don't return our calls. You don't make calls—"

"I didn't think there was anything to say," Wolf interrupted.

"Hello, how's it going, nice to hear your voice, son."

"That goes without saying."

Maverick lifted a brow, expression quizzical. "Does it?"

Wolf sighed inwardly. Maverick could be relentless. "You know I'm not a phone guy."

Maverick glanced into the dining room, where the drafting table dominated half the space. Wolf followed his gaze, and saw the huge bin of rolled-up plans and papers. More plans covered the drafting table. It looked cluttered to Wolf, and that bothered him.

"I really am working," Wolf said. "And you know if you need me, I'm there."

"What about the others?" Maverick answered.

For a moment Wolf thought of Andi, and then pushed her image aside. He shouldn't be thinking of her. No good would come from thinking about her. They weren't going to get together. She wasn't the kind of woman interested in a one-night stand, and that's about all Wolf wanted. Hot, satisfying sex, followed by a quick, satisfying goodbye.

"Like who?" Wolf asked. "Lincoln seems good."

"Lindsay," Maverick said. "I'm worried about her. She and Mom have been having issues for a while, but now it's getting worse."

Wolf suddenly felt the need for a beer. He went to the fridge and drew out two bottles, putting one down on the counter next to Maverick's cocktail sauce and carrying the other back to the wall he'd been propping up. Wolf used the underside of his heavy silver ring to pop the bottle cap. "What's going on?"

"Mom thinks Lindsay needs to get a job, or do something besides stay in bed all day, and Lindsay thinks Mom needs to stop telling her what to do."

Wolf's lips quirked. "But that's your mama's special gift."

Maverick popped his own beer cap. "Mom's tough. Nothing is going to break her, but Lindsay . . . not sure she can handle Mom's helpfulness." He made air quotes around the word *helpfulness*.

"No one is making Lindsay stay there."

"Do you really want her and Charlie on their own?" Maverick turned around, faced his dad, muscular arms folded over his broad chest. "Mom can be difficult, but she takes care of Charlie. Makes sure he's looked after."

"You make it sound as if your mom is doing the parenting."

"She's doing more than she planned on."

"Your mom feeling resentful?"

"Mom's fed up."

That would lead to trouble. A resentful Jess wasn't pleasant company. "When did you last talk to her?" Wolf asked.

"Who? Mom, or Lindsay?"

"Both."

"Talked to Mom yesterday while I was shopping at the fish market, and talked to Lindsay briefly this morning. I called just when they were sitting down to Mom's Christmas brunch, so we couldn't talk long."

"Your mom still does those big holiday brunches?"

"She still thinks she's Brennan's. Only thing missing from her menu is the turtle soup."

Wolf smiled. Jessica had grown up without a lot of money, just outside Baton Rouge, and she'd envied Wolf's childhood in New Orleans's fabled Garden District. She'd practically swooned the first time he showed her his grandparents' mansion on St. Charles Avenue. "If you only spoke to Lindsay for a moment, how do you know she's not doing well?"

"Because I can tell. She sounded tired. Depressed. Here it's Christmas morning and there's no emotion in her voice, none whatsoever."

Lindsay had been low for a long time now. Even Wolf knew that much.

"Do you want this in a cocktail glass? Or deconstructed?" Maverick asked, gesturing to the platter of crabmeat and shrimp.

"No cocktail glass," Wolf answered.

"Then come help yourself," Maverick said. "I'm going

to put the yams in the oven and when they're ready, I'll cook up the steaks."

Wolf liked watching his son move about the cabin kitchen. He was comfortable, confident, relaxed. But then, Maverick didn't let very much get to him. He'd been twelve or so when Wolf and Jess divorced, and while he hadn't been happy about the divorce, he also didn't make a fuss, and kept his teenage drama to a minimum. Now, Lincoln, Wolf's middle son, had made it hard. Linc was a hard-ass just like Wolf's father, Wolfgang Enders II.

"Dad, when did you last talk to Lindsay? And Charlie?" Maverick tossed the potatoes into the hot oven. "You promised them both you'd be there."

Wolf shifted, restless. Those were pretty strong words coming from his youngest. But then, Maverick had never had any problem speaking his mind, not to Wolf. Not to anyone. Perhaps being the youngest gave him the most confidence. "I was there end of summer," Wolf said.

"Summer. Four months ago. Which might as well be forever to a three-year-old." Maverick gave him a steady look. "Unless you don't care if your only grandson remembers you."

"Don't be an asshole."

"Me? The asshole? Dad, I talk to Lindsay every week. I FaceTime regularly with my nephew. I've gone out there—"

"Alright, fine. You're a paragon of virtue. I should be more like you."

Maverick looked disgusted. "You couldn't if you tried. I'm good with people. You're not."

"I don't need people, not like you."

"It's not that I need people, but I understand people. You, on the other hand, seem perplexed by the human race."

Wolf suppressed his smile. Maverick had always been smart, not just book smart, but people smart, street smart. "So what are you working on now? Anything you can tell me?"

"No." Maverick lifted his beer and took a swig. "I'll be

heading overseas, though, end of this week. Things are getting hot. Not sure when I'll be back."

Those weren't the words a dad liked to hear, not even a dad who'd spent almost twenty-five years serving his country. "Stay safe."

"I try."

Wolf had been home between deployments when he'd heard Maverick compared to Superman for the first time. Maverick had only been a junior in high school, but he was strong, muscular, with thick brown hair, blue eyes, dimples, and his ridiculous square jaw. Like his older brothers, he played all sports, and played them well, but unlike his brothers, Maverick wasn't deeply invested in high school. He rarely dated, didn't want a girlfriend, didn't care about school dances. He had other things on his mind, bigger things, like learning Mandarin and Russian, and studying advanced mathematics. He earned a full ride to Tulane, where he played football, but again football wasn't his passion. He just happened to be good at it. He had his sights set ahead, on life beyond college, adding more languages to his study of chemistry and electrical engineering. When Maverick shared with his dad that he was working on Korean and Arabic, Wolf had a pretty good idea of what his son planned to do. Maverick chose not to share the language studies with his mom, and she was perplexed by his decision to move to Glynco, Georgia, after graduation, but Wolf knew that's where the Federal Law Enforcement Training Center was for the CIA.

"Your mom can't lose another son," Wolf said gruffly.

"You're not as tough as you sound, old man," Maverick replied, giving his dad a small, sympathetic smile. "You can't handle losing another one, either."

ON CHRISTMAS MORNING MARGOT AND ANDI TOOK A walk after Margot's brunch of cinnamon roll French toast with lots of crispy bacon. It was either walk or go back to bed, and Andi was determined not to gain weight over the holidays.

They bundled up and headed out, sun shining, air crisp, cold, invigorating. They decided to walk up to the top of the mountain while it was early and they had energy, and use the downhill to their advantage on the way back. Margot told Andi about her job, and her boss, Sally, who'd been married five times and had finally decided she'd had enough men. But Sally had learned something from each of her marriages, had come out financially smarter, too, and was the owner of one of the top property management firms on the Central Coast.

"She's very savvy," Margot told Andi as they took a rest on the side of the road. Sunlight streamed through the tall trees, casting long shadows on the asphalt. "But a year ago she bought this small theater complex—it had been on the market for years, and it had been turned into a storage facility when she bought it—and she has this plan to make it a thriving arts center, for tourists and locals."

"You'd be perfect for that," Andi said.

"I'm not touching it. Not getting involved. I have given up theater. I have no desire to help run a community theater," Margot said grimly. "I can't even drive past the place without shuddering."

"Is it in such bad shape?"

"Sally's spending a fortune restoring the theater complex. There's an adjoining café and an old brick courtyard that probably was once beautiful, but after years of neglect, it's just sad. As soon as it starts to warm up a little, the new landscaping goes in, and that will help, but I think she's wasting her money. Cambria is such a small place, and the theater doesn't even seat one hundred. I'm not sure how she'll ever earn her investment back."

"Maybe it's a deduction kind of thing? Maybe she needs the write-off?" Andi suggested, slightly out of breath but pushing on, as they weren't far from the top now.

Margot thought about it for a moment then nodded thoughtfully. "Maybe. I never considered that."

They fell silent, both needing to conserve energy until they reached the summit. Andi was perspiring, and breathing heavier than she liked. She was out of shape. It wasn't good for her. She didn't need to have a heart attack like Kevin.

"What a view," Margot said, doing a slow circle. "Looks like there was a fire here at some point."

"There were cabins up here a long time ago. Burned down in a fire, never rebuilt." She pointed to some of the blackened trees. "But I think those are from a more recent fire. Poor California and all the wildfires."

Margot nodded and they picked their way through a clearing to sit on a fallen log. "What's that lake?" Margot asked, pointing.

"That's Lake Arrowhead." Andi hunched her shoulders against the icy wind. "I haven't been up here in years. Kevin and I used to do this hike in summer. We'd go in the morning before it was hot."

"You said your cabin is a family cabin on the McDermott side," Margot said. "Does that mean it'll go to Luke one day?"

"It's actually already in his name. But Luke isn't interested in it. He's planning on selling one day." Andi glanced at Margot. "Just hope it won't be for a number of years. I'd like to spend time up here again."

"I would if I were you. It's so peaceful."

But the peace was disturbed by the crunch of footsteps and the bark of a dog.

Wolf, Jax, and a younger man who was every bit as big as Wolf, with dark hair and dark stubble, appeared on the mountain, coming from the opposite direction. Jax let out another short bark. Wolf put one hand on the top of Jax's head, keeping him at his side.

Margot gently elbowed Andi. "Do you see what I see?"

Andi's pulse raced. Her mouth dried. "I do," she said, taking a quick drink from her thermos.

"There's two of them now."

Andi had noticed. "I think that's his son. He has two. I haven't seen either of them in years, but I'm guessing that's the younger one."

"He's gorgeous."

Andi wrinkled her nose. "Maybe if he shaved?"

Margot laughed. "You don't like beards?"

"He just looks like trouble."

"Like his dad." Margot flashed Andi a wicked smile. "You've got to appreciate a bad boy."

"Do I?"

There was nowhere to go, and no polite way to pass without each acknowledging the other. Of course Margot had to greet them first, stopping them.

"Merry Christmas," Margot sang out, smiling widely. "It's a gorgeous day, isn't it?"

The men stopped and Andi and Margot stood. Wolf did the introductions. "Margot, this is my son Maverick. Maverick, this is Margot, Andi McDermott's friend, and I'm sure you remember Andi?"

"Your dad's archnemesis," Andi said, smiling ruefully and extending her gloved hand to Wolf's son. "It's nice to officially meet you. I've just seen you from afar."

Maverick's hand closed around hers, giving her a firm shake. "Nice to meet you as well, Andi." Maverick had light blue eyes and dark brown, nearly black hair, and when he smiled, a dimple deepened in his cheek. Put him in blue tights and a red cape and he could pass for Superman. He shook Margot's hand next.

Margot seemed dazzled by Wolf's son. "I understand there's another one of you," she said. "Does your brother look like you?"

Maverick's expression didn't change, but Andi felt the energy shift.

"Lincoln's not as good-looking," Maverick said easily, still smiling. "And his hair is lighter. He's more fair, like Mom."

Margot and Maverick talked for another minute or so. Andi glanced up, her eyes meeting Wolf's. Their gazes locked and held. He wasn't in a hurry to look away. If anything, he seemed to be drinking her in, taking his fill. She forced her gaze away, even as her cheeks grew hot. A ripple of sensation, part tingle, part shiver, coursed down her spine.

Okay, she wasn't afraid of him, but she wasn't comfortable, either.

Jax whined once, bored by the conversation. Wolf patted him and then, using Jax as an excuse, he and Maverick continued on.

Margot faced Andi in the clearing. "Wow," she murmured. "That was a Christmas treat."

Andi laughed. "You might say you've given up acting, but you still have a very dramatic flair."

"I just appreciate good-looking men, and Wolf and his son are gorgeous. Seriously sexy. How old do you think he is?"

"Wolf? Or Maverick?"

"Wolf," Margot said. "Maverick's too young for me."

"Are *you* interested in Wolf?"

"Yes, but only if you're not." She hesitated, looking at Andi expectantly. "Do you care? The last thing I want to do is upset you. Your friendship is important to me. *You're* important to me."

Andi didn't know how to answer. She wasn't interested in dating Wolf, but she couldn't wrap her head around the idea of Margot dating Wolf, either. But Margot was waiting for an answer and Andi forced a smile. "I have no claim on him. He's just a neighbor. Wolf is all yours."

Margot grinned and soft creases fanned at her eyes. "Don't say I didn't ask you."

"Come on, let's head down. I need to warm up. My feet

are freezing." But as they walked back to the cabin, Andi let Margot talk, the words rushing around her, while she wrestled with her feelings.

Of course Margot would be able to capture Wolf's attention. Margot was young, slim, beautiful. She was also smart and funny, as well as outgoing. She had a confidence Andi would never have.

Andi's hands knotted into fists. Her chest felt tight with frustration. She hated feeling this way. Rattled. Emotional.

It was almost as if she was jealous of Margot.

But why be jealous? Andi wasn't attracted to Wolf . . . was she?

As they approached Andi's cabin, Margot circled back to the topic of Wolf. "How old do you think he is? Wolf?"

Andi suppressed her negative emotions and sense of inferiority. Margot deserved better. "I don't know. That's a good question."

"If you look at his body, I'd think he was late thirties," Margot said, stamping a clump of dirty snow and ice off the soles of her boots. "The gray in his hair and beard make me think early fifties."

"He couldn't be early fifties, not if Maverick is late twenties, and he's the younger son. I think Wolf is probably my age. Midfifties. Possibly a little older."

Margot peeled her knit cap off her head and ran a hand through the straight blond strands, fluffing it. "I might walk over and say hello tomorrow." She looked at Andi. "But only if you won't feel abandoned."

"I won't feel abandoned," Andi assured her, trying to mean it.

"Okay. We have a plan."

Margot disappeared into the cabin, and Andi took a moment to straighten the benches at the picnic table, and then took the broom and swept pine needles, twigs, and crunchy leaves from the deck.

As she swept she thought of Wolf, and now and then

glanced toward his cabin. You couldn't see his place from hers—you literally had to climb that awful hill, or the long, steep driveway, to reach it. But her cabin was closer to the road, and Wolf passed it every time he went to town or returned.

Kevin had hated it in summer when Wolf and his biker friends would roar up the road, polluting the air. Andi would agree with him that the noise was intolerable, and that life in the mountains had been far nicer before Wolf Enders moved in, but privately, she couldn't help being intrigued by their mysterious neighbor. What exactly had he done for the military? And since he'd apparently retired, what did he do now?

She was still curious. She wanted to know and it killed her a little bit that Margot would find out all those answers first.

ANDI AND MARGOT PREPARED THEIR CHRISTMAS DINNER together. They were having a big salad—roasted chicken, greens, candied pecans, goat cheese, pomegranate seeds with a homemade tangy dressing courtesy of Margot, who said she could make brunches and salads, and that was it—and they talked as Margot chopped the chicken breast and Andi candied the pecans.

"You need to come up and see me next time," Margot said, sliding the chicken into a bowl. "We could go wine tasting, and stay at a fun hotel. A lot of the wineries now have their own hotels and restaurants."

"I've never been there," Andi said, keeping a close eye on the pecans so they wouldn't burn.

"What about San Luis Obispo?"

"I've been to Santa Barbara, and Monterey, but never anyplace between."

"When I was born it was still pretty much ranch land. But Paso Robles has become a wine destination. Lots of tourism. I'm surprised Kevin never took you there. You said he liked good wine."

"He was a wine snob. It was Napa or nothing."

"Napa wines are overrated."

Andi laughed. "Those would have been fighting words for Kevin. He considered himself a wine expert. He was the one who always chose the wines. He liked throwing parties. Big parties."

"Did you like them, too?"

"Not as much as he did. He was very social—" Andi paused, swallowing the rest of the words. Kevin wasn't just social, he was usually the life of the party. He had so many friends, people she didn't know. As the years passed she felt less and less like his best friend, and more like an outsider. He used to say she was being sensitive, and maybe she was. But she didn't need as many people as he did. She really just wanted him.

Margot reached out, touched Andi's arm. "Did I make you sad?"

"No. I just . . ." Andi struggled to find the right words. ". . . realized what we had in the beginning wasn't what we had at the end. Relationships change. We changed. There were no big fights, but we had less in common. At least it seemed to me that we did less together."

"Did he mind?"

"Not as much as I did."

"You still miss him."

"I miss being married. I loved being married. I never wanted to be alone."

They ate on the couch, in front of the fire, with a music channel playing classic carols in the background. The Christmas tree looked adorable with the red balls, gingham bows, and wooden toy soldiers, and Andi thought the cabin had never looked warmer, or more welcoming, than it did this Christmas. She was happy. At peace.

The salad was also the perfect thing for dinner. Lots of

flavor and crunch, perfect with warm baguettes and Margot's choice for wine.

"This is such an amazing place," Margot said, snuggling into her side of the couch, balancing her plate on her bent knees, and setting her wineglass on the end table at her side. "It's a real log cabin. Not like the cabins at Lake Tahoe that call themselves a cabin but are all big windows and drywall."

"Drywall has its place," Andi said wryly, drawing the footrest closer to her chair. "And drywall doesn't require chinking."

"Chinking?"

"That's the filler between the logs, keeping the cold air out."

"Important stuff."

"Indeed."

Margot layered some chicken on her baguette and took a bite from it. She glanced around the room as she chewed. "If this was my place, I'd spend every Christmas here. It's like an old-fashioned Christmas. Rustic and charming."

"Kevin's family did when he was young, but that's because they liked to ski. But when Kevin and I moved to California from Texas, Kevin preferred being on the water instead of the slopes. We'd come up in summer, but not regularly, and then even less after all the drama with Wolf."

Andi's phone rang and she pulled it from her quilted vest pocket and glanced at the screen. Bruce. Sighing, she muted the call and put the phone back in her pocket. It was the second time Bruce had called today. She suspected he just wanted to wish her a Merry Christmas, but she dreaded the conversation, not knowing what else they'd say.

Things had been tense ever since he'd wanted to stay over earlier in December. She wanted to end things, but didn't know how. He wanted to move things forward, and was panicking at her resistance.

"Was that Luke?" Margot asked.

Andi shook her head. "No, it was Bruce." She leaned

forward and picked up her baguette slice with the pat of butter. She loved bread and butter. She'd be twenty pounds lighter if it wasn't her favorite comfort food. "He called earlier, too. I'm avoiding him."

"He's the one you've been dating since September."

Andi nodded. "But let's talk about you. Are you dating anyone?"

"Nope. Don't have time, and let's face it, the Central Coast isn't a hotbed for single men my age."

"Are you only interested in men your age?"

"I'll date younger, I'll date older. My only criteria are he must be gainfully employed, and normal. No guys in the arts, no musicians, no writers, no actors. No egos." She exhaled, grimaced. "I'm not desperate to date, either. I've realized not everyone is meant to be married. I didn't think I'd still be single at forty-five, but I've come to accept that I'll probably always be single. Motherhood certainly isn't in the cards, not unless I want to do it solo, and I don't. I don't think I'm wired that way . . . not patient enough, not strong enough—" She broke off, and looked at Andi. "You didn't get to be a mom, either, did you?"

"I did get to help raise Luke," Andi answered.

"Not much, from what I understand." Margot hesitated. "And I know it's none of my business, but as your friend, I'm still angry that he treated you that way. Just bailing at the last minute on Christmas—"

"Luke has lots of family and commitments when he comes to California, and he doesn't come often—"

"Don't make excuses for him. What he did was wrong, and you went to so much work. You deserve better. You must know that."

Andi didn't answer immediately. "I really want to be a grandmother, and if he cuts me off, I'll never have the chance."

"Have you thought about becoming a foster mom?"

"I actually looked into adopting, but I'm viewed as pretty old."

"You're not old."

"Close enough to sixty that it limits my options. But maybe it would be different for fostering a teenager. It's a good idea. I'll have to look into it."

"Even if you don't, Andi, maybe it's time to stop trying so hard. Maybe it's time to focus on surrounding yourself with people who make you feel good. You're a wonderful person. You have a huge heart. Protect it. It's a special one."

Andi's eyes suddenly burned and her throat thickened with emotion. "Thank you." She leaned across the couch, gave Margot an awkward one-arm hug. "I'm grateful you came into my life. I needed you."

Margot nodded and lifted her wineglass. "To friendship, and all the adventures we'll have this year."

"Amen."

In the kitchen, Andi topped off Margot's wineglass, and then half filled her own, aware that if she had too much she'd end up with a headache tomorrow. She loved red wine, but it didn't always love her. And then, just because her conscience was nagging her, she texted Bruce, wishing him a Merry Christmas.

He immediately phoned. She hesitated a moment before answering.

"Hi," she said. "How are you?"

"Good. Better. Now that I've heard your voice."

Andi felt a pang. "What did you do today?"

"Spent most of it with Holly and Mike and the grandkids. It was fun, but by dinner I was ready to come home. How did dinner go with Luke and Kelsey?"

"It didn't work out," she said lightly, before adding, "and so my friend Margot drove down from Paso Robles and we're spending Christmas at my cabin near Lake Arrowhead. You met Margot."

"The actress friend?"

"Yes. She had a week off between Christmas and New Year's and so we're doing a girls' Christmas in the mountains."

"Be careful. I heard on the news tonight that we have a winter storm coming."

"I haven't heard that, but then, I haven't had the news on."

"It's forecast for end of the week, around New Year's. You might want to leave early, just in case."

Andi felt a wave of annoyance. She knew Bruce meant well, and was just trying to be helpful, but as an intelligent woman, capable of making good decisions, she didn't always need input from men. It was bad enough Kevin had always told her what to do, and how to do things, but dates? Boyfriends? No, thank you. Of course she didn't say that, though. She was too well trained not to be rude, and he was just trying to show he cared. "Good to know. I'll keep an eye on the weather."

Margot suddenly appeared in the kitchen doorway. She put a finger to her lips and tiptoed to the counter, where she snagged a bar of chocolate and disappeared just as quickly.

"I don't want to keep you," Bruce said, "but I know there was some tension these past few weeks, and things have been a bit strained, but we can work through our issues. Relationships don't just happen. They take some effort, some give-and-take."

Andi closed her eyes. Maybe it was her age, maybe it was going through years of grieving, but she wasn't excited about dating if it took effort. She had a job. She went to work. She didn't want spending time with someone to be work as well. Spending time with someone should be fun. It should make her feel good.

Like Margot said.

"Bruce, I think taking a break was good for us. It gave

us some perspective. It gave me perspective. I'm not sure I'm ready—"

"Don't give up on us. We've just hit a bump in the road. All relationships have bumps."

"You deserve someone who can give you more."

"I can't accept that we're over. I like you, Andi. I really do. I could spend the rest of my life with you."

Andi couldn't speak. The words she wanted to say would only hurt him, and she didn't want to be hurtful, not today, not on Christmas. "You know I like you, too."

"Good, so let's just leave it there. Let's not say anything more, and when you're back we can meet for coffee, go for a walk. We'll slow it down, talk everything through. There's no reason we can't make it work."

Except she didn't want to make it work, not anymore. He wasn't her person. He was a good person, but not the one for her.

"Merry Christmas, Bruce."

"Merry Christmas, Andi, and call me, please, once you're home."

Back in the living room, Andi dropped into her corner of the couch and groaned. "I hate dating. I hate this part of dating. I'm going to hurt him, and I hate that, too."

"Disappointment is just part of life. There's no way around it."

"He deserves a good person."

"It's not your job to make him happy, Andi. It's your job to make yourself happy, because if you don't do it, no one will."

THERE MIGHT NOT HAVE BEEN A CHRISTMAS TREE, OR A wreath, or gifts, but for Wolf, it was probably the best Christmas he'd had in years. Maverick was good company, and after dinner they played cribbage, a game Wolf's dad had taught him, and Wolf had taught his sons. They played and drank decaf coffee liberally spiked with Baileys, taking a break at one point to enjoy the Southern-style bread pudding Wolf had made for their Christmas dessert.

"Your neighbor, Andi, she looks different," Maverick said. "Haven't seen her in years but she looks almost younger. She hasn't had work done, has she?"

"I don't think so. I just think she's dressing differently now that she's on her own."

"How are things between you guys?"

"Cordial. I have no beef with her."

"Her friend reminds me a little bit of Mom."

Wolf grimaced. "Because she's blond? That's the only resemblance I see."

"You don't think she's pretty?"

"She's very pretty. She's an actress. Spent the past twenty years on Broadway. But I'm not looking for anything serious and she's young enough she'd probably like a husband. I've been there, done that, and not doing it again."

They started a new game and played until midnight, when they called it a night. "I'm going to be gone early," Maverick said, as they prepared to part in the hall. Wolf's room was upstairs. Maverick was taking a bedroom in the new wing. "I'm not going to wake you up, so this is goodbye."

Wolf hugged his son hard, and then let him go. He didn't like goodbyes, better to get them over with quickly. "Keep in touch," he said gruffly.

"That's a two-way street, Dad. You can pick up the phone, too."

"I will," Wolf promised. "I'll do better."

Maverick was gone when Wolf woke the next morning at six. He'd heard the truck start—it had still been dark—and Wolf had gone back to sleep, but dressing and heading down to his kitchen, Wolf felt the loss of Maverick's company.

Maverick and Lincoln were good people, and the fact

that they had turned out to be such good people was due to their mom, certainly not him.

As he cooked his steel-cut oatmeal, he thought about their conversation yesterday, the serious one about how Wolf was failing Lindsay and Charlie, and then as he ate, he replayed it again. Maverick was right.

Three-year-old Charlie needed more than a visit from his grandfather once or twice a year. He needed his grandfather to be present. Visible. Last night in bed, Wolf had texted Lindsay, wishing her a Merry Christmas. She hadn't answered yet, and that was unusual. Wolf had a good relationship with his daughter-in-law, but perhaps he had been too distant lately, too preoccupied, immersed in his work.

To be honest, Wolf wasn't comfortable thinking about Lindsay. He hated the guilt, and pain, that haunted him whenever he saw her or spoke to her. They'd been married for only eleven months when Stone was abruptly taken from her. She'd never had a chance to have a real marriage, going from bride to widow in less than a year. She'd been young to start with, but now to be a single mom?

Wolf stepped out the kitchen door onto his deck and looked up at the bright blue sky. The air was cold. He shivered slightly. He should phone her. A text was cheap. A text was easy and careless and impersonal. She deserved better. He hadn't sent gifts; he hadn't finished shopping. He'd picked up Lincoln Logs for Charlie at Target in town, and a box of Duplo at the mall's Lego store, but then Wolf got stuck, indecisive about what he should buy for Lindsay. He'd asked a girl working at Nordstrom, what's a good gift for a young woman? She rattled off suggestions. Yoga top and leggings. A cashmere wrap, like the one behind her. Cute pajamas. Or maybe a gift card?

All the suggestions just confused him. He failed to purchase any. And because he had nothing for her, he hadn't mailed the gifts to Charlie.

Wolf sucked at being a husband, he sucked at being a grandfather. Feeling like shit, he called Lindsay now. The phone rang and rang and just when he thought it'd go to her voice mail, she answered.

"Hello?" she said, sounding groggy.

"Lindsay, it's Wolf. I'm sorry I didn't call yesterday. The day got away from me."

"That's okay. It was a weird day. I'm just glad it's over."

She did sound bad. Wolf used his heel to break the small patch of ice on the deck. "What about Charlie? Did he have a good Christmas?"

"I think so. Lincoln was here, you know. He brought his new girlfriend, Anna. He played for hours with Charlie. Charlie loved it."

"I bet he did."

Lindsay's voice deepened, growing husky. "Linc is nothing like Stone, and yet I can't help thinking that this is how Stone would have been with Charlie. Can't help comparing everyone to him."

For a moment Wolf didn't know what to say. Stone wasn't like anyone else. "Linc still there?"

"Not here at the house. He and Anna are staying in the French Quarter. They head back to DC tomorrow, I think. Lincoln wants to be back for a New Year's Eve party. It's a fancy officers' ball, something for West Point alumni."

"What do you think of Lincoln's girlfriend?"

"Have you met her yet?" Lindsay countered.

"No," Wolf said. Lincoln was private. Reserved. Of his three sons, Lincoln was the least like Wolf, and the one most like Wolf's dad. "You think she's a keeper?"

"Hard to say. She's pretty, very smart, works with the UN. It's obvious he likes her, but I'm not sure he's ready to settle down."

That made Wolf feel better. Sometimes he felt as if he was still on the outside, looking in. The boys were protective of their mom. They took good care of her, and he was glad. She'd been an excellent mom, and she deserved their respect. "I have some gifts," he said. "I'm sorry they didn't arrive on time."

"It's okay. I'm not really that into gifts anymore."

"What about Charlie?"

She sighed. "Fair enough. He's crazy about them. He destroyed his pile of gifts this year, tore off the wrapping paper so fast. Jessica wanted a Christmas like you see in the movies, but instead she got us. Christmas with the Tasmanian devil."

Wolf smiled. "Sounds like my kind of Christmas. You should have been with me."

"I was thinking the same thing, Dad."

Dad. She didn't call him Dad very often. Wolf's chest tightened, heavy with love and pain. "Do you have anything planned this week?"

"Nothing." Her voice cracked. "Absolutely nothing."

"I might come spend a few days in New Orleans. But I don't want to impose—"

"Never. Unless you're planning on staying here? Jessica might have something to say about that."

Wolf laughed shortly. His ex would lose her mind.

So would he.

"Don't worry, I'll stay at my usual place. Tell Charlie Pops is on his way."

Chapter 4

WOLF WAS GOOD AT IGNORING PEOPLE AND THINGS.

Even as a kid he had the ability to shut off, detach, which proved useful when everyone was losing their minds. No matter the circumstances, he hadn't lost his.

It had served him well professionally, but it hadn't helped his relationships. Stone's death changed that, tearing a hole in his armor, just as the roadside bomb had torn through Stone's vehicle, killing him instantly.

Wolf arrived in New Orleans late on the twenty-seventh, picked up his rental car, and drove to his hotel on the edge of the French Quarter. There were few people he'd drop everything for, but Lindsay was one. Three-year-old Charlie was another.

Despite the time change, he woke early, got coffee and an egg sandwich from the hotel restaurant, and then drove to the Garden District, where he walked the neighborhood, killing time until he could show up on Jess's doorstep. His ex would not be happy to see him. By the time they divorced when Maverick was in seventh grade, they were no longer speaking, Jess choosing to communicate with him via brief messages, messages that eventually the boys or her lawyer would give to him.

Even though Wolf had been in California for years now, New Orleans was still home. He'd grown up in the Garden District, in an 1850 home on Prytania. It hadn't been the biggest home on their block, but it had history, and that was what mattered to his mom, a New Orleans native raised in the Garden District, too. Wolf took himself on a self-guided tour of his childhood, passing first the home he'd been raised in, and then his mother's parents' huge mansion on St. Charles Avenue.

In New Orleans, ancestry mattered, as did one's wealth, especially where and when one earned that wealth. Old money was superior, and the Bordelons were old money. Being part of New Orleans's established, elite society was equally important. Wolf's maternal grandfather could trace his family back to the late 1700s. Wolf's maternal grandmother to the 1820s. They'd had four children and only one, Wolf's mother, Delfinia Bordelon, lived to thirty, making Wolf their sole grandchild.

Wolf wasn't interested in money, not even family money. He'd never tapped any of the trust set up for him. Wolf had been determined to make it in the world on his own, and he had, but now he was back, standing on the doorstep of the house he'd once shared with his wife.

The cone-shaped topiaries flanking the glossy black front door were underplanted with red and white flowers and trailing ivy. A large fragrant wreath with clusters of little red berries hung on the door. Everything was elegant. Polished and restrained. Jess had finally achieved her dream—she'd become his mom.

He rapped the brass knocker, a lion's head, against the glossy door and waited. He didn't have to wait long.

The front door opened a fraction, and then swung all the way open. Jess stood in the doorway, as beautiful as the day he'd met her thirty-some years ago on a Frontier jet. Her blond head cocked, blue gaze narrowed, expression unsmiling. "Hello, Beast."

"Hello, Jess."

"What are you doing here?"

"Had some business in the area and thought I'd stop by and check in." It was mostly true. His business was Lindsay and Charlie, but he didn't need to explain that.

"How unfortunate."

He ignored the barb and glanced up at the ornate trim work above the front door. "House looks good."

"I know how to take care of my things." Her gaze roved over him, expression disdainful. "I keep the people and things I love close to me." Her head slowly tipped back and she looked even more slowly into his face, gaze locking with his. "Unlike some."

He deserved that and more. "Can I come in?"

"It's not a good time. Lindsay is asleep and Charlie is finally, thankfully, watching a show."

"I'd like to see Charlie."

"I finally have him settled. It's been a wild morning."

"I can hang with him. You go do your thing."

She arched a brow. "My thing?" she repeated. "Surely you jest, as my thing now is taking care of my grandson since his mom can't. Lindsay hasn't been functioning for a long time. She's given up on life. She's giving up on Charlie."

"I wish you would have told me," he said.

"And what? Have you rush in and play the knight on a white horse?" She laughed. "You're no knight. We both know that."

He felt the insult, but it wasn't new. He'd finally accepted that his ex would always be angry. "Lindsay loves Charlie," he said quietly. "And we love both Lindsay and Charlie. We both want the best for them."

"Stone didn't have to join the Marines." Her voice dropped, cracked. "You could have convinced him that there was something else for him, something better, greater. Like West Point."

And here was the source of her hatred. If Stone hadn't become a Marine. If Stone had gone to West Point, as their middle son, Lincoln, had, then Stone would still be alive.

So many words not spoken, but so much communicated without being said.

"If you'd called, I would have told you this isn't a good time," Jess said. "Tonight's my annual holiday party, and I have a cleaning service coming, and a caterer, but I haven't finished setting up. I can't get everything done, not with Charlie getting into everything, making a mess of everything."

"So let me help."

"Why is it always too little, too—" She broke off at the sound of glass breaking from within the house. "Dammit. Charlie!" Jess pushed open the door and disappeared into the house.

Wolf followed, closing the front door behind him. They'd only lived here five years together before Jess asked him to pack up and leave, but he remembered it well, as it was a house he'd hoped would bring them closer. It did not.

Wolf found Jess in the living room, kneeling in front of Charlie even as she picked up shards of bright red glass from around Charlie's bare feet. "What were you thinking?" she scolded. "You know these are glass. You know they break. You're not supposed to even be in here—"

"I just wanted to touch it."

"But you didn't touch it. You broke it. There's glass everywhere. You could have sliced your feet into ribbons."

"Ribbons?" Charlie repeated, wide-eyed but unafraid.

"Yes, ribbons." She was on eye level with him. "And we'd have to take you to the hospital and you'd get lots of shots and it would hurt—"

"No." Charlie shook his head, skeptical. "I don't think I'd have lots of shots."

"You would if you had to get stitches."

"Like this?" Charlie said, biting into his lip to show off his chin with a thick scar beneath his mouth.

"Yes, just like that."

"Hmph."

"You should listen to your gram," Wolf said, scooping the boy into his arms. "She knows. She's had a lot of experience with little boys and emergency rooms."

"Pops!" Charlie cried, throwing his arms around Wolf's neck, giving him a fierce hug.

Wolf kissed Charlie's forehead. "Is this room off-limits?" he asked the preschooler, wanting to sound severe, but Charlie was Stone in miniature and as rebellious as Wolf had been as a small boy.

Charlie shrugged. "I wanted to see the Christmas tree."

"But if Gram said no—"

"Charlie calls me Gigi," Jess interrupted, standing. "And I'm going to throw this away and get the vacuum. But, Charlie, you know the rules. I'm not happy with you."

Charlie stuck out his bottom lip. "I just wanted to look."

"But you didn't just look, you touched." Jess swept past them and Wolf waited for his ex to disappear to speak to Charlie.

"You have to listen to Gram—Gigi. No means no."

"Yes."

Wolf looked down into Charlie's face. The boy was mischievous, all smiles, his light blue eyes his daddy's eyes. Wolf kissed Charlie again on the forehead. "You don't want to make Gigi mad," he whispered in Charlie's ear. "You won't win."

Jess returned with the vacuum, plugged it in, and turned it on. "Maybe this will wake up Lindsay, and you could get them both out of the house so the cleaners can clean."

Wolf glanced at his watch. It was almost nine thirty. "What time does she get up?"

Jess didn't even look at him as she carefully ran the vacuum over the hardwood floor, picking up the smallest shards of glass. "Depends on what time she went to bed, and if she took a sleeping pill or not."

"Who gets up with Charlie, then?" he asked.

Jess looked at him, incredulous. "Who do you think?" She turned the vacuum off. "I love her, and want her here, but she has to do her part. She has to *try*. I know she misses him, but giving up on life won't help her, and it won't help Charlie."

Wolf and Jess rarely agreed on anything, but he agreed with her on this.

"He needs structure," Jess added. "Limits. Boundaries. If he was my son—"

"He's not."

"At the very least he should go to preschool a couple days a week," Jess said, wrapping the cord and straightening. "He'd benefit from activities and being with other kids. He needs to play with people his age."

Wolf privately agreed, but wouldn't say anything until he talked to Lindsay first to get her thoughts. "How about I just take Charlie, then?" Wolf suggested, noting the boy was still in his pajamas. "We can get out of your hair until early afternoon."

"What would you do with him all day?"

"Go to City Park. Eat lunch. Play with him until he tires out."

"That won't happen. He has endless energy—" She broke off, bit her lower lip.

He knew what she was going to say. Like Stone. Just like Stone.

Stone might be gone, but he haunted them still.

"He'll need snacks," Jess added, looking away, her voice husky. "A change of clothes just in case. He's potty-trained, but he still has accidents now and then—"

"I don't," Charlie interrupted, making a face. He caught Wolf's face in his hands, forcing Wolf to look at him. "I don't, Pops. I'm a big boy now."

Wolf's chest tightened. His eyes narrowed and he focused on the sunlight pouring through the tall windows, the morning light bouncing off the gold and glass ornaments on the tree. Jess had always taken care of Christmas for the family, buying the tree, setting it up, handling the gifts, making the dinner. She'd been an excellent homemaker. She'd taken care of the kids, the house, the yard—all of it, really. Obviously when he was home he did his part, but he'd been deployed for much of his career, serving overseas where he was needed most, leaving Jess to raise the kids.

"We'll get lunch while we're out," Wolf said. "Chicken nuggets still his favorite?"

"Yes," Charlie said, wiggling on Wolf's arm. "Chicken and French fries."

"Limit the fries," Jess added. "And milk, not apple juice. He doesn't need the sugar." She put her hands on her hips, accenting her toned frame. She was still as slender as when he'd met her, with a small waist and sensational curves. Even in her fifties, Jessica was a beauty. "I'll get him dressed and send his backpack with you. I'll let Lindsay know you're off to the park. She might want to join you."

Lindsay didn't join them, but she did send a text at noon while Wolf and Charlie were having lunch at a little place near Storyland. *Just waking up,* the text read. *Jessica is having a party tonight. Want to have dinner with Charlie and me?*

I'd love it, he answered. *What about the Camellia Grill?*

Yes, came the immediate response. *I've always wanted to go.*

When Wolf and Charlie returned in midafternoon, Charlie was asleep in his car seat and Wolf carefully unbuckled his grandson and carried him into the house. Charlie threw an arm around Wolf's neck, holding tightly. Wolf hated the heaviness in his chest, emotion he didn't want or need. He wanted to love Charlie without pain, wanted to enjoy him without grief. It seemed impossible when his grandson was so much like his dad.

Wolf let himself into the house. The cleaning crew was just leaving, one of the women mentioning that Mrs. Enders was upstairs, and the other Mrs. Enders, the young one, was in the kitchen. Wolf headed to the kitchen and found Lindsay standing by the microwave warming a cup.

"How did you get him to sleep?" Lindsay asked, crossing to Wolf's side and standing on tiptoe to kiss his cheek.

He put his free arm around her to hug her. She'd become so thin she felt like air and bones. "Ran him hard," Wolf answered, letting her go. He was worried. Nothing was right here.

"Jessica said you took him to City Park. He must have been thrilled. He loves to go there." Lindsay returned to the microwave to retrieve her mug. The coffee smelled burnt. But Lindsay didn't seem to mind. She sipped her coffee and settled into the booth in the corner of the kitchen. "I should take him more. I just don't seem to have enough energy lately," she said, her long light brown hair drawn back in a tangled ponytail, shadows beneath her dark blue eyes. For someone who'd slept until noon, she looked like hell.

"You've lost weight," he said flatly, the words out of his mouth before he could think them through.

"Fashionably thin," she said, flashing a teasing smile, but the smile didn't reach her eyes and her breezy tone was off.

"Are you trying to lose weight?"

"I just don't feel like eating. I don't have an appetite."

"You're not doing any of that bingeing and purging, are you?"

Lindsay's jaw dropped. "I don't have an eating disorder, Wolf. I just miss my husband."

He didn't flinch, but the rebuke stung. They all missed Stone, but of course she struggled the most. She'd never planned to be a single mom. She hadn't married Stone to be widowed less than a year later. She patted the upholstered bench. "Bring Charlie here. He can sleep next to me. I'm not going anywhere for a bit. At least, not until dinner."

Wolf gently eased the boy onto the soft padded bench. It was still the blue-and-white-checked fabric from when Jessica redid the house, their first remodeling project together. They had a list of things they planned to do: kitchen first, boys' bathroom, and then the master bath. They were in the middle of tackling the master bath when he chose to re-up. Jessica had been pressing him to retire, but Wolf wasn't ready. Jess was livid, insisting that he couldn't go away, not again, not so soon, not when the boys were getting older and needed a real dad, one who showed up at their school and athletic events.

He'd been on the ground in Baghdad just two days when she called him and said she was done. Don't come back.

"Do you want to pick us up for dinner, or should we meet you there?" Lindsay asked Wolf even as she smoothed Charlie's fair hair back from his brow. "What's easiest for you?"

He rubbed his eyes, suddenly very tired. "What's easiest for you?"

"Pick us up? Charlie's car seat is already in your car."

Wolf let himself out of the house and climbed behind the steering wheel of his rental car. For several minutes he just sat there, a hand on the steering wheel, the other on his left thigh. The little voice in his head was whispering again, the voice that hadn't left him alone since Stone died, blown to smithereens by a roadside bomb.

What if Wolf hadn't re-upped?

What if he hadn't returned to Iraq?

What if he'd stayed home and been a proper dad?

What if he'd shown his sons that there were other options, other careers, other ways to lead? To serve one's country?

What if.

Would Stone still be here today? Would Charlie have his dad?

Wolf started the car and drove back to his hotel. He'd take Lindsay and Charlie to dinner tonight, and he'd give them a good meal, and they'd act like a family, and he'd slip her money, and then he'd be back on a plane to California early tomorrow and at his cabin by dusk.

MARGOT GAVE ANDI UPDATES DAILY ON WOLF'S AB- sence. She'd first walked up to his cabin on the twenty- sixth, and had returned, reporting that Wolf's Land Rover was gone, the cabin was dark, and there had been no bark- ing dog.

Every day she'd walk up that long, steep driveway to see if he was back.

Andi continued to wrestle with ambivalent emotions, and was secretly glad Wolf wasn't there but knew it was just a matter of time before he'd return. Margot was supposed to leave early on New Year's Eve, and as the days passed, and her departure day loomed, Andi made sure they did as many fun activities as they could, going to the movies in Blue Jay, lunch in Twin Peaks, dinner at a resort restaurant overlook- ing the lake. They went shopping and got manicures and pedicures and squeezed in everything they could think of before Margot had to leave.

Every morning, though, Margot dragged Andi out the door for a walk, or hike, and Andi knew Margot was right, exercise was important, but she dreaded huffing and puff- ing. Fortunately, they could talk as they walked, and Margot asked Andi questions about Kevin and how they met. Andi was happy to talk about Kevin. They met her freshman year at Clemson. It was fall, and Andi was new on campus, and flattered by the invitation to a fraternity party. Kevin was talking to some girls when she arrived, but when he intro- duced himself later—he was the social chair and in charge of the party—she was instantly smitten. He was handsome and charming, and unlike the other guys in the frat house, he wasn't Southern but a Californian, from Newport Beach, no less. He'd grown up on the beach, and he rowed. In fact, he was there at Clemson on a rowing scholarship. At six foot one he was tall and muscular, with sculpted biceps, very straight white teeth, and sun-streaked brown hair. Kevin wasn't just athletic, he was academic, on the dean's list every semester.

Kevin called her after the party, asked her out, and Andi never dated anyone else again. When she finally introduced Kevin to her parents, still living in Maryville, just outside Knoxville, they loved him, too. He proposed at Christmas her junior year. He'd be graduating the next semester and wanted to get a ring on her finger, so they married after he graduated, and when he was offered a job in Houston, she dropped out of school to follow him to Texas, and then later to Southern California, where he was from. His parents were aging and as his only sibling, a sister, had died in a car accident a few years before, he wanted to move back to be closer to them.

Andi had enjoyed living in Texas, and had made some good friends, but Kevin was happy to be back in Orange County. He got back into rowing, joining the Dana Outrigger Canoe Club in Dana Point, and began doing half marathons as well.

Because Kevin, a high-level chemical process engineer, was an excellent provider, they had plenty of money, and she never needed to work. But as they had no children, her days often felt empty, and so she volunteered every day somewhere just to stay busy. Kevin used to brag at cocktail parties that his wife was the most giving woman he knew, but she only volunteered as much as she did because she had no children of her own.

She'd wanted them, too, badly.

It was almost like rubbing salt in a wound when they built their dream house and Kevin insisted on it being five bedrooms. She didn't understand why it had to be so big—who needed all that space?—but Kevin said it was necessary for resale value. He was already looking down the road, protecting their investment. It took two years just to get the plans right. The house was Kevin's vision, but when he couldn't get away from work, he'd send her in his place. The contractors preferred when she was on-site, as Kevin could be short tempered. He had a low tolerance for fools and work done slowly or incorrectly.

And now she lived in that huge house on her own. The huge house was too much for her, but it was a tie to Kevin and she couldn't bring herself to sell it . . . yet.

But she was thinking about it, she told Margot, as they made the loop in the woods and started back. "Someday, before I die, I need to have a place that feels like me." Andi glanced at Margot. "That probably sounds spoiled—"

"No. I agree with you. One of the things I love about being back on the Central Coast is that housing is affordable and I can have my own place . . . a place that's mine. I can decorate it the way I want. I can cook the way I want. I can live the way I want. No compromises."

Andi darted a glance in Margot's direction. "But you're open to marriage."

"Yes, but I don't *need* to get married. I'd like to marry if it's right, but honestly, it's better to be single and happy than in a relationship and miserable."

"But can't you have both? A relationship and happiness?"

"Of course you can." Margot's voice quavered slightly, before she managed a wry smile. "I just haven't had that in years, and I'm not blaming anyone but me. I was the one who chose to stay with someone who clearly didn't love me, but I was foolish and made excuses for him. For years. How pathetic is that?"

"You loved him."

"I was scared to be on my own." Margot looked at her, her gaze briefly meeting Andi's. "I was afraid I'd never meet anyone else—"

"How can you say that? You're so pretty, and so interesting—"

"With horrendous self-esteem." Margot shrugged. "Acting didn't help. Being on the road all the time, away from Sam, made me anxious. Sometimes I wondered if he was cheating on me. Sometimes I'd get this feeling that he wasn't faithful, but I never had proof, and to be honest, I didn't want proof. Because if I had proof, I'd have to take action, and I didn't want to do that. I loved Sam and I thought we were perfect for each other." She sighed, shook her head. "I got caught up in the fantasy of two creatives living in New York, being artistic together. Once I realized I was just being played, I wanted out. I came home. And I want nothing to do with acting or the theater ever again. It's time for a normal life. Time to just be . . . me."

Chapter 5

WITH JUST TWO DAYS REMAINING IN DECEMBER, ANDI was dreading her return to San Juan Capistrano, but at the same time looking forward to seeing Elizabeth, who'd invited Andi to her annual New Year's Eve party.

After waking up and dressing, she headed downstairs. In the kitchen the coffee pot was half-full, the coffee still hot, and Andi poured a cup and wandered into the living room to see if Margot was there. Margot wasn't. But her car was in the driveway, parked right behind Andi's. She had probably gone for a brief walk. It was something she tried to do once or twice a day so she could get some steps in and clear her thoughts, creating a "positive, peaceful outlook for the day." Andi wasn't sure how one meditated while walking, but the mountains were perfect for quiet reflection, and Margot always returned cheerful and full of energy.

Slipping on her fleece-lined boots, Andi pulled on her puffy white winter coat and stepped outside with her coffee. She sucked in a short breath, the cold air bracing, and walked down the stone path to her driveway, and then beyond.

Reaching the street, she glanced both directions looking for Margot. She loved Blue Jay, loved that this community had over 120 acres of forest lands and trails, an area fiercely protected by the community, committed to preserving the older cabins and preventing destruction of the forest.

Andi couldn't see Margot anywhere on the road, but she did hear voices, a male voice and a female voice. The woman sounded like Margot, but Andi didn't recognize the male voice. Andi didn't have many neighbors on her long winding lane; there were just three cabins at this junction of the road, but there were a dozen or so at the turnoff below.

Andi walked down the road, following the voices, and discovered Margot at the next bend speaking animatedly with a man in his mid to late forties. The man was a little heavyset but attractive, with dark eyes, and dark, somewhat thinning hair, going gray at the temples.

Margot spotted Andi and waved her over. "Andi, not sure if you two have met, but this is Jeff Daria. Jeff and I went to school together. He graduated the year before me, but he's another Paso theater kid."

"My cabin's on Whispering Pine," he said to Andi. "You're on White Dogwood?"

Andi nodded. "I can't believe you know each other. What a coincidence."

"We go a long way back," he said. "We did a number of shows together, including *Hello, Dolly!* my senior year. Of course Margot was Dolly. I was just a supporting player."

"That's not true. You were Horace Vandergelder, one of the male leads," Margot corrected.

Jeff smiled, looking pleased. "You have an amazing memory. After all these years, and all the shows you've been in." He looked at Andi. "My wife and I have seen Margot in a number of productions, traveling and on Broadway.

Once when we were in New York, Margot gave us a back-stage tour. My daughters were thrilled."

"I'm glad I could make you look good," Margot teased. "But that's all behind me. I've given it up. No more acting. No more theater. I've a new career now, one that lets me be close to Dad."

"You said that earlier," Jeff said. "Real estate? Property management?"

"Yes. Managing a pool of rentals, both commercial and residential," Margot answered.

"In Paso?"

"Cambria."

"That's not far," he said.

"No," Margot agreed. "Just a half-hour drive and so I can see Dad a couple times a week." Margot glanced at Andi. "Our dads used to work together for the sheriff's department." She looked back at Jeff. "How is your dad?"

"He's doing well. Playing a lot of golf. I think Mom misses him working. He's always in her way now, needing attention."

Margot laughed, and the two talked a bit more, exchanged numbers, and then Jeff headed down the road toward his cabin.

Margot shook her head. "What a small world," she said. "I go for a walk, and who do I bump into? My high school crush. Unbelievable."

"You didn't mention that earlier."

Margot smiled. "It was a long time ago. I'm sure he's forgotten."

"You haven't."

"Because he was my first."

Andi's eyes widened. "Really?"

Margot nodded. "After the Sadie Hawkins dance, my junior year."

"You two were serious."

"No." Margot wrinkled her nose, cheeks turning pink. "I liked him far more than he liked me. We went out while we were rehearsing for *Hello, Dolly!*, but after the show ended, it was over. He was graduating. Heading to college."

"He's followed your career, though. He sounds like a fan."

"You don't want people to like you because you're playing a part onstage. You want to be liked for who you are in real life." Margot shrugged. "I'm not that Margot Hughes anymore. I'm just plain old Margot now."

"Never plain, and not old."

"You are so good for my ego," Margot said, smiling.

"That's what friends are for."

They walked in silence for almost a minute. Margot sighed, not quite as cheerful as she'd been before. "I'm thinking I'm going to get on the road today. I know it's a day early, but it's supposed to snow tomorrow, and I don't have chains. I'd rather head home while the roads are clear."

Andi's heart fell. She'd thought they'd have all day together and had been thinking about where they should go for lunch, but at the same time she could understand Margot's fears. Andi wasn't a fan of driving in poor conditions, either.

Margot glanced at her, worried. "Would you mind?"

"Of course not." Andi reached out, squeezed Margot's arm. "I will miss you, but I think you're smart. Bruce said something about a storm, but I haven't heard anything on the news."

"We haven't exactly been paying attention to the news," Margot said as they reached Andi's driveway. "But Jeff said his family was looking forward to lots of fresh powder. They all ski and snowboard."

"What can I do to help you get ready?"

"Nothing. I'll just pack, it won't take me long, and then I'll strip the sheets—"

"Don't do that. I can."

"I don't want to leave more work for you."

"I've nothing else to do," Andi said, meaning it. "I'd rather you get on the road soon so you can make it home before dark."

Inside, Margot disappeared upstairs, and Andi walked to the living room and gazed out the windows at the trees with the little collars of snow. The big trees shaded her yard, keeping the snow from melting, but the main roads were all clear, and would remain clear, until it snowed, which sounded imminent.

Andi blinked hard, unable to believe she felt like crying. It was silly for her to be this upset. Margot was only leaving a day early. But it had been such a nice week, and now it was over.

Andi wasn't looking forward to returning to real life. When she got home she'd have to take down all the decorations there, although she still had another week before having to be back at the university with the other administrative staff. Teachers and students returned the following week.

Hard to believe her Christmas vacation was nearly over. Time had passed so quickly this week, and Andi and Margot had grown even closer. Andi felt lucky to have a friend who could come spend holidays with her. If it weren't for Margot, she would have been all alone.

Margot appeared a few minutes later on the stairs, and carried her bags to the front door.

She had her coat on and her sunglasses perched on top of her head. "I think I have everything," she said.

A lump filled Andi's throat. She gave Margot a big hug. "I am so glad you joined me. It was such a fun Christmas. A girl Christmas. Thank you."

"We'll have to do it again," Margot said. "Maybe next year come join me in Paso. There are so many restaurants and wineries. We'd eat and drink our way through the holidays."

"Sounds fun."

Margot picked up one of her bags and Andi reached for

the other. Together they exited the house into the bright morning sunshine.

Margot dropped her sunglasses over her eyes. "When do you head back home?" she asked, using her remote to pop her trunk open.

"Tomorrow morning. I'd like to be on the road by noon at the very latest," Andi said. "I just have to clean up a bit here, empty the fridge, and turn everything off. Don't want my pipes to freeze."

"Will you be going to Elizabeth's New Year's Eve party?"

"I've RSVPed yes. Paige and Jack will be there and I'd love to see them before they head off to Tanzania for the winter break."

"Jack's back in California?"

"Just for the holidays. He's teaching his final year at Princeton, and Paige is spending her winter break in Arusha working with math teachers."

"When do you start back at Orange?"

"I've another week off, and then the students return mid-January."

"I envy your school schedule. Three weeks off for Christmas? Must be heaven." Margot slammed the trunk closed and opened the door to the driver's side. "Come see me next time you have a long weekend."

"I'll check the calendar," Andi promised.

Margot gave her one more quick hug, and then she slid behind the steering wheel, closed the door.

Andi waved goodbye as Margot shifted into reverse. Margot blew her a kiss and was off.

Andi shoved her hands into her coat pockets and watched until Margot's car vanished. In just a year and a half Margot had become one of her best friends, if not her best friend. The twelve-year age gap didn't matter. What mattered was the kindness, the conversation, the laughter, as well as availability. As neither of them had husbands or children, they had flexibility—and time—mothers and married women didn't have.

Andi looked up at the sky as she headed back inside. It was a wintery blue with scattered clouds. Nothing threatening. Was there really a storm on the way? If so, Andi should begin dismantling the tree now and running the laundry so she could leave early in the morning before the storm moved in.

The rest of the day was cleaning and organizing. She carried the tree out, leaving it on the side of her cabin, washed the sheets, remade the beds, hauled the plastic tubs of decorations into the attic just above the two upstairs bedrooms. But once she was done with her tasks, she felt a little lost, missing Margot's company and quick laugh. It was these in-between times that were hard on Andi, these moments when she struggled to remember who she was, and where she belonged. As a wife, she belonged with her husband, in their home. But single?

Antsy, Andi put on her hiking boots and bundled up to take a walk through the beautiful woods. Dogwood Canyon really was a magical place, so different from the rest of Lake Arrowhead, and as she walked, she breathed in the cold crisp air. The pale blue winter sky had given way to gray, the gray like a low ceiling, heavy and cold.

It wasn't supposed to snow until tomorrow, but the temperature was dropping, the air already icy. If she didn't know better, she'd think snow was imminent. Maybe she should head home today, leave before it started snowing. But again, the idea of being home, in that big house, gave her pause. It didn't feel like her home without Kevin. The house had been all him—his style, big, impressive, lots of Mediterranean arches, columns, and marble. He'd grown up in a similar house in Newport, with a soaring entry and an ornate wrought-iron banister. Personally, she liked more of a cottage style, wood siding with pretty windows and wraparound porches. If she sold her San Juan Capistrano home, she could downsize, finding a two- or three-bedroom house with a pretty garden and maybe a pool. She did like a pool for the summer months. Come home from work, pour an iced tea, sit on the steps in the shallow end, and relax.

But selling the house felt like a betrayal to Kevin. She'd loved being married, even though their marriage wasn't perfect. How could it be when she and Kevin weren't perfect? But such was the beauty, and challenge, of marriage. Two imperfect people come together, and learn to make a life together.

Kevin had been a true provider. He'd worked to create a new lifestyle. They owned a lovely home. They had quite a few friends. And when it was just the two of them, he loved being taken care of. Spoiled. He enjoyed her cooking, complimented her style, appreciated how she worked so hard to make him comfortable, and happy.

If there was any disappointment, it was the fact that she never had a baby of her own. Kevin had fathered Luke his senior year of high school, and had always thought he'd have more children, but Andi couldn't conceive. They tried and tried, but Kevin's faith—he was very Catholic—shaped their lives. He thought it wasn't God's will for them to have a baby, so they didn't try in vitro. They looked into adoption, but in the end, Kevin wasn't comfortable with it. Andi begged Kevin to just go to an appointment with a fertility specialist, just to better understand why she couldn't get pregnant, but Kevin said he was content with the child he had.

It was a bitter blow for her.

If she and Kevin fought, it was over children. Her inability to conceive, her desire to be a mom, her emptiness without a child of her own. Kevin didn't relate.

He chose not to relate, which hurt her immensely. She could have let the issue drive a wedge between her and Kevin, or she could accept that things didn't always work out the way you'd hoped. So, over the years, Andi learned to suppress the longing and need. Motherhood wasn't in the cards. She'd have to find other ways to feel important, and needed, and she did, later, when she went to work at Orange. There were so many young people on campus having questions, needing help, missing home, struggling to find their place in the world. She loved the students, and was grateful she could give them her time and attention.

The snow began to fall before she'd even turned around to start back home. The flakes were small, light, a lovely, delicate powder tumbling from the sky. Andi didn't push on, but instead headed down the mountain, walking with her head tipped back, welcoming the snowflakes on her face. She stuck out her tongue and caught one, and then another.

Growing up in eastern Tennessee, they'd get snow each winter, three or four inches, but not necessarily at Christmas. A white Christmas therefore had been special, magical. Even now, when it snowed, she felt like a kid, excited that something wonderful was happening. The world was full of possibility again.

The snow was falling harder, the flakes thicker. She zipped her coat up all the way to the throat as a wet snowflake slid down her collar. It wasn't a long way to her cabin, just fifteen minutes or so, but in the time it took to walk back, the delicate flakes had become a true snowfall. She was able to see, but it was like looking through a veil of white lace. Thick flakes stuck to her eyelashes. Her lips felt chilled. She enjoyed the walk down the quiet paved road, but wondered what it would be like driving down the mountain. Would she need chains? Could she make it without them?

If she left immediately, she'd probably be fine, but the curves of the narrow highway would be difficult in a flurry of white. She hated driving in fog. Driving in a snowstorm wouldn't be much better. Worse, the road would be slipperier with the new layer of powder.

Approaching her cabin, she noticed the transformation. Everything was white. The ground, the driveway, the trees, the porch, the steep shingle roof.

She heard a bark and turned toward the sound. Wolf and Jax—unleashed, of course—emerged from their driveway and were walking to her.

Andi let them come, her pulse doing a wild tattoo that made her feel nauseous. She did her best to stand her ground and look calm, but it wasn't easy when just looking at Wolf made her feel strange.

"The storm is moving in," he said, voice deep, pitched low. "Has your friend Margot left?"

She nodded. "A couple hours ago." Andi hesitated. "She was hoping to see you before she left."

"I got her message," he replied.

Andi didn't know what to say to that. She hadn't realized Margot had left him a note, and she shouldn't care. She really shouldn't care, but for some reason, she did.

"And you?" Wolf asked. "How much longer will you be here?"

"I head home in the morning."

"You might want to rethink your departure. It's going to get a lot worse."

That put fresh butterflies in her middle. "I didn't think we were going to see snow until tomorrow."

"It's catching everyone off guard."

"How do you think the roads will be?"

He glanced at her car tires. "You don't have snow tires. You'll need to chain up."

She wasn't very good at putting on chains. "And visibility?"

"Not ideal, but at least it's still daylight." His brow furrowed. "Are you a nervous driver?"

Yes. "Not usually, no."

"Would you like a hand with your chains?"

Yes. "Thanks, but no. I've got it."

He nodded once, his expression grim, and then returned to his driveway, Jax dashing ahead, enjoying the snow.

In hindsight, Andi should have left then.

In hindsight, she should have accepted Wolf's offer to chain her up and see her off. Instead, she went inside and made a cup of tea, and stood in front of the fire, warming herself. Bruce had texted her while she walked, telling her the weatherman was saying the storm would be bad, and he hoped she was being smart and had gotten on the road. Bruce's choice of words—*hoped she was being smart*—annoyed her. She didn't need a man talking to her as if she was a child.

But she was also not going to let her ego make her stupid.

She should go. Maybe she could get by without the chains until the pull-off on the highway and someone from Caltrans could help her.

Andi packed her car, running in and out of the cabin as the wind howled, sending the snow swirling sideways. She just needed to get on the highway and the snowplows would work their magic.

She locked the cabin door, climbed in her car, buckled up, and shifted into reverse to slowly back down her driveway.

Her wheels slid. Her pulse jumped and she pumped the brakes. It didn't matter—it didn't slow or stop her. Her car kept sliding, down, sideways, until she bumped into a massive tree stump that marked the junction of her driveway with Wolf's. She hoped she hadn't dinged her car or scratched her paint.

Andi turned off the engine and closed her eyes, feeling like an idiot.

She shouldn't have been so proud. She should have accepted Wolf's offer to get chains on her car.

If she was going to come up to the cabin in winter, she needed a car with four-wheel drive. Or snow tires. Or both.

Andi opened her door, and the wind immediately caught her hair, snow swirling around her. She grabbed her purse, and lugged her suitcase back to her cabin, slipping on the steep driveway. She still had a box of food in the car but would deal with that later, when she could see past her nose.

Back in the safety of her cabin, she turned the heat on, turned the fire back on, and stared out the kitchen window at the blinding white world outside. So this was a blizzard.

Andi made the second trip to the car before it was dark, wanting her milk, half-and-half, eggs, cheese, butter, and bread. She shivered on her way out, and shivered on her way back, but she was also laughing. The whirling snow was wild and enchanting. She felt like Elsa in *Frozen*, and having never been in a snowstorm at the cabin on her own, it was like being part of a grand adventure, the snow piling swiftly on the railing, covering the teak picnic table, powdering the trees.

Andi made herself a grilled cheese sandwich for dinner and sat on the floor before the fire. So what if she didn't make it down the mountain tomorrow? So what if she missed Elizabeth's party? This was exhilarating. She was having fun.

Her phone buzzed with a text. She picked it up. Safely home! read the message from Margot.

Glad to hear, Andi answered. You were wise to leave early. It's already snowing, and hard.

Send pictures, Margot replied.

I will in the morning, Andi typed back. And then, since her phone was there, Andi scrolled through her messages, rereading the last several from Bruce. She didn't know what to do about Bruce.

No, that wasn't totally true, she knew what to do. She'd already told him what she wanted—to end things—but he hadn't wanted to accept her decision.

It was time to make a clean break, she thought. Do it now, for the new year.

Hi, Bruce,

I've been thinking about you a lot, and I value your friendship, but don't think we should continue dating. I believe there's someone else out there for you and I want you to find her. All the best in the new year.

Andi

She hit send. She'd done it. She was free.

Chapter 6

IT SNOWED ALL NIGHT. ANDI WOKE IN THE NIGHT TO USE the bathroom and glanced out the window to her driveway; the snow was still steadily falling. Her car had disappeared under the snow, and the low rock wall bordering the cabin was gone, buried in a sea of white.

It was magical, serene.

She climbed back in bed and snuggled beneath the still-warm covers, thinking it'd be a very different New Year's Eve.

Andi's bedroom was freezing the next time she woke up and left bed to use the bathroom. She always turned the thermostat down at night, but set it at a comfortable sixty-seven. It was not sixty-seven in her room, or in the hall, or anywhere in the house. When she turned on the light to try to adjust the heater, it didn't come on. She tried another one. Nothing. The power was out.

She hurried back to pull heavy sweatpants over her pajama bottoms, adding a thick hooded sweatshirt and then a coat and gloves over that. Outside the snow was still falling.

The flakes were coming down more slowly, but the fat white flakes still tumbled steadily from the pale winter sky.

She lit the gas fireplace in the living room, turning the flames up high, and then lit the gas stove in the kitchen to boil water for coffee. Thank goodness for the carafe. She could make almost everything on the stove, so she'd be fine today until power was restored, but was everyone impacted, or was it just her?

Last night she'd read in bed for an hour before falling asleep, and failed to plug her phone in. It was at fifty percent now. There were new text messages, too, from the power company and internet service, both alerting her that services were down and crews were working on it. It could be a couple hours. Could be a couple days. Looking at the sheer amount of snow that had fallen in the past eighteen hours, Andi suspected it'd be the latter.

The water boiled, and Andi poured it over the grounds in the cone filter in the carafe, and while waiting for it to drip through, she bundled her arms over her chest and studied the snow-covered picnic table. The layer of snow had to be at least fourteen, maybe sixteen, inches deep. If it was that deep everywhere, she'd be going nowhere for quite some time. And that was fine, she reassured herself, grateful for coffee and all the food she had left over from the holidays. She wasn't going to go hungry. And if she stayed near her fireplace, and made up a bed there, she wouldn't freeze, either.

Andi read by the fireplace for the rest of the morning, and then when her phone battery dropped to below twenty percent, she turned it off, wanting to preserve it. She made a grilled cheese sandwich for lunch, and then cut up an apple, and in theory she was comfortable. Andi wasn't too cold, or too hungry, but she was beginning to get the restless feeling, the one she usually managed by walking, or doing something.

She could shovel her front porch, and work her way to

the driveway, clearing a path to her car. The community association would handle keeping the main road clear, but her driveway was her responsibility. But when Andi found the shovel in the mudroom and headed out, she discovered her work had been done for her.

A path had been shoveled from the main road, up her driveway, up her porch steps, to her front door. Her car was still buried, but she had a path through the deep snow, giving her access to the road.

Andi stood rooted to the spot, completely caught off guard.

There was only one person who could have, would have, done this, and it was the one person she continuously rebuffed.

Andi drew a slow breath, torn between gratitude and guilt. Why had he done it?

She studied the cleared path. It was very impressive— deep, clean, with clear, straight edges. It had to have taken him hours.

She'd have to say something.

That sounded awful.

She wanted to thank him, and in the ideal world, she'd do something for him in return. Bake a loaf of pumpkin bread, or make gingerbread, just something to show appreciation, but her gas oven wouldn't light without electricity. She'd once made a delicious chocolate cake on the stove, using a Dutch oven, but the recipe required a lot of eggs and she wasn't going to use up all her eggs for a cake that her neighbor may or may not eat.

Maybe just a thank-you note. Was that sufficient?

Or should she think of something else to make?

Andi returned to her kitchen, a snug little room that had the best of appliances because she spent a lot of time in there. Kevin had appreciated her cooking and liked her food better than going out to eat. Andi wished they ate out more, but understood that after a long day at the office or, later, after rowing, Kevin just wanted to come home and eat and be comfortable.

She scrutinized her supplies. She still had some apples, oranges, a banana, plus the pantry basics she'd brought up with her.

She kept looking at the apples. Two honeycrisps. One Fuji. She checked her pantry supplies. Oats. Brown sugar. Cinnamon. Pecans. Butter.

She had everything she needed for a small apple crisp, one cooked on the stove in a small cast-iron skillet. She'd do the topping first, then sauté the apples in butter, sugar, and spices and sprinkle the topping on. It wouldn't be as good as made in the oven, but it'd be something she could do and, coupled with a note, would show effort and appreciation.

As she always did for her family, she doubled the topping recipe because honestly the crumbly buttery sugary topping was the best, and then while that cooled, she cooked the chopped apples, making sure those were tender before covering with the crumble.

She wished she could slide it below the broiler to crisp up the topping further, but she'd done her best, considering.

While the dessert cooled, Andi washed her face, aware that her hot water would soon cool, too, and combed her hair, adding a little bit of makeup, her favorite touches always mascara and eyeliner. She wasn't planning on seeing Wolf, just leaving the dessert and note on his doorstep, but should he come out, she didn't want to be caught looking disheveled. Back downstairs, she drew out a sheet of paper from the old-fashioned desk in the hall and scrawled a quick note.

Thank you so much for clearing my front porch and walk. You went above and beyond.

Andi McDermott

She studied the note a moment, wondering if it was too casual, if the tone was fine, and then decided not to obsess. She folded the note, slipped it in an envelope, and tucked it in her coat pocket. After covering the still-warm skillet with foil, she pulled her mittens on, lifted the skillet, and headed outside, walking carefully down her cleared path.

It was *cold*. The snow had finally stopped, but the frigid air cut into her lungs, making her cheeks burn and her eyes sting. She was glad she'd worn her hiking boots, as they had the best tread, but she paid attention to her steps, not wanting to fall as she walked down her driveway to reach his.

She hadn't been to Wolf's cabin in years, not since she'd gone to ask if he had jumper cables, but it wasn't hard to find his driveway. He'd cleared almost all of it, and she wondered if he had a snowplow, or something to make the shoveling easier.

His cabin had been built ten years before the McDermott cabin, and a previous owner had added some rooms to it, including a second story. When Wolf bought it, the entire thing was falling down, but it looked welcoming as she approached. The paned windows were painted a dark blue-green, the front door was the same color, and the logs were a warm brown. The porch was clear of snow, as were the dozen wooden steps leading to the front door.

Andi had hoped to slip up to the cabin, leave the note and apple crisp, and sneak away undetected, but Jax must have heard her and began barking. She prayed Jax was secure in the house because the last thing she wanted was to come face-to-face with the dog. Quickly, she hurried up the steps, placed the foil-wrapped skillet on his doormat, propped the note against the skillet, and had just turned around to leave when the door opened and Jax growled.

Andi froze, petrified. Wolf commanded the dog to sit.

Andi couldn't move.

"He's not going to bite you," Wolf said, his deep voice laced with amusement.

She slowly turned to face him, hands tucked in her coat pockets. Her gaze swept from the dog to the man. "He doesn't like me."

"He did that to Maverick, too. It's not personal."

"Do you need such a scary dog?"

"Shepherds are intelligent and loyal. They're good companion dogs."

She looked at Jax again. His eyes were so gold it was eerie. "What do you think he's thinking right now?"

Wolf glanced down at his dog. His eyebrow quirked as he looked back at her. "Is he going to get a treat when he goes inside?"

Andi couldn't help smiling. "Really?"

"He loves his treats."

She laughed softly. "As long as his treats aren't small children."

Wolf's straight white teeth flashed in a rare smile. "He's quite a picky eater. I don't think he'd like them." Wolf bent down, picked up the card and then skillet by the handle. "What's this for?"

"It's a thank-you for clearing a path for me." She hesitated. "At least, I assumed you did it. I don't know who else would."

"I did," he admitted. "I still need to finish your driveway. I'll use my tractor snowplow for that, but it's noisy and I didn't want to wake you."

"You did all that early this morning?"

He nodded.

Her insides did a crazy somersault and her heart beat a little faster. He was already tall, but standing four steps above her, he seemed huge, and intimidating in every way. Muscles and tattoos and intense pale gray eyes in a striking face.

She hoped he wasn't interested in Margot. Hoped they hadn't been on the phone, making plans. "That was very kind of you. The apple crisp isn't my best, but hopefully you'll enjoy it. I did what I could on my stove as my power's out—" She broke off, noted the yellow light coming from inside his cabin. "You have power."

"I have a backup generator. Living here year-round, I've been through this before."

"How long before you think we get power back?"

"A couple days."

"What?"

He nodded. "Last time it was three days, and the snow wasn't half this thick."

"But why?"

"Downed power lines. Downed trees. Folks can't dig out of their houses to work. Everything is going to be closed for a few days. It doesn't help that tomorrow is New Year's Day, a holiday. Everyone has it off."

She shivered. "My phone's almost dead."

"You could charge it here."

"You wouldn't mind?"

"Not at all."

She retrieved it from her pocket and handed it over. She'd already turned it off for the sake of the battery. "I'll come back in an hour or so."

"I can bring it to you."

She felt prickly and hot and strange. The landscape was so powdery white, all sound swallowed by the thick layers of snow. The world felt different—icy, still, mysterious. Here, high on the mountain, it felt as if she and Wolf were the only two people alive. "You've gone to enough trouble," she said, teeth chattering. "I'll be back."

She hustled down the stairs, anxious to escape, but in her haste, she stepped too quickly on a slippery patch and went tumbling down, slamming an elbow and hip. She must have cried out because Jax barked and Wolf was immediately at her side.

Andi didn't even have a chance to sit up before Wolf was lifting her to her feet. "Did you hurt yourself?" he asked, his arm wrapping around her, supporting her.

She shook her head, dazed, partly from the hard fall, but also from the strange intimacy of being held against him, her body pressed to his side. He was hard. Strong. He felt warm even through the layers of sweater and coat and she tipped her head back to see his face.

His gaze caught hers, held, and her heart did a double beat, making her light-headed. The world was icy cold and yet she felt hot, skin sensitive, lips tingling. "I'm okay," she murmured, the tip of her tongue touching her upper lip. Her mouth suddenly dry,

He must not have believed her because the next moment he scooped her into his arms and carried her up the stairs to his cabin, her cheek against his chest, a masculine scent of spice and cedar tickling her nose.

He smelled like the woods, and Christmas. He smelled crisp and fresh and she drew a deep breath, unable to remember the last time anyone had carried her anywhere. Maybe as a bride? Maybe after the car accident in Houston when she'd been broadsided and slammed her head against the steering wheel? In those days there were no airbags. In those days you didn't always wear a seat belt. In those days you took hard hits and hoped you'd survive.

"I really am okay," she said as he walked through his cabin, past a dark kitchen and into a living area with a high ceiling and dark rustic beams. Like in her cabin, the walls were logs, and the fireplace had a similar stone hearth— square-cut stones, light gray with touches of gold—stones quarried from the area in the twenties and thirties.

"Maybe, but I'm not sending you back to a freezing cabin when my place is warm," he said, setting her on her feet, not far from the blazing fire. He kept one hand on her elbow, checking her balance. "What hurts?"

She was probably sore somewhere, but she couldn't focus on bruises when adrenaline rushed through her veins.

She liked him.

She'd liked him for a long time, but she'd been too stubborn and proud to admit it.

Andi looked up at him, saw something in his eyes that

made her hold her breath, and couldn't look away. Desire coiled within her. Her pulse raced. She went hot, and then cold, a delicious shiver racing down her spine. And in all that time, Wolf never looked away.

Something was happening here. Something she couldn't wrap her head around, but she liked it . . . wanted it . . . whatever it was.

He reached out to her, cupped her cheek. His palm was warm, calloused. The hair rose on her nape, sensitive, so sensitive. Common sense whispered she shouldn't encourage this, but another part of her, a part that was so tired of being good and proper, of taking care of others, of not asking for too much, wanted *this*.

"What hurts?" he repeated.

She shook her head. "Nothing," she whispered.

His thumb stroked her cheek. She sucked in a breath, feeling dizzy.

He touched her mouth with the pad of his thumb.

Her lower lip quivered. Her legs trembled. For a split second she thought he might kiss her. The tension felt electric. *She* felt electric.

She wanted him to kiss her.

She hoped—

His head dropped, the silver glint of his eyes making her heart race. His mouth covered hers.

There was pressure, and touch, pleasure and sensation, and Andi's head tipped back as Wolf's mouth nipped along her neck, and then lit flames beneath her skin as his tongue traced her collarbone. She didn't even know how her clothes—all those layers—came off, but they were falling away, one by one, until they were on the floor, on a sheepskin rug in front of the fire. It wasn't making love—it was hot and hard and carnal, Wolf's body filling hers, thrusting into her, making her feel alive in every cell and every atom of her being.

Usually she had to focus, concentrate, to come, but Wolf

seemed to know just how and when to touch her, and she shattered just before he came. It wasn't until much later that she thought about protection, and questions about health. Was he . . . safe? Was there anything she should know? But that all came later, because first there was the mind-boggling fog, and the intense physical release that wrung her out and made her almost want to cry. The pleasure had been that good. The sensation, the pressure, the fullness of him with her, that satisfying. She couldn't even remember if it had ever felt that way with Kevin.

There was nothing safe about Wolf, and the sex hadn't been safe, and the way he took her wasn't safe, and she couldn't cling to modesty or proper behavior. She couldn't do anything but feel and feel, and it wasn't until she lay spent, in his arms, that she realized this was the first time in years since she'd felt anything in her body, anything in her soul.

Her spirit had been numb. Dead. Her body had felt numb. Dead.

The tears she'd held off filled her eyes, and she wiped them quietly, not wanting Wolf to see.

Thank God she couldn't get pregnant. At least that wasn't a risk.

"I SHOULD GO HOME," SHE SAID LATER, SITTING UP AND glancing around Wolf's bedroom, before remembering her clothes were still downstairs by the fire. They'd come upstairs after round one, and in the throes of passion it had all felt easy and natural, but now she was self-conscious and shy and more than a little shocked by her behavior.

"Why?" he asked, an arm behind his head, the arm thickly muscled. Wolf looked impressive dressed but was awe-inspiring naked. She'd never met a man with so many defined muscles. "Your cabin will still be cold."

"I can't just stay here until power comes on."

He shrugged. "You're not in my way."

"Once I'm out of your bed, I will be."

Creases fanned from his eyes as he smiled. "I had no idea you had a sense of humor."

"That's because we've never been neighborly," she said, the sheet and duvet pressed to her chest, hiding herself. She could use a shirt. And underwear.

"I wondered what you'd be like in bed."

She squirmed inwardly, disconcerted. "You thought about that?"

"Of course."

"Even though I was Kevin's wife?"

"I didn't dwell on that part. He wasn't my favorite person."

"Nor you, his."

"The feud was stupid, and unnecessary. Axel never attacked any of the dogs here, let alone that white fluffy thing down the canyon."

She hesitated. "He was a very aggressive dog."

"He was a trained member of the armed forces. He wasn't interested in little dogs, let alone Muffy."

"Misty," she corrected with a faint smile. Her smile faded. "It didn't help when you invited all those bikers up for the weekend. You had to know it would be upsetting."

"Your husband could have talked to me instead of spreading lies about me."

"You let your dog chase him off your property. Kevin was terrified."

Wolf made a guttural sound in the back of his throat. "Axel wouldn't have bitten him. All he had to do was stand his ground. Be a man."

"Not everyone is comfortable with big dogs, especially when they're growling and salivating."

Wolf laughed softly, and reached out to trail a fingertip from her shoulders, down her spine, to the cleft in her bottom. She hissed a breath, arching with pleasure.

"You're beautiful," he said.

She blushed, body tingling. "I'm almost fifty-eight."

"When's your birthday?"

"February thirteenth." She shuddered as he leaned close and lifted her heavy hair to kiss the back of her neck. "When is yours?"

"April seventh."

"An Aries," she said, closing her eyes as he lightly raked his nails down her back, making her sigh. He was no amateur in the bedroom, she thought, even as he wrapped her hair around his hand and pulled her back down onto the bed.

"Whatever that is." His voice was husky, and his narrowed gaze swept her, lingering on the fullness of her breasts, before he stretched out over her and kissed her deeply, stealing her breath, as well as all thoughts.

She was still wet from earlier and when he parted her thighs to thrust into her, she gasped as shock waves of pleasure rushed through her. He'd felt good the first time, but this second time was even better. They were making love missionary style, but there was nothing missionary about it. With his hand still grasping her hair, he tipped her head back, exposing her neck to his mouth and tongue while he rocked her world, teasing her senses, heightening her pleasure, drawing it out so that she couldn't come quickly, refusing to give her release, but when she finally did, she bucked against him and cried out, climaxing violently.

Andi couldn't catch her breath. Her heart raced. Her legs quivered. She felt completely drained.

Wolf stroked her hair back from her damp brow, kissed her, and rolled onto his side, closing his eyes.

Within minutes he was asleep.

Although exhausted, Andi couldn't sleep, overwhelmed by everything she felt. Her body was a little sore, a little tender, and her skin felt sensitive everywhere. But it wasn't just her body that surprised her. It was her mind, her thoughts, her *choices*.

She'd wanted this to happen. She'd been curious and aroused and almost desperate for him to touch her. She'd wanted every bit of pleasure he could give her, and it had been considerable. And yet she'd never fallen in bed with anyone before. Even with Kevin there had been no back-to-back sessions. She wasn't sure she'd ever orgasmed twice in a half hour. She didn't think she could.

Andi must have finally fallen asleep because when she opened her eyes it was dusk, and the room was strange and it took her a minute to figure out where she was, and then it all came flooding back.

Wolf. Sex. His body on hers, in her, his hands wrapped around her wrists, holding her down, making her feel . . .

Andi pushed back the covers and left bed. Wolf had placed all her clothes on a chair in the corner of the room. She dressed and headed down the stairs. It took her a moment to locate Wolf, but eventually she found him at a large drafting table in what might have been a dining room. He was wearing jeans and a dark gray flannel shirt layered over a white thermal. The rest of the room was dark, but a bright desk lamp illuminated the plans he was working on. She didn't think she'd made any noise, but Jax, in a dog bed in the corner, lifted his head, growled softly. Wolf looked at her over his shoulder, expression inscrutable.

She had no idea what he was thinking, no idea what he was feeling. He was a stranger. Despite the hours spent today in his bed.

"I'm going to head home," she said.

"Your house will be freezing."

"I'm planning on sleeping in front of the fire."

"You're welcome to stay here."

He was saying the polite thing, but she knew they'd both be happier with her at her own place. "Thanks for . . ." Her voice trailed off and she frowned, not sure what she was thanking him for. The orgasms? His time? Reminding her she wasn't frigid?

He lifted a salt-and-pepper brow, waiting. The amused light was back in his eyes.

Seconds dragged by. She remembered his mouth on her nipple, his hands cupping her butt, his thigh between hers, his teeth scraping the sensitive skin down her neck.

"For everything," she concluded, smiling ruefully. "Good night."

She was nearly out the door when Wolf called her name. "Wait," he added, following her to the door. "Your phone," he said, handing it to her.

She wasn't sure what she thought he wanted from her. A kiss goodbye, maybe? Instead she took the phone, nodded once, and then—

He had her up against the wall, his broad chest pinning her to the rough logs. His mouth captured hers, his tongue taking hers, tasting her, making her whimper as heat and need exploded all over again. And then he was drawing away. "Stay here," he commanded. "I'm going to get my coat and walk you back."

"I can—"

"Don't," he interrupted. He grabbed his coat off the hook by the door, slid his feet into lined boots, tightened the laces.

Jax joined them at the door and they stepped out into the cold, still night, surfaces glowing beneath the moonlight, the snow reflecting light to the sky. The snow seemed to sparkle. More magic, Andi thought, chest tight and hot, filled with emotion.

Her cabin was dark as they approached, the orange glow of flickering flames in the living room the only light. He walked her to her door. Tiny icicles hung in a delicate line above the door.

"You're not nervous, are you?" he asked her.

"Nervous of what?"

"Of being alone. Of not having any power."

She shook her head. "I'm alone every night. It doesn't

bother me anymore, and there's no one up here but you and me."

"Your cell phone isn't getting coverage. If you need something, you're going to have to come to me, unless I bring you one of the walkie-talkies."

Andi smiled. "Thank you, but I'm fine. I don't need it. I'm just going to lock up, make some dinner, and have a campout in the living room."

He kissed her. "You have the best lips," he said, drawing away.

She shouldn't be so flattered. "Thank you. Good night, Wolf."

"Good night, Andi."

She watched him walk away, the big dog silent at his side, and she felt a stab of pain, and a rush of panic.

Were they done?

Was it over?

"Wolf—" she called out breathlessly, not yet ready to let him go.

He paused on the steps, looked at her.

"Want to come over for breakfast?" she asked, hoping her voice sounded stronger than she felt. Desperation wasn't attractive. She prayed she didn't sound desperate.

"You don't have to do that."

A prickly heat filled her. Things were already getting awkward. "I know. I want to."

His cool gaze locked with hers. "I have no expectations, Andi."

Was that a rebuff?

The heat surged up, from her ankles, through her hips, chest, neck. Her face burned. Her eyes stung, her emotions not in control. "I don't, either." She swallowed hard, squared her shoulders, refusing to let anxiety make her feel shame. "I was simply inviting you over for some eggs. Thinking eight might work. But if you'd rather not—"

"I didn't say that."

She held on to her temper. She wasn't going to make this a big thing. "If you're up, and hungry, drop by. If you're busy, don't give it another thought." She flashed him a smile. "Thank you for walking me back."

It wasn't until she'd closed and locked the door and headed to the kitchen for water that she saw that her kitchen sink was on, just a trickle, but on, and the cupboard doors beneath the sink were open. She didn't remember leaving them that way.

Andi went to the bathroom and found the same. The water slowly trickling out. The upstairs bathroom had both the sink and shower going.

She hadn't thought to leave the water on. But just like the shoveled driveway earlier, she knew who'd done it. Probably when she was sleeping in his bed.

There was no point asking why. She knew the why—he didn't want her pipes to freeze. But why hadn't he mentioned it?

Why did he do these things to help her, when she got the sense that he didn't want her?

Correction, he wanted her body. He just didn't want to deal with the rest of her.

Chapter 7

HE WAS NOT GOING OVER FOR BREAKFAST. THERE WAS no way he could go. He had work to do, and a schedule to keep. And after the trip to New Orleans, Wolf needed downtime. Alone time.

Yesterday with Andi wasn't supposed to have happened. He wasn't even sure how it had happened. He'd cleared her walkway because he didn't want her trapped. It wasn't safe, being buried by all that snow. He'd woken early, made a path for her, and that was it.

But then she'd come over with her apple crisp and . . .

What the hell happened?

He didn't just fall in bed with women. He might be an ass, but he didn't just bed women right and left. And he certainly didn't bed women who were inconvenient.

Andi was the very picture of inconvenience.

She might live next door, but that wasn't a plus. Her physical proximity was a negative. Sleeping with a woman who lived walking distance to your place was stupid. It complicated—no, ruined—everything. Wolf loved his cabin, his solitude, his detachment from society. Sleeping with a neighbor changed all that.

If only the sex had been terrible. If only he'd felt relief when she left. But he didn't feel relief as he walked her back to her place; he felt torn.

Confused.

Sex with Andi had been pretty damn perfect. She was soft, warm, sweet, and responsive as hell. The chemistry between them had been off the charts. For a brief point in time, he'd lost himself in her, and it had been a relief.

Passion, pleasure, but also peace.

He never felt peace. But he had, briefly, with her.

For a moment in time he was just a man with a beautiful woman and he hadn't wanted it to end. The calm, and comfort. The release.

But of course that didn't last. Waking up next to her, he'd felt . . . strange. He'd . . . felt . . . feelings, and God help him, Wolf didn't do feelings. He didn't do relationships. He wasn't cut out for relationships.

And so he'd left her in his bed, and showered and dressed, and returned to his office downstairs to work. But sitting down at his desk, he thought of her place, dark, cold, and he realized she probably hadn't left her water running. She was probably going to go home to burst pipes.

He'd headed to her place immediately. The door was open and her cabin, even with the fire burning, was freezing. Her pipes hadn't frozen yet, and he turned the water on to a thin stream in each of her bathrooms as well as the kitchen sink before returning to his cabin and getting back to work.

He was glad when she'd appeared an hour later, fully dressed, glad she was returning home, glad she'd be out of his place. It was done, over, and yes, he'd had a lapse in judgment, but he'd be up-front, direct, and make it clear that this was a one-off. A mistake, if you will, and it wouldn't happen again.

He wasn't going to take her to his bed again. And he wasn't going to become neighbors that borrowed sugar from each other. There'd be no breakfast with her in the morning. No coffee and chat.

Back home, Wolf had worked, wrapping up with one job and beginning another. It was after midnight when he fell into bed, and he should have slept well. He didn't. He couldn't, not when his senses were still stirred, his body hard for her. They'd made love twice and yet he wanted more. He woke up hungry for her. Normally this didn't happen. Normally he could walk away and be good for weeks, if not months. Instead he lay on his bed, one hand wrapped around himself, trying to convince his body to relax. Forget her.

It didn't seem to matter if his eyes were open or closed; either way, he could see her, feel her. She was nothing like Jess, nothing like the women he'd been seeing these past five, ten years, but maybe that was what made her remarkable. Andi was pretty, kind, sweet, and funny. She had a warm, self-deprecating sense of humor and bright eyes that made his chest grow tight, fearful he'd hurt her. He was the kind of man who would hurt her. He should have stayed away.

But she had that accent, and those lips, and that smile. He'd always had a weakness for Southern girls, and even if she'd lived in California for decades, she remained a Southern girl.

So, no, he wasn't going for breakfast.

He wasn't going to encourage this, whatever it was, between them.

HE WASN'T COMING OVER.

She told herself he wouldn't come over when she woke up, and she told herself he wouldn't come as she made coffee, but of course, she hoped.

Andi was glad she'd showered at Wolf's place yesterday because she had no hot water, and washing her face in ice water was bad enough. There was no way she'd immerse all of herself in ice water. But she styled her hair, smoothing the wild curls into a thick ponytail, and put on clothes she hoped were somewhat flattering. And then covered those clothes with her puffy coat because the kitchen was freezing.

He wasn't coming, she told herself as the minutes ticked by, but even then, she waited a half hour more, just in case.

At eight thirty she cooked herself a scrambled egg, and toasted a slice of cinnamon bread using tongs over the flame of a gas burner, then ate her breakfast standing at the counter, near the stove, which warmed the kitchen a little, keeping her from freezing. She stared out the window at the snow-covered world, the snow still so thick she could only make out rough shapes, like that of the porch railing, and that of the picnic table.

She told herself not to feel hurt, and not to be embarrassed, as she boiled water to wash her dishes. Wolf wasn't an ordinary man. She'd known that for the past ten years. Just because he knew his way around her body didn't mean he'd be good for her heart. Which meant she couldn't—wouldn't—get attached. He wasn't one of those men she'd consider a keeper. He wasn't going to be part of her future. Which meant she wasn't going to go by his place. She wasn't going to drop in, or ask him to charge her phone. She'd survive a few days without her phone. She'd survive a few more days up here, without him.

She was shocked when Wolf showed up late that afternoon.

"How are the pipes?" he asked when she opened the door.

His hair looked wild. His beard looked wild. There was a fierceness in his eyes that matched the set of his jaw. Something was up, she just didn't know what. "Fine," she said cautiously. "How are you?"

"Just making sure you're alive."

"I'm here, doing well." She gestured to the living room behind her. "Want to come in? I hate letting the heat out."

He stepped in. She closed the door. He towered over her, glowering at her.

"What's wrong?" she asked, trying not to be put out because *he'd* come to her; *he* was interrupting her. There was no reason for him to be frustrated with her.

"I wasn't going to see you today," he said bluntly.

"I know." She tipped her chin up, meeting his gaze. "You don't do relationships. You don't like entanglements. And you're sorry you slept with the lady next door."

He growled his displeasure. "You're not just a lady next door. You're Andi McDermott—"

"Kevin's wife. Yes, I know." She crossed her arms over her chest. She was wearing four layers today. A silk camisole, a long-sleeve T-shirt, a cashmere turtleneck, and a thick down vest. Those layers plus the fireplace were just enough to keep her warm. "You didn't like Kevin, and now you don't know what to do about me."

Heat flared in his eyes. His voice dropped, deepening. "I know what I want to do with you."

"I have a feeling it's not conversation."

"I hate conversation."

"I've picked up on that," she said dryly. "So what brings you here?"

"I can't get any work done. I've spent the day worrying about you. I keep thinking I can't protect you if you're not under my roof."

He sounded seriously aggrieved. "You shouldn't be worried. I have shelter, Wolf. I have a fireplace. A stove. Running water, thanks to you."

"Come up for dinner."

"I don't think that's a good idea."

"What do you mean?"

"I don't regret yesterday, but I don't think it's smart to

continue. Being with you is playing with fire. I'm thinking a little self-preservation is in order."

"If we follow the rules, no one will be hurt."

"But I don't know the rules. You'll have to explain them to me."

"I will over dinner."

"So says the spider to the fly."

His mouth slowly curved. "I'm inviting you to dinner. I'm not going to have you for dinner. I promise you'll leave unscathed."

"Can I ask you a question?"

"Of course."

"Besides your marriage, what is the longest relationship you've had?"

"You mean, after my divorce?"

She nodded.

He thought for a moment. "A month or two. But that was a couple years ago."

"You don't do relationships?"

"No."

"But you like sex."

"Very much."

"You don't plan on getting married again?"

"Never. I've no interest in supporting a woman."

"Emotionally, or financially?" Andi asked, feeling offended on behalf of all women.

"Both."

"I see." Her eyes narrowed as she studied him. His words were clipped, cold, but it was good for her to hear this. Just because he'd been a very generous lover didn't mean he'd be a good partner. Just because he'd made her feel amazing didn't mean he wouldn't break her heart. She didn't want to care about him, but somehow, she did.

His jaw tightened, a small muscle pulling near his ear. "It's not personal—"

"Always a good answer."

He glared at her. "You're starting to piss me off."

"Don't take it personally. I'm just being honest."

"What's wrong with you?"

"You. You seduce me, you make me feel so many things, and then you tell me I'm not to get attached, that it's only sex and it's nothing else, and I have no desire—"

He cut off her stream of words by covering her mouth with his. Wolf pulled her close, his arms wrapping around her, his tongue parting her lips in a deep, fierce, possessive kiss. He kissed her as if he was starving. Kissed her as if he couldn't get enough of her.

Andi couldn't resist him, either. He made her feel alive, made her nerves dance and her pulse race, desire flooding her veins. She couldn't remember ever feeling pleasure like this, couldn't remember ever wanting anyone like this. It was madness, but the madness was addictive. . . . She wasn't sweet, safe, reliable Andi, but fire. Dangerous. Exciting.

By the time Wolf lifted his head, Andi was up against the wall, with one of Wolf's hands beneath her clothes, cupping her breast, and the other on her butt, making her feel delicious things.

She wrapped her arms around his neck. "That wasn't supposed to happen, you know."

"You wouldn't stop talking."

"Today I vowed to keep you at arm's length," she said, voice husky, lips tingling, body throbbing. She loved his hand on her breast, loved his hand on her butt, loved the pressure of his erection against her thighs. "And look at us now."

"And I vowed to focus on work, and instead I spent the afternoon chopping and browning meat and vegetables."

She laughed, but the laugh turned to a gasp when his warm hand cupped her bare breast, his fingers tugging lightly on her nipple. Intense sensation flooded her, melting her. "I don't know how to keep things platonic around you."

"You can't." His lips brushed her earlobe. His teeth pulled on her sensitive skin. "Just as I can't keep my hands off of you. It's your fault, you know."

She closed her eyes, breathless, weak. "Mine?"

"Apparently, I have a thing for your big brown eyes and your soft, sweet mouth. Can't work, can't focus, can't relax. You've gotten under my skin and it's annoying as hell."

"If you'd been terrible in bed, we wouldn't be having this problem today," she said, amused.

"You're blaming me, then?"

"Yes. Yesterday was amazing. On a scale of one to ten, it was a ten. Make that a ten plus. But I'm not sure that it's smart to continue—"

"I made you dinner. You need to eat."

"I have canned soup here."

"Don't tell me you'd rather have canned soup over homemade beef burgundy."

"But if I come over, I can't sleep with you this time. If I come over, it's as your neighbor. As a friend."

"You said I was a ten plus."

The corners of her lips lifted. He looked boyish and hopeful, handsome and charming, and yesterday afternoon when he put his mouth on the tender skin of her inner thigh, she'd nearly lost her mind. Kevin didn't like "mixing it up." He'd enjoyed receiving oral sex but didn't reciprocate. Wolf had . . . well, he'd nearly given her her third orgasm, but she'd stopped him just before she climaxed, feeling guilty, and confused. Was sex supposed to be this good? And was this just sex, or was it more? Because being close to him, being held against him, made her feel things that she hadn't felt in oh so many years.

"You were," she said, adding, "And I imagine you still are, but I'm new at this. Dating the second time around is different. You know what you're doing. I don't. I have to be careful, Wolf. If I'm not, I could lose my head."

"I'm inviting you for dinner. And to take advantage of my hot water, as well as recharge your phone while you're there." He hesitated, expression almost grim. "I promise not to take advantage of you. Nothing will happen that you don't want."

That was the problem. She already wanted him. If she came over, they'd be naked again, fast. She wasn't going to tell him that, though. She was going to make him work a little bit. "It'll be awkward coming over and eating in silence." She gave him a look. "You said you don't like to talk."

"We can talk about some things."

"We've already exhausted the weather as well as the economy. I'm not much for sports, although if I'm watching college football, I always root for the Southeastern Conference—"

"What do you want to talk about?"

"I want to know who you are. I want to know where you're from. I've been your neighbor for ten years, but I know nothing about you."

His lips brushed hers and he trailed a finger down her ribs to her waist. "You drive a hard bargain, but you have a deal."

YESTERDAY SHE'D SPENT A HALF DAY IN HIS CABIN, BUT most of it had been upstairs. Tonight she was staying downstairs and she was intrigued by the differences between his cabin and hers. Both were built in the late twenties to early thirties, and both had additions, but her cabin was much smaller, whereas his had a wing attached to the back, space for his sons, he explained.

Wolf didn't have a dining room, either, having turned that into an office. One entire wall was covered in books, shelf after shelf of books. She turned and looked behind her. The doorway was framed with more shelves, all filled with books.

She approached one wall and studied some of the titles. Histories. Biographies. Politics. Current events. She moved down the wall, still reading. Novels. More novels.

"Whose books are these?" she asked him, drawing out a novel she'd heard about but had never read.

"Mine," he said, watching her.

Andi slid the book back to its place. "Have you read most of them?"

"I've read all."

Andi hid her shock. All these years she'd made so many assumptions about Wolf Enders based on the way he looked. She thought his size, wardrobe, transportation, and tattoos meant he was rough. Brutish. And yet these books, and the music playing in the background, classical music—she didn't recognize the work or the composer—weren't choices an uneducated man would make.

All these years she'd felt a superiority . . . she and Kevin were the good ones, Wolf and his aggressive dog were the problem. But maybe she and Kevin had been the problem. Maybe they'd been ignorant and judgmental.

She felt incredibly shallow, as well as unkind. What had Wolf actually ever done to them? What had he ever done to *her*?

WOLF COULDN'T REMEMBER THE LAST TIME HE'D PRE-pared a dinner for someone. Yes, he'd thrown steaks on a grill, but that was different. That was easy. The chopping, the sautéing, the browning had kept him in the kitchen, away from his computer, but he wanted to do something for her. Wanted to feed her. Make sure she was warm, safe.

It was the most ridiculous desire. Andi McDermott was

not starving in her cabin, nor was she going to turn into an icicle, but it didn't matter. He felt compelled to go to her and ask her to join him. He wanted to see her by the fire, her thick dark curls framing her face, her warm brown eyes smiling at him.

She was beautiful and intriguing and he'd missed her today. And that frustrated him.

He didn't miss anyone. He didn't need anyone. He was happiest alone, doing his thing. At least, that's how it usually was. Today was different. Today he couldn't stop thinking about her; and the fact that she was so close, just down the driveway in her own cabin, drove him crazy,

"Do you remember when you and Kevin wore matching outfits?" he said as they finished dinner, which they'd eaten in the living room in front of his fire.

"We never wore matching outfits."

"Alright, matching shirts." He saw her shaking her head, and he nodded. "You did. You both had these blue plaid shirts—his was more masculine, but it was the same plaid. And then one Christmas you each had matching sweaters. The kid had one, too—"

"We'd just gone to Santa's Village for a family photo," she interrupted. "You can't count that."

"But the plaid shirts? The baseball shirts?"

"The baseball shirts were only worn on game day. We were baseball fans. We supported the Angels."

"It was cute."

She rolled her eyes. "Funny how you don't make it sound cute."

"Were you happy with him?"

Andi's expression shifted, becoming more wary. "Yes."

"It was a happy marriage?"

"We had our disagreements, but it was a good marriage. I loved him. I liked being married."

"Why?"

She shrugged. "I liked being somebody's person. Maybe

I'm old-fashioned, but I liked being a wife. *His* wife. I liked being the one he came home to, and shared things with. I think that's what I miss the most now. I have new friends, people who care about me, but . . . there's no one I belong to. No one at night who looks for me to come through that door. No one to smile at me . . ." Her voice wavered. "Or to hug me. I don't think I realized how much those hugs mattered until there weren't any. I mean, a hug is a hug, right? But it isn't. A good hug from the right person is everything. The right hug is comfort with love and acceptance. The right hug means happiness."

ANDI WATCHED AS WOLF ROSE AND COLLECTED THEIR big bowls and dinner plates. He carried them into the kitchen and then returned, standing in the doorway to look at her.

"You didn't like marriage?" she asked.

"I'm divorced."

"Was it ever good?"

He hesitated. "I don't remember."

"Honestly?"

He returned to his chair and sat down, extending his legs onto the old coffee table. "Have we talked enough now? I'd like to kiss you." His gaze slowly swept over her, lingering on her lips, and then lower, on her breasts. "And other things."

Andi flushed. "We're still getting to know each other."

"I think we know each other."

"Is there something else you're interested in right now?" she asked.

He looked at her, silver-gray gaze hot. "You."

Her skin tingled. Her cheeks felt warm. "I was dating someone until recently," she said, ignoring what he'd said, "but it was awkward. I'm discovering that dating the second time around is every bit as bad, if not worse, than the first time."

"That's why I don't date."

She looked at him, her eyes locking with his. "You just . . ."

"Yes. I just do . . . you." He gestured, wanting her to go to him.

She felt a tremor within her. She wanted to go to him, but the attraction was overwhelming. "Dating is like Goldilocks and the Three Bears. Nothing feels right. Everything is either too big or too small."

"But what if you found the right bed, and the right chair, and the right bowl of porridge? What then?"

"I don't know. That's a good question. I hadn't planned on remarrying."

"No?" He rose, crossed to her, pulled her to her feet. "You're avoiding me."

"I'm trying to stick to the rules," she whispered, mouth going dry, pulse racing.

He dropped his head, kissing her temple, and then her cheekbone and then the corner of her lips. "I think you would remarry," he said. "You are the marrying kind."

Her legs wobbled. Her insides felt hot and shivery. "I'm not trying to replace Kevin, but I'm open to love. I'm open to falling in love."

He tilted her chin up, kissing the tender spot just beneath her jaw. "If you met the right person," he said.

Her body no longer seemed to belong to her. She felt sensitive and strange . . . wildly alive. "If," she echoed breathlessly.

"Tell me about the men you're dating," he said, bringing her close, shaping her body to his.

Andi exhaled. She couldn't think. Couldn't remember his question, not when his hands were on her hips, palms sliding to cup her backside. His hands felt good, and his kisses were making her dizzy. "Maybe," she said, dazed, "we should stop talking."

"Finally."

*   *   *

THEY MADE LOVE ON THE SHEEPSKIN RUG IN FRONT OF his fire.

After, Wolf held Andi in his arms, her back to his chest, his arm wrapped around her, cupping her full breast. He relished her softness and the way she fit against him, long curls tumbling over his arm. He liked her smell—lavender, citrus, and honey—and the scent of her warm, damp skin. Her modesty when he kissed her—everywhere—made him harder, made him hungrier, even more determined to please her and feel her shatter for him.

If he'd met her years ago, before he was who he'd become, he'd find it hard to let her go. But he wasn't young, and his scars and wounds and walls were permanent, protecting others from being damaged by him. Because that's what he did. He was destructive. The beast.

He thought she'd dozed off, but then she whispered, "You said you were going to talk to me. Tell me about you. But all we've done is talk about me."

"I thought it was a good conversation," he said.

"No. I want to know you. Where did you grow up? Before you retired, what did you do? What was your wife like?"

"That's a lot of ground to cover."

"Start with your wife. Maverick's mom."

"She was from Louisiana, born and raised just outside Baton Rouge."

"What was her name?"

"Jessica. Jess."

"Do you miss her?"

"No." He paused, realizing how harsh that sounded. "As I said earlier, we didn't have a good marriage. We didn't see eye to eye. I'm sure I didn't make it easy for her. She wasn't happy, and she wasn't happy with me. The divorce—which happened when Maverick was young—was a relief for both of us."

Andi tucked a hand beneath her cheek. "She was a good mom?"

"She was a great mom." He said nothing, before shrugging. "And I was a shit dad."

"How did you meet?"

"On a plane. She was the flight attendant in first class."

"You were in first class?"

"No. I was in the front row of economy—bulkhead—and there was a flimsy curtain between us, but I managed to get her number, and the rest, well, you probably figured out."

Andi looked up at him, eyebrow arched. "No. I haven't. That's not even a story."

"I don't really tell stories."

"I'm sorry."

"That I don't tell stories?"

"That the only thing you remember about your wife is that she was a flight attendant."

He laughed because Andi was funny and he hadn't expected that. "There's plenty to remember," he said dryly. "That's all I chose to share."

"Where did she live? Why did you fall in love with her?"

"You don't give up."

"I try not to."

Again he smiled. He didn't like to smile, but she was doing it to him. "You want the truth?"

"Yes."

"I fell in love with her body. She was gorgeous. A beautiful blond with a smoking-hot body. Is that what you want?"

"If it's true."

He looked at her, thinking she was a little bit crazy. "Why are you so interested?"

"Until this weekend, all I knew about you is that you ride motorcycles, own big scary dogs, and live like a hermit."

"What's wrong with that?"

"You also read books and make great beef burgundy."

Wolf looked away, fighting annoyance. This was the part of dating he didn't like. He didn't enjoy being pressed and prodded. He didn't want to share feelings. He didn't want to expose the past, or give away pieces of himself.

Why did women think conversation created intimacy? Sex was far more satisfying than conversation.

"I know you mean well," he said after a lengthy, uncomfortable silence. "But this kind of talking, and sharing, isn't part of what I do."

"What do you do?"

"Sex, no strings attached."

He waited for her to cry, to rail, to get up and stomp off. Instead she just looked at him. The silence made him even more irritated. Her silence. She should say—do—something.

"Please don't feel judged," she said, putting a hand on him.

"I don't."

"I'm just curious because I like you."

"You shouldn't like me."

"Probably not. But I do. I'm sorry."

Wolf looked down at Andi and traced her lovely brow bone, cheekbone, and lips. "I met Jess on the flight after my dad's funeral. He died in a car accident. It was unexpected and we hadn't been talking at the time of his death. I went back to New Orleans for the funeral, and then three days later was heading back to Camp Pendleton, and Jess was on that flight. She was young, blond, with legs that went on forever. I wasn't the only one watching her pass out drinks and snacks to the window seat, but I was the one that got her number."

"Of course you were."

"The next time she had a layover in San Diego we hung out, and . . ." He shrugged. "That was that. We married six months after we met. Three months later I was deployed for eighteen months. I came home and finally met my son."

At first Jess was good waiting for him, especially as she had Stone, named after Wolf's favorite band, the Rolling Stones, and then came Lincoln, who was named for his favorite president, and then finally Maverick, simply because.

But by the time Maverick arrived, Jessica had had enough of being a single mom. She wanted Wolf to retire from active duty and be the husband and father he'd said he would be. She wanted the home he'd promised her, the handsome house in the Garden District.

Wolf bought her the house she wanted, a three-story pale green Queen Anne Italianate, with tall windows, ornate trim, and a wide covered porch. The house had black shutters and a glossy black front door. There were wrought-iron window boxes beneath the upstairs windows, gas lanterns, and a grand staircase leading to the second and third floors. He'd liked the house, too, and it was a stretch but ultimately a good investment. They settled in the house, enrolled the boys in the local school, and then Wolf was off again, for close to a year this time. The Middle East was a hotbed of terrorism and extremism and Wolf did sensitive, highly classified work that he couldn't discuss with anyone, even her. She just knew he had a very private life, a very dangerous life, one that involved rigorous training that not every soldier survived. He did, of course, as Jessica reminded him on a call once. He lived such a charmed life that the world could implode around him and he'd come out unscathed, walking tall.

By the time she filed for divorce, she loathed the sight of him. She wanted all of his things out, and removed all the pictures of him from the house, although the boys kept their photos of him in their rooms.

The boys grew up. Stone went to Tulane, earned a degree in engineering, even as he committed to the Marine Corps, wanting to follow in his father's steps. Jessica was beside herself. She railed at Wolf, begged him to talk some sense into Stone, cried herself to sleep for nights because she loved her oldest and feared he was too good and too kind to survive the life his father had lived. She knew in her heart he wouldn't lead a charmed life.

Her fears had been correct.

"So you have two sons," Andi said, snuggling in his arms.

He hesitated. Three, but he wouldn't talk about Stone. "Yes."

"Do you miss your work?"

"It took me awhile to settle into civilian life. Did a stint as a defense contractor until I earned my drafting degree and started my own business. I now work for myself."

"What is a drafting degree?"

"My degree was in technical drafting and design technology. I work with architects, contractors, builders, and homeowners who know what they want and don't want to pay architect fees."

She rolled onto her back, and he moved onto his elbow to look down at her. The firelight illuminated her profile. Her dark hair spilled across the sheepskin rug. She looked like a sexy cavewoman. His, but not his.

He kissed her, because she looked kissable, but also, he was tired of talking, tired of remembering. He wasn't a fan of the past, and he hated talking about himself. Far easier to make love to Andi again, to get lost in her warmth and forget everything for a brief period of time.

But later, Andi stirred and said she should go home, as they'd both sleep better in their own beds. It was true.

He needed to say something before she left, to clarify things. He wanted her to understand he wasn't relationship material. But what to say? He'd told her he didn't do relationships and yet he'd been so into her, acting like a lovesick teenager. "I enjoyed myself. I hope you did, too."

She gave him an odd look even as she sat up, pulled her undershirt on, and then the flannel over it, skipping some layers. Her gaze locked with his. Her chin tilted up. "It was great." But, judging from her expression, great wasn't good. Her face was pale, jaw set. She looked as if she felt sick. Or about to be sick.

He hated that. He didn't want to hurt her.

Wolf reached out, tugged on one of her wild curls. "Maybe I didn't say that right."

"No, you said it fine. You're right. It was fun, and now it's over. Right?"

Yes. No. "Let's just skip it. We can talk in the morning—"

"No, let's do it now," she said, holding the flannel shirt closed over her chest. "Let's get this done. I've been worrying about this. Just tell me. Pretend I'm someone else, someone you've just met in a bar, or a bike rally—"

"A bike rally?" He flashed his smile.

"Isn't that what you call them?"

"I don't do bike rallies. I just ride my motorcycle. Usually on my own. Sometimes with a few friends."

"Okay. So you've met me in a bar and we had a night of hot sex. What happens next?"

"I walk you out, or I walk out of your place."

"And?"

"It's over."

"How do I know it's over?" she persisted calmly, and yet there was a shadow in her eyes.

"I'd remind you that there's no getting attached. This isn't a relationship. This is about convenience. We had a good time, but it's over." He paused, looked at her. Her eyes were wide; she was listening, taking it all in. "So we won't exchange numbers. We won't make plans. There's no future."

"No more hooking up then?" she asked.

"That's right."

"Because you're on to your next hookup."

There was no light in her eyes anymore. Just sadness. "Because I don't leave doors open," he said bluntly. "I don't like entanglements. I prefer things neat, clean. So this, what we're doing, ends when you go home. When do you head back?"

"In the morning," she answered huskily.

Silence stretched. Andi wasn't looking at him. He saw her swallow and draw a deep breath. "Will you help me get chains on my car in the morning?" she asked. "Just help me with that and we'll be done."

HE DIDN'T SLEEP WELL THAT NIGHT BUT, AS PROMISED, woke early to help Andi with the snow chains, and then she was gone.

Wolf returned to his cabin, dragged his snow-crusted boots off and left them just inside the door before heading to the computer adjacent to his drafting table. Thank goodness for the software that made his job easier, streamlining the technical drawings required by both city planners and builders. In the beginning, when he was just starting out, he did it all by hand, not trusting the dimensions would be right, but now he couldn't imagine trying to do it all himself. He still pored over the final plans, double-checking dimensions before handing them off to the builders and contractors, but he had more confidence in the software than his own measurements.

Wolf switched on the desk lamp and picked up the plans ready to be mailed to the architect in San Clemente. With the snow, it might be easier hand delivering. If so, he'd leave in the morning and just drive them down. He could visit the bank, take care of some errands, and be back the same night.

And then instead of his schedule, he pictured Andi climbing into her car, and then driving away. She hadn't looked back at him. Hadn't waved.

And he hated all of this, but a clean break was the best way to go. Honestly, the only way to go. She wasn't good for his calm, and control. She knocked him off-balance, disturbed his focus.

There was something about her that got to him. She had a strange way of breaking down his walls, getting him to feel, and God knows, he didn't like feeling. His head would always rule his heart. It was the way he was wired.

He wished he hadn't opened up yesterday about his marriage. He shouldn't have talked about Jess. Thinking of his ex-wife always made him feel like a failure. He'd loved her, and he'd hated her, but he'd mostly loved her.

And he couldn't think of her without thinking of Stone.

She'd never forgive him for Stone's death, just as she'd never forgive him for leaving her all those years to raise three little boys on her own.

She'd never forgiven him for choosing to serve the country over being home to take care of her.

She'd never forgiven him for being the kind of role model that made their sons want to sign up and fire guns and put their lives in harm's way.

The thing was, he couldn't blame Jess. She had a right to be angry. He hated himself, too. Stone had been the best of the best. He'd been smart, a great athlete, polite, loyal, loving, and a damn good soldier. A damn good leader. He'd done it all right and then it had gone all wrong and it didn't matter that he'd earned a Purple Heart posthumously. The Marine Corps could keep all of its damn medals, damn awards. They could just give him back his son.

Wolf got up and went to the fridge, opened it, looked at the beer. It was too cold for a beer. He closed the fridge and rubbed his eyes. He missed Stone. The other boys, Lincoln and Maverick, they were good boys, too, really good boys, and they tried hard to keep an eye on their mom. They tried hard to fill the gap that Stone had left, but Stone had been larger than life, and even now, four years on, they missed him so much.

Chapter 8

ANDI WAS NUMB AS SHE DROVE HOME TO SAN JUAN Capistrano.

It was over. Whatever had been between them was over. She'd suspected it'd be short-lived, but after so much heat, and so much passion, he was able—willing—to break it off completely?

Her eyes stung, watered, but she blinked hard, refusing to give in to tears.

She wasn't going to fall apart, not now, not driving. She turned on the radio, flipped between the seventies and eighties channel on her satellite radio, and heard ELO's "Don't Bring Me Down" and turned it up. Loud.

She sang the lyrics as she drove, angry, not just at him but at herself, because she really should have known better. All the warning signs were there. She'd just chosen to ignore them.

But oh, the pleasure. She hadn't felt anything close to that in years. Her last orgasm with a partner had been with Kevin, a month before he died. She should be grateful Wolf knew what to do with her, knew how to satisfy her, but why did it have to end *now*? Why couldn't they still see each other sometimes?

What was wrong with occasional dates?

Andi wiped away a tear, still determined not to cry, still determined to be strong. She'd been through so much worse. She wouldn't break now.

But she'd liked him. And she liked him still.

WOLF WORKED LATE MONDAY, TRYING TO GET CAUGHT up, wanting to wrap up the Seifferts' plans so he could drop those off tomorrow as well.

He didn't have his phone near him, not wanting to be distracted, but when he got up to stretch his legs and refill his coffee, he looked at his phone and saw missed calls from virtually everyone in his family.

What had happened?

He began scrolling through the texts. Jess hadn't sent a message, but Lindsay did. Houston, we have a problem, was the first.

Then, Get me out of here.

Followed by: Please help! I'm going crazy.

Wolf glanced at the time. Eleven his time, one in the morning there. He texted back. Just seeing your messages, are you okay?

No. She answered almost immediately. Can Charlie and I come live with you?

Wolf set his phone down. He needed time before he answered that one. His first instinct was no, because he couldn't imagine anyone living with him, much less a young woman and a child. Even if that child was his grandson.

Maybe *because* that child was his grandson.

But at the same time, he owed Stone. He owed Stone big-time.

Wolf picked up his phone. I've got to drop off some plans tomorrow and then I'm on my way.

Lindsay: Is that a yes or a no, Wolf? I need to know.

Wolf: We'll talk to Jess tomorrow. But the plan is to pack up your car and drive you and Charlie home with me.

IF JESS HADN'T BEEN HAPPY TO SEE HIM A WEEK AGO, she was even less welcoming now. "You're enabling her," Jess said tightly, facing him in the kitchen. He'd caught her in the middle of doing dinner dishes. It was takeout—the cartons were on the stove—but, knowing Jess, they'd used real plates.

"She wants a change. I don't think that's a bad thing," Wolf said, standing inside the kitchen door. Jess hadn't asked him to sit, and he wasn't interested in lingering, or getting into a war of words. It had been a long travel day, and tomorrow would be even longer if they started the drive to California. If they could get on the road tomorrow.

"She doesn't know you, though," Jess added furiously. "She doesn't understand what life will be like with you. She has this idea that California will be all sunshine, beaches, and amusement parks. She thinks you'll be there for her—"

"I will be."

"You won't."

"I'll try."

She laughed bitterly. "Famous last words."

Wolf raked fingers through his beard, holding on to his own temper. After landing earlier, he'd gone to his hotel, showered, put on clean clothes, and driven over to Jess's. Lindsay had given Jess a heads-up that Wolf was coming, which had just given Jess time to fume. "I can't change the past, Jess. I can only do better now."

She gave him a long look that said more than words ever could. "If things get hard—and they will get hard—you are on your own. I'm not going to rescue you."

Wolf sighed, exhausted. "Good night, Jess. I'll see you in the morning."

Back at the hotel, he put on a worn, soft T-shirt and light-weight sweats before stretching out on the bed. He was tired, but he couldn't sleep.

He shouldn't have come back. He shouldn't have done this. He felt trapped. Obligated.

But how did he say no to Lindsay? How did he take away her hope?

Jess was right—from his conversation earlier with Lindsay, it was clear she believed life would be better in California. She had this idea that things would be easier and she'd be happier. She'd never lived in California, but to be near the beach? To go outside and pick oranges anytime you wanted? And then there was Hollywood. Universal Studios. Disneyland.

And then there was the fact that she'd be living with him, and not Jessica, who tried to run her house as if it was a military base, and Lindsay didn't want the authority, or the rules.

Jessica had been outraged that he'd show up today and play hero. It had made Jess even more upset that Lindsay calmed down once he was there, and Charlie, too. Wolf had promised Jess that he wouldn't take Lindsay away tomorrow, but give them a day to discuss everything and come up with a plan. Lindsay had a plan, and felt as if Jess wasn't listening, or didn't care because it wasn't her plan. Jess wanted Charlie in a preschool program somewhere, learning.

So tomorrow would be more negotiation, more conversation, more decisions. Now he just wanted to sleep so he'd be prepared for the battle.

The battle began early with a loud breakfast at Jess's. Charlie was running wild, taking advantage of the tension, trying to upstage his mom, who was arguing with his grandmother Gigi.

Listening to the two women yell, Wolf was glad he'd never had a daughter. He couldn't imagine years of this.

Since neither woman wanted to listen to him, he wasn't going to stay. He'd go, get coffee, and return when things were calmer. If things could settle. But Charlie shrieked when Wolf headed to the door and then everyone chased after him, Lindsay crying, Charlie still shrieking, Jess shouting.

He held up one hand. "Enough," he growled, fed up. "This is ridiculous. I'm not going to do this, and if you want to, you can continue without me."

"Don't go, Wolf," Lindsay begged, catching his arm. "Please, I need you here."

"Sure, Wolf, leave. It's what you do best," Jess said, hands at her hips.

"Stop making that noise," he said to Charlie, picking him up.

Thankfully, Charlie stopped.

Wolf looked at Jess and Lindsay. "I'm going to go for breakfast. You're welcome to come with me, but no more fighting. It stops now."

"I'd like breakfast," Lindsay said meekly.

"Me, too," said Charlie, smiling up at Wolf.

Wolf looked at his ex. "Jess?"

She shook her head. "No."

"Why not?" he asked, keeping his tone neutral. "You can pick the place. You used to love Silver Whistle Café—"

"I have a Mardi Gras committee meeting in a couple hours, and I need to dress. It's a special luncheon and I can't show up like this." Her lips compressed. "But can I ask that no big decisions get made until we all talk this afternoon? Can we do that?"

"Yes." Wolf had no problem agreeing to it. He glanced at Lindsay. "Where do you want to go for breakfast?"

"Can we go back to Camellia Grill? I loved that place."

Wolf agreed, and fifteen minutes later they were in the

car, and another fifteen minutes passed and they were seated. Camellia Grill, a New Orleans institution, had been a favorite of his when he was a boy, his grandfather taking him, and now here he was with his grandson. Wolf put Charlie in a high chair, thinking it would help contain the boy while they ate. Charlie wasn't a fan, though, and squawked a protest.

Wolf dropped down, eye to eye with Charlie. "That noise stops now. You're not a baby anymore. You need to stop screaming and use words. Got it?"

Charlie stared back at him, as if assessing the danger.

"He's just hungry," Lindsay said, putting a hand on Charlie's arm. "He'll calm down as soon as we eat."

"Didn't he have anything earlier?" Wolf asked, sitting down at the table.

"I don't know. Maybe." She frowned. "Probably."

"Lindsay, I'm going to be honest. You should know. You're his mom. Not Jess."

"Jess has taken over. She makes all the decisions, and overrides my decisions."

"She cares about you," he said, drawing Charlie's high chair closer to the table, not liking how close a server was walking with a tray of food.

"She thinks I'm a terrible parent. And she's told me so, several times." Lindsay looked at Charlie, who was playing with a straw. "At the same time, I know she loves Charlie. She's very attached to him, which makes me feel guilty for wanting to leave—because she has been good to us. Better than my mom."

"You don't want to live with your mom?" Wolf asked.

Lindsay shuddered. "She's got a new boyfriend. He's worse than the last one. He's okay when he's sober, but he's not sober that often. Mom's afraid to kick him out."

"It's that bad?"

"She's always attracted to losers. I swear, I will not be like her. I won't. I'd never expose Charlie to the stuff I saw growing up. It's why I accepted Jessica's offer to live with her after Stone died. It seemed stable. Like a good environment. But it's become toxic. I have no confidence left."

"Would you rather live on your own?"

"Someday, but I don't think I can right now. I'm just so sad so much of the time." She looked at Wolf, tears filling her eyes. "He's not coming back, is he?"

Wolf didn't need to ask.

A hard knot thickened his throat. It had been three years, eleven months, and a handful of days since Stone had died, blown up by a roadside bomb in Afghanistan. "No." Wolf glanced at Charlie, who'd begun to play drums on the table with the available cutlery. Charlie, blond like Stone, with the same light gray eyes. Wolf removed the silverware from Charlie's hands and when Charlie opened his mouth to yell Wolf gave him a hard look and said no.

Charlie closed his mouth.

Wolf focused his attention back on Lindsay. "What do you need? What do you want?"

"Stone back." She grimaced and wiped her eyes with the restaurant's cloth napkin—a point of pride to the Camellia Grill—and then glanced around the restaurant, packed as, usual. "And Charlie healthy and happy."

"He is healthy and happy," Wolf said, noting Charlie's cunning expression. The three-year-old was planning his next mission of destruction. "He's a very bright boy."

She managed a watery smile. "Like his daddy."

"And his mom," Wolf corrected.

Lindsay said nothing for a long moment and then shook her head. "I want to come live with you and maybe take some classes, and finish my degree. It's going to take some time, but Stone always wanted me to finish, and I should, not just for him, but for Charlie, and me. With a college degree I could get a better job, have a career, provide for him the way I should."

She took the pink napkin and scrubbed her face dry.

"And yes, I could do that here. Your ex said she'd watch Charlie while I take classes, but I don't want to do this tug-of-war with her anymore. Jessica raised her sons. She had her turn. I want to do things differently than she does, but whenever I suggest something, she snaps at me. I'm always afraid I'm going to do something wrong, or Charlie will be loud or messy and that will set her off. She forgets that Charlie isn't Stone. Charlie doesn't have to be a little military man—"

"No one's wanting that."

"But she goes on and on about discipline, and how I've spoiled Charlie too much." Lindsay reached out and ran a hand over her son's thick blond hair. "She even took him to get his hair cut, despite me saying I liked his hair long. But no, she had to have him get one of those little-boy haircuts that I didn't want."

Wolf knew Jess, and she had good intentions; she was trying to step in and help, but Jess was very black-and-white. It was her way or the highway.

"I've looked into schools," she added. "There are several community colleges near you, as well as universities—"

"Lindsay, I live in the mountains, in a cabin, and there are schools near me—community colleges as well as Redlands, Cal State San Bernardino, UC Riverside—but they can be a long, difficult drive in winter, or when we get our fog."

She frowned. "What about your house? The one near the mission?"

"I've been renting it out. I've got people in it for months."

Her mouth opened, closed. "I didn't know." She looked crushed. Her eyes watered again. "All this time I was thinking you were there."

"I've been at the cabin for a couple of years now. I get more done there."

She nodded slowly. "Is there room for us at the cabin?"

He pictured the ice and snow, the lack of fences, the remote location on the mountain. "Charlie would love it in summer. I don't think he'd like being so cooped up this winter." He didn't add that he couldn't imagine trying to work with them there, too. It had been hard enough with Andi in her cabin next door, never mind a grieving Lindsay and a three-year-old trapped in the cabin with him.

"So you don't think we should come," Lindsay said in a small voice.

He knew he'd told Jess that no big decisions would get made, but that was before he understood just how dire the situation was. "No, I'm taking you and Charlie back with me tomorrow. You finish packing and I'm going to make some calls. I need to rearrange things so we can make this work."

Chapter 9

IT WAS HARDER SETTLING BACK INTO THE WORK ROU-
tine than Andi expected. Even after two weeks, she still
missed Wolf. She physically missed him, missing the feel
of him, the weight of him, the way he'd wrapped his arms
around her, holding her.

She couldn't quite remember his smell, but it was fresh,
crisp, masculine, and she'd liked it. She'd breathed him in,
burying her nose in his neck, smelling his throat, kissing
his chest. She'd liked the rough hair on his chest, and the
strength in his arms. She'd liked how tall he was and how
he'd press her back against the wall, or the bed, capturing
her body with his.

She missed all of it. She missed the tension and the energy and the sensation. She missed him. *Him*, Wolf, that
most awful and exciting of men.

So what was she to do? Just get over him? How?

It was one thing when Kevin was taken from her. There
was no option but to move on. He was gone, forever gone,

but Wolf wasn't gone. He was just an hour and a half's drive away. And everything in her wanted to go back up that mountain and demand more. Demand another night, another day, another forty-eight hours in his bed.

At his table.

In front of his fire.

For the first time in a long time she couldn't eat. For the first time in a long time she couldn't sleep. For the first time in a long time she felt like a girl—crazy, confused.

She needed someone to talk to, but who?

Her friend Paige wasn't at Orange when Andi returned, as Paige was in Tanzania teaching until spring semester began. Andi liked Elizabeth a lot, but wasn't comfortable seeking her out just to discuss men and sex. And Andi couldn't call Margot, not to discuss Wolf, not when Margot had been so interested in him.

She probably needed to say something to Margot about Wolf, but didn't know what, or when.

Maybe, if she was lucky, she wouldn't have to say anything at all.

Margot was the one who called her. It was the last day of a three-day weekend and the new transfer students were to move in to campus housing the following day, with the rest of the students returning a week later.

"Haven't heard from you in ages," Margot said when Andi answered. "What's going on?"

Andi's heart hurt. She felt guilty, and torn. Should she say something? Had she betrayed Margot's trust? "Nothing much. How about you?"

"I haven't talked to you since New Year's. Were you snowed in?"

"For a few days, yes." Andi took a quick breath. "Wolf dug me out and put chains on my car so I could get back home." She walked across her kitchen to the instant hot faucet on her sink and topped off her herbal tea. "There was so much snow. It was incredible."

"That was nice of Wolf," Margot said. "Did he offer, or did you ask him for help?"

"A little of both." Andi chose her words with care. "He's not as bad as I thought. You were right. Given the right circumstances, he can be . . . neighborly."

Silence stretched for a moment and then Margot laughed. "How neighborly?"

Margot might be laughing, but Andi wasn't sure she'd laugh if she knew Wolf had given Andi a half dozen orgasms in a handful of days. "I lost power, but he had a generator so he'd charge my phone for me, and my last night up there he made dinner."

"What did he make? Let me guess. Chili? Stew?"

"Stew," Andi said, thinking it was close enough. No need to make this a bigger deal than it needed to be. "But once I left, communication ended. I can't even imagine the next time I'll see him."

"You could always go back to your cabin."

"I'm back to work. No more running around for me, not for a while."

"Not until you come see me for your spring break. When is that? Have you checked the dates?"

"Looks like the third week of March."

"And you'll come see me?"

"I promise."

But after hanging up, Andi looked at the phone where she'd put it on the counter and it crossed her mind that they hadn't discussed Margot, or her work, or her life, at all. They'd only talked about Andi. And Wolf.

Even though there was no Andi and Wolf, not anymore.

NORMALLY WOLF WOULD DO THE DRIVE FROM NEW Orleans to Southern California in two days, a fifteen- or sixteen-hour day for day one, and then eleven or twelve hours the next day, but Charlie would never survive that many hours being strapped in his car seat, and Wolf wouldn't survive Charlie's frustrated tears, so they turned it into a three-day drive, with the first day breaking in San Antonio after nine hours, the second day stopping in Tucson, and then the third waking early to get home before dark.

Charlie was still in his pajamas when they loaded the car and set off for the last leg home. The rising sun painted the desert floor rose and gold, illuminating the tall saguaros. It was a beautiful morning and Wolf sipped his black coffee, grateful Charlie had fallen back asleep, and Lindsay sat curled in her seat, her winter coat draped over her chest, while she watched the scenery, absorbed by the view.

Wolf was grateful for the silence. He wouldn't say it was a terrible road trip, but it wasn't one of the best. Charlie had been bored these past two days, even with an iPad propped in front of him, and Wolf had begun to see how much Lindsay relied on the iPad to keep Charlie entertained, whether in the car, at the motel, or while eating at a restaurant. Wolf didn't want to weigh in, certainly not yet. But it did concern him.

A lot of things concerned him.

Charlie didn't like scrambled eggs, he didn't like vegetables, he didn't like meat that wasn't a hot dog or chicken nuggets. He liked strawberries, and sometimes a banana. He liked bread and butter. He liked syrup. If you could put syrup on it, he'd eat it. Pancakes, waffles, French toast, but otherwise, he'd just have Froot Loops for breakfast. Or Goldfish.

Lunch was nuggets and fries.

Dinner was more nuggets and fries.

None of Wolf's sons had been picky eaters, maybe because Jessica wouldn't allow them to be, or maybe she'd been creative in her approach, finding ways to cook healthy things without the boys knowing they were eating healthy things. Regardless, he wanted Charlie to get more variety in his diet. Drink more milk, less juice. Juice was full of sugar. Way too much sugar. The fact that a three-and-a-half-year-old loved soda as much as Charlie did bothered Wolf. His sons didn't drink soda until they were older, and even then there was more iced tea at their house than soda.

They drove along the Mexico border for an hour, the landscape monotonous, but Lindsay was fascinated that Mexico was just right there, on the other side of the highway.

Wolf broke the silence as they approached the California state border. "Should we talk about what's going to happen when we get to my house?" Wolf said.

Lindsay turned her head, looked at him. "Your house or your cabin?"

"My house. I've managed to take it back."

"I thought you had it rented out."

"I did. I refunded everyone their money, at least for the next six months."

"And then I'll be gone?" she asked.

"I didn't say that. But who's to say you will like living with me?" He wouldn't let himself say the other part, the part where he wasn't sure he'd like living with her, because it kind of didn't matter. He'd made a commitment to Lindsay and Charlie, and in his mind they'd be together for at least the next year. But there was no point saying too much about the future, as the future wasn't here. "I haven't been inside the house for a couple months. I went by and did some repairs in November, and had a cleaning company come this morning and change the sheets and run the vacuum, but it's not set up for us, it's set up for renters. I'll need to pull some things out of storage, turn one of the bedrooms that has a queen bed into a room for Charlie. Does he still sleep in a crib? Or is he now in a twin bed?"

"No cribs," Charlie said, having woken up. "I'm not a baby."

"I know," Wolf agreed. "You're not a baby. You're a big boy."

"Right," Charlie agreed.

"But you do know what that means, don't you?" Wolf glanced up, looked at the boy in the rearview mirror. Charlie was staring back at him with a serious expression. "It means you're big enough to help out now. Big enough to have some jobs around the house. Big enough to listen to your mom when she asks you to do something; you do it."

Charlie put a hand on his forehead and sighed heavily. "I'm not an adult. I don't have a job."

"You don't have to be an adult to have a job. Kids have jobs. Everyone helps out. That's the way it should be. In a family everyone contributes."

Charlie closed his eyes, apparently pained by the conversation. Wolf checked his smile, and looked at Lindsay. "You are responsible for yours and Charlie's laundry. I do my own. Same thing with sheets and towels. We will take turns with dinner. Some nights will be my night, other nights it will be your night. I haven't had a roommate in years. Jess was my last roommate, and as you know, she kept things tidy. I do, too. I never leave dishes in the sink. I will not like coming into the kitchen and seeing pots or pans on the stove, or the dishwasher always full. You do your part, and I'll do mine, and we should get along just fine."

Lindsay didn't look very confident. "I have a feeling I'm going to disappoint you." Her voice grew husky. "I disappointed Jessica all the time."

Wolf heard the pain in her voice and he didn't know what to do to comfort her. He wasn't good at comforting. He'd never known the right thing to say. His words only irritated Jessica. She called them excuses. Maybe they were. Or maybe he just didn't know how to be who she needed him to be. She'd grown up with three sisters, no brothers, and Wolf had been an only child. As a teenager he discovered sex was easy. Tenderness, that was something else.

"Just do your best," he said. "You're an adult, and I'm going to try not to be an asshole. Deal?"

She nodded, worry still shadowing her eyes.

He reached out, touched her shoulder, giving it a quick squeeze. "You've got this. I believe in you."

"But Wolf?"

"Yeah?"

"I don't know how to cook."

"I'm not expecting gourmet meals, Linds."

"No, I can't cook. Mac and cheese, and frozen pizzas, and microwaved burritos, that's all I can do. Are you okay with that?"

No, he wasn't okay with that. And neither was Charlie. "So Jessica cooked every night when you were with her?"

"Or we'd get takeout. We'd have dinner delivered three or four nights a week. She'd cook the other nights. She'd make a lot of salads. We both liked salads."

"And Charlie?" he asked, shooting her a troubled glance. "He likes salads, too?"

She wrinkled her nose. "No, I'd just boil him a quick hot dog."

Wolf counted to five, and then ten. This . . . this kind of helplessness, laziness, was going to end. He'd made sure his sons could cook. He'd make sure Lindsay could, too. "I'll teach you," he said. "You're smart. Cooking isn't that hard. You'll be glad you learned."

She didn't look encouraged. "But then there's the shopping."

"Yes."

"It all just takes a lot of time."

He had to bite his tongue, because really, what else did she have to do right now? She had Charlie, and . . . ? But he wouldn't say it. He wouldn't be that guy.

Not yet. They were only on day three.

He wished he had more coffee. He needed more coffee.

"It's not as time-consuming if you get in the habit of making a list of what you're going to cook, and then do your shopping once for the week, so you don't have to make daily trips to the store."

"But how do you know what you will want to eat later in the week? I don't even know in the morning what I'll want for dinner."

"Dinner isn't entertainment. It's just food. Fuel."

Lindsay sighed, closed her eyes. "Of course you'd say that. You're a guy."

Wolf winced. He said nothing else, ending the conversation.

ANDI FROZE, HANDS TIGHT ON THE SHOPPING CART. IT couldn't be . . . no. There was no way.

But who else had a beard and a tattoo of a snake wrapped around thick, tan biceps? Who else had more ink creeping out of the neck of a T-shirt?

It had been a month since she'd last seen Wolf, and spotting him across the grocery store felt as if she'd touched a live wire. She felt zapped, electrified.

Seeing him made her feel intensely; it was such a visceral reaction, too.

The chemistry, the energy, the awareness.

The ache.

She'd spent weeks going about her day, passing men, working with men, feeling absolutely nothing, no awareness, nothing. And then just one look at Wolf and her insides melted into a quivering mass of need.

This could not be normal.

Was this why she'd been so afraid of him all these years? She wasn't afraid of him, but the attraction. Afraid of how she responded to him.

Like when she'd gone to ask about jumper cables and

he'd looked at her as if he was a wolf, and she was a little rabbit. He was powerful. She was prey.

She'd felt that power then. She felt it now, across the store, beneath the bright lights of the produce area, felt it through the shoppers and the carts and the employees re-stocking bins.

She hoped he wouldn't see her because she just wanted to watch him, drink him in. Oh, he looked good, Hand-some, yes . . . Margot was right. He was handsome and rugged, and that face of his, when he turned his head . . . that profile. The brow, the cheekbones, the nose, the chin.

The mouth. Those lips.

How he'd kissed her with that mouth. How he'd made her feel . . .

Her heart raced, her body shot with adrenaline.

Look at me, don't look at me.

Look at me, don't see me.

It would kill her if he saw her and just walked away. It would break her heart.

Don't break my heart.

He was dressed so casually, jeans, a T-shirt, black boots, as if he'd just climbed off a motorcycle. Maybe he had.

He added a couple bell peppers and onions to his hand-basket. Grabbed some avocados. Examined squash, and then bagged up three of those, adding them to his basket, too.

She felt like a kid standing outside a candy store. She wanted . . . she wanted . . . him.

Wanted more time with him.

But he wasn't hers. He was no one's. But most definitely not hers.

Andi pushed her cart around the corner, disappearing before Wolf could see her. It wasn't that she hadn't made an effort today—she had, she always did—but seeing him made her feel everything all at once, and it was too much.

Andi grabbed some yogurt, a carton of creamer, eggs, and Swiss cheese and then decided to just leave.

Andi did the self-checkout, anxious to escape. She'd just stepped outside, late afternoon sunlight making her blink, when one of Kevin's old friends from the canoe club stopped her and gave her a hug, asking about her. Andi hadn't seen Vince for a couple years and would normally have enjoyed catching up, but all she could think about was Wolf exiting through those same doors and bumping into her.

Finally, Vince said goodbye and he walked into the store and Andi crossed the parking lot for her car, but slowed when she spotted Wolf's distinctive Land Rover parked not far from hers.

Again, her heart fell.

She stopped, stared. A young woman with long light brown hair was sitting in the passenger seat while a little boy stood in the driver's seat, twisting the steering wheel, pretending to drive. The young woman was smiling at the child and Andi's heart seized, leaving her shaky.

Who were they?

Was this why Wolf couldn't see Andi anymore? Was he in a relationship? Did he have another family?

She felt anxious, breathless. Heart pounding, she put her groceries in the car and left the parking lot quickly. Everything felt wrong. And nothing made sense.

IT WAS ANOTHER WARM MORNING, THE SANTA ANA winds blowing hot air over the mountains, toward the ocean, the dry air gusting through the eucalyptus trees surrounding Andi's house. It wasn't even eight yet, but temperatures were rising and Andi dressed lightly for her Saturday morning walk, wearing stretchy walking pants and a T-shirt with a thin hoodie to wrap around her hips.

She'd slept badly, again.

Seeing Wolf at her local grocery store had thrown her, just as much as seeing a young woman and child in his car, waiting for him. There was so much she didn't know, so much she didn't understand. She needed to move on. They weren't supposed to be attached. He didn't want a relationship with her, so why was she still spending so much time thinking about him?

How did one weekend upend her whole world?

How had he hooked her heart like this? She'd dated a half dozen different men this year and none of them had mattered. Why did Wolf mean so much to her? It was ridiculous. They were opposites in every way. They had nothing in common . . . other than sharing a property line in Blue Jay.

She had to stop this, had to stop obsessing. It was exhausting, and it wasn't helping. Time to go walking and walk him out of her heart and head.

Andi grabbed her water bottle, put a hat on to shield her eyes and skin, and set off, walking from her house, down the long curving road to Del Obispo, and then along the busy road until she could turn left and cut through the park, walking to Hidden House Coffee. Just like at the cabin, she enjoyed the walk down the hill. The walk back up wasn't too bad on a cool day, but it'd be warm, if not hot, when she returned. But she'd survive. Sweating might just be what she needed.

The yellow coffeehouse was literally in a house, a 120-year-old house on Los Rios Street. The coffee was always strong, the customer service wonderful, the setting special. Los Rios was the historic district, and a reminder of what old California must have been like, before everything became big houses and palm trees.

Andi had come to love California. She hadn't thought she would, and it had taken her years, but it was now home. She was happy in this place with orchard-covered hills and Spanish architecture. She loved the university where she worked. She had a good life, she knew good people, and one day she'd find her person. One day she'd meet a man who wanted her, a man who'd make her feel safe and desired, and not just put her in a car and send her on her way.

Goodbye.

She hated goodbye.

Andi entered through the wooden gate, walked beneath the trees, leaves crunching underfoot. She could smell the coffee and cinnamon from here. Climbing the front steps, she stepped aside so a mom pushing a stroller could exit first, and then waited another moment so that a girl on a phone could get past her, the girl upset about something a boy had done or said.

Andi smiled sympathetically, feeling the girl's pain.

Inside, she ordered her coffee, gave her name, pocketed her small wallet, tucking it into her vest, and then stepped away, waiting for her coffee to be made. The interior of the coffeehouse had lots of dark wood and cream walls. Pastries and muffins filled the glass display. She loved the cinnamon rolls here, but then, she loved all things butter and sugar.

She was tempted to get a cinnamon roll and then remembered her vow to lose ten pounds. She needed to lose more, but really, ten was necessary, and she wouldn't lose a single pound if she indulged in pastries and sweet rolls.

"Enders," the barista said, calling a customer's name.

Andi startled at the name, wondering if she'd heard right. She glanced around and there was Wolf, rising from a corner table, again dressed casually in a T-shirt, jeans, and boots. He'd just cut his hair. Thursday it had still been long. Now it was cropped close, highlighting the angle of his cheekbones, the light eyes.

She stepped back as he retrieved his coffee from the counter. She watched him walk, heart falling, tumbling to her feet. She couldn't believe it. Again? Twice in one week? What were the odds?

If it were anyone else, she'd greet him, make conversation, work through the awkwardness by being friendly, but Wolf made her feel too many things, and he'd been quite clear . . . no contact, no emails, no texts, no calls.

But now he was here, again, invading her calm, upending *her* world.

Her jaw firmed, she turned the other way, not interested in making eye contact or having a conversation. But after picking up his coffee he approached her.

"Morning," he said.

She remembered the grocery store, and the young woman and the boy in the car. She remembered the shock of seeing him then, and now again, the shock was overwhelming. "What are you doing here?"

"Getting coffee."

She still needed her coffee. She couldn't just walk away. And to be honest, she didn't want to walk away. She wanted to know what he was doing here, wanted to know why he was torturing her when they'd agreed they wouldn't see each other again.

"How are you?" he asked.

She nodded slightly. "Fine." She swallowed hard. "Surprised to see you here."

"Why? It's my favorite coffeehouse."

"What? No. It's mine."

He seemed amused. "It can't be mine, too?"

"Not when you live in Blue Jay." She gave him a searching look. "Isn't it a long way to drive for coffee?"

"I suppose, but I didn't drive here. I walked." His light eyes glinted at her. "I live in Los Rios, just a couple blocks over."

"What about your cabin? You're not there anymore?"

"I'll still go up some weekends, but I'm needed here for now."

Andi wasn't following. He lived just blocks from her? How was this possible?

How had she never known?

"I saw you at the grocery store," he said.

She arched a brow.

"You were avoiding me," he added.

"I wasn't—" She saw his expression and shrugged. "Maybe I was."

"Why?"

"Why?" Andi laughed incredulously. "You made it clear you didn't want to see me again, or speak to me again—"

"You're taking that a little far."

"I am? I spend two days so close to you and then wham. Done. You're not fair, Wolf. Not at all."

The barista called Andi's name and Andi was grateful for the distraction. She collected her cup and added a sugar before glancing at Wolf. He was standing there, waiting for her. So annoying. She gave her coffee a vigorous stir before picking up the cup and exiting the coffeehouse. Wolf followed her. She wasn't going to do this with him. Talk, make nice, act like he hadn't hurt her heart, because he had.

"Slow down," he growled as she skipped down the steps, charging ahead. "We need to talk."

She turned on the sidewalk and shook her head. "No. I'm tired of you making all the rules, deciding how things will be. I don't like the way you play." She sniffed and held up her cup, a mock salute. "I'm not playing."

Wolf sighed and slipped his sunglasses on, hiding his eyes. "You're making this personal—"

"How isn't it personal?" Andi took a furious step toward him, closing the distance. "There was you, and there was me. And you decided it was over and I had to suck it up and accept it, and I'm trying. I am, but I'm not as good at being a coldhearted beast as you."

His lips thinned. "Jess calls me that. Beast."

Andi sniffed again, fighting tears. "She's right, you know. You're awful."

"I didn't want to hurt you, Andi."

She shot him a look of disbelief and began walking, unable to stand there and do this.

He caught up with her, putting a hand on her arm to stop her. "Andi, wait. Please?"

The *please* gave her pause. She blinked the tears away, grappling with her composure. "What would we talk about?"

"Maybe tell me how you're doing—"

"Terrible."

He smiled faintly. "Is that my fault?"

"Yes."

"I'm sorry."

"You're not. You're an expert at breaking women's hearts."

"I didn't break your heart."

She stepped off the narrow sidewalk so that a couple could get past her. She noticed Wolf didn't move. He owned the world, and everything in it. "I should have kept my distance. I knew better. I did."

"You're being awfully hard on yourself."

She wanted to kick him. He was so smug.

He nodded at the empty picnic table overlooking the quiet street. "Can we sit?"

She shouldn't have. She should have been strong enough to go. Instead she took a seat facing the camellias in full bloom, the red and white flowers reminding her of valentines dipped in white chocolate. Her mother grew camellias, and azaleas, and was always so proud of them. Her mom died of Alzheimer's six months before Kevin died and Andi had never had time to properly grieve her before she was grieving for her husband.

Maybe she should plant some camellias at her house.

Wolf sat down at the table, facing her, his big body filling the space. She looked at his muscular arms, at the snake and dagger curving around his thick biceps. There was more to the tattoo, but his black T-shirt sleeve hid it.

The ink reminded her of the scars on his chest. The scars on the other arm. The scar on his thigh, running down his knee, to his shin. The man was a walking battlefield. "I don't understand you," she whispered, looking away, focusing on the pepper tree above them and the leaves blowing in the warm wind.

"I did not want to hurt you, Andi."

"Why hook up with me just to cut me out?"

"Because I wanted you."

"And then you were done—"

"It's not that black-and-white. I still feel everything I felt then. I'm still attracted to you. I still want you—"

"Then why?"

"Because I'm not the right man for you. I'm not good for you. You deserve someone wonderful. Someone kind. I'm neither. I'm hard, and selfish, and I let people down. *All* the time."

She blinked back hot tears. "Then stop letting people down."

"It's not that easy. I don't like who I am. But it's too late to change—"

"Why?"

"Because the damage has been done. I can't undo who, or what, I've become."

Andi reached across the table and plucked his sunglasses off, placing them on the table between them. She needed to see his eyes. She needed to see *him*. "What have you become?"

He didn't answer immediately.

"What, Wolf?"

"You already said it. Beast. Monster. Destroyer."

"Now you're just being boastful." She brushed tears away. "Surely, you're not all those dreadful things."

"I've been trouble my whole life. I chose to be trouble. I knew right from wrong, but I just enjoyed being bad. I liked stirring things up . . . upsetting the status quo. But most of all, I liked pissing my dad off."

"And your mom?"

"I loved her. But she wasn't going to leave my dad refused to be a divorcée, not in New Orleans polite society—and so I did everything I could to make my dad suffer."

"Was he that awful?"

"He was a military man, a West Point man—"

"You're a military man."

"Enlisted in the Marines. Totally different." He took a drink of his coffee. "He didn't deserve my mom. She was way too good for him and so I found my own path, my favorite pursuits, rebellion and pleasure. I loved flouting his rules. I delighted in doing all the things he'd forbidden—smoking and drinking starting in middle school. Fighting for the fun of it. Discovering sex in the arms of a pretty but lonely married woman down the street whose husband was never home."

Andi's eyes widened. "Why?"

He shrugged. "I was a bad seed."

"No."

"Growing up, I played sports. I was decent. In high school I had college scouts watching me. There were full-ride scholarships being dangled in front of me. Dad bragged about me to everyone, because finally I was making him look good. I hated how superficial it all was . . . hated being part of society who craved approval and acceptance, since I didn't—don't—need them, or want them." Wolf fell silent. His brow furrowed.

Andi didn't know why her heart hurt so much. If Wolf was as bad as he said, why had his arms felt so good?

Why had he made her feel so safe? "Which college did you go to?"

"I didn't."

"Why?"

"Because someone dared me to drive my car into the high school swimming pool, and I decided to do one better." The corner of his lips lifted. "I drove my father's beloved Opel GT into the pool instead. And just like that, I was expelled. The scholarships disappeared, and I was kicked out of the house. Dad had finally had enough."

"Your dad was ashamed."

"Everyone was ashamed. But me. I thought it was awesome. I wish I'd thought of it myself."

"Where did you go after that?"

"My maternal grandparents, who also lived in the Garden District, took me in, found a program for me so I could graduate."

"That's good."

"And then the week of graduation, I enlisted with the Marine Corps and never looked back. The first time I returned to New Orleans was for my dad's funeral five years later."

"Your poor mom," Andi murmured.

"My dad was an ass."

"I meant, losing you like that. How devastating for her."

Wolf glanced away. "I never thought about it that way." After a moment he looked back at her. "See? A bad seed."

"You were a teenager filled with testosterone and anger. No better, no worse than any other eighteen-year-old making impulsive decisions."

"You're blaming my lack of a full frontal cortex?"

She laughed, unable to help herself. "I bet you were a good dad to your boys."

"Jess wouldn't agree, but I loved them. Unconditionally."

The sincerity in his voice touched her, and just like that, her eyes smarted with fresh tears. She was on a teeter-totter of emotion, up and down. "That's the way it should be," she said huskily, taking her cap off, smoothing her wild curls, and putting the cap back on. "Love should never be conditional."

"But I wasn't there," he added ruthlessly. "I spent much of their lives overseas, and when I was home, I was often away training."

"And yet Maverick came to see you for Christmas."

"Maverick doesn't keep score."

"But your other son does?"

"I actually have three sons. Only two are alive today."

Andi circled her coffee cup with her hands and waited.

"My oldest, Stone, was MARSOC. He died overseas four years ago, just before Charlie was born."

"Charlie?"

"My grandson."

It was beginning to come together. The woman and the little boy in the Land Rover.

"Lindsay and Charlie are living with me now. That's why I'm in town. It's better for Charlie here than in the mountains."

So that's who they were. Some of the knots in her stomach eased. "How is it going?" she asked.

He shook his head. "Not well."

ANDI WALKED HOME IN A FOG.

She'd loved Kevin and lost him and that made sense, in a terrible way.

But this, what she felt for Wolf, made no sense. She shouldn't need him like this. She was practical and sensible and well-behaved. She made good decisions, smart decisions, decisions with her head, not her heart . . .

But her heart was overruling her head. Wolf was trouble. Wolf had spent his life fighting the world, the rebel without a cause.

She didn't need trouble, and she didn't need pain, but something in him called to her, something in him felt right, something felt like . . . hers.

Even with all his secrets and scars, she wanted him.

She wanted all those things she thought she disliked. His height. His muscles. The tattoos. The big biceps. The gray beard. The hair he'd recently cut, cropping it closer to his head. He was tan and rugged and virile, and he'd rocked her world when they were at the cabin. And now she was just bumping into him as if he was an ordinary man, but he wasn't ordinary, far from it.

He would never be just anyone, and she was quite certain she would never be able to be around him and act like he was no one. It was so frustrating, so painful. It would be easier to not see him. It'd be easier not to ever see him again than to just bump into him and have to act as if she had no feelings, when she was overwhelmed by feelings.

She couldn't go to Hidden House Coffee again. Couldn't shop at her favorite grocery store again. Not if she ran the risk of bumping into him, wondering, each time she shopped, if he might be there.

She couldn't handle that wishing, and hoping. Hope was the worst. Hoping she'd see him, and hoping he'd want to talk to her and spend time with her. Hoping for something that would just hurt.

So she wouldn't return to her favorite grocery store, and she'd find a different place for coffee, and she wouldn't go look for his house.

She wouldn't drive up and down the streets in the Los Rios District—such a small neighborhood, just a few streets, less than twenty houses—looking for his Land Rover or his motorcycle. She wasn't going to torture herself like that because she knew what would happen if she found his place.

She would be compelled to drive by. Again and again and again.

She'd be compelled to look for him.

More hope and wishing.

It would've been better if he'd stayed in the mountains. Because that way, she might have gotten over him. This way, he'd keep hijacking her heart and thoughts.

Chapter 10

WOLF LOOKED AROUND THE LIVING ROOM LITTERED with toys, dirty dishes, and a basket of laundry needing folding. The TV was on, but no one was in there. Lindsay's voice came from the bedroom down the hall. It sounded as if she was on the phone. Where was Charlie?

He set the bag of groceries on the kitchen counter and went in search of his grandson. He glanced into Charlie's room. Empty. Went to Lindsay's. She was lying on her bed, phone to her ear, deep in conversation. No Charlie. He continued to his room, heard the sound of water.

Wolf found Charlie sitting on his bathroom sink counter, bare feet in the sink, splashing water. He had shaving cream on his face, shaving cream in his hair, and more shaving cream on the mirror.

"Pops," he said, delighted to see Wolf. He lifted his face, showing off his foam-covered cheeks. "I've got a beard, too."

"I see. What are you planning on doing?"

Charlie lifted the razor from next to his hip. "I'm going to shave."

Wolf exhaled, relieved he'd come home now before Charlie hurt himself, but also ticked off. Where was Lindsay? Why wasn't she watching her son?

He picked up Charlie, shaving cream and all, and carried him to Lindsay's room, depositing him in her arms. "I'm going to make dinner. And then you and I are going to talk tonight after he's in bed."

Wolf boiled the new potatoes and grilled the salmon steaks he'd picked up, adding the asparagus spears to the grill for the last few minutes.

Charlie wouldn't love any of these foods, but he knew Lindsay would get some bread and butter out, and maybe slice a banana for him, adding some peanut butter. She could make him kiddie food if she wanted. He wasn't going to create a separate dinner just because he wouldn't eat anything Wolf had made.

Dinner was pretty quiet. Wolf didn't know if Lindsay had scolded Charlie or not, but Charlie looked remorseful and tried the smallest bite of salmon before returning to his bread and butter.

While he did the dishes Lindsay put Charlie to bed. He was done in the kitchen when she emerged from Charlie's bedroom. She sat down on the couch, facing Wolf. "Just say it," she blurted. "Just say whatever it is you want to say."

"What do you think I'm going to say?"

"That I was irresponsible. That I should have been watching Charlie. That Charlie could have been hurt—" She broke off, bit into her lip, and looked at him. "Yes?"

"Yes."

"Are you going to kick us out?"

"No."

She pulled her knees up to her chest, wrapped her arms around them. "I've let you down."

"You've let yourself down. You're letting Charlie down."

"Thankfully, he didn't get hurt."

"That's not the point." Wolf glanced around the still-messy

living room. He'd decided not to clean it up this time. It wasn't his mess. And yet, he'd been home two hours and she hadn't picked up the toys, or the dirty dishes, or folded the laundry. He had a feeling everything would just sit there until he said something, or did it himself. "You're supposed to be pulling your weight."

"I had a bad day."

"What's going on?"

"I'm lonely. I'm angry. I didn't want to be a single mom. None of this was my plan—"

"You can love Stone, and still function."

"So says the man who won't even talk about him. And he's your son."

"I talk about him."

"Really? To whom? Not to Maverick, or Linc. And certainly not to me."

"It's been four years, Lindsay. Life goes on."

"Not for me." Her eyes were pink, shiny. The tip of her nose was pink. Her lower lip trembled. "And maybe you can box everything up, but I can't. Do you know what tomorrow is?"

Wolf thought, shook his head. "No."

"February thirteenth. Do you know what happened that day?"

Wolf shook his head again.

"Stone proposed. I thought he was going to propose on Valentine's Day. He'd made reservations at this nice restaurant and I was so sure he was going to do it then that I made an appointment for a blowout before dinner, but he didn't propose on the fourteenth. He proposed while we were watching *Seinfeld*." She shook her head and glanced down at her ring finger. It was a stunning diamond solitaire. "I was shocked. He was laughing. He thought it was hilarious as I was caught completely off guard."

"Did you go to dinner the next day, at the fancy restaurant?"

"We did. And I had my blowout, and a manicure." She balled her hand into a fist, hiding it. "Five years tomorrow since he proposed."

"Do you want to do something special?"

"Like what? Watch *Seinfeld*?"

"We could. Or we could go to dinner somewhere. I know you like Indian food."

"Charlie isn't a fan of Indian food."

"I'm sure he'd eat rice and naan."

She smiled crookedly. "As long as there are no peas in the rice. But yes, I'd enjoy going out. Today I felt like I was losing my mind."

It crossed his mind that maybe she needed more than a fresh start. She needed more than sunshine and beaches and oranges picked right off the tree. "Do you . . . have you . . . thought you might want to talk to someone? Professionally?"

"Like a therapist?"

He nodded.

"Maybe." And then she rose from the couch, looked around the room, picked up the white plastic laundry basket, and carried it to her room.

Wolf heard her door close and after a moment leaned back in his chair. He was in over his head. He didn't know how to help Lindsay, didn't know how to give her the support she needed. He loved her and Charlie, but he wasn't tender, or patient. He didn't know the right things to say. He didn't even know where one would start to look for a proper therapist. He'd never gone to a shrink, never wanted to spill his guts to anyone, but if it would help Lindsay, he was all for it, because nothing else had worked.

It wasn't until he was getting in bed later that night that he remembered why February thirteenth stood out in his mind.

He was fairly certain it was Andi's birthday.

He should have sent her flowers.

*   *   *

ANDI WAS WAITING SUNDAY MORNING FOR ELIZABETH and Paige to arrive. They were on their way to pick her up for a birthday lunch. She'd bought a new blouse, a red tunic, to reward herself for losing five pounds. It was flattering and she felt good in it. When she was a little girl her mom always surprised her with a new outfit for her birthday, and when she told Kevin, he continued the tradition, taking her out shopping so she could pick out something she liked.

Andi didn't need a new blouse. She had a closet full of clothes, but they reminded her of a person she wasn't anymore.

She didn't know who she was, but she wasn't Kevin's wife anymore. And she wasn't Kevin's widow. She was becoming someone else, both exciting and terrifying.

The doorbell rang. Andi grabbed her purse, and a light wrap, not sure if it would be needed, and opened the door.

Wolf stood there with an enormous bunch of red roses. "Happy birthday."

Her lips parted, shocked. "You remembered."

"I did, yesterday, but it was too late to get anyone to deliver flowers to you on a Sunday."

"You kept my address?" she asked, remembering when he'd sent the sympathy card.

"No. I asked Margot. She gave it to me."

The realization that he and Margot were still in touch dimmed some of her happiness. "Thank you. That's very kind of you."

"Heading out?" he asked.

She nodded. "Friends are taking me to lunch."

"Glad I caught you, then."

She glanced past him, looking for his car. "How did you get here?"

"Motorcycle." As if sensing her confusion, he gestured

behind him. "The bike is noisy so I left it on the street. You have a very long driveway, by the way."

"Rather like yours up in Blue Jay."

He smiled, gray eyes glinting. His beard was shorter, trimmed to match his hair, and he looked good. Civilized. Sexy. "The flowers will need water. Sorry."

"They traveled by bike, too?"

"Tucked them inside my jacket."

She couldn't imagine how they looked so good, considering they'd been zipped inside his black leather jacket. But then, she wouldn't have minded being tucked inside his jacket. Andi set her purse and wrap on the hall table. "Should I take them?"

"Please." He handed the roses to her, and then leaned down, kissed her cheek. "Happy birthday, Andi."

His lips were cool against her hot cheek. He smelled like cedar and spice and her stomach clenched, her throat aching with emotion. "Thank you, Wolf."

"I'm glad your friends are taking you out."

His voice was so deep it sent shivers through her. "Me, too."

"You look beautiful. I like you in red." And then he was walking away, all long legs, dark denim, and black leather.

She watched him go, air bottled in her lungs. He was without a doubt the most fascinating, impossible man she'd ever met.

Andi had headed to the kitchen to put the roses in a vase when her doorbell rang for a second time. She went to the door, greeted Paige and Elizabeth with hugs, and thanks, as they'd also brought her flowers. Gorgeous flowers—tulips and freesias, roses and lilies—an extravagant, feminine arrangement. Thankfully, they didn't need a vase.

"Can you give me a minute?" she said, smelling the fragrant freesias. "A friend just dropped off some roses and I need to put them in water."

Paige and Elizabeth exchanged glances.

"Was your 'friend' riding a motorcycle?" Elizabeth asked.

Andi blushed. "Yes."

"He's smoking hot," Elizabeth added.

"Yes," Andi said, unable to hide her smile. "He is."

"Are you guys dating?" Paige asked.

Andi's smile faded somewhat. "No. *No*. Just friends."

At lunch her friends wanted to know how Andi had met her friend, and so she gave them a short version, that he was her neighbor up at Blue Jay, and she thought she'd escaped without divulging too much when Elizabeth suddenly clapped a hand to her chest.

"Wolf," Elizabeth said. "Margot told me all about him."

Andi suppressed a sigh. Of course Margot had. Margot liked him.

But Paige, the mathematician, was putting the details together. "Isn't he the one Kevin had a problem with?" she asked. "You stopped going to your cabin because your neighbor's dog attacked another dog—"

"I don't think his dog attacked Misty. Kevin thought Axel did. But knowing Wolf now, I doubt any of his dogs would do such a thing."

"I wish I'd gotten a better look at him," Paige said. "I was too busy talking."

"He does look interesting," Elizabeth said. "Happy birthday, Andi."

SHE DID WHAT SHE HAD VOWED SHE WASN'T GOING to do.

She went looking for Wolf's house.

Los Rios was a tiny neighborhood, bordered by Trabuco Creek, the train tracks, Del Obispo, and Ramos, or Mission Street, depending on how you thought of it.

As she drove the narrow streets without curbs, with small houses set on large lots, shaded by immense trees established years ago, she kept asking herself what she was doing, and what she thought she'd accomplish. Just because Wolf dropped off flowers for her birthday last week didn't mean he wanted to see her showing up on his doorstep.

Was she really going to stop if she found his house?

Maybe she shouldn't be driving. Maybe she should park her car and walk. That way if he spotted her, she could say she was just out for a walk—

She braked.

That had to be his house. She could see the Land Rover in the driveway, and the motorcycle with the giant ape hanger handlebars parked in front, between the car and the garage. She'd passed this house dozens of times over the years and she'd never known it was his. How ironic that they were neighbors in Blue Jay and San Juan Capistrano.

As she watched, the front door opened and the young woman—Lindsay, was that her name?—appeared with the little boy, Charlie. Charlie raced down the stairs, across the lawn, to the wooden swing hanging from the gnarled limbs of a huge oak tree. The young woman followed more slowly.

Andi knew she should leave. She was feeling very stalker-ish, but before she could go, Lindsay looked at her, forehead creasing.

"Can I help you?" Lindsay called to her, somewhat wary.

Andi had been caught. She didn't want to lie, or make Lindsay nervous. "Is Wolf home?" she asked.

"He's out for a run. He should be back in a half hour or so." Lindsay's head tipped. "Can I help you with something?"

Andi felt foolish. "Yes, um, tell him Andi stopped by. I just wanted to thank him. For the flowers."

"You're welcome to wait, if you'd like."

And that would have been utterly mortifying. "No, don't want to intrude. Thank you, though. Have a good day." Andi waved and drove on, face hot, stomach queasy. What had she just done? Had she lost her mind?

Where was her self-control?

She shouldn't have gone looking for him. But come on, she also knew she would . . . it had just been a matter of time.

THE ROAR OF THE MOTORCYCLE MADE ANDI LOOK UP from the stove. What? Was that . . . ?

She froze, listening, the motorcycle growing louder. This wasn't on the road. She went to the sink just in time to see Wolf flying up her driveway to her front door.

Her stomach fell.

Her heart raced.

He was back.

Andi met him at the door. He'd left his helmet on his seat outside. His leather coat hung open. He looked glorious. "Hi," she said.

"Lindsay said you came by."

"I just wanted to say thank you for the flowers. That was really nice of you."

"You could have sent a text."

"I don't have your number."

"Let's rectify that, shall we?" He pulled out his phone. Typed out a quick message, pressed send. "Now you do."

"How do you have my number?"

"Margot."

"She's very helpful," Andi said, more than a little annoyed with her friend.

He smiled. "Yes, she is."

Her heart did a little double beat. He had the most gorgeous smile. "Mind if we talk in the kitchen? I'm in the middle of making dinner and don't want it to burn."

"No problem."

He followed her down the hall, his boots ringing on the black and white marble parquet floor. His gaze swept the living room, the dining room, taking it all in. "Quite a formal house," he said as they entered the kitchen.

"Kevin built the house."

Wolf pulled out a stool at the island and sat down. "You weren't part of it?"

"I met with the contractor almost daily, but it was Kevin's design. His dream."

"Not yours?"

"Someday I'll build my own house," she said, turning the chicken breasts over and adjusting the heat down a bit lower. "I've saved all these issues of *Southern Living* and have lots of ideas. But it's a lot of work, building a house. After we were done here, I swore never again."

"It is," he agreed. "Lots of decisions."

"Every day," she said. She glanced at him over her shoulder. He'd taken off his coat and was wearing a faded gray thermal shirt. The shirt was a bit worn and baggy, revealing his collarbones. "Why did you cut your hair?"

He lifted a hand, ran it over his nape, and then his beard. "Lindsay said I looked like Bigfoot's cousin. She thought I needed to clean it up a bit."

"You do look nice."

He sat up, broad shoulders squaring. "Thank you."

She gestured to the frying pan. "Hungry? I've got enough to share. It's just, uh, chicken."

Wolf smiled. "You're funny."

"I'm not." But she was smiling back at him. He looked good in her kitchen. But then, he looked good everywhere.

"It's my night to cook, so I can't stay long. But maybe another time."

She'd like that, although she wasn't sure how any of this fit the rules. Were they even following his rules anymore?

"You met Lindsay," he said.

She nodded.

"I need your advice," he said.

She waited.

"I'm having a difficult time," he said. "I'm not sure how to help her. I thought—" He broke off, exhaled. "I don't know how to help her, and she needs help. Jess warned me. Jess said that Lindsay has issues, but I thought the issues were just between her and Linds. I should have realized it was so much more than that."

"Jess is your ex-wife."

He nodded. "Lindsay has lived with her for years, ever since Charlie turned one. It was supposed to be temporary, just until Lindsay got on her feet, but Charlie will be four this summer and Lindsay is just . . . a mess." He looked at her, troubled. "I've never had a daughter, and I wasn't as involved with my kids as I should have been. This is all new territory for me. I don't know what to do."

Andi wasn't sure what to say. Kevin had never asked her for input when it came to Luke. But she had plenty of experience with the college students at Orange, many of them seeking her out for advice. Sometimes just a smile or a hug. "What do you mean by a 'mess'?"

"She can't really look after Charlie. She doesn't leave the house often. When we moved here we talked about all the things she could do with Charlie—the beaches, the parks, the libraries. But she doesn't do anything. She can barely drag herself outside to push him on the swing."

"Is she suffering from depression?"

He shrugged. "I don't know. But she does need help. I'm not sure how to tell her, though, and I'm not sure what kind of therapist she should see. Does she need a psychiatrist, or a psychologist, or just a family practice kind of counselor?"

"There are counselors who specialize in grief. I saw someone after Kevin died. I didn't think I needed to, but about a year after his death, I wasn't sad anymore. I was angry. I mean, crazy rage anger, and I didn't understand the rage. It was isolating because I couldn't let anyone else know that I was jealous of them, and their marriage, that I hated they still had a spouse, that their lives were still wonderful while my world was shattered and it would never be the same."

"Not to pry, but did you ever . . . take something? Or did you just get better by talking to someone?"

"I did take something for about six months, and it helped me cope a little better while I continued with the therapy. Eventually I stopped the antidepressants, and then after a year, stopped going to counseling, although every now and then I think I should go again. It's good to have someone objective to talk to."

"What do you mean by cope better?"

Andi shrugged. "I was able to start sleeping better, and I didn't feel so emotional. I just felt more even."

"I thought if Lindsay just got out of the house, or found a part-time job, her mood would improve. But it's bigger than that."

"You've mentioned counseling to her?"

"I did. A week ago."

"And?"

"She said maybe. Maybe it'd help." His powerful shoulders shifted. "But 'maybe' isn't action, and in the meantime, I worry about Charlie. He's a very bright boy, and he needs to be challenged. He needs structure and I can't believe I'm saying this, as I sound like Jess, but he should be in a preschool, at least a few days a week."

"Can she afford it?"

"*I* can afford it. I'd like him to go, and it'd give her time to go to the gym or meet some friends."

"She probably hasn't made friends here yet."

"She won't if she doesn't leave the house."

Andi covered the chicken with a lid and moved it to a cool burner. "How old is she?"

"Twenty-seven? Twenty-eight? She was young when they married."

"Tragically young to be a widow." Andi drew out a stool

and sat down not far from him. "So what advice are you looking for?"

"Where do I start? Do I start by insisting she get help? Do I start by insisting Charlie enroll in preschool? Because my suggestions go nowhere. My suggestions are always met by a 'mmm, interesting idea,' and then nothing. She shuts me down, and if she didn't have a son that would be one thing, but Charlie is going to escape the house one of these days, or play with knives, run with scissors. He's going to get hurt, and I can watch him part of the day, but not all day."

"Do you want me to research possible preschool programs? Good places near here?"

"Yes," he said firmly. "Yes, that would be huge."

"So maybe that's your first step."

"And getting Lindsay help is next."

Andi reached out, touched Wolf's corded forearm. "I think you've got a plan."

He nodded. "I do."

"I'll start looking into preschools tonight, and then tomorrow I'll make some calls."

"You've got work, don't you?"

"I can make a few calls from work. Dr. Nair won't mind."

"Thank you. I really do appreciate it."

"I know you do."

He rose. "I better go. God only knows what's happening at the house while I'm gone."

Andi walked him to the front door. He hesitated there. "Would you want to come over for dinner?"

She searched his eyes. What about his rules? All those rules? But if he was willing to ignore them, then so was she. "I'd like that."

"This week?"

"Thursday or Friday?"

"Let's do Thursday. And call me tomorrow if you find a program you like."

"Wolf, I never had a preschooler. I don't know the things to ask."

"But if you had a preschooler, what would you want to know?" He smiled at her, a crooked devil-take-all smile. "Tomorrow. Call me. You've got my number."

"What if I haven't found a program?"

"You can still call me."

ANDI USED HER LUNCH TO RESEARCH PRESCHOOLS IN San Juan Capistrano. There were many, ranging from big schools to smaller programs in private homes. Andi pored over websites, looked at reviews, compared programs and prices, left messages at several places, had conversations with some staff, coming up with a list of programs that could be possibilities for Charlie. She also paused, then created a list of things she'd want at a school for her own child.

Small class size, credentialed teachers, friendly and fun staff, creativity, flexibility, lots of outdoor play time, introduction to alphabet and numbers.

She then compared her list to the list of schools with openings, and put together a top five list for Wolf. And because he said money wasn't an issue, she wasn't going to rank them by most affordable but by the programs that truly impressed her.

Dr. Nair was in a meeting at midafternoon and Andi used the time to call Wolf. "I've found some interesting places that have openings for Charlie." She picked up her notepad, scanned her list and all her notes. There were a lot of notes. She'd been very thorough in her research. "Would you want me to type it all up and send you an email, or talk it through with you? What would be most helpful for you?"

"That was fast."

"You said I was to call you tomorrow."

"Because I wanted to hear your voice, but you didn't have to work so hard today."

"You sounded desperate."

He laughed softly. "Not desperate. I am never desperate."

"Do you want my list or not?"

"I want the top three. Actually, just tell me your favorite and why it's your favorite."

"It might be my favorite, but I haven't visited in person. You'd have to go in person and check it out. It might be disappointing once you're there."

"What did you like about it?"

"Big outdoor play structures. Swings, climbing walls, a fort, a castle, slides, poles—it looked like paradise, but indoors is just as impressive. They have a very solid educational program, with a strong focus on linguistic development, and literacy and numeracy skills. I spoke with the school's director and she was really passionate. She personally hires every teacher and member of the staff and believes a preschool is to be warm, comforting, supporting every aspect of childhood development."

"I imagine you looked at reviews."

"I did. Pretty much five stars across the board. And the only reason they have a spot for Charlie is that a family is moving soon. I don't think the spot will remain open long."

"I don't suppose it's walking distance to the house."

"For you. Not sure Charlie would like the walk. But it's not that far. Five-minute drive maybe."

"Text me the director's name and number. I'll sign him up today."

"You don't want to go visit?"

"I'll have a look around when I meet the director. I'm planning on meeting her today."

"Sounds good," Andi said.

"You're still coming to dinner Thursday?"

She hesitated. "Is this smart?"

"What do you mean?"

"From the sound of things, I'm not sure Lindsay will welcome having a stranger around."

"She might welcome a friendly face," Wolf said, sounding tired. "She's lonely and tough to love right now, but maybe having some female company might help. Jess was never Lindsay's friend. Jess was her mother-in-law, an authority figure, with strong opinions. Lindsay could use the friendship of a kind woman, a woman who has no skin in the game. You're both widows—"

"I don't think that would matter to her."

He hesitated. "So will you come Thursday? Six?"

How was she going to turn him down now? It'd be impossible. "Can I bring anything?"

"Just yourself."

WOLF WAS TORN. ON ONE HAND HE WAS REALLY GLAD Andi was coming for dinner tonight. But on the other, Lindsay was in a terrible mood, still very upset with him for signing Charlie up for preschool without her permission. She'd stormed out of the living room last night, and had given him the silent treatment most of today.

Thankfully he'd had a lot of experience with silent treatments. Jess had taught him how to deal with them—ignore it. Don't talk. He preferred the silence anyway.

But when Lindsay appeared in late afternoon, eyes red from crying, Wolf knew they needed to call a truce. Andi would be arriving in ninety minutes for dinner, and he didn't want her walking into a battlefield, although he suspected she could handle it. Andi might be beautiful, but she wasn't a delicate princess.

"Preschool isn't a punishment," he said to Lindsay, gesturing for her to sit; whether it was a counter chair or the little banquette by the window, he didn't care.

She didn't move, arms folded over her chest. "He's my son."

"Yes, but his dad was my son, and Charlie is smart, smart like Stone. He needs to be challenged. He's causing mischief because he's bored. He's ready to learn. He's ready to make friends—"

"I'd like to make friends."

"What's stopping you?"

"Everything."

Wolf clamped his jaw tight, fighting for patience. No wonder Jess was so brittle. Lindsay had worn her down. "If Charlie was in preschool three mornings a week, you'd have those mornings free to do things for you. You could join a gym, take classes, paint ceramics—"

"Who does that?"

"People around here. There's a ceramics studio by the park. They're always busy. And next to the ceramics studio is a yoga studio, and then there's a jujitsu place. You could take martial arts, or check out classes at the college—like you said you wanted to do. Lindsay, the world is out there, and it's waiting for you."

Lindsay was about to protest, but Charlie ran in and flung himself at Wolf. Wolf picked him up, held him high above his head, and gave him a couple throws, sending Charlie even higher. Charlie loved it. The higher you threw him, the happier he was. The more risk involved, the more exciting.

Charlie was a miniature of his father. He was rambunctious and busy and into everything. He didn't like the word no, and refused to walk, wanting to run everywhere, all the time. The more you scolded him, the more difficult he became, taking perverse pleasure in defying rules, thriving on the energy.

Wolf admired Charlie's fearlessness. He understood it. Growing up, he'd resisted society's rules and limitations. He had no desire to behave. Why behave? Where was the fun in being good?

Society wanted to suppress you, restrict you, take your freedom.

Charlie took pleasure in rebelling.

Run naked, grab things, throw them, make your voice heard. Live.

Wolf's eyes burned, his chest hurt. He missed Stone, how he missed Stone. He hugged Charlie. He wasn't going to fail him. No way.

"I have a friend coming to dinner tonight." Wolf set Charlie down. "She's my neighbor up in Blue Jay. Not sure if you and Stone ever met her."

"The crazy lady next door?"

Wolf's lips twitched. "The husband was crazy. She just happened to be married to him."

"And you're friends now?"

"Crazy husband died."

"Ah." Lindsay gave him an arch look. "You like her."

"We're friends."

"Wolf, you're not friends with anyone."

"Hey."

"You know what I mean. You don't have just anyone over, into your space."

"We were snowed in together over New Year's. I helped dig her out."

Lindsay grinned. "I bet you did."

"Linds."

She scooped up Charlie and carried him to the pantry, pulling out the bag of Goldfish so that he could reach in and take a handful. "Is she the one who stopped by wanting to thank you for the flowers?"

He'd forgotten about that. Dang it. No getting around that one. "Yes."

"Why did you send her flowers?"

"It was her birthday."

"What did you send her?"

"I don't remember."

"I'll ask her, then."

"She won't remember."

"Wolf, a woman always remembers when a man sends her flowers." She put Charlie down and handed him the bag of crackers, letting him wander off. "And since you're being so cagey, I bet it was something . . . romantic."

"No."

"Roses."

He sighed, pinched the bridge of his nose. "You win. Yes, roses."

"Red?"

"She's a woman—"

"And pretty."

"Okay, I need to make dinner."

"What are we having?"

"Steak, potatoes, simple stuff."

"Are you making one of your famous sauces for the steaks?"

He was, actually. "You're impossible."

"Does she know how much you like her?"

"Lindsay, I will throttle you—"

"I'll set the table. Where do you want to eat? Inside or outside?"

"Outside? It's a nice night."

"And that way you can have a romantic fire in the firepit."

"Are you having fun?"

She laughed, the first laugh he'd heard from her in forever. "Yes, as a matter of fact. I am." She stuck her tongue out at him. "And don't worry, I'll make it look nice."

Chapter 11

ANDI WAS AN EASY GUEST, AND DINNER COULDN'T HAVE been more relaxed. The night was mild, and the sky remained light until six. The fire in the firepit was unnecessary, but it added atmosphere. A fat candle flickered on the table. Andi had brought a bottle of red wine and was enjoying herself, sipping wine and talking with Lindsay while Charlie played on the grass, kicking a soccer ball from one end of the yard to the other. Wolf wasn't the only one keeping an eye on Charlie. It had taken Jax a few days to warm to Charlie, but now the dog was protective. He, too, watched Charlie run around the yard and when the ball would roll close to the fire, Jax would jump up and stand between the ball and the fire.

With his chair positioned so that he could see Charlie and the firepit, Wolf was content to sit with his beer, and listen. Lindsay had taken to Andi practically straightaway, and she'd talked to her tonight of everything. Andi was good at listening, too, knowing how to keep conversation flowing, asking the right question, giving the right feedback, her expression warm.

Her tone warm.

It had taken him awhile to understand Andi's gift, as everyone had something special, and Andi's gift was being real. Genuine. She was authentic—sweet, caring, kind.

Kind.

Maybe that was the biggest difference between Andi and the other women he'd been attracted to. Andi lacked sharp edges. She didn't play games. She was considerate, patient, understanding. She didn't have a thick skin, though. It would be so easy to hurt her. He didn't want to hurt her.

Wolf still desired her, but the desire was tempered by the knowledge that inevitably he'd do, say, be the wrong thing. That's why he ended things early, before everything could go south, before he showed his true colors.

He always showed his true colors.

Every. Single. Time.

He took a swig of beer and swallowed before glancing over at the girls. Andi looked at him at the same moment, and smiled, a small private smile, and it hit him square in the chest. How beautiful she was. How loving. Wonderful in every way.

She was good for him. But he'd be bad for her.

Pain replaced the warmth inside him, and he drank again. He couldn't do this now, wouldn't do this now, not tonight when he felt a moment of peace. It had been a long time since he'd felt peace. All he wanted was a night of this. A week. A month. Unrealistic, he knew, but one could sometimes hope.

Charlie's soccer ball came flying toward the table and Wolf leaned over, scooped up the ball before it could crash into them. He tossed it back to Charlie, who shouted, "No hands! No hands in soccer!"

"Goalies can throw the ball," Wolf said.

"You're not a goalie!" Charlie shouted back.

Wolf smiled, amused by Charlie's confidence. For a little guy he was fierce, far fiercer than Stone ever was. Or maybe Stone just had more discipline. Jessica didn't mess around. "I can if I want to be."

Lindsay and Andi had been listening to the exchange and Lindsay shook her head as he sat back down. "He's got you wrapped around his little finger, Wolf."

"I think he has us all wrapped around his little finger," Wolf countered.

"He is adorable," Andi said. "And very bright."

Lindsay glanced at her. "You think so?"

"You can tell by his vocabulary and sentence structure."

"You have kids?" Lindsay asked.

"I do. A stepson. I don't see him as often as I'd like, though. Luke's a doctor and lives on the East Coast."

"That must be hard."

"It is," Andi agreed.

Wolf knew Andi well enough now to know this wasn't a conversation she enjoyed. Her smile was forced, her tone brittle. Luke was a sensitive subject for her.

Wolf's phone rang. He reached into his pocket to silence it but saw the name and number. It was Aaron Larkin, an architect he worked with on a lot of projects, commercial and residential. Aaron was conscientious and never called after hours unless it was urgent.

"I need to take this," Wolf said, rising. Leaving the table, he headed to his office garage, where he could have quiet but also still see Charlie. Jax, who normally would follow him, stayed next to the fire, watching everyone.

"What's happening?" Wolf asked the architect, taking the call.

"We have a problem with the Richardson plans. The contractor just alerted me that the mechanical drawings don't coordinate with the electrical drawings. I'm on Catalina right now. It's Leigh's birthday and I didn't bring any work, thinking I'd be fine for a night, but we need to get this figured out. We can't have electrical conduit running straight through steel beams."

"That's impossible."

"Exactly. But for some reason, some of the subs' plans are different from what I recall us doing. Can you pull them up, and get a hold of Larry? They're pouring concrete in the morning and all the subs have been scheduled. Larry's anxious to hear from you."

"Don't worry. I've got it."

Wolf hung up and returned to the table. Charlie had crawled onto his mom's lap and was yawning. Andi and Lindsay were laughing at something. The bottle of wine looked close to being empty. Wolf worried about the amount of alcohol Lindsay drank. He worried about the pill bottles in her room, and more bottles in her purse. She did a lot of self-medicating, and he understood why—a lot of vets did, too—but he was concerned about her not being fully present with Charlie.

"I'm afraid I'm going to have to excuse myself," Wolf said. "One of the jobs has a problem and I need to sort it."

"Go," Lindsay said, waving him on. "Andi and I are good here. We're just chatting."

Wolf looked down at Charlie, whose eyes were getting heavier by the moment. "I think your boy would like to sleep in his own bed."

"He's fine here," Lindsay said.

Andi looked up at him, big brown eyes wary. "Would you like me to leave?"

"No," Lindsay said a little sharply. "Don't go just because Wolf is being the big bad. He's not going to eat you."

Wolf looked at Andi, a dark eyebrow lifted, a hint of something heated in his expression. "You never know," he said.

Andi blushed, bit her lip. She was remembering the cabin, too.

"You don't have to leave right now," he added. "But when you do, will you be okay to drive?"

Andi nodded. "I'm fine, I promise."

"I drank most of the wine anyway," Lindsay said, raising her hand. "Is that okay, Dad?"

Wolf swallowed his retort, hung on to his patience, reminding himself that Lindsay had a good buzz going. She wouldn't normally be so confrontational. "Of course, you're an adult, Linds. Good night, Charlie. Good night, Andi."

ANDI WATCHED HIM WALK AWAY, JAX AT HIS SIDE, AND felt a wave of regret. Wolf wasn't happy with Lindsay, but after everything Wolf had shared with her about Lindsay, Andi thought Wolf didn't need to play quite such the heavy with her, especially since she clearly craved company, girl company.

"He's a little scary sometimes, isn't he?" Lindsay said, kissing the top of Charlie's head.

"I'm sure he means well," Andi answered, remembering her impression of Wolf before she knew him. He could be scary. And intimidating.

"Lincoln's intense, too. Wolf and Lincoln butt heads, and I've heard it's because Wolf thinks Lincoln is a lot like his dad, but honestly, it's that Lincoln is a lot like Wolf."

Andi didn't know what to say.

"You know, Stone looked after Wolf," Lindsay added. "He understood him, said his dad needed him. Stone had this ability to see the best in everyone. Like me." She pressed another light kiss on sleeping Charlie's head. "I didn't trust many people when I met Stone. To this day, I never understood what he saw in me, but he changed my world. He lit it up, lit *me* up, made everything magical. Those three years we had together were perfect. He was perfect."

A lump filled Andi's throat.

"It's weird being here with Wolf. We actually don't

know each other that well. He tries, but he's not a girl dad. But what do I know? I never had a real dad—" She broke off, shook her head. "Obviously I had a dad, but I never knew him. He left when I was a baby. My mom was never single long. I had a half dozen different stepdads and boy-friend dads before I was eighteen. Growing up was aw-ful, but then came Stone and wow. Just wow. To be loved like that. To feel safe like that. Unreal." Lindsay's voice dropped. "Unreal."

"How did you meet?" Andi asked.

"At the coffeehouse where I worked in Sneads Ferry. Stone showed up one day with two friends. They were all in uniform, but Stone . . . he was the only one I saw. Our eyes met, and wham. Struck by lightning. I started shaking. I couldn't even make the coffees, my hands were trembling so bad. I've never felt anything like that. I swear, it was love at first sight."

"He asked you out?"

"No. He left with his friends, and I was devastated. All I could think about was him. He was a Marine, but Camp Lejeune is huge. There are almost one hundred and forty thousand soldiers there. How would I ever find him?"

"You didn't catch his name?"

"No. I was too nervous. But later, just before my shift ended, he returned, and gave me his number. He said to call him if I ever felt like talking. *Talking*." She shook her head. "He meant it, too. For the first month we just talked, on the phone, every night. I was in school then, taking classes at Coastal Carolina Community College, and working and didn't have a lot of time, but I couldn't wait to talk to him every day. Soon I was telling him everything, about my mom, and her boyfriend, and how bad it was at home and so I was staying with friends, sleeping on their couch. I told him stuff I'd never told anyone." Lindsay went silent. "And despite that, he loved me. Loved *me*."

Lindsay was breaking Andi's heart. "Where did you get married?"

"On base, by a chaplain. It was supposed to be just the two of us, but all thirteen of the Raiders on his team showed up. All these guys in their formal uniform. They were not just his best men, they were my best men, too. That's the thing I learned—I didn't just marry Stone, I married into his Raider family. They're still my family, even with Stone gone. They continue to check in on me and Charlie."

"I don't know what a Raider is."

"The Marine Raiders are special ops. It's the most elite division of the Marine Corps. Wolf was one before they called them Raiders. He did special reconnaissance for the Marine Corps, spending almost twenty years in security and direct action. You could say he was the prototype for today's MARSOC. That's why Stone wanted to be a Raider, because of his dad."

Andi sat with this for several moments. "I know so little about Wolf's time in the military."

"He doesn't talk about it," Lindsay agreed. "Stone was more open—I mean, he didn't ever reveal anything classified, but he knew I needed to be part of his world, as much as I could, so he would reassure me that things were well, and that he was always careful, and he had really good people with him, the best people." She stopped talking then, suddenly quiet and pale.

After a moment she rose, carefully shifting Charlie onto her shoulder. "I'm going to put him to bed."

Andi nodded, and collected the wineglasses, carrying them into the kitchen where the rest of the dishes were on the counter.

While Lindsay got Charlie into his pajamas, Andi did the dishes. Her heart felt heavy, though, and she felt guilty for having thirty years with Kevin when Lindsay had only had, what? Three with Stone?

It wasn't fair, especially since Lindsay adored Stone so much. Needed him so much.

Her eyes burned as she rinsed the last of the pans, and she was drying the last wineglass when Lindsay returned to the kitchen.

"Wow. You're already done?" Lindsay asked, glancing around an immaculate kitchen.

"There wasn't much to do since Wolf grilled the steaks."

"I hate dishes."

"I don't mind dishes, but I hate laundry." Andi smiled at her, and then impulsively crossed to her and gave her a hug, holding her tightly. "You're amazing," Andi whispered to her. "You're truly amazing and I'm lucky to know you."

Lindsay hugged her back. "Can we stay in touch?"

"Absolutely. I'd love that. I'll text you my number now. What's your number?"

FRIDAYS WERE ALWAYS BUSY AT THE UNIVERSITY. TODAY was no exception; it was after one and Andi was at her desk, her lunch still uneaten, when her phone buzzed with an incoming text. She saved her work on her computer and checked the message. It was from Wolf. Sorry I disappeared on you last night.

She answered: It's okay. I had a really good conversation with Lindsay. I like her a lot.

Wolf: Everything was okay then after I left?

Andi: More than okay. We did fine without you. ☺

Wolf: She's been through a lot.

And not just with Stone, Andi answered. Sounds like her homelife was terrible.

Wolf: That concerned Jess, too. She wasn't happy Stone proposed to her.

Andi thought about this for a moment before replying. Is this why they had no family at their wedding?

Wolf: Probably.

There was nothing for a moment, and then she saw the little dots dancing. He was writing another text. Do you like Mexican food?
She stretched and smiled before answering, It's only my favorite food.

Wolf: How about we go out this weekend? Do you have time?

Her heart felt ridiculously warm. Always have time for you.

Wolf: Saturday?

Andi: Yes.

Wolf: I'll pick you up at six.

Andi: Can't wait.

HE TOOK HER TO EL ADOBE DE CAPISTRANO ON CAMINO Capistrano. It was yet another of her favorite places in downtown San Juan, the building recognized as a California State Historical Landmark, just two blocks from the mission. The northern section, built in 1797, was a home, and the southern half, built in 1812, was a former jail and court.

Tennessee had history, but it was so different from Southern California's history, and Andi, who'd grown up thinking chile powder was only for chili, immersed herself in San Juan once they moved, going to lectures at the college, visiting exhibits at the mission, and taking cooking classes downtown.

"This is my favorite tree," Andi said, pointing to the huge tree outside the restaurant. "I'm not sure if it's a laurel, but every time I see it, I feel calm. Imagine how long it's been here. Imagine the things it's seen."

Wolf hugged her. "You make me feel calm."

She tipped her head back. "I do?"

"And you make me smile." He smiled then, creases fanning from his eyes. "I hate smiling."

Dinner was cozy and perfect. Wolf had managed to get them a table in a corner, giving them a little privacy from the rest of the restaurant. She had a margarita, and he a beer. "Don't you like margaritas?" she asked.

"I try to stay away from hard liquor."

"And wine?"

"Just don't like it."

"Is there a reason you avoid the hard stuff?" she asked.

"Makes me an ass. And I don't need help with that."

"You're so hard on yourself."

"Have to make sure I don't make the same mistakes."

Andi studied him, beginning to know him, beginning to see him, which meant seeing past the walls and masks, the air of detachment and indifference. He was exactly the opposite of who she'd thought he was. His silence wasn't coldness. His silence was his attempt to keep from caring too much . . . feeling too much. "If you were this horrible person, your sons wouldn't stay in touch, or come see you at Christmas." Her gaze locked with his. "It's obvious from what you told me that Maverick loves you. I don't know Lincoln, but if he's anything like Maverick, he loves you, too. And Lindsay wouldn't want to live with you if she didn't feel safe with you."

"Jess thinks I'm going to screw up Lindsay."

"Maybe Jess is jealous that Lindsay wanted to come live with you?"

"No, she knows me. She knows the things I'm capable of."

"What do you do that is so horrible?"

He shook his head. "I don't want to ruin tonight."

He looked haunted, his eyes shadowed. Andi reached across the table, touched the back of his hand. "Let's drop it. We're having such a nice time. I don't want to make you sad."

"I'm not sad, I just . . ." He shook his head, but he turned his hand over, letting her hand slip into his. ". . . destroy."

Wolf's palm was calloused and warm, and when his fingers encircled hers, Andi realized she was lost. Not just now, but forever.

She heard his words, but her heart overrode them. She heard what he was saying, but her heart was louder.

She loved him.

She loved him, for the good and bad, and she'd love him for as long as he let her. If he would let her.

"I believe in you," she said carefully. "And I see the good in you."

He drove her home, and when he shifted into park, she summoned her courage and asked him in. "Spend the night with me."

"I can't stay all night."

"Then stay until you need to leave."

He leaned across the car and kissed her, and it was a kiss like the kisses he gave her in the mountains, a kiss full of hunger and heat. She clung to him, body weak, pulse slow, heavy.

Wolf lifted the hair back from her brow, kissing her

temple. Then close to her ear, and finally the corner of her mouth. Each of the kisses sent a fresh shiver through her.

"This goes against the rules," he said.

"Everything about us goes against the rules," she answered, catching his face in her hands. "Can't we just change the rules?"

"I don't think it works that way."

"Sure it does. Just let me write the playbook."

She fell asleep in his arms, but sometime in the night, he left, managing to sneak out without waking her. Andi woke in the early hours of the morning and reached her hand beneath the covers, across the sheets, and could feel where he had been. It was still warm. She shifted into his spot, pulled the covers up to her chin, and closed her eyes, remembering being with him.

She wouldn't be afraid.

She wouldn't look too far ahead.

She would learn, for the first time in her life, to live in the now.

ANDI HAD LUNCH ON CAMPUS WITH ELIZABETH AND Paige a couple days later. It was a spur-of-the-moment invitation, but Andi needed some time with friends, wanting to be distracted from her world. But Elizabeth and Paige had different plans. They were interested in quizzing her about Wolf.

What did Wolf do for work?

How often did they see each other?

Were things getting serious?

The last thing Andi wanted to do was talk about Wolf, not because there was anything bad to say, but because she felt so much it was difficult to talk about him, never mind the future.

Now that they'd "broken the rules," was there a future? And what would it look like?

Instead of talking about Wolf, Andi told them about Wolf's three sons, and how Stone had died after only three years of marriage, leaving Lindsay to raise Charlie on her own. She added that Lindsay and Charlie had come to live with Wolf in San Juan Capistrano, and that Charlie was adorable. He'd be four at the end of June and Jax, Wolf's dog, who didn't like anyone, seemed to have adopted Charlie.

Andi had only been back at her desk for an hour when she received a text from Lindsay.

Wolf and I had a fight last night. We're not talking today and I need to talk to someone. Can I trust you?

Andi hesitated only a minute. Of course, she answered. When is a good time to call?

When is good for you? Lindsay replied.

Andi: I'll call you as I drive home from work. Around five?

Lindsay: Thanks, Andi. I appreciate it.

LEAVING WORK THREE HOURS LATER, ANDI CALLED LINDsay on speaker as soon as she was out of the university parking structure. "Hi, Lindsay, it's me. What happened?"

"Wolf can be such a jerk." Lindsay's voice was rough. She sounded exhausted. "He went through my stuff. He had no right to go through my stuff—"

"Why would he do that?"

"He said he was looking for drugs."

"What?"

"He thinks I'm doing drugs."

"I can't believe that. Why would he think that?"

"I was super stressed out so I took some Xanax yesterday.

Xanax can make me sleepy and I took a long nap. Wolf freaked out. He woke me up and demanded to know what I was on. He accused me of doing drugs. I don't do drugs. I have a prescription for Xanax that's legal, and mine, given to me by a doctor in New Orleans. I was livid with Wolf for opening my purse without permission. I would never go through his things. What gives him the right to go through mine?"

"I think he's just worried about you."

"What he did was wrong."

"He didn't handle the situation right," Andi said. "He should have had a conversation with you, letting you know he was concerned, without accusing you of anything, or going through your things."

"He literally dumped my purse out on the coffee table." Lindsay's voice sharpened. "I feel so disrespected. I am not a druggie. I don't abuse my body."

"Where is he now?"

"He's in the garage working. We haven't talked since last night."

Andi held her breath, not sure what to say.

"He's enrolled Charlie in preschool. Said Charlie has to go or we can't stay with him any longer."

Andi winced at the ultimatum. No one liked them, and she wished Wolf had approached the subject of preschool with Lindsay differently. "Maybe he just thinks preschool would be good for Charlie. Maybe he isn't phrasing things well."

"Maybe he's a jerk."

Andi tried not to laugh. "Everyone's a jerk sometimes."

"Wolf's the biggest one."

"Would you and Charlie want to come to my house? I'm not that far from your place and we could order pizza, keep it super casual."

"I'd love that, but Charlie can be hard on houses."

"My house can take it, and I've got toys in the garage. I can bring them out."

"Oh, don't go to trouble for us. I'm just glad to get out of here for the evening. It's so awkward."

"It wouldn't be trouble. It would make me happy to see everything I kept get played with. But maybe we should tell Wolf you're coming over? I don't want him to think I'm interfering."

"You tell him, then. I'm not talking to him."

Andi said goodbye, called Wolf, he didn't answer, and so she left a brief message, letting him know that Lindsay and Charlie were coming over for pizza, and he was welcome to join them, too, if he desired.

Wolf replied with a text as Andi parked in her driveway. I have a meeting with clients tonight. Enjoy your pizza.

Andi turned off the engine and responded. Do you mind that Lindsay and Charlie are coming over?

Why would I mind? he asked.

Andi hesitated. Lindsay said you had a fight.

Wolf: Did she tell you why?

Andi wasn't sure how to answer. She got out of her car and headed to the front door. As she unlocked the door she decided truth would be the best. You thought she was taking drugs?

Wolf called her then. "Is that what she told you?" he said, temper evident in his voice.

Andi wasn't feeling particularly charitable with Wolf at the moment. "You went through her purse looking for drugs . . . without her permission."

"I respect privacy, but this was serious. I came home and Charlie was gone. The gate was open. Lindsay was passed out on the couch, TV blaring, and Charlie was nowhere to be found."

"Was Jax missing, too?"

"No, he'd been with me. But we immediately went out looking for Charlie. We drove up and down the neighborhood, and then over toward the mission. We returned home, left the car, and searched for him along the train tracks, in the garage by the theater, stopped by the little animal zoo over by Hidden Coffee House. And the whole time I was trying not to think the worst, praying he hadn't gotten into anyone's car, that he hadn't been hurt by anyone. I finally found him the second time I went to Los Rios Park. He was talking to an older Hispanic man who was there with his granddaughters. Charlie had approached them and asked if he could have some of their crackers because he was hungry. The old man realized Charlie was lost and was trying to find out where Charlie lived so he could get him home. Thank goodness he was a good person. It could have turned out very differently. So yes, I was angry with Lindsay. I still am."

Andi didn't know what to say. Had she made a mistake inviting Lindsay and Charlie over? "Should I suggest they come another night?" she asked Wolf. "Maybe this isn't the best night."

"It's up to you. I don't care if they come over. It would probably do Lindsay good to get out of the house for the evening."

Hanging up, Andi texted Lindsay that she'd love to see them, and to come over as soon as she was ready. She sent her address in a separate text and then, after changing her clothes, she headed to the garage to begin pulling down the boxes filled with Luke's old toys. Lego and Matchbox cards, a huge tub of them, plus die-cast airplanes—oh, he had dozens of military planes, planes she'd bought for Luke, thinking he'd like them—and there was more. Pieces of an elaborate castle complete with outer walls, tower walls, and a working drawbridge. There were little play people that went with the castle. Horses with plastic armor. Shields and helmets, too.

Andi was soon surrounded by tubs of toys. She didn't want to overwhelm Charlie, but there was so much here, so much she'd bought for Luke, things she hadn't been able to throw away, hoping one day when he had kids, they'd enjoy the toys.

She lugged the two castle totes into the living room, and then brought in the Matchbox cars, and finally the airplanes. Surely he'd find something in these to entertain him. Luke had liked the castle for a few years, but he'd never shown interest in the planes or cars. She was interested in seeing how Charlie would respond to the cars. She wasn't an expert on children, but she had a feeling he'd like them.

Lindsay and Charlie arrived within the half hour, and the toys were a hit, and while he liked everything, the military airplanes were the clear favorite. Charlie zoomed planes from one end of the long marble hallway to the other, through the kitchen, around the living room, across the backs of sofas, over coffee tables, around dining room chairs. The planes soared up, and down, dive-bombing to destroy the enemy. Sometimes pilots died, sometimes the heroes survived. For someone not yet four, Charlie had a love of all things battle.

When the pizza arrived Andi brought out her pool plates and they ate in the living room, with Charlie sitting on the huge blue and green Oriental rug. He chewed bites of pizza in between building the castle, and then the outer castle walls. He had his own idea of how it should look, and he lined all the little plastic people on the walls so they could shoot the bad guys on the other side.

"They didn't have guns then," Andi told him, vastly amused, as Luke had never shot anyone or anything, nor did he like battles or war. Charlie was the opposite. War seemed to be in his DNA. "They would have fought with arrows, and maybe spears, and then if the bad guys got inside the castle, it would be swords and clubs. That's why the little soldier people have armor. They needed it for protection."

Lindsay sat curled up in one of the big overstuffed chairs, taking a slice of pizza apart, eating cheese, and then a mushroom and then a pepperoni. She'd been pretty quiet tonight, and her face still looked puffy and swollen as if she'd cried her eyes out earlier. "I'm sorry you didn't have kids," she said. "You're a natural."

"I wanted them," Andi said, helping Charlie to another slice of cheese pizza. "I couldn't get pregnant, though."

"And the doctors . . . ?"

Andi shook her head. "Kevin didn't believe in in-vitro and those things. He was a very devout Catholic."

"He went to church a lot?"

"No, but he had strong beliefs, and since he had a son, he felt fulfilled as a parent."

"I think that's pretty selfish of him. But men can be that way." She nibbled on some crust. "Where on the East Coast did you say your stepson lives?"

"Luke's just outside Washington, DC."

"Lincoln's in DC. Not entirely sure what he does. It's military, but not CIA. Lincoln's pretty private. Doesn't share much."

Like Wolf, Andi thought.

"Is your Luke single?" Lindsay asked.

"No. He's engaged to a fellow doctor. They're getting married this spring—" Andi broke off, realizing it was March second. Kelsey's bridal shower was supposed to be in February, and that had come and gone.

Andi hadn't been invited. Luke hadn't called or tried to introduce Kelsey. Andi had a feeling an invitation to the wedding wasn't coming, either.

The sting of rejection made the air catch in her throat. Her eyes burned, too, but she smiled, and held it, keeping the ache in. Lindsay didn't need to know. No one needed to know. It didn't matter. Luke, she realized, had let her go, and Andi had to move on. That was how life worked. Change.

Change was inevitable. And at fifty-eight Andi understood this quite well, but she wasn't going to cut Luke out of her life. She couldn't. She might not be his birth mother, but she loved him, and he was still her son, even if they weren't close.

"Wolf thinks Charlie should go to preschool," Lindsay said, abruptly changing the subject. "He's pretty much insisting, but I don't know why Charlie has to start school already. He's only three."

"It's not really school proper, is it?"

"You have to line up, sit down, do what you're told."

"You mean, listen?" Andi teased.

"I just feel betrayed. Jessica—Stone's mom—wanted Charlie to go to preschool, too. She said it would expose him to art and activities, and help him make friends. Now Wolf is saying the exact same thing and Charlie is supposed to start in the morning. I haven't even told Charlie yet."

"Will he have a hard time adjusting?" Andi asked.

"No. He'd probably love it. But I don't like being pressured, and I feel pressured."

"Tell Wolf that—"

"He doesn't care. He's used to making decisions, being the boss, but he's not the boss of me. He's Charlie's grandfather, and that's it."

Andi hesitated. "Do you want me to talk to Wolf for you?"

"No, then he'd just get mad at you and that's not fair to you."

"Maybe you could create a preschool for Charlie at home? You could plan activities for him . . . have an art hour, and read, and play—"

"You're joking."

"Charlie doesn't have to go anywhere. You can be his teacher. Lots of moms do it."

Lindsay made a choking sound and shook her head. "I don't have the energy to teach him. If I had the energy, I'd go back to school. Get my degree—"

A crash in the corner had them both on their feet. Charlie had just destroyed his castle with a metal fire poker he'd found next to the living room hearth. He stood now in the middle of the ruins, poker still in one hand, a smile of satisfaction on his face.

"I won," he said. "The bad guys are all dead."

Andi diverted Charlie's attention even as she eased the poker away from the child, making a mental note to hide all the fireplace tools, and better boy-proof the room for future visits. Lindsay helped clean up the castle, putting the pieces and people in the appropriate tubs. Charlie didn't want to go home. He said he loved Andi's house.

"You can always come visit me again," Andi told him before carrying the plastic plates and pizza boxes into the kitchen, hoping they would. She liked the company. It had been food for her, too.

Lindsay stepped out of the powder bath between the living room and kitchen. Her eyes were pink and watery.

Andi impulsively gave her a hug. "What's wrong?"

"You're so nice to me."

Andi gave her another hug. "You're nice to me. I loved having you here. Please come again."

"You mean that?"

"I do."

"Why?" Lindsay said, drying her eyes.

"Because I like you."

"Thank you," Lindsay said, taking Charlie's hand and walking him to the door. But at the door Charlie didn't want to relinquish the two airplanes he held in his free hand. "You can't take them home," Lindsay said. "They're not yours."

"I don't mind," Andi said, crouching down to look Charlie in the eyes. "Not as long as you take care of them and bring them back. Would you do that?"

Charlie nodded enthusiastically.

"Good." Andi kissed his cheek. "Let's plan another playdate soon."

Chapter 12

ANDI WAS EATING A SMALL BOWL OF STRAWBERRY ICE cream and watching a show when her phone rang. She knew without looking it was Wolf. She could feel it in her bones.

Reaching for the phone, she saw she was right. "Hi," she said, muting the TV. "How did your meeting go?"

"Fine. How did your night go?"

"Really well. Charlie loved Luke's old toys. It was so fun to watch him play. He's a big fan of battle."

"Yes, he is." Andi could feel Wolf's smile over the line. "And Lindsay?" he asked. "How was she?"

"Kind of teary." Andi paused, searched for the right words. "I think she's struggling because you two aren't getting along."

"I know she misses Stone, but she has to snap out of it. She has to move forward. Now I know why Jess wouldn't leave her alone with Charlie. Lindsay doesn't watch him. She's not responsible."

"Maybe she has too much free time. Maybe she doesn't know what to do with herself."

"She could take Charlie to a park, or to the children's museum. They could take a walk on the beach and look at tide pools. They could go have lunch at the mall, or story time at the library—"

"But those are all things with Charlie. Things for him. But maybe she needs to do some things for herself."

"She'd have time for herself if she let him go to pre-school."

"I have a feeling she will. She doesn't like you mad at her." Andi hesitated. "And then there's the fact you gave her an ultimatum."

"Charlie could have been hit by a car, or kidnapped, or molested—"

"But you found him, and he was safe—"

"Thank God."

"Exactly. But don't take it out on Lindsay. She's doing the best she can. She never planned on being a single mom. She loved Stone. He was her world."

"Stone wouldn't be happy with her parenting—"

"Wolf, don't ever say that to her. That's not fair. It's not easy on women to be left behind while men go off to work, whether it's downtown or across the world. My dad was a traveling salesman—he sold copiers for Xerox—and we were lucky to have him home for a week a month. My mom was lonely a lot. I vowed if I got married, I'd never be left behind."

"Kevin didn't have to travel for work?"

"He was a chemical engineer, so no, not often, and when he did travel to a conference or regional meeting, he'd take me. We were lucky." Andi hesitated. "I was Lindsay's age when I married, but I was never on my own, and never with a baby on my own. Try not to be so hard on her. She doesn't want to feel this way. She doesn't like beating herself up—and she does. Constantly."

"Then she needs to get help."

"I agree."

Wolf was silent for a long minute. "I thought she'd do better here with me, but it's the opposite. She was better with Jess. At least, Charlie was safer with Jess."

"I'm sure it will never happen again."

"Doesn't matter. It only takes one time. One lapse of judgment. That's it. And maybe it's not fair of me, but I wouldn't be able to forgive her—or me—if something happened to him while they stayed with me. Yesterday was such a bad day. I haven't felt fear like that in years. I was sick with it, sick that something terrible had happened to Charlie. He's just a baby. He's so innocent. He has no idea what can happen to him in the real world."

Andi felt Wolf's pain and she closed her eyes. For a moment there was just silence, and the silence pulsed with unspoken pain.

"But you found him," she said finally, chest tight and heavy with emotion. "You didn't give up—"

"I'd never give up."

"Then don't give up on Lindsay. She needs you."

"Would you come to dinner here, soon? I need you here. I need a buffer until I can work through my anger."

"When?" she asked.

"Let me check my schedule, but maybe tomorrow, or Sunday?"

"Just let me know."

ANDI DRESSED FOR SUNDAY NIGHT DINNER AT WOLF'S. He'd mentioned that his son Maverick might drop by, but it depended on traffic and whether or not Maverick had a date.

Andi had seen a framed photo on Wolf's living room mantel of his three sons when they were just boys, all dressed in navy and gray school uniforms, backpacks at their feet. It was the only photo in the house and when she asked Wolf about it, he said that because the San Juan house was a rental house he didn't keep personal things out. The framed photo was one he kept at the cabin, and he'd brought it to town with him.

It was easy to know who was who in the photo. Stone was the tallest, and smiling. He had big shoulders and fair hair and a beautiful smile. He seemed charming, easygoing.

Lincoln looked a lot like Stone, blond and lean, but unsmiling. If anything he glowered at the camera, clearly not pleased that he was being forced to take a picture.

Maverick, then just ten or eleven, had a wide smile, deep dimples, a mop of dark hair, and blue eyes. He was puffing his chest out, trying to look bigger, while flexing one arm.

Wolf's boys who'd become men.

Andi had made a chocolate cake and she carefully put it in the car and drove to Wolf's. A huge black truck was in the driveway. Was Maverick here?

Jax barked as she entered through the gate, but he didn't rush at her. Rather, he met her and then walked with her through the open front door. "Good boy," she said to him, giving him a tiny pat on his gold and black head once she set the cake on the kitchen counter.

A tri-tip in marinade sat on the counter. The salad had been made but hadn't been dressed yet. She glanced out the kitchen window into the big backyard.

Wolf was at the grill, cleaning it, and Maverick was in a chair talking to Lindsay. Maverick was huge. She had forgotten he was that big. He had to be even taller than Wolf, his shoulders every bit as broad, but he was fit, his body honed, sinewy muscles everywhere.

She watched Maverick and Lindsay talk; Maverick appeared to be mostly listening. Lindsay appeared upset. She reached up to wipe tears away. Her hands gestured as she talked, emotion in those, too.

Just then, little Charlie flew past the window, at a full

sprint, the die-cast airplanes in his hands. Jax had abandoned Andi and was running next to Charlie.

Andi smiled faintly, heart aching just a little bit. It was bittersweet watching the Enders family from inside the kitchen. They were their own tight unit, and she was most definitely the outsider, looking in.

Before Andi could even go outside, Maverick rose, said something to his dad, lifted Charlie, hugged him, and headed to his big truck.

Andi wanted to talk to him, but thought it'd be weird to just rush out and introduce herself. Instead she shifted to the dining room and watched him open the gate at the driveway, back out, and then climb from his truck to secure the gate.

He made a call as he climbed back into his truck, and was speaking to someone as he drove away.

Maverick's profile was Wolf's, just years younger.

Wolf entered the kitchen, wrapped her in his arms. "You missed Maverick," he said, dropping a kiss on her lips.

She leaned into Wolf, feeling a little overwhelmed by emotions she didn't fully understand. "I saw him leave, but he seemed to be in a hurry."

"He's picking someone up from the train depot. She's come down from San Luis Obispo, I think."

"She took the train down?"

Wolf nodded. "They're grabbing dinner and heading up to the cabin for a few days."

"Maverick must like her."

"Maverick's having fun." Wolf picked up the tri-tip. "I'm going to put this on the grill, but then I've got to work for a half hour. Are you okay keeping Linds and Charlie company until dinner?"

"You two doing better?" Andi asked, curious.

"It's not great, but it's not terrible. We'll survive."

They walked outside together. Wolf lifted the lid on the barbecue, set the meat on the hot grill. It sizzled and he lowered the lid, adjusted the temperature, and kissed her again. "Glad you're here," he said. "Sometimes I don't know what the heck I'm doing."

She hugged him, and held on. "This is a big change for all of you, and you're doing great. Stay positive. Everything is going to work out."

He smiled reluctantly. "You're endlessly optimistic."

"There's no reason not to be. Now go work so you can come hang out with me later. I miss you."

Wolf disappeared into his office in the garage and Andi crossed the lawn to sit in the chair Maverick had vacated.

Lindsay gave Andi a wan smile. "Hi."

"How are things?" Andi asked.

Lindsay shrugged. "We're talking . . . barely. It's still pretty strained."

"It'll just take some time. Try not to let it get to you. People don't always see eye to eye."

"Charlie went to preschool Friday."

"Oh? What did he think?"

"He loved it. He has a crush on his teacher. He said she looks like a princess."

"Does she?" Andi asked, intrigued.

"She's young and very pretty, with long red hair and big blue eyes."

"Which princess would that be?"

"Ariel, I believe."

Andi had to think. "*Little Mermaid*?"

"Yes." Lindsay turned to watch Charlie try to throw a ball to Jax without putting his planes down. "I'm afraid Charlie's a romantic. One day at preschool and he's going to marry Miss Brittney."

"He is darling," Andi agreed.

"Stone was sweet, too. Not like Wolf. Wolf is tough. He means well, but I forgot just how hard he is. He doesn't forgive easily, either."

"But most of the time he's good company, isn't he?"

"I'm not so sure. He likes to boss me around, and it's annoying. I'm not his employee. I don't work for him. And if he doesn't want me here, then he should tell me that, and not be so cold."

Andi felt a shaft of sympathy. For both Lindsay and Wolf. "Have you tried to talk to him about it?"

"I'm not sure how to start. Where do I start? I don't mind his rules. Those are fair. They make sense. Keep things tidy and we have no problem. Use up something from the refrigerator, put it on the shopping list or replace it, no problem. But when I try to talk to him, he looks . . . bored, or irritated, or both. He doesn't like listening to me."

"Try not to take it personally. I work with a lot of men, and, without generalizing too much, I've found that a lot of men don't have the same listening skills women do. I thought this was just Kevin, but after four years at Orange, I realized that when men hear my voice, they think I need help, or they assume I need someone to make a decision for me. I'm trying to communicate, but all they hear is that there's a problem and they believe they need to solve it. Many men don't realize that many of us women need to share. It's how we feel close to someone, or how we express our thoughts—"

"And feelings." Lindsay glanced toward the garage. "Wolf doesn't like feelings, and avoids them at all costs." She tugged on a lock of her long hair, twisting the light brown strands. "Wolf told me this morning he thinks I should go talk to someone because I have too many feelings. But I don't want to go talk to someone, I was trying to talk to *him*."

Andi stifled a groan. "That must have been frustrating."

"And hurtful. He's a caveman. I don't know why you like him so much."

"Because, despite all his rough edges, I think he has a good heart. He has integrity. He's loyal to his family."

"Maybe if he'd had a daughter instead of all sons he'd be more comfortable with me here."

"Give him credit for trying."

"You should have seen his face when I told him I'm lonely. He was exasperated, and rather than giving me a hug, he rattled off a list of things I could do to meet people. I could go to a park, I could join a gym, he told me there had to be mom groups out there, some that probably meet with their kids at the park. He said if I take Charlie to a library, I might meet other moms. He made it sound so easy. Just go out, say hello to people, be open and friendly, put a smile on your face. Make an effort. Try." Lindsay's voice cracked. "The thing is, I *am* trying. And I do talk to other moms, but, Andi, most women my age aren't widows. Most women my age have a husband at home waiting for them every night. Moms my age don't relate to me, and to be honest, I can't relate to them. I'm angry. I resent them. They have what I don't."

She used her sleeve to rub her eyes dry, adding, "I'm so tired of this. I'm tired of feeling different. I'm tired of not being me. I haven't been me for years. I'm Stone's widow. I'm Charlie's mom. But who is Lindsay? I don't know anymore. I'm lost. I don't even know how I got this life. I met Stone, fell in love, married, certain we'd have a happy-ever-after. Instead we had a wedding and he was dead. He was overseas when I found out I was pregnant. He knew a baby was coming, but he never met Charlie."

"Do you ever think about dating again?" Lindsay said nothing and Andi leaned forward. "You're young and beautiful. It's okay to want company. It's okay to fall in love again. It's okay to get married again someday and add to your family."

"You haven't married again."

"I'm twice your age, almost sixty. Too old to have children, and financially secure enough that I don't feel a need to rush into anything. So no, I don't need to marry again."

"I don't need to marry again, either."

"You wouldn't want to give Charlie brothers or sisters?"

"Not unless I met someone truly wonderful, someone every bit as special as Stone, and I'm not sure that man exists. I'm going to compare every man to Stone. There was only one Stone, and I will never love anyone the way I loved him."

Andi clasped Lindsay's hand. "I wish I had known him, and I hope you'll talk to me about him, as often as you'd like. I love hearing about Stone. I love how you bring him to life."

Lindsay gave Andi's hand a little squeeze. "You make it easy to talk about him. You make it comfortable, and I'm grateful. Thank you for being my friend. You know, you're my first friend in California."

"We are friends, aren't we?"

Lindsay nodded, smiled.

"Even though I'm old enough to be your mom?" Andi teased.

"I don't care about age. Age is stupid. Some people are mature when they're young, and others can be old and incredibly immature. My mom was a young mom. She had me at sixteen. She didn't know how to be a mom, and even today, she's unreliable. Unavailable. When Stone died I couldn't go live with her. It wouldn't have been good for Charlie, and it wouldn't have been safe for me. The guy she is with now—Conrad—is such a loser. The last time I saw him he wouldn't stop hitting on me. It was creepy and uncomfortable. I mentioned it to Wolf, and he said if Conrad ever came near me again, to tell him and Wolf promised me I'd never have a problem with him again."

Andi's eyes widened. "Wow."

"Fortunately, I went to Jess's in New Orleans and never

had to deal with creepy Conrad again, but Wolf meant it. He doesn't mess around, and you don't, ever, mess with his family."

"So you know he loves you."

"He has high expectations for me, and sometimes I disappoint him, and that's hard."

"He'll get over it. You have to move forward, too. And you will. You've overcome a lot, and you've faced challenges that many people never have to face, and you do it with courage, and humor. I'm a fan, Lindsay, I am. I can see why Stone fell in love with you. You're special. And remember, even if Wolf is brusque, even if he doesn't say the right words, he wouldn't have asked you and Charlie to live with him if he didn't want you with him."

"But he didn't ask. I asked him. I put him in a position he couldn't very well refuse."

"Oh, come on. I don't see anyone making Wolf do anything he doesn't want to." Andi's heart did a little flutter then, realizing this applied to her as well. Wolf wouldn't invite her here, to join him, if he didn't want her here. If she didn't matter. He was protective of his family, and for him to include her in family dinners, that meant something.

She meant something. Even if he didn't say so in words.

As if able to read her mind, Lindsay said, "He's into you, big-time. I've never seen him like this."

Andi flushed, heat rushing through her. "It's not serious," she said, because there were no promises, no talk of the future. Yes, Wolf showed her by his actions that he cared, but Andi was no naive girl. A man could change his mind at any time.

"That's not true. Wolf's told both Lincoln and Maverick about you. He has fallen for you."

Andi glanced down and then off toward the garage. Her insides flipped, and her heart raced. "Well, let's just keep that between us," she said unsteadily. "I'd hate to jinx anything."

* * *

SOMEHOW, WITHOUT A LOT OF DISCUSSION, THEY FELL into a routine, where one night a week Andi would have dinner at Wolf's house, and then another night he'd take her to dinner or they'd go to Andi's, and then Lindsay and Charlie would spend part of Saturday with her, giving Wolf time to work at home undisturbed. But when Lindsay confided in Andi that she wasn't feeling strong, and wondered if going to a support group for grieving widows would help her, Andi said she'd take Charlie anytime, and that, outside of her work hours, she had nothing else to do.

"The thing is," Lindsay said slowly, "I was wondering if you'd maybe go with me. I'd feel better if you went with me. I'm nervous about going on my own."

"And Charlie?" Andi asked.

"Maybe Wolf could watch him? Or, better yet, maybe I could hire a sitter, and the sitter could stay with Charlie here so Wolf doesn't have to know? I'd prefer that, actually. I don't really want Wolf knowing everything, because he'll just worry and it will be suffocating again."

"Have you looked into any of the groups? Have you found something that would work?"

Lindsay nodded. "There's a group that meets at a church in Irvine on Saturdays. It's for widows and widowers. There are seventy-six members, but apparently only a dozen or so attend regularly. There's also a group that meets locally, in a church on Del Obispo. They meet Tuesday nights at seven."

"That would be a lot more convenient," Andi said. "You wouldn't have to spend any money paying for a sitter, either. Wolf would be happy to stay with Charlie. He could read him a story, and then just put him down to bed."

"Wolf will think I'm crazy."

"No, Wolf will respect you for taking care of yourself.

Talk to him and let's plan on attending this coming Tuesday. I can pick you up and we'll drive together."

"I'll pick you up," Lindsay said. "You're on the way."

THAT EVENING ANDI AND WOLF WERE SUPPOSED TO GO out, but Andi was tired, unusually wiped out, and asked Wolf if he'd mind coming over and just hanging out with her. He arrived and made dinner for them—a delicious pasta dish with chicken, sun-dried tomatoes, and artichoke hearts. He had a beer and she had a glass of white wine, and they ate in front of the TV, although the TV was muted.

It was a comfortable evening, the kind of evening Andi needed, where they didn't talk but just sat close, her hand in Wolf's.

She and Bruce would do this—have dinner, watch TV, hold hands—but Andi had never felt this way with him. There was no tingle of pleasure, no joy, no sense of gratitude and peace. With Wolf, she felt lucky. Blessed. Bruce was a nice person . . . but he wasn't her person.

As Wolf gathered their plates and carried the dishes to the kitchen, it crossed her mind that if they broke up, she wouldn't date again. She wouldn't want to.

When Wolf didn't return right away to the living room, Andi got up to see what he was doing. He was putting the final touch—dabs of butter—across a topping in a Pyrex dish. "It's a secret family recipe," he said deadpan, putting the dish into the oven.

Andi turned one of the empty cans around. Sliced peaches. He'd made a peach cobbler from canned peaches, a box of white cake mix, and what looked like a cube of butter.

"How much butter did you use?" she asked.

"As much as I needed to." He kissed her and cleaned the rest of the mess. "Haven't made this in years. Let's see if I remembered how to do it right."

An hour later Wolf served up his cobbler, and added a scoop of vanilla ice cream. They ate at the kitchen island, and Andi realized the "cobbler" was what Andi's mom called a "dump cake," and instead of peaches, Andi's mom used cherry pie filling.

"It's delicious," Andi told him, taking a tiny bit more of the still-warm, buttery, sweet and salty topping. The topping combined with ice cream and warm sweet fruit was heavenly. "And I do believe you're the first man who has ever made me dessert."

"I don't know what kind of men you've been dating, but clearly the wrong ones." He took her empty dish and put it in the sink.

"Dating isn't fun. But this year I tried. I thought it was time."

"Meet anyone special?"

"You."

"Good answer," he said, lifting her up and setting her on the island counter as if she was just a five-pound bag of flour. He caught her hair in one hand and drew it away from her neck. He kissed the side of her neck, and then lower, kissing down to her collarbone.

Her nerves danced. She struggled to keep breathing, shivering at the intense sensation. "You're dangerous," she murmured weakly as he pushed the collar of her blouse to the side. He unbuttoned the blouse, and kissed lower, unhooking her bra to take a taut nipple in his mouth. The things he could do with his mouth. The pleasure he gave her. Andi sighed, hot, impatient, eager.

Her clothes came off, and he laid her back on the marble counter, his mouth moving down her belly to the apex of her thighs. His hand was already there, and she arched as he kissed her where she was most sensitive. He was so good that she came, quickly, not just once, but a second time.

Dazed, Andi looked up at her kitchen ceiling, noting the dark beams against the creamy stucco. The house was supposed to look old; instead it just looked like someone had a lot of money to burn.

"I don't like this house," she said, still trying to catch her breath.

Wolf's laugh was low and husky. "I don't like this house, either, but that's not what I'm thinking about."

She dragged herself up into a sitting position, conscious of the cool marble against her bare backside. This was a first for her kitchen. "What are you thinking about?" she asked.

"I'm trying to decide if I want to do you here, like this, or turn you over, and do you from behind."

Andi flushed so deeply she could feel the heat rising up from her chest. "You're wicked."

"You like it."

"I do," she agreed, pushing her heavy curls from her nape, letting her skin cool. "But I think it's because I like you."

"Or maybe you like me because of what I do to you."

She grabbed him by the waistband of his jeans and pulled him toward her, so that he was standing between her thighs. "You could take away the sex, and I'd still love being with you."

Wolf stared into her eyes. "Why?"

"I don't know. I just have a thing for you."

They ended up making love in her room because her bed was huge, and the sheets were clean and cool. Andi loved the feel of him with her, in her. She loved his skin and his smell and the weight of him on her.

She fell asleep in his arms. And as always, he was gone when she awoke.

WOLF AGREED TO PUT CHARLIE TO BED ON TUESDAY nights so Lindsay and Andi could have a "girls' night." Wolf never asked them what they did on Tuesdays, and so Andi never told him they were in a meeting room at a nearby church listening to men and women of all ages share their thoughts and emotions, many crying as they talked, others crying as they listened.

It was after the second meeting that Lindsay told Andi that she was beginning to understand what the grief group was for. "They're trying to make us feel normal. We're not alone in our pain. We're not crazy, or broken. We're just missing those we love."

They went to a restaurant across from the mission for cappuccinos, as Lindsay was restless and not ready to go home. Andi suggested they drive into town and find a place they could talk.

"You know Marcia, the lady running our group?" Lindsay said as they were seated with their coffees. "I'd like to do what she does. Grief counseling. I'd like to be a therapist and help people."

"I think you'd be good at it," Andi said.

"Did you ever get counseling after your husband died?"

"I did, briefly. I should have gone longer. I needed to talk to someone, but I stopped going, thinking I was fine. Thinking I had it together. I didn't." Andi shrugged. "It took me a long time to feel okay again."

"What changed things?"

"I got a job. I slowly started making new friends. No one at my new job knew about Kevin, and my new friends weren't his friends, and so I could escape him, and the grief, for a little bit every day, but then when I came home, I'd walk into that big silent house and hate it all over again."

"You should have moved."

"I should have." Andi smiled. "I might move yet." She added another packet of sugar to her coffee. Even though the cappuccino was decaf, it was strong. "Are you thinking about going back to school, then?"

Lindsay hesitated. "I've been doing some research. There are a couple universities in the area that have good psychology programs. Obviously, I'd need a master's degree if I wanted to be a therapist, but earning my undergraduate degree is the first step."

"This is exciting, Lindsay!"

Lindsay blushed, suddenly bashful. "Please don't say anything to Wolf. I'm still trying to figure it all out and I don't want him to weigh in or try to influence me."

"I won't," Andi agreed. "But I'd love to help you, any way I can."

"Maybe on Saturday when I come over, we could look at the admissions process? See what I'd need to do?"

"That sounds wonderful."

"I'll bring my laptop," Lindsay said.

"Yes, but please, don't forget Charlie. I love my Charlie playdates."

It was true, too. Andi looked forward to Saturdays with Charlie.

Luke had never been a child who got on the ground and pushed cars around or built forts with blankets and chairs and couch cushions. He hadn't liked Play-Doh, he hadn't wanted to finger-paint, he didn't want to bake. He liked his toy microscope and his books and his coin collection that his grandfather had started for him. Charlie was the complete opposite. He loved all the things Luke hadn't. Each visit he couldn't wait to get his hands dirty. He loved getting messy, and Andi felt the same.

Charlie made her feel young, and happy, especially when he climbed onto her lap and threw his arms around her neck or planted wet sloppy kisses on her cheek. Maybe the best part of all was that she had no expectations. She knew she was just borrowing him, enjoying this little human being, and it was a gift really. God knew she'd needed a chance to love, and He was giving it to her, in abundance.

On Saturday after Charlie and Lindsay arrived, Charlie started lining up tiny green army men outside a Lincoln Log fort he'd built on his last visit, and Andi made Lindsay a cup of tea and then handed her an admissions packet from Orange University.

"I stopped by Admissions yesterday," Andi said. "This is where I work. Orange is a small, private school, but they have an outstanding psychology program. They're still accepting transfer applications until April fifteenth."

"That's soon."

"Three weeks from now. Plenty of time if you're serious." Andi pushed a wayward curl behind her ear. "I'm not a professor, I'm the assistant to the math chair, Dr. Nair, but I work with him and other faculty, and students, and I think you'd love being on a university campus. It's a different feeling than a community college. Most students are there full-time, and there's a great energy on campus. It's stimulating. You'd be surrounded by people working toward something important."

"You don't think I'm too old?"

"*No.* Would you look around and see students younger than you? Yes. But you'll have an advantage over them. You know yourself. You're not a green girl. You've lived."

"I didn't earn my associate's degree, but I did meet a lot of my core requirements. I had pretty good grades, too."

"Where? At high school or Coastal Carolina?"

"Both."

"That's great. If you have solid grades, and a decent SAT score, you'll have lots of options for schools here. There are quite a few universities within driving distance. Cal State Long Beach, Cal State Fullerton, Cal State Marcos, UC Irvine, plus all the private ones."

Lindsay thought for a moment. "And it's not too late for fall semester?"

"Maybe for a few of the schools, but a lot of schools are flexible for transfers, and that's what you'd be. The important thing is to make a list of schools you're most interested in, organize applications by deadline date, and start tackling applications so you have a shot at going to school this fall."

Lindsay pushed her tea away from her. "Do you really think I can do this?"

"One hundred percent."

Lindsay reached for her laptop and opened it. "Let's do this."

Chapter 13

THEY BEGAN TO GET TOGETHER TWICE A WEEK TO work on Lindsay's college applications, using the Tuesday nights to go to the grief support group, and then another hour for college apps, and then on Saturdays, Lindsay would work at the dining room table, while Andi and Charlie would play.

On this Saturday after Charlie was happily lining up the Matchbox cars, one after the other in an enormous line across the dining room floor and into the kitchen, Lindsay asked Andi about the scholarship section for the Orange application. "I don't think I qualify for financial need," Lindsay said. "I personally don't have a lot of money, but there is Stone's trust. I haven't used any of the money yet, but I will one day, to help Charlie and me buy a house, and put Charlie through college. But what about this part, where it says, would I like to be considered for any scholarships?"

Andi leaned over Lindsay's shoulder to read the screen. "It looks like Orange has some merit scholarships, which I believe are based on talent, and not always financial need. I don't see why you wouldn't want to be considered?"

"It is a pricey school," Lindsay said. "I can't believe tuition."

"You said Wolf promised to help."

"In theory. We discussed it when we were still in New Orleans. He doesn't know I'm applying to schools now."

Andi sat down in a chair next to Lindsay. "When do you think you'll tell him?"

"I still want to surprise him. If I got in somewhere . . . he'd be pleased, wouldn't he?"

"He'd be over the moon."

Lindsay laughed. "Wolf, over the moon? Just who are we talking about?"

Andi smiled. "Okay, maybe not over the moon, but he'd be proud of you."

"That's why I don't want to tell him, not until I get in somewhere. Otherwise, he'll feel sorry for me if I don't get in somewhere and I don't want that. It just adds too much pressure."

"Do you have enough in the trust to cover tuition at a private university?"

"Yes."

"For all four years?"

"Wolf set up a trust for each of his sons, and Stone left his trust to me, so I'm okay."

"Of the schools you're applying to, what are your top choices?"

"Long Beach State would be my first choice if I had to go to a public school, but I won't get in-state tuition for another year. And if money isn't an issue, both Chapman and Orange look really good. They're still accepting applications from transfers, so those would be my top two, and Orange would probably be my number one choice, simply because it's so close to home. I could be at school in, what? Fifteen minutes?"

Andi nodded. "Sometimes less."

"I hope I get accepted."

"Me, too. Then we could carpool together." Andi realized then how silly that was. Andi was staff, and worked eight thirty to four thirty, and Lindsay would be a student with very different hours. "Probably not carpool, but I could meet you on campus for a coffee or lunch sometimes."

"You're getting me excited."

"I'm glad. It's time you embraced the future. There is so much opportunity out there, so much life to live."

"If I graduate, I'll be the first woman in my family to graduate from college."

"Then let's get you back to school. I can't wait to see you receive your diploma."

"YOU AND LINDSAY HAVE BEEN SPENDING A LOT OF TIME together," Wolf said to Andi. They were walking hand in hand in his quiet neighborhood, closely following Charlie, who'd just learned to ride a bike, and had only needed two weeks to go from training wheels to no training wheels.

Wolf had gotten Charlie the bike, using their Tuesday evenings together to teach him how to ride. No one had expected Charlie to be such a natural, least of all Wolf. But then, Wolf hadn't taught his sons how to ride a bike. That had been Jess.

"We're friends," Andi said simply. "We enjoy each other's company."

"What do you do together?"

"On Tuesdays we go to this support group together. On Saturdays I play with Charlie. Sometimes Lindsay stays and hangs out, and other times she does errands, or goes for a run. She's trying to take care of herself. Not sure if you've noticed."

"You both go to the support group?" Wolf asked, glancing at her.

"Lindsay hasn't mentioned it?"

He shook his head.

"It's for widows and widowers. It's free and informal. Lindsay was nervous about going on her own, and she asked me to join her for the first time. I realized it was good for me, too, and so we've both continued to go."

"Why didn't you tell me before?"

She gave him a look. "Why have you never told me about your work, or the years spent in the military? Why have you never talked to me about your marriage, or how you got all those scars—"

"Because it's in the past," he answered, looking from her to Charlie, who had climbed off his bike and was trying to fix his shoe. Wolf let go of Andi's hand and crouched next to Charlie, helping ease his heel back into the shoe. He rose and reached for her hand again, but Andi put it in her pocket, and faced him.

"I understand you're private. I understand you don't feel the need to discuss the past, but I don't even know how you became a draftsman. How does one leave the Marine Corps and do what you do?"

"Katrina," he said.

Her eyebrows rose. "Can you please use that in a complete sentence."

He laughed. She was funny. And good company. "I put off retiring as long as I could. I didn't want to leave active duty because I didn't know what I'd do. But then Katrina struck, and so much of the South suffered damage. People were homeless. Homes were destroyed. I had to help, so I responded to a call put out by a vet I'd served with. We worked together in New Orleans and then we headed to Mobile. I was in Mobile for a few years, clearing debris, scraping lots, working with the city, helping with the rebuilding process, and I realized this was something I wanted to do professionally. I went back to school, earned my drafting degree, apprenticed in New Orleans, but New Orleans isn't where I belong, and so I headed here, having once been stationed at Camp Pendleton, and happy here."

"Isn't Maverick in the area, too?"

"When he's not traveling, yes."

"But he travels a lot."

"He does."

Charlie was getting tired and ready to return home, so they turned around at the next corner and headed back.

"If you could design any house you wanted for you, what would it be?" Andi asked as they approached his house.

This was easy. "I like the way houses were built in the South, with the tall doors and windows to let in cool air and allow hot air to escape. I like how tall windows let in the light. I like porches. High ceilings that allow heat to rise, keeping it more comfortable below. I like the aesthetic as well—from the coastal houses you'd find in the Carolinas to Louisiana's Creole cottages, to the ornate balconies you find in the French Quarter."

"Pretty houses," Andi said, smiling up at him.

"They're functional."

"But pretty," she said, leaning against him. "But that's good, because I like pretty houses, too, houses with charm, houses with verandas and thick crown molding. I prefer cozy and charming . . . and the only place I really like marble is in the kitchen on a counter, and maybe the bathroom."

Wolf opened the gate, and Charlie abandoned his bike and raced toward the house, flinging his helmet as he dashed inside. Wolf picked up the small green bike and carried it in one hand. Andi picked up the helmet and followed Wolf.

"I agree," he said, "less is more, at least with a home. Up at the cabin I did add a wing for the boys, thinking we'd need the space for them when they grew up, as they'd maybe bring their families for Christmas or summer. It hasn't really turned out that way." He placed the bike near the garage. Jax appeared from within the garage, sniffing them, tail drooping, clearly not happy that he hadn't been included in the walk.

He patted Jax's side. He hadn't been as attentive to Jax as he used to be. There seemed to be more people to take care of now. Charlie needed attention and then there was Lindsay, who still remained difficult to read.

"That's not to say it couldn't still happen," Andi said, referring to family get-togethers at his cabin. "Lindsay has Charlie, and if Maverick and Lincoln marry one day, you'll want that space."

"I'm not sure how long Lindsay is going to be here," he said, turning off the light in his garage office and firmly closing the door.

"Why do you say that?" Andi asked as they headed to the house.

Andi was staying for dinner, and tonight she'd brought a lasagna with her. It had been baking while they were out walking. "I'm a hard-ass," he confessed.

"You are," Andi agreed, pressing a kiss to his upper arm. "But that's why we love you."

"I'm not trying to make her life miserable. I just think she'd be happier getting a job and doing something. She needs to get out. Meet people. Be active. Sitting in her room all day, or watching shows all day, isn't going to help her adjust to life here."

In the kitchen Andi peeked into the oven and lifted a corner of the foil on the lasagna. She liked what she saw and the foil came off and she closed the oven door. "She's working on it," Andi said, facing him.

"How? By going to grief support group meetings? Hanging out at your house while you take care of Charlie?"

She gave him a reproving look. "You're being a little judgmental."

"Then tell me she's using her time better and I'll feel better."

"She's using her time better," Andi said firmly. "Trust me."

Wolf studied her expression—the firm press of lips, the tilt of chin, the fierceness in her eyes. He appreciated Andi's faith in Lindsay, and he didn't necessarily doubt her, but he knew Andi was a softie. She tried to see the best in everyone.

Hopefully Andi was right.

Hopefully Lindsay was making positive strides in the right direction. Not just because she was getting older and needed to mature, but also because Charlie was a bright boy. He needed a mom who could properly care for him.

AFTER DINNER, WOLF WANTED TO TAKE JAX FOR A QUICK walk. Usually Lindsay would use that time to give Charlie a bath and put him to bed, but tonight Charlie wanted to go on the walk with Wolf and Jax.

Andi saw Wolf hesitate. He glanced at Lindsay, but Lindsay was waiting for him to make the decision.

But when Charlie came in with Jax's leash, and Jax was at Charlie's side, tail wagging wildly, Wolf couldn't say no. "A short walk," Wolf said. "It's getting late and you have school tomorrow."

Jax was patient while Charlie hooked the leash to the collar and then the three of them left the house, with Charlie walking Jax.

Andi had never seen anyone else walk Jax, but the dog doted on Charlie, and watching the two together was terribly sweet.

"I think Jax has adopted Charlie," Andi said to Lindsay as they disappeared from view.

"Jax sleeps in his room now," Lindsay said. "Well, for the first part of the night, and then when Wolf goes to bed, he switches to Wolf's room. Charlie hasn't been around very many dogs, so I was surprised at how quickly he took to Jax."

"I didn't think Jax liked anyone but Wolf," Andi said.

"I know. But I have a feeling Charlie is a mini Wolf." Lindsay sat down on the couch, and pulled a soft blanket over her. "Jessica used to say the same thing, but as you'd expect, it wasn't a compliment."

"I think it's a huge compliment." Andi sat at the opposite end of the couch. She should go. She was tired. She had work in the morning. But the idea of returning home didn't appeal. She wished she could just crawl into bed with Wolf and sleep. It would be nice to have him with her all night, not just for a few hours.

Lindsay was tired, too. She smothered a big yawn. "Did you know you're the only one I can talk to about Stone? I can't talk about him with anyone but you. Why is that?"

"I don't know. Maybe it's because you know I care about you, and I'm here for you. And I promise you, I will never judge you. I have a feeling you've had more than enough of that."

"Why couldn't you have been my mom?" Lindsay said huskily.

Andi tipped her head against the couch and sighed. "I have a feeling parenting twenty-four seven isn't easy. I'm sure I'd let you down, just as your mom has disappointed you."

"No matter what happens with you and Wolf, promise me you'll always be my friend. Promise me you'll always—"

"You don't even have to ask. I am your friend forever. I am on your team, here for you and Charlie, no matter what."

"No strings attached."

"No strings attached. Cross my heart."

Wolf and Charlie and Jax returned not much later, and Andi gathered her basket with the lasagna pan and salad bowl and Wolf walked her to her car. He kissed her good night and she drove away, but as she made the trip home, Lindsay's words, *No matter what happens with you and Wolf,* echoed in her head.

No matter what happens with you and Wolf . . .

Andi was sure Lindsay hadn't meant anything by them, but they held a note of doom, and troubled her. Was something going to happen with her and Wolf? What could possibly happen to drive them apart?

Andi's feelings were so strong, she couldn't imagine ever just walking away from him. So if they ended, it would be because of Wolf, and that was terrifying. She'd known going into this there were risks. She'd known Wolf wasn't someone who made commitments, but things had been going so well, and they were both so happy. Why couldn't they just remain happy?

Chapter 14
~~~~~~~~~

WOLF HAD WARNED ANDI THAT HE'D BE LESS AVAILABLE in the coming week, due to a project that needed attention, and he needed to unplug to focus. Andi understood and was happy to welcome Lindsay and Charlie on Saturday, having invited them for the whole day instead of just part so that Wolf could have fewer disruptions.

When Lindsay arrived at nine Saturday morning, she mentioned that she'd love to get a manicure and a pedicure, and she also hoped to do some shopping, if Andi was comfortable with Charlie being there that long without her. "I can also pay you," Lindsay offered awkwardly. "The last thing I want to do is take advantage of your generosity."

"I don't want your money," Andi said, trying not to be offended. "I think of you as family. Please take as long as you like. Charlie and I can watch a movie today after lunch. It's been years since I got to watch a Disney or Pixar movie."

Lindsay hugged Charlie goodbye and then was off. Andi and Charlie did some painting on the easel Andi had bought, and then they read some books, had lunch, and watched the movie with popcorn. Lindsay hadn't yet returned so Andi suggested they make cookies, which Charlie thought was an excellent idea.

When Lindsay arrived, the first tray of cookies was still in the oven.

"Come in," Andi said, gesturing for Lindsay to step inside. "Charlie can't leave without his cookies."

"What kind are they?"

"Peanut butter with chocolate chips, since Charlie couldn't decide if he wanted peanut butter or chocolate chip." Andi led the way to the kitchen. "Tea? Coffee? Water?"

"I'm good."

Andi looked at her from across the island. Lindsay did look good. Her hair was silky smooth and she was wearing a little bit of makeup. But it wasn't just that. She was almost . . . glowing. "Did you get a blowout?" Andi asked her.

"Along with a few new highlights," Lindsay answered, blushing faintly.

But there was something else, Andi thought, something else making Lindsay radiant. "Did you have a date?"

Lindsay's brow creased and she shook her head. "It wasn't a date." She met Andi's gaze, adding, "But I did meet a friend of Stone's for lunch. Zane was out from North Carolina so he called me, wanting to check up on me."

"I'm glad. I'm really happy you had a chance to have lunch with a friend. Is he doing okay?"

Lindsay nodded, her smile returning. "He is. It was nice catching up. He took me to Laguna for lunch. I hadn't been to Laguna Beach yet. It's nice. I wouldn't mind living there."

Lindsay leaned forward, trying to read the spine of a cookbook lying on the counter. "What is that cookbook? I'm sure Jessica has the same one."

Embarrassed, Andi pushed the book across the marble to Lindsay. "It's *The New Orleans Cookbook*. I just bought it. It's supposed to be a classic."

Lindsay smiled at Andi as she flipped through the pages. "You don't have to win Wolf's heart through his stomach. He's already crazy about you."

"I like to cook. I thought it would be fun to try new recipes."

"How much do you know about Wolf's family in New Orleans?"

"Virtually nothing."

"You should ask him to show you his childhood home, and his grandparents' home. Both are featured on the Garden District historic walking tour, but his grandparents owned one of the oldest, biggest, and most impressive homes in New Orleans. And you know, he was their only heir. He basically inherited everything."

"Wolf?"

"Yes, and he walked away from all of it. He doesn't touch the money. He never has, and he never will. He pretty much took his inheritance and put it all in trusts for his sons. And of course he took care of Jessica."

The timer went off and Andi put on a mitt and took out the cookie sheet, placing them on the stove. "Wolf doesn't seem to care much about money."

"He doesn't. And he doesn't like to draw attention to himself."

Andi slid two more cookie sheets into the oven. "And yet everything he is sets him apart. He's like no one else I've ever met."

"They're all that way." Lindsay's expression turned wistful. "You should have seen them together, Wolf and his sons. They were like their own special forces. Amazing. Intimidating. But they loved each other. You knew they would do anything for each other. I think that's why Wolf takes Stone's death so hard. He would have gladly, without a moment's hesitation, given his life for Stone. But he couldn't."

Andi had always thought that, and felt it, but to hear it from Lindsay was something else. "Considering you had such a complicated relationship with men growing up, you weren't intimidated by Stone, or his family?"

"Stone made me feel safe. Wolf isn't always easy for me, but I understand he's trying. He's not a nurturer. He's a fighter. I mean, all the Enderses are fighters, but when they come together, they're never hard. They're not bullies. They have their own family dynamics, this code of conduct, and it's loving, honest, but respectful. At home together they let down their guard and can just be . . . themselves."

Lindsay moved around the island to take part of a warm cookie. She blew on it, and put it in her mouth. "Good. Very good."

"I'll send them all home with you," Andi said.

Lindsay took the other half of the cookie from the sheet. "I think Jessica resents Wolf because he is so close to his sons. She feels as if she did everything for the family, and yet the boys idolized their dad. Wolf was their hero. Wolf was everything. Leader, commander, mentor, protector. Wolf made them want to be brave, strong. He never asked it, either. He never wanted them to follow in his footsteps. They just did."

"You have a lot of amazing insight into them."

"I love them. I love this family. Spend enough time with them and you want to be part of them."

"But you found it hard living with Jessica."

"I find it hard living with Wolf. They're both really strong people. I don't know how they ended up together."

"I heard she's beautiful."

"She is. She looks a lot younger than her age. She's still quite slender, too. I've been with her and strangers ask if she's a model. She loves it, of course." Lindsay made a face. "I shouldn't be critical. She took us in when I couldn't remain on base any longer and had nowhere else to go."

Andi began moving the cookies to a wire rack. "Why did you have to move?"

"The military lets widows remain in their housing for a

year after the death of the military spouse, which was good, because I couldn't have gone anywhere, and didn't want to leave my friends, all wives of Raiders. But when it was the first anniversary of Stone's death, I had to go. My time was up."

"That had to be difficult."

"I felt like I was losing Stone all over again. Lincoln knew I wasn't doing well and he reached out to his mom. Jessica invited us to New Orleans and we ended up living with her for two years. But it wasn't a good fit. Jessica isn't a warm woman, or forgiving. She hates Wolf. Hates, hates, hates."

"He's never said anything bad about her."

"He won't. He respects her as the mother of his sons and is protective of her, considering how awful she treats him."

"Do you think Stone's death changed her?"

"Probably. It changed all of us."

"What does she like?"

"Besides her sons, and Charlie?" Lindsay thought for a moment. "She loves her house. She loves being Delfinia's daughter-in-law. She's taken Delfinia's place on committees and in social clubs. She has a position in society and it's important to her." Lindsay paused. "I get the feeling she didn't have that growing up. She needs to be someone. I relate to that. I need to be someone, too."

"You are someone," Andi said firmly.

"But I want to do something with my life. I want it to have meaning. If I've learned anything from my mom, or Jessica, it's that no one else can make you happy. You have to do that for yourself."

"Bravo." Andi walked around the island and gave Lindsay a fierce hug. "You're an inspiration, Lindsay. You've got this. You're on your way."

WOLF SHOWED UP AT ANDI'S HOUSE AT NINE THAT night. Andi had been watching TV and flipping through saved copies of *Southern Living* and the doorbell startled her. But when she saw it was Wolf on her doorstep she threw the door open and hugged him. "This is a wonderful surprise," she said. "Come in, come in."

"I missed you," he said, closing the door behind him. He held up a colorful bag. "Brought dessert. I know you have a sweet tooth."

She saw the bright logo for the Cheesecake Factory. "Oh, Wolf, you didn't."

"I wasn't sure which kind was your favorite so I brought several slices." He headed to the living room, sat down in the middle of the couch. "What are you watching?"

"Nothing special." She muted the TV and sat next to him.

Wolf opened the bag and drew out three containers, each with a slice of cheesecake topped with whipped cream.

"How's your project?" she asked.

"I finished it."

"Yay! That's great. So we're celebrating."

"Yep." He leaned over, kissed her. "Celebrating by seeing you."

She couldn't hide her smile. His words warmed her, making her feel cherished. Special. "You are too sweet."

"I'm not sure anyone has ever described me that way before." He picked up one of her magazines with the stickie notes. "What's this?"

"My collection of favorite houses." She could see he was interested so she added, "They're not very grand houses, but they're my dream homes." She watched as he flipped through the magazine, pausing at one of the houses she'd earmarked. "I've heard about your childhood. Lindsay said you grew up in an important house in New Orleans."

"My grandparents' home on St. Charles was the important house."

"Tell me about it."

"Which part?" he asked. "The thirteen bedrooms or—"

"Thirteen bedrooms?"

"Or the ballroom that could hold fifty waltzing couples, or the two-story library, or the orangery with its fruit trees from all over the world, including guava, mango, papaya, and pineapple."

"Is either house still in the family?"

"No, they both sold years ago, but I could pull them up on the internet, show them to you sometime if you're interested."

"I'd love to see them."

"Now tell me why you like this house," he asked, returning to the magazine with the stickie note.

She leaned against him, looking at the magazine. "It's cozy, comfortable. I like the windows, and I love the porch. I'm a sucker for a wraparound porch."

He reached for another of her magazines on the table, flipping through pages to find another house she'd put a stickie note on. "And this one?" he asked.

"I don't know what style you call it, farmhouse or cottage, but again, it has lots of tall windows, a steep roof, a covered porch, and master suite on the main floor, with French doors that open to the garden."

While they ate their cheesecake, Wolf continued to flip through the magazines, studying some plans intently, skipping over others. While he studied the houses, she studied him, feeling happy.

It was nice having him here, hanging out on her couch, having dessert with her, looking at dream homes. He looked good on her couch, biceps bunching as he fed her a bite of his cheesecake—banana cream something delicious—and when he smiled at her, as he wiped the whipped cream from her lip, her heart did a double beat, her tummy full of butterflies. He still gave her butterflies. He still took her breath away.

When Kevin died, she'd been certain life as she knew it

had ended, and in many ways it had, but as she began to inch her way forward, working through her grief, windows opened. Doors opened. Her heart opened.

She'd found love again, and she appreciated it even more this second time around.

"What are you doing Sunday? Any plans?" Wolf asked, stroking her hair.

"I was going to sort through some things in the closet. I've decided it's time to purge things I will never use, but the purge can wait. What do you have in mind?"

He wrapped her hair around his hand. He loved to touch her hair, he seemed fascinated by the curls. "It's a surprise, nothing big, but dress in layers, bring comfortable walking shoes. I'll take care of the rest."

"You're going to make me exercise?"

He pulled her onto his lap. "You'll be fine. Trust me."

"I'm not, you know, as fit as I should be. I huff and puff going up the stairs."

His lips brushed her temple. "You do not. At least, you don't huff. You might puff."

Andi laughed, snuggled closer. "Don't you have a birthday coming up?"

"Yeah, but we all have birthdays."

"Yours is coming soon, I think. It's in April. I've forgotten the day."

He tipped her chin up, his teeth scraping her tender earlobe. "What a terrible girlfriend you are. Forgetting my birthday? The first year we're together?"

She squirmed at the delicious sensation. "I didn't forget it. I just don't remember the exact date. And am I your girlfriend?"

"If you're not mine, whose are you?"

"No one's. But we've never discussed this."

"We are now."

"True." She hesitated. "Are you my boyfriend?"

He lowered his head, kissed her, and the kiss deepened.

By the time he lifted his head she was breathless and oh so warm. "I hope I am," he said.

She slipped her arms around his neck. "I'm happy."

"Good."

"So happy I'm afraid something is going to go wrong."

"Don't say things like that. We have a good thing. A really good thing."

She thought of Kevin driving to Dana Point one morning and never coming home. They hadn't said a proper goodbye. She'd been in the shower and he was rushing. He shouted he'd see her soon, and have a good day, and that was it. "There are no guarantees."

"I know."

"I try not to think negative—"

"So don't. I'm careful. I don't take risks. I had a physical for my sixtieth, and I passed with flying colors. I'm more settled than I've ever been. I have Lindsay and Charlie to take care of. And then there's you. I want to be here for you. Nothing's going to happen."

"It's just that I haven't felt this way in so long, and I know how lucky I am to have this second chance—"

"You're making yourself anxious. There's no need for that. I'm here. I'm not going anywhere."

She held his face between her hands. "I'm crazy about you," she whispered.

"I feel the same way about you."

WOLF PARKED IN HER DRIVEWAY SUNDAY MORNING right at eight thirty on the dot.

Andi had been ready for an hour. She'd probably had too much coffee, but she was excited to spend the day with him. When she opened her front door, she flung herself at him, happy.

When Wolf put her back on her feet, Andi did a quick twirl, showing off her jeans, T-shirt, lightweight sweatshirt, and vest. He'd said to dress in layers. She hoped this was what he meant. "Is this right? Does this work?"

His gaze slowly drifted down, taking in everything before an equally slow perusal back up. By the time he looked into her eyes, her cheeks burned. "You follow directions very well."

"I have three layers on and you just made me feel naked."

"That's because I was picturing you naked."

She lifted a sneaker, pointed at her toe. "I just hope you're not picturing me naked in this elegant footwear."

"You make me laugh," he said.

"I hope that's a good thing."

"It's a very good thing. I've gone years without laughing."

The sudden huskiness in his voice made her heart ache, and she realized that he might be this big tough guy, but he hadn't had the easiest path. She wondered who had really loved him, who had really been there for *him*. "So what are we doing today?" she asked, hoping she didn't sound as emotional as she felt.

"You'll see."

Wolf drove north on the 5, and she looked out the windows, watching them pass exits, trying to guess which direction they were going. When he headed east on 91, she wondered if they were going to the mountains, but there were a lot of places they could go this way . . . Riverside, San Bernardino. She was pretty sure of their destination when he turned onto the 18. The 18 was what she drove to reach Blue Jay.

Indeed, when he took the Waterman exit, she smiled. "We're going to the mountains."

"Yes. You know why?"

"You want to check on your cabin?"

"Try again."

"You want to check on my cabin?"

"You get one more guess."

"You want to make love in one of our cabins?"

Wolf flashed her a grin. "That is a good idea and will probably happen, but that's not why we're going up there."

"Good. It's an awful long way to go for an orgasm, especially when you do that quite nicely back in San Juan."

Wolf shook his head. "You're shameless. I had no idea."

"I think you made me shameless."

"I think it was always there. The adventurous girl was buried beneath the prim and proper good girl."

"Prim and proper? You make me sound like a prude wearing pearls."

"You used to wear pearls all the time. What happened to them?"

"Those were gifts Kevin gave me. I gradually stopped wearing them after he died."

Wolf glanced at her. "Why?"

Andi didn't answer immediately. "I didn't really like pearls that much."

Wolf's jaw dropped slightly. He gave her an incredulous look. "You wore them every day. With cardigans, your prissy little blouses—"

"Hey, I resemble that!" She laughed because it felt good to laugh, just as it felt good to shed the old Andi image. It had never felt very much like her anyway. Her mom had never been a pearl girl, and Andi wasn't sure why Kevin liked them so much, but she had tried to be the wife he wanted, tried to conform into the woman he wanted her to be. Elegant, polished, classic. At least that was what he said he liked—even though the women he hung out with down at the canoe club were casual, sporty, fit, natural. "I'm more comfortable in how I dress now. Or maybe I just don't care as much. Or maybe it's just that I'm heavier than I used to be and I can't fit in all those clothes I used to own. No more fitted skirts and trousers with belts. Nothing tucked in. I'm all about comfort."

"You think you're heavier?"

"From five years ago? Oh, twenty pounds heavier. I lose a few and gain five, lose a few more, gain another five. And I'm sure if I disliked food I could be thinner, but I like to eat and drink and have fun, and so here I am."

"Fifty and fabulous," he said, shifting gears as they were climbing now, approaching the steep turns.

"Closer to sixty than fifty."

"Oh, you're just fishing for compliments now."

Andi laughed. "Why not? I'll take another, if you're doling them out."

"I'd say sixty and sensational, but that's just way too cheesy."

"And Wolf Enders is never cheesy."

He glanced at her, creases fanning from his eyes as he smiled. "Not if I can help it."

Thirty minutes later, as they entered their Blue Jay community, Andi soon realized why Wolf wanted to drive up to the San Bernardino Mountains today. The dogwoods were waking up, the first of the white blooms unfolding on bare branches. The woods were filled with dogwoods, a stunning lacy understory to the big trees. The creek was full, icy water rushing downstream, with delicate purple wildflowers popping up between seedlings.

Wolf had planned a long but relatively easy hike for them on one of the many trails, with the path curving around the mountain rather than steep ups and downs. He'd brought a backpack, which he'd packed with a picnic lunch, thermoses of water, and snacks. She was glad he carried it, and she was even happier when he stripped off his long-sleeve shirt, shoving it in the backpack, exposing his muscular arms and broad chest. It was shallow, and maybe a little vulgar, but the man's body blew her mind. He was just hot. And he was into her. She wasn't going to question it, either. Why look a gift horse in the mouth? She would just enjoy him. She loved him. There was no walking away from him now. She was all in, completely committed with all of her heart.

Wolf knew where he wanted to stop for lunch. It was a pretty spot near the creek in a clearing buzzing with butterflies. A massive tree had fallen years ago, and part of the fallen log was shaded, the other half in sun. The sun shone warmly, and Wolf wanted a spot on the log with sunshine. She felt warm and wanted shade. They sat down on the log exactly where the sun and shade came together.

Andi ate her turkey and Swiss sandwich on whole grain bread. He'd put lettuce and a tomato slice on it, with salt and pepper, and it was delicious. Maybe the best sandwich she'd ever had. Maybe it was amazing because he had made it for her. Or maybe she was hungry. Or maybe it really just was a fantastic sandwich.

Wolf knew how to pack a lunch, too. He brought chips and apples, a container of grapes, plus cookies. They were store-bought little gingerbread cookies with icing. Andi loved molasses cookies and gingerbread everything. When she finished her first water, he pulled out another thermos for her. "I'm not taking yours, am I?"

He reached into the backpack and pulled out another. "I come prepared."

Andi leaned across the log to kiss him. She could feel the sun on her cheeks, the dazzle of light across her eyelashes as she closed her eyes. Her fingers crept around his nape. His hair was crisp, his skin warm, his mouth cool from the ice water he'd just drunk. He felt like nature, and life. He felt like everything she needed and wanted. "Thank you," she whispered.

He pulled her onto his lap, and the kiss continued. When the kiss finally ended, she needed to adjust her bra and tug down her shirt. She felt breathless and young. Love made her feel young—like a girl with a world filled with possibilities. And maybe the possibilities were always there and she just hadn't seen them before.

* * *

WOLF HAD MORE TIGHT DEADLINES FORCING THEM TO take a break until the next weekend. Andi kept Charlie on Tuesday night so Lindsay could attend the support meeting. But Lindsay returned late from the meeting, and her cheeks were flushed, and her eyes were bright. Andi couldn't tell if she was happy or sad, but something was happening. Or something had happened.

"Was it okay being there on your own?" Andi asked her, as Lindsay lifted a sleepy Charlie in her arms and carried him out to her car.

"It was fine." Lindsay buckled him in, and straightened. She carefully closed the passenger door but didn't quite look at Andi, her attention focused on a point past Andi's shoulder.

"Charlie was so sweet tonight. He held my hand while we watched a show. He said that's what couples do." Andi laughed. "He said he can't marry you, but maybe he'll marry me."

Lindsay smiled reluctantly, but the smile didn't reach her eyes. "He does love you. He told Wolf you're his girlfriend."

"What did Wolf say to that?"

"I don't know." Lindsay's eyes watered and she drew a big breath before sighing. "I should get home."

"Drive safely."

"It's only a few blocks," Lindsay said.

Andi gave her a hug. "You've been working hard on those applications. When they're done we'll celebrate."

"I only have UCI left. I don't think I have the grades or test scores to get in there. Not sure if I should bother."

"You won't know, though, if you don't try. Set that bar high."

"I'm trying." Lindsay got into her car and Andi stepped back and watched her drive away.

Andi waited until the red taillights disappeared before going inside. She wasn't worried about Lindsay, but Lindsay did seem a little off.

A little sad.

Maybe the discussion at the support group had touched a nerve. Maybe someone's pain had resonated with hers. Maybe it was just hormones and Lindsay was a little more emotional.

Andi locked the front door, tidied the kitchen, turned out the lights, and went upstairs for bed.

Still thinking about Lindsay, Andi sent her a text as she got into bed. I'm so proud of you. xox

Chapter 15

SOMETHING WAS RINGING.

What was it?

It took Andi a moment to register it was her phone ringing. She opened her eyes, looking at the clock next to her bed. Eleven forty-seven. She'd only been asleep for a little over an hour.

Andi reached for her phone charging next to the bed. It was Wolf. For him to call now, it couldn't be good.

"Wolf?" she said, sitting up.

"I have an emergency. Can you come here?"

"Yes. On my way." She asked nothing else, just dressed fast, grabbing a sweatshirt and pulling it on over her pajamas.

An ambulance was at Wolf's house when Andi arrived, red lights spinning. Paramedics rolled a gurney out of the house. Lindsay's long light brown hair spilled off the gurney. Andi froze, stunned. Lindsay was still. An oxygen mask covered her face.

Wolf emerged from the house behind the paramedics. He'd pulled a baseball hat on and had his keys. "I don't know when I'll be back," he said.

Andi gave him a quick hug. She wanted to ask questions, but this wasn't the time. "Don't worry. Charlie's in good hands. Call me as soon as you know something."

Wolf nodded and headed to his Land Rover. The ambulance closed the doors and drove off, siren off until they exited the neighborhood.

In the house, Andi closed the front door and put her purse on the end of the couch. She stood there for a moment, numb, cold. What had Lindsay done?

She went to the kitchen, put the kettle on, and then, while the water heated, she went to Lindsay's room and peeked in.

She could smell a candle—it had recently been extinguished—and the covers were rumpled, but the sheets weren't exposed.

Andi glanced around the room, trying to understand what had happened. There was nothing out of the ordinary. Well, there was a wine bottle and a wineglass on the bedside table, but the bottle was half-full, and the wineglass wasn't empty.

Andi saw Lindsay's phone facedown on the side of the bed. She picked it up. It was locked. But there was one missed call and several messages. Andi knew she'd sent one message. Who were the others from? And who'd called her?

The kettle whistled in the kitchen. Andi hurried back to the kitchen to take the kettle off the burner. A cup of tea in hand, she sat down on the couch, pulled a blanket over her, but she couldn't get the picture of Lindsay so still on the gurney out of her head.

Andi texted Wolf an hour later. How is she?

She should survive, was his answer.

Andi had a million questions but didn't think now was the

time. She left the couch, went to check on Charlie. Jax lay next to his bed. He lifted his head, growled a little, before putting his head down again. Charlie slept through it all.

Andi had forgotten all about Jax. Despite all the drama tonight, he'd remained at Charlie's side. The vigilant protector. What a good dog.

She returned to the couch, covered herself with the blanket again, and closed her eyes, intending to rest for only a few minutes.

She was still sleeping when Wolf walked through the front door five hours later. "Hey," she said, sleepily. "How is Lindsay?"

"Resting," Wolf said, taking off his cap and hanging his keys on the hook by the front door. Jax appeared, going to Wolf, pressing against him.

Wolf gave him a pat and then sat down on the couch, slumping backward. He looked deeply tired.

"Is she out of danger?" Andi asked.

"For now."

She quietly went to the kitchen, filled a glass of water, and returned to the living room. She sat next to him, took his hand, and just held it. He'd tell her what he wanted to tell her when he was ready.

Finally he started talking, and he told her that Lindsay had overdosed, emptying a bottle of Xanax and Ativan, a deadly combination of benzos.

"If I hadn't checked on her then, if I hadn't smelled that candle . . ." He shook his head. "She wouldn't be here. It would have been too late."

"I didn't see any bottles in there."

"I grabbed all the bottles, took them with me, thinking doctors would need them."

Andi's thoughts raced. She thought back to earlier in the evening, when Lindsay picked up Charlie. She'd seemed emotional, but not necessarily in a bad way. Or had Andi just read the signals wrong?

"So close," he said. "So close to being dead."

"I just can't believe she'd do that, though. She's been happier. Positive. Not at all suicidal."

"She had us both fooled, then." Wolf exhaled and ran a hand across his face, rubbing his brow. "She needs help. I have to get her help. She needs to go to a treatment facility, someplace that will watch her better—"

"And Charlie?"

"He'll stay here with me."

Andi struggled to piece this together. "You're going to send her away from Charlie?"

"I don't like it, Andi, but she's not well."

Andi left the couch, paced the room, exhausted, stressed, confused. Andi had seen Lindsay earlier. She remembered how Lindsay had carefully carried Charlie to the car, and buckled him into his seat. Lindsay loved Charlie, needed Charlie. "She's his mom. Don't separate them."

"She dumps him off at your house every Saturday—"

"She doesn't dump him, Wolf!"

"She leaves him with me on Tuesdays."

Andi fought her outrage. "We thought you enjoyed time with him."

"I can't play ostrich, Andi. I can't pretend everything is fine here when it's not fine. She's in trouble."

But none of this lined up with what Andi knew, and she'd spent a lot of time with Lindsay these past two months. "Something must have happened. Something doesn't add up. This isn't Lindsay. She wouldn't hurt herself."

"I appreciate your optimism, but in this case, it's just denial, which isn't helpful, not for her, not for anyone."

Andi tried to slow her racing thoughts and gain control over her temper. Wolf was tired, she was tired, this wasn't the time to try to make sense of it all. They needed to hear from Lindsay. They needed to find out from her what was going through her head. "I think we have to talk to her when she's awake. Ask her what happened, don't project—"

"Andi, sweetheart," he interrupted, his tone flinty, contradicting the use of *sweetheart*, "Lindsay nearly died tonight. She swallowed a handful of pills. She was this close to death." He held his fingers up, showing her the tiniest space. "It doesn't matter what she thought happened. Her opinion is no longer important, not when she nearly orphaned Charlie."

"I'd like to talk to her, though," Andi said in a small voice, not wanting to argue with Wolf, but feeling protective of Lindsay. Now wasn't the time to come down on Lindsay. Now was the time to offer love, and support. "I'd like to just be with her, at the hospital, if they'll let me."

Wolf rose from the couch, went to the kitchen, and began to make a pot of coffee. Andi followed him, but she was uneasy. Wolf's posture was rigid, his jaw set. He looked angry; he looked like he was barely hanging on to his temper. Why?

What was he thinking? What was going on in his head?

"You okay?" she asked, watching from the doorway, not wanting to get in his way.

"Yes."

But he didn't look at her, and his tone was harsh.

"Why are you making coffee now?" she asked, as he pushed the brew button. "Why don't you go to bed, get some sleep—"

"I'm not going to bed. I'm heading back to the hospital once Maverick is here."

"Maverick's on his way?"

Wolf faced her, leaned back against the counter. "He's going to stay with Charlie while I handle things."

"Can I go to the hospital with you?" she asked, still trying to decipher his expression and tone.

"I'm going to ask you something," he said instead, "and I need you to tell me the truth."

"Of course."

"No, not of course. Because I don't think you always tell

me the things I should know. I don't think I'm aware of half of the things going on with my daughter."

Andi's legs felt weak. She suddenly went cold, dread seeping through her. "I'm always honest with you."

"Then tell me, has she ever talked about being depressed? Has she ever said anything about being overwhelmed, or hinting at death, or wanting to die?"

She wished there was a chair in the kitchen, or a stool like she had in hers. It would be easier to have this conversation sitting. It had been a long, long night. "We both know it's hard for her without Stone. She's never made a secret out of that."

"That's not what I asked."

"I wasn't finished talking, Wolf." Andi's voice hardened. She met his cool gray gaze and held it. "I'm trying to explain."

"I don't think a lot of explanation is required. It's either yes, or no. It's that simple."

"But it's not that simple. When women talk to each other, we share things, private things, because it helps us heal—"

"So she mentioned dying before."

"She mentioned that if it weren't for Charlie, she might have hurt herself in the past, but she wouldn't do it because she'd never do anything that would hurt him."

"And you didn't tell me?"

"She said it was in the past. I assumed it was at Jessica's."

"When did she tell you this?"

"A couple weeks ago . . . a month ago? We talk a lot, Wolf, we share things."

"But you never shared any of that with me."

Andi had never, ever heard him take that tone with her. It was harsh. A little terrifying.

"I promised to keep it between us—"

"For Pete's sake, Andi, you're not a doctor or a lawyer.

There is no client privilege here. She's Stone's wife. *My* daughter-in-law. You should have come to me straightaway. You should have told me."

"I thought she was doing better."

"Again, you're not a doctor. You're not an expert."

"I'm sorry."

"I'm shocked. I trusted you."

"But she's been doing well, Wolf. We still go to those group sessions, and she doesn't cry every time. Sometimes when we leave she's only concerned about the others. She talks about how she wants to help people who are grieving, and how she feels for them, and hopefully they'll keep going so they can get better."

"Grief sessions are good for people grieving, but not for people who are suicidal!"

"But she's not. I swear, she's not."

"What else are you hiding from me?"

"Nothing."

"I want to know, Andi. I need to know. We nearly lost her tonight and I blame myself for not being more involved, for not paying more attention. But that's over. My eyes have been opened. We have a problem and we're going to deal with it, head-on."

Andi put a hand to her middle, pulse racing, stomach queasy. She felt like throwing up. "I don't understand any of this. I've seen a lot of Lindsay lately and she's been happy. She's been working hard. There have been no signs of anxiety or depression."

"Where does she go all the time?"

"My house."

"Why?"

Andi hesitated. "Lindsay's been working on college applications. She decided she wanted to study psychology and she researched schools and is applying to five, but there are only three she's seriously interested in."

"Have the applications gone in?"

Andi nodded. "She's completed four, and is working on the fifth."

"Didn't she have to pay fees?"

"I covered them."

"Why?" he demanded. "You're not her mom, not her family."

"We thought you'd be pleased."

"Why didn't she talk to me about school? Why haven't I been part of any conversations? She's living with me, not you."

"It was supposed to be a surprise. She thought you'd be proud of her. It's a lot of work, filling out all the applications, and she knows it might be a long shot getting in to her preferred schools, but she wasn't trying to be sneaky. No one was being sneaky. Lindsay just hoped she'd have some good news to share with you for Father's Day."

"Instead she's in the hospital, getting her stomach pumped."

"But Lindsay wouldn't do that. She wouldn't hurt herself. We talked about it and she knew how much Charlie needed her—"

"I can't believe you. Who are you?"

Andi's chest tightened. Her eyes burned. "Wolf, I've only tried to help her. I've done nothing but be supportive."

"No, not true. You came between us, Andi, and you cut me out."

"I didn't. I swear."

"Then why all the secrecy? Why did I not know what she's been doing this past month? Why did you pay the fees?"

"Lindsay told me that you guys talked about her going back to school when she was still in New Orleans. She said you discussed colleges and how you said there weren't many near Lake Arrowhead."

"Yes, there was one conversation, months ago. I had no idea she was moving forward with it."

"You should be happy."

"I had three sons, and they all went to college, and they've all been successful. I might not always have been the best dad, but I loved them and helped them whenever they needed me. But ever since you came into the picture, Lindsay doesn't talk to me, or spend time with me, she just runs to you—"

"Are you jealous?" Andi asked, interrupting him.

"Not jealous, livid. You manipulated the situation, took advantage of her when she wasn't strong."

"That's not what happened. You asked me to be her friend. You asked me to give her support. I did."

"You're done now, though. You're out. We're cutting the cord."

"You can't mean that." Andi drew back, her throat sealing, her lungs burning, making it hard to breathe. "Wolf, I love her."

"I don't care. I don't want you anywhere near her, or Charlie."

"Can I at least see her? Just to check on her."

"No. You've done enough damage. You were reckless and irresponsible and I don't trust you, not around my family. Stay away from us, from all of us. And please go before Maverick gets here. He doesn't need to be part of this."

ANDI CALLED IN SICK TO WORK THAT MORNING, WHICH wasn't a lie, since she cried herself sick once she was home.

She couldn't sleep, not even after she took an icy shower, trying to make herself stop crying. She was in shock. It was like a nightmare. Lindsay being wheeled out of the house. Wolf returning, saying she'd overdosed. Wolf's questions. Andi's answers, even as she felt increasingly helpless.

She knew halfway through the conversation it wasn't going to get better. She knew from his face that he'd shut her out. He wasn't listening. He just wanted to be angry and blame someone, and so he blamed her.

Did she deserve the blame? That was the question . . . that was what kept her from falling asleep, and staying asleep.

Had she failed Lindsay?

Had she missed a sign that Lindsay wasn't doing well?

Later that day, after taking a shower at noon, and trying to eat a few bites of something, Andi called Lindsay, hoping against hope that she had her phone with her.

But Andi's call went unanswered.

Andi leaned on the kitchen island and thought about calling Wolf. She had a feeling he wouldn't answer, but she was anxious for news about Lindsay. She needed an update.

Tomorrow was Thursday. It was a very long day, with no news about Lindsay.

Andi called the hospital Thursday afternoon, asking for Lindsay's room. Andi was informed that the patient was no longer there.

Andi hung up, chewed on her lip, trying to ignore the churning sensation in her gut. It was good that Lindsay had been released. It meant she was doing better.

But if she was home, why didn't Lindsay respond to the message Andi had left her yesterday? Maybe it didn't record. Andi sent a text. Checking in on you, my amazing brilliant girl. Sending you so much love.

Andi told herself it might be awhile until she heard back, but Lindsay didn't respond, not that day, nor on Friday.

The days passed in a blur. Andi couldn't look at food. She felt sick, poisoned; everything in her hurt. She made herself go to work, but she made so many mistakes that even patient Dr. Nair gave her a scolding and told her if she couldn't do the job, it would be better if they got someone else.

She knew he meant temporarily, but still, the rebuke stung.

That evening she'd had enough. She phoned Wolf, but he declined her call immediately. She waited an hour and tried again. Same thing. Andi followed up with a text. Just tell me if she's okay. You can do that much at least.

He answered with a brusque text. She's okay, no thanks to you.

Andi turned off her phone, pressed the heels of her palms against her eyes, holding back tears. She couldn't keep crying. There was no point in crying. There was also no point going to work when she was this much of a mess.

Andi called Margot. "Spring break is next week, can I still come up to visit?" Her voice wasn't steady, but she wasn't sobbing at least.

"What's going on?"

"Everything."

Margot was silent a moment. "Elizabeth said that Paige said you're having a hard time."

"Very hard," Andi agreed. "I think I'm having a nervous breakdown."

"Do you want me to come get you?"

"No. I'll be okay driving."

"Are you sure? It's a long drive when you don't feel good."

"I'll leave early in the morning, before traffic starts."

"At four?"

"Maybe three. Doesn't matter. I'm not sleeping. Maybe I'll feel better once I'm there. I need a change of scenery."

Hanging up, she sat for a moment, thought about going to Cambria, where Margot had just moved into a rental house, and pictured being far from San Juan Capistrano, where everything reminded her of Wolf and Lindsay, and sweet funny Charlie. But she'd never told Margot that she and Wolf had dated, and it would be hard not telling her. . .

It would be just as hard telling her.

And yet, Andi needed to get away. She needed a friend. She needed Margot.

Andi sent an email to Dr. Nair, asking him if it would be possible for her to take the rest of the week off. She knew the following week was spring break, but she could use a long break, and he was right, she was useless at the moment. With his permission, she'd like to get some rest so she'd be ready to return on the Monday following break.

Dr. Nair answered within a half hour. I'm glad you're taking care of yourself, he wrote. I will be happy to welcome you back after the break.

Andi went to bed early, and was on the road by three thirty. It was dark, but traffic was light for Los Angeles. She made it out of the valley before the sun rose, and reached Ventura just as the sky lightened to blue and gold.

Even with a fifteen-minute break in Santa Barbara, where she got coffee and a breakfast sandwich, Andi made it to Cambria in less than five hours. Margot was home, waiting for her, having arranged her schedule so she could be there to meet Andi.

"You've lost so much weight," Margot said, hugging Andi as Andi climbed out of the car. Margot stepped back to examine Andi's face more closely. "You look terrible, though. You haven't been sleeping, either, have you?"

"I can't eat," Andi said. "I'm too sad, and I can't sleep, because I cry in my sleep."

"What's going on?"

"I feel dead inside. I hate it."

Margot picked up Andi's small suitcase, looped her arm through Andi's, and walked her inside. "Tell me. You can't keep it all bottled in."

Andi brushed a hand over her face, her eyes gritty and dry, her mouth equally dry, the lack of sleep catching up to her. "If I start talking, I'll cry and then I won't be able to stop. You'll regret inviting me here."

"You told me you've got the next ten days free. We have ten days to talk. You don't have to tell me anything right now. Just let me know what you want, and I'll make it happen."

"Could I get some water and take a nap? I'm so tired."

"Absolutely. Let's get you settled."

Andi loved the cool, darkened bedroom with the black-out shades. After a quick shower she fell into bed, closed her eyes, her body and head aching. Andi pulled the fluffy feather comforter around her, hiding from the world. She felt as if she had jet lag from flying halfway around the world, instead of driving up the Central Coast. But at least she wasn't alone. At least, when she woke up, she'd be with Margot.

Andi slept and slept and slept, unaware that Margot checked on her twice, just to be sure she was okay. Placing a fresh water bottle at her side, just in case Andi woke up thirsty.

It was dark when Andi emerged from the bedroom. Margot was working on her laptop at the small round dining table, spreadsheets all around her.

"She lives," Margot said, closing her laptop and rising. "I've been worried about you."

"I was so tired," Andi said, groggy, but rested. She didn't ache in every bone anymore. Her eyes didn't feel like she had sand in them. "Sorry to waste your whole day."

"You didn't. I just worked from here."

"You can do that?"

"All the time." Margot glanced at her watch. "Are you hungry?"

Andi nodded. "That's what woke me up."

"Feel like going out? I made us reservations at a little place near here, but I can cancel them, if you'd rather stay in. We can always go out another night."

"Let's go," Andi said. "I haven't been out in ages."

Andi's hair was a mess, the tight curls knotted from days of not washing it, or brushing and detangling, and so she swept it into a big, wild ponytail and let it go. She knew Margot didn't care about her hair, or her sloppy sweater and baggy trousers.

Margot had chosen a small French restaurant in downtown Cambria. The restaurant was cozy and the food was amazing. They sat in a little bay window and sipped their wine and watched the world—the view framed by outdoor trees covered in little white lights—go by.

"You don't have to tell me anything you don't want to tell me," Margot said as the waiter walked by and topped off their wine. "We can just relax and not worry about anything. It's wonderful having you here. I've missed you. Haven't heard much from you, not since January."

"Has it been that long?"

Margot nodded. "I didn't think you were still going to come for your break."

Andi felt remorseful, especially as she hadn't planned to come, thinking she'd probably be doing something with Wolf and his family instead. "I haven't been a very good friend," she said.

"I wouldn't say that. We have jobs, and lives, and we always catch up eventually."

Andi nodded, grateful Margot was so easy. Just one more reason why Andi appreciated her so much. Not everyone was as fun, interesting, and undemanding. "I've been seeing someone," she said carefully, worried how Margot would react to the news that Andi had been seeing Wolf all this time. "Someone new—"

"Someone named Wolf?"

Andi couldn't believe it. She stared at Margot, incredulous. "How did you know?"

"I suspected."

"Aren't you mad at me?"

"Why would I be mad at you?"

"You liked him. You left him a note with your number."

Margot pursed her lips, trying not to laugh. "I never wanted him for me. I wanted him for *you*. I thought you secretly liked him and were just too shy to make a move."

"And the note?"

"It had your phone number." Margot was still smiling. "Okay, it also had my number, just in case he needed to know your favorite color, all your favorite foods, things like that."

For a moment Andi couldn't speak, overwhelmed by the realization that Margot had been trying to help her date Wolf, and all this time she'd been worried about telling Margot that she and Wolf were seeing each other. "We did go out," Andi said. "And I liked him, a lot. Things were good, from January until just recently, but it's over now. I messed everything up."

"What happened?"

"It's a long story, and I don't think I can talk about it just yet, but I ruined everything, and Wolf hates me—"

"I'm sure he doesn't hate you."

"No, he does. He most certainly does." Andi paused, picturing Wolf's hard expression and the ice in his voice. "But what's hard is that due to my mistake, I didn't just lose him, I lost Lindsay and Charlie—"

"Who are they?" Margot interrupted, confused.

"Wolf's daughter-in-law and grandson. I became close to both, but when he ended things, he told me I wasn't to contact any of them again."

Margot looked outraged. "I don't think he can decide what his daughter-in-law can or can't do."

"But in this case, he can." Andi's head ached, and her eyes burned, and she wondered if she'd ever feel okay. "I don't want to say more. Just believe me when I say, if I could go back and change things, I would."

THE DAYS PASSED QUICKLY. MARGOT WENT IN TO THE office each morning and worked until noon, when she returned to do things with Andi. Most afternoons they walked the boardwalk overlooking Moonstone Beach. When the waves were good they'd stop and watch the surfers, and when it was low tide, they'd go down onto the sand, take their shoes off, and explore.

On the first weekend Andi was in Cambria, Margot suggested they do some sightseeing and, after packing an overnight bag, Margot drove them to Paso Robles, where they spent the day wine tasting. They could have gone home that evening—it was just a half hour away—but Margot wanted Andi to meet her dad, and so the three of them had dinner, and then when he went to bed, Andi and Margot sat in the living room and binge-watched episodes of *Project Runway* before calling it a night.

On Sunday they had brunch with her dad, and he came along when Margot drove Andi around, showing her downtown Paso Robles. After Margot dropped her dad off, it was time to return to Cambria.

The next week passed even more quickly, with one night spent at the refurbished Cambria Playhouse and another night at a jazz club, and one night Andi and Margot were taken to dinner by Sally, Margot's boss.

Sally was hilarious . . . salty, sassy, and she definitely ran the show. Andi could see why Margot enjoyed working for her so much. Sally was smart, and strong, and through the years had become very successful. Sally was pretty open about her success, too, saying her first husband had left her some money, she'd invested it well, worked hard, and was now very comfortable financially. No actual numbers were mentioned—that would have been tacky—but Sally did casually drop into the conversation that she owned more real estate in Cambria, San Luis Obispo, and Pismo than any other individual. "Husbands two through five have all tried to take a piece of what I own, but my prenups are ironclad, and I don't suffer fools."

"I still love men," she added, draining her cocktail, "but I'm not trotting them off to the wedding chapel every time I fall for a pretty face."

"So it was you who wanted to marry each time?" Andi asked, fascinated by Sally's stories.

"Oh yes, I'm a softie. I love the idea of being married. I love to love, but when you have as much as I do, not every man has pure intentions. I understand it, though. Money is attractive. Money is an aphrodisiac. That's why before I go out at night I dab it behind my ears." She saw Andi's expression and chuckled. "No, I don't do that anymore. I've turned over a new leaf. I'm not footing the bills anymore. I'm not going to set my love up in business. I won't bankroll his grandkid's college education. I'm going to play hard to get from now on. I need to be wooed, and won."

Andi exchanged glances with Margot. Margot was smiling, an indulgent smile that showed just how much she liked Sally.

"I've sworn off men," Andi said. "It's too hard."

"Not if you don't fall in love; then it's quite easy." Sally signaled to the waiter that she wanted another martini.

"But how is dating fun, then?"

"You don't have to be in love to have a satisfying orgasm. Find someone who makes you feel good, someone unselfish in bed, and don't worry about the rest. If you want to have dinner with him, have dinner. If he wants to buy you something pretty, thank him prettily. But if all you want is good hot sweaty sex, then keep it at that. It's your life. You're in charge. You make the rules."

You make the rules.

Just like that, Andi was back in Blue Jay with Wolf. She could feel the cold, and see the snow, and remember how he looked, naked above her, his powerful body silhouetted by the flickering fire.

He'd made the rules, though, and then he'd broken his own rules, and now after falling for him so hard, it was over.

Sally was still talking and Andi looked up, and focused, trying to catch up on what was being said.

Fortunately, the waiter appeared with the dessert menu and the conversation shifted. Sally was a firm believer in dessert, and dithered between the flan and the flourless chocolate cake.

Margot leaned close to Andi, her voice dropping. "Are you okay?" she whispered.

Andi nodded.

"Good. I got worried about you for a minute."

"All good," Andi said, forcing a smile. "I'm thoroughly enjoying myself."

A half hour later they were waiting in the parking lot for the valet to bring around the cars. Sally gave them each a goodbye hug, but gave Margot's back an extra pat. "Isn't she amazing?" Sally said about Margot. "In just a few months she's organized the office, hired someone to create new software, updated our database, and designed a new website. I knew she was pretty, but I didn't realize she was also brilliant."

Margot shifted uncomfortably. "I didn't do that much. I just made a few changes, put technology to work so you didn't have to do as much."

"She's being modest. For the first time in years, I don't have to worry about the business. I could die tomorrow and Margot could take over."

Margot paled. "That's not funny. I don't want your job. I wouldn't enjoy your job. I'd ruin everything, so don't even joke about such a thing."

IT WAS TIME FOR ANDI TO HEAD HOME. SHE WASN'T ready to go, though. She felt good being at Margot's. Safe. The problems in San Juan Capistrano felt far away. But she'd also promised Dr. Nair that she'd be back on Monday, and in good form, ready to work. She needed to get back to work. Finals were approaching and the end of the school year. The end of the year was always busy.

She had today, and then tonight, and early tomorrow morning she'd drive back, spending the rest of her Sunday unpacking, going through mail, doing errands, picking up groceries, and just settling back into her routine at home.

For Andi's last night, Margot had made a reservation at another of her favorite places, this one a hotel restaurant fronting Moonstone Beach. They arrived before sunset and sat at a small table with a heat lamp above them and the ocean before them. The waves crashed, and fog rolled in, mysterious, haunting, eventually swallowing the sea, turning their world quiet and misty.

"Are you ever going to tell me what happened between you and Wolf?" Margot asked, after they'd placed their order with the handsome young waiter who'd given Margot a long once-over. "You might as well tell me. We've nowhere to go."

"It's complicated."

"I think I can handle it."

Andi tried to smile but couldn't. "The short version is that I got too close to Lindsay."

"Wolf's daughter-in-law?"

She nodded. "In the beginning, Wolf wanted me to be nice to her. He seemed to like that we got along, and that she enjoyed talking to me. Over time I was there at Wolf's once a week for dinner, and then Lindsay and Charlie came to my house on Saturdays so Wolf could work undisturbed. Lindsay and I discussed grief counseling and she asked if I'd attend a Tuesday support group with her—"

"Did you?" Margot asked.

"I did. We were still attending every Tuesday when the . . . thing . . . happened."

"What happened?"

"Everything." Andi's eyes burned and she blinked. "I forgot myself. I forgot I wasn't family. I was so busy trying to help her that I kept important information from Wolf. And because of that, he nearly lost her."

"What do you mean? He nearly lost her?"

Andi couldn't speak for a long time. She didn't know how to say the words, didn't want to say the words. They were so harsh, so desperate, so final. She looked at Margot, wishing Margot could just read her mind and understand.

Margot couldn't, and then maybe she did, because she abruptly sat back. "Lindsay didn't hurt herself, did she?"

"She swallowed a bottle of Xanax Tuesday night, after she'd been to our support group. Thank God Wolf found her. He called an ambulance. They rushed her to the hospital and pumped her stomach. She's home with him—" Andi broke off, realizing she didn't actually know where Lindsay was. Was Lindsay at Wolf's, or had he sent her somewhere? The idea of Lindsay being separated from Charlie made her chest seize in pain. "I don't know for sure where she is. She was discharged from the hospital, but whether she's at Wolf's or somewhere else, I don't know."

"I don't understand how he can blame you, though. You didn't buy the pills for her, did you?"

Andi shook her head. "No, and after the first week, I didn't drink with her, either. No wine, no cocktails. We stuck to herbal teas and decaf coffees."

"Then why is he blaming you? Sounds as if he should thank you for trying to help her."

"I kept things from him. I didn't report to him on all our activities." Andi tried to make it a joke, but the words came out sharp and flat, and she felt bruised again. "Lindsay had confided in me a lot, but there was nothing said to indicate she was in trouble, that she would swallow a bottle of pills. She'd been happy, and working hard, filling out college applications so she could return to school this fall."

"Surely Wolf appreciated that."

"No. He felt left out. Shut out. I think he was jealous that Lindsay and I had developed a close relationship and he and she weren't seeing eye to eye."

"But she was living with him?"

"Wolf is tough, and he could be tough on her. Jessica, his ex, was the same. When I first met Lindsay, she didn't have a lot of confidence. She felt judged and criticized. What she needed was a friend, and I became that friend. I didn't do it for him, though. I didn't even do it for her. I did it for me. I liked her, and I came to love her. Lindsay wasn't weak. She's just young, and still grieving."

"I'm glad you were there for her. You did the right thing."

"I just wish she'd told me she was having a hard night. I would have been there. I would have picked her up and taken her to my place and talked to her, or listened."

"Maybe she didn't mean to. Maybe it was an accident."

"That was actually my first thought," Andi said. "Maybe she forgot she'd already taken something, but that's also not healthy. She's a mom. She has a three-and-a-half-year-old. She can't just . . . take stuff. Not even if she's in pain."

"What a terrible situation."

"I'm devastated."

"I knew this had to be more than just a breakup. I knew something awful had happened."

Andi exhaled slowly. "Talking about it makes me feel terrible. It will be so strange going home and not seeing any of them anymore. Wolf and his family became a big part of my life. I'm going to miss them, all of them."

"You fell in love with him, didn't you?"

Andi wrapped her cashmere shawl around her shoulders, tucking it closer to her neck. "I did, but I wish I hadn't. If I could go back in time, I'd leave those mountains the day you did; I'd leave before New Year's Eve and spend the evening at Elizabeth's with normal, civilized people."

"Instead you tried to tame the beast."

"Stupid, stupid me."

ALTHOUGH ANDI HAD PLANNED ON AN EARLY START, she'd slept in, and then Margot had made them breakfast, including mimosas with fresh-squeezed orange juice. They'd sat at her table in the backyard and talked, further delaying the departure. But the return home couldn't be delayed any longer.

She carried her bags to the car, stowed them in the trunk, put her purse on the console next to the driver's seat, and turned to face Margot, who was wearing a navy linen sheath dress and looking adorable. "I hate to leave," Andi said. "But I know I have to. I'm sure you'd like your life back, too, but oh, Margot, you've been so wonderful. You were a lifeline. You saved me."

Margot still held the water thermos she'd filled for Andi, and the paper bag of snacks. "You don't have to leave. You could just stay."

"If only."

"I'm serious," Margot said. "Why don't you move here? It'd be an adventure. What's keeping you in San Juan?"

"My job. My friends. My—" Andi broke off, picturing Wolf, picturing Lindsay, picturing sweet wild wonderful Charlie. She hadn't seen Charlie in over two weeks, hadn't heard from Wolf or Lindsay, either. Andi had been so sure Lindsay would reach out, but there had been nothing, just silence. "I can't imagine leaving San Juan. I loved it there."

"But Wolf is just a few blocks away. Isn't that going to be hard for you? Knowing he is so close? Thinking you could bump into him at any time?"

Yes. It'd be awful. Intolerable. "I just can't believe how quickly it went from wonderful to over. I felt like I had everything . . . and now I have nothing."

Margot handed her the water and snacks. "You have me. I'm here, and should you want a fresh start, I'll help you. We can find you a job, and a beautiful home, and we'll go explore the area, have little adventures. Don't look back, look forward. You deserve all the happiness in the world. You deserve better than Wolf."

"That's a big move," Andi said.

"Think about it."

"I will." She put the water and snack bag in the car, gave Margot a last hug. "Thanks for everything, my friend. You're a star."

Chapter 16
~~~~~~~~~~~

"SHE SAID IT WASN'T INTENTIONAL," MAVERICK SAID, standing next to his dad in the backyard of Wolf's house. "She's angry that you don't believe her."

Wolf closed the grill on the tri-tip and faced his son, who was holding a beer; by all appearances everything looked normal, but nothing was normal. "You weren't there," he said. "You didn't see her as they took her to the hospital. This is serious."

"People make mistakes."

"An overdose is not a mistake."

"She'd only taken a couple Xanax. The Ativan was already empty. She had a bad reaction, coupled with the wine—"

"So she says."

"Yes, Dad, and I believe her."

Wolf couldn't remember ever feeling this tired. Or angry. He seethed all day, every day. Ever since that terrible Tuesday night where he'd smelled the candle burning and entered Lindsay's room to find her facedown on her bed, barely breathing, nothing had been okay. He'd assured Jessica that Lindsay would be safe with him and he'd been wrong.

"I still think she needs an inpatient treatment program," Wolf said. "Most of them are for ninety days—"

"You can't make her go. And if you try to force her, she'll leave, and she'll take Charlie and they'll both be out of your life. Is that what you want?"

"Stone would want her to get help."

"Stone helped her by loving her."

"Well, Stone's not here, is he?"

"No, but I'm here, and Linc's available."

Wolf squared his shoulders, eyes narrowing. "What does that mean?"

"We're not going to let anything happen to her. We're a family. We all love her."

"You're going to take her? We're going to pass her around like a hot potato?"

Maverick shook his head. "This is Stone's wife. Would you talk to Stone about her this way?" When Wolf didn't answer, Maverick added, "She needs us, but we shouldn't be talking about her as if she's a child. We consult her, don't talk down to her. If she tells us something, we believe her."

"You can't put your trust in an unreliable narrator."

"Dad, I know you're old-school, but enough with the blame game. Give her a chance to tell us what she wants and needs."

Wolf looked across the lawn to the lounge chair in the shade where Lindsay was sitting with Charlie, reading him a book. Instead of her usual glass of wine she had a diet cola. There was a sweetness to the scene that belied the tension and exhaustion of the past two weeks. "But is any of this fair to Charlie?" he asked quietly. "Are you and Linc thinking of him?"

"You and Mom had plenty of problems, but, Dad, you never once threatened to take us from Mom, and she wasn't always well. She had her moods. She'd go through periods where she was drowning her stress with afternoon cocktails. There was a year where she used to drive me to football absolutely wasted. Or she'd pick me up from practice and as soon as I opened the door, you could smell the alcohol."

"You never told me."

"You were in Libya or Iran. What were you going to do from there?" Maverick drained his beer and set the empty bottle on the side of the grill. "You left Mom to do her best, trusting her to do her best, and she did. Sometimes one's best is good enough, and sometimes it's barely good at all, but for heaven's sake, give Lindsay some credit for trying."

Wolf swallowed, his throat tight, his gut hard with bottled emotion. "I love her. She's my daughter—"

"Then treat her like your daughter. Give her respect. It's demoralizing to hear you talk to her, and about her, as if she's damaged. She combined benzos with alcohol. Bad move. She learned a lesson, and I can promise you, she'll never make that mistake again."

"And what happens if it happens again and I'm not there to save her?"

"Like Stone?" Maverick asked quietly.

Wolf looked away, jaw jutting, chest aching. "I owe him."

"Do you know why Stone married Lindsay on base? Because he wanted to protect Lindsay from all our bullshit. He wanted her to be loved, feel important, feel special. That's what he'd want us to do for her—now and forever."

Trust good old Maverick to tell him like it was.

"Anything else you want to say?" he asked his son, the corner of his mouth curving.

"Stop talking about sending her away. She's already promised to see a therapist. She's promised to work on her anxiety and the panic attacks. She realizes she can't be dependent on benzos to calm her, especially as she wants to return to school in August."

Wolf glanced over at Lindsay and Charlie again. They'd

finished the story and Charlie was resting his head on Lindsay's chest, and she was stroking his hair, gently smoothing it back from his face. "Do you think she can handle it?"

"Linds? Come on, Dad. She's an Enders now. I'd never bet against her."

ANDI HAD BEGUN TO THINK SHE'D NEVER SEE OR HEAR from Lindsay again, but then one day when Andi least expected it, Lindsay was waiting on Andi's doorstep when Andi returned from work.

Andi stepped from her car, uncertain as to how she should greet Lindsay. But then Lindsay rushed to her, and hugged her. Andi's eyes filled with tears.

"I'm sorry," Lindsay whispered, squeezing tighter. "I'm sorry for everything. It's all my fault."

"Do you have time to come in?" Andi asked.

Lindsay nodded. "Maverick and Wolf have Charlie."

"Maverick's still in town?"

"He's home for a while. He's supposed to be staying at his own place, but he comes over every day." She made a face. "I think he's been told to babysit me."

"Oh no." Andi unlocked the front door and ushered Lindsay inside. "That bad?"

"Wolf's upset."

"Still?" Andi asked worriedly, turning on lights, peeling off her knit sweater jacket.

"He's actually worse now than when I first came home from the hospital." Lindsay followed Andi to the kitchen. "But that's not why I'm here. I wanted to see you, and talk to you. I wanted you to hear from me what happened, not what Wolf has told you."

"I haven't talked to Wolf since the night you went to the hospital."

Lindsay sat down on one of the tall counter stools. "Seriously?"

Andi wasn't sure what Wolf had told her, or not told her, but the last thing she wanted to do was come between Wolf and his family. "He loves you."

"What does that have to do with him not talking to you?"

"I broke his trust. I think that's the bottom line."

"You didn't do anything." Lindsay's voice rose. "That doesn't make any sense."

"He thinks we kept things from him. He thinks . . . I . . . kept things from him." Andi drew a breath, remorseful. "And in hindsight, I did."

"Andi, I didn't even tell *you* everything."

Andi wanted a drink, badly.

"I didn't go to the support group that Tuesday night," Lindsay added. "I had dinner with Zane." She looked at Andi, brow creasing. "Do you remember me mentioning him?"

"A friend of Stone's?"

"Yes. Him. We had dinner that night." She looked away, down. "And then went back to his hotel."

"He didn't . . . hurt you, did he?"

"No, oh, *no*. He was a gentleman. There was no pressure, no coercion. We'd had some drinks and I had a little buzz, and I was into him. But after . . . I freaked. I didn't know why I did that."

"Sleep with him?"

Lindsay covered her face with her hands. "What was I thinking?"

"You were attracted to him."

"I betrayed Stone."

"You didn't."

"Zane was one of his best friends."

Andi was processing it all. "You felt guilty."

"I loved Stone with all of my heart. I have missed him so much—" Her voice broke and she pressed a hand to her trembling mouth. "I can't forget him. I can't let him go, because then he'll be really gone. And who will tell Charlie about his dad? Who will keep Stone's memory alive?"

"You, Wolf, Maverick, Lincoln, Jessica. Stone's platoon." Andi came around the counter, drew out a stool, and sat close to Lindsay. "And Charlie, of course."

"Charlie never even met his dad."

"But Stone lives in him. And Stone lives in you, and even if you fall in love and marry one day, Stone will always be part of your life." Andi gently rubbed Lindsay's back. "It's been four years since you lost him. It's okay to move on—"

"*No.*"

"Is that why you took the pills?"

Lindsay's head jerked up. Her eyes were pink and watering. "You think I tried to kill myself, too?"

"No. Absolutely not. I'm just trying to piece together what happened between when you left me and when Wolf called and asked me to come over."

"It's actually ridiculously simple. I came home, a mess, and then saw Zane had texted me to make sure I got home okay, and he told me how much he liked me and hoped to see me again, and I lost it. I started crying and couldn't stop. I took two Xanax—"

"Is that a lot?"

"It would be probably for you, but I've had a prescription ever since Stone died and I probably have a higher tolerance. So I took two pills with some wine. Then I answered Zane's text and said that I'd made a mistake and I couldn't see him again. Then I blocked him." Her voice quavered. "Because I didn't want to be tempted. I can't do this to Stone . . . can't move on, not yet. If I were single that would be different."

"But you are single, sweetheart," Andi said.

"Not in my heart."

Andi understood that. For years after Kevin died she still felt married, still felt like his wife. "Did you take more medicine?"

"This is where it gets a little fuzzy," Lindsay said. "I

think I forgot I'd taken Xanax already, and I took two more. I was just so sad, and so upset with myself. All I wanted was to calm down. Sleep. Forget."

"So four Xanax can kill someone?"

"I think it was all the alcohol. Cocktails, wine at dinner—"

"You shouldn't have been driving."

"Probably not," Lindsay agreed. "And then more wine when I got home."

"How much did you drink once home? Half a bottle?"

"Less than that. It was already open from the night before." Lindsay closed her eyes. "I screwed up, I did. I understand it's time to make changes, and I am. I'm getting off the Xanax and Ativan. Cutting out alcohol. I've started counseling, not group stuff, but therapy just for me." She looked at Andi. "And since I'm being honest, I might as well let you know those were Wolf's conditions for me to remain at his house."

"But you're okay with them?"

Lindsay nodded. "He's right. It's time to get my act together." She reached out to Andi, touched the back of her hand. "But how is any of this your fault? How can Wolf blame you?"

"I did keep things from him."

"Because I asked you to keep it between us. I asked you, and you gave me your word. And you kept it."

"I love you. I will never not love you. I will always be in your corner."

Lindsay hugged her. "I love you, too."

"How is my Charlie?" Andi asked. "Has he forgotten me?"

"No. He still talks about you all the time. Would you want me to bring him by?"

"I'd love that. Bring him by soon."

LINDSAY BROUGHT CHARLIE SATURDAY MORNING. CHARlie was so happy to see Andi, he threw himself at her, and when they went into the house, he insisted on sitting on her lap, wanting hugs, wanting to tell her about a little girl at preschool who liked him but he told her that he already had a girlfriend he was going to marry.

"You know, Charlie," Andi said gravely. "It's okay if you like both of us. I won't mind if you have a preschool girl-friend."

He looked skeptical. "I can't hold her hand, though. I can't kiss her, either. There's no touching."

Andi and Lindsay exchanged glances. Lindsay was trying not to laugh. Andi fought her smile. "I think that's a good rule," Andi said. "Preschool is about learning. And it's a good idea to keep your hands to yourself."

Charlie spotted the castle tubs across the room, stacked by the fireplace. He slid off her lap and ran to the toys, leaving Andi and Lindsay to talk.

"He misses you," Lindsay said, watching Charlie pull the tops off the bins. "Wolf is sullen and moody and not patient at all."

"Sounds like he needs a vacation. Maybe he should go up to the cabin, have some time to himself."

"Why don't you go to your cabin, and then I'll suggest he go to his—"

"I appreciate your efforts to smooth things over, but Wolf wants nothing to do with me, and tricking him into a meeting will only make it worse."

"Wolf doesn't know the whole story."

"He knows enough, and he doesn't care."

"He didn't have an easy childhood," Lindsay said.

Andi rolled her eyes. "You didn't and you don't blow up at people and say cruel things."

"Can I tell you a story?"

"As long as it's not about Wolf."

Lindsay grinned. "You know me so well."

"I don't care about Wolf."

"Now, that's not true. I've gotten to know you pretty well

and you love him. And you two were so happy together, and would have remained together if it weren't for me."

"I don't want you to blame yourself."

"For purely selfish reasons, I want you two to get back together. You were good for him, and he was good for you. You brought out the best in each other, and . . . I got to see you a lot. I got to spend time with you, and I love spending time with you. You're like the mom I always wanted but never had."

Andi sighed. "Tell me your story. But I doubt it will change anything."

"It's a long one." Lindsay gave her a smile. "But it's interesting. At least, *I* think it's interesting and I doubt anyone else has told you about Wolf's mom and dad."

"I'm listening."

Lindsay's smile widened. "I think you already know that Wolf comes from one of the oldest, most influential families in New Orleans. His mom, Delfinia, was the youngest, and very beautiful. She had older brothers and one sister, but none of them made it to thirty, and so she became her parents' whole world. As you can imagine, she was spoiled, but she was also charming and vivacious. But instead of falling in love with someone from her elite social circle, Delfinia met an army officer visiting New Orleans for Mardi Gras."

"Wolf's dad?"

Lindsay nodded. "Wolfgang Enders was as dashing as Delfinia was beautiful. He was tall, with blond hair and light gray eyes. His family was originally from Prussia, where his grandfather had been a famous general. Wolfgang's parents emigrated between World Wars, settling in upstate New York. The family wasn't treated well during World War Two, which is why their oldest son, Wolfgang, chose a career in the US Army, wanting to prove that he and his family were good citizens."

"Wolf's dad had blond hair?"

"Wolf gets his dark hair from his mother. Delfinia had

black hair and blue, blue eyes. But remember, Stone was blond, Lincoln's blond. Maverick is the only one with Wolf's and Mémé Finn's coloring."

"Mémé Finn?"

"That's what the boys called Delfinia."

"Fascinating."

"I think so, too. I come from nothing, but Stone? His family has *history*."

"Were Delfinia and Wolfgang happy?"

"Sadly, the honeymoon stage didn't last long. Delfinia's parents disapproved of Wolfgang, not just because he was German—"

"He was American."

Lindsay shrugged. "You're dealing with an old New Orleans family where ancestry is everything. They never thought he was good enough for her, and then later, his true colors showed. He was arrogant, cold, and self-centered. To keep her close, her parents gifted the newlyweds with a home just two blocks from theirs, ensuring that their only child would remain in their lives. Wolfgang resented his interfering in-laws, but resented his bride's refusal to become a traditional army wife, following him around the world, even more. Wolfgang and Delfinia went months without seeing each other, an arrangement that suited Delfinia fine but enraged Wolfgang, who believed in duty before all else. When he finally retired and returned to New Orleans to find work in the private sector, Wolfgang took out his anger on his wife and son. Apparently Delfinia handled his rage with icy silence, perfecting the art of the cold war at home."

"What about Wolf?" Andi asked.

"Because Wolfgang couldn't control his wife, he focused on Wolf, taking his anger out on him, but the more he punished Wolf, the tougher Wolf became. Wolf refused to cower. He wouldn't apologize, either, for things he hadn't done."

"Sounds like Wolf," Andi muttered.

"Stone told me a story about an incident Wolf's senior year. Wolf had broken curfew and come home drunk—I think it was the middle of football season and he'd been out celebrating a win. Wolfgang was waiting up, and he took a bat to Wolf, intent on teaching him a lesson. Only Wolf, now almost eighteen, was taller and stronger; after wresting the bat away, he gave his dad a couple whacks before dropping the bat and walking out.

"He lived with his grandparents for a month," Lindsay continued, "until his mom begged him to come back for the holidays. Wolf returned for her in time for Christmas, but in February, on Fat Tuesday, he drove his dad's car into a pool, and that was that. He was thrown out, and he went back to his grandparents', to finish school, but the week he graduated he took a bus down to the Marine Corps recruiting office for Jefferson Parish and enlisted, aware enlisting in the Marine Corps would devastate his dad, as Wolfgang, a West Point officer, looked down on the Marines. In his mind, the Marines were the lowest of the low, and the fact that Wolf wanted to be one was the nail in the coffin. They never spoke again."

So much of this lined up with what Andi had already heard, or what Wolf had told her.

"When Wolf left for boot camp," Lindsay added, "he walked away from everything in New Orleans—the family, the money, all of it. He can do that. Sever ties. Cut everyone off. He's never done that with his kids, but once Jessica wanted the divorce, he was done."

Andi heard what Lindsay was saying.

Wolf was done.

Or, Wolf might be done.

Andi wasn't sure if she had a chance to make him listen to her, but she'd have to try. She didn't just walk away from people. And she didn't walk away from love.

"Talk to him," Lindsay said. "He's proud and he's hard—sometimes too hard—but he has a soft spot for you. I know he loves you. He hasn't been himself since all this started."

Those were the words Andi wanted to hear. She wanted to believe that Wolf still cared, and that Wolf just needed someone to extend the olive branch. She wanted to believe that there was hope, and he could, and would, forgive.

"Don't give up," Lindsay pleaded. "Please."

IN HINDSIGHT, ANDI SHOULDN'T HAVE LISTENED TO Lindsay.

Andi should have remembered that Lindsay had good intentions but not necessarily the best judgment. But listening to Lindsay's story, Andi softened, weakened. The truth was, she wanted to be persuaded. She wanted a chance to see him and try once more to smooth things over . . . to make amends.

But when she saw his expression when she arrived at his house, she should have immediately returned to her car and gone home.

She should have had some self-respect. But she didn't. She was stubborn, and hopeful, and just one look at him made her heart ache. She missed him. She loved him. She wasn't ready for it to be over.

Entering through the gate, Andi crossed the lawn to the driveway where he was drying off his Land Rover. She stood there for at least a minute without him acknowledging her. She counted to five and ten, determined to be patient.

They could make this work, if they both could just talk. If he'd stop shutting her out and would make an effort to communicate.

Another minute passed and it was just getting more and more uncomfortable. He knew she was there. The least he could do was look at her. Say hello.

He tried to pass her to dry the other side of the car, but

she stepped in front of him. "Wolf, please. Please talk to me."

"There's nothing to say, Andi." His voice was hard. His expression rough. He looked at her as if he despised her.

She swallowed the hurt. She wouldn't be proud. He was worth it. She just wished she was worth more to him. "There's still so much confusion about what happened, or what you think happened. Lindsay didn't try to hurt herself I'm sure you know this now. She mixed wine and her anxiety pills and had a reaction. She came to see me and wanted me to know that she'd never do that—"

"It doesn't matter what she said or did. What matters is what you said and did. You broke my trust."

"Are you really that rigid? Is everything so black-and-white in your world that you can't forgive, can't allow someone who loves you to make a mistake?"

"I hate games. I hate manipulation. I did this with Jessica and I won't do it with you."

"I'm not Jessica!"

"I hate dishonesty. I can't get past the lies."

"I *never* lied to you."

"You also never told me the truth."

He was making her mad, so mad. And he wasn't even trying to listen. He enjoyed being mean. He wanted to be a bully. "Do you even know the truth? Has Lindsay told you what happened that night? Or are you so busy intimidating her and threatening her that she's afraid to trust you?"

Andi stepped closer, hands knotting. "Three weeks ago I would have begged you for a second chance, but I just realized I'm lucky you showed your true colors when you did. Because I was falling for you, and picturing a life with you, but I didn't know you, did I? You're ruthless, Wolf. And you're the one that can't be trusted, not me."

She gave him a moment then to speak, to try, to care.

She gave him one last opportunity to be a decent human being.

But he just went back to drying his car, dismissing her as if she was no one . . . as if she wasn't even there.

It hurt. He made her hurt. But she was done. No more pleading or groveling. No more loving someone who couldn't—wouldn't—love her in return. "Goodbye, Wolf. I won't bother you again."

Once home, Andi paced her house, her courage deserting her, her anger fading as she realized it was indeed over. It had to be over. She couldn't do this with him anymore.

She shouldn't do this anymore. It wasn't even about pride, but self-preservation. She shouldn't have to hurt, either. There was no reason for him to punish her like this.

So it was done. She was done. She was permanently closing the door on the relationship. She wasn't interested in making amends or reconciling. She felt disillusioned, but even more importantly, she felt let down. By Wolf. He was loyal—but only to a few, and that small tight circle didn't include her.

Hands shaking, Andi shot Margot a text. I think I might be ready for a move. If you hear of any job openings that might suit me let me know.

Not that finding a well-paying job for a fifty-eight-year-old would be easy, but at this point Andi would take just about anything if it gave her the impetus to make the move.

Chapter 17

WITHIN HOURS OF SENDING MARGOT THE TEXT, ANDI got a phone call from Lindsay. "What did you say to Wolf?" she asked when Andi answered. "He's destroying the punching-bag guy in his garage. He spent an hour beating the dummy up, and then he went for a run, and now he's locked himself in the garage punching poor dummy dude again. He's been at this for hours."

"This is a Wolf thing, Lindsay, it has nothing to do with me."

"Are you sure? Because he was a lot calmer before you came by."

"Our conversation didn't go well."

"Clearly." Lindsay exhaled, exasperated. "I thought you went to see him to patch things up."

"Unfortunately, we are beyond that. There's no smoothing things over, or patching things up, not now."

"Why?"

"Because he was impossible, and I don't want to be the one to always apologize and fix things. I've done this before.

I've bitten my tongue before. I've let things go and held things in and avoided conflict so there would be more peace, and maybe I didn't mind at twenty. Maybe I didn't mind at thirty and forty, but I'm heading toward sixty and I realized today that I now very much mind. I want to be an equal with a man. I want to be respected. I want him to listen and set aside his ego now and then. And if he can't do that, I'm not interested."

"Did you tell this to him?"

"No. He did most of the talking—well, there wasn't actually that much talking—it was a brief, unpleasant meeting. He didn't want me there, and he said the same thing he told me the night of your hospitalization, which is I broke his trust."

"But Andi, *you* didn't do anything wrong. He's being unfair and projecting his anger onto you. He doesn't like that he felt helpless that night, he doesn't like that I disappointed him, so he's taking it out on you."

"You are going to be such a good therapist one day." Andi held her breath, holding the wave of emotion in. "Have you heard from any schools yet?" she asked, changing the subject.

"No. I'm on pins and needles."

"I bet you are. I am, too."

"Andi?"

"Yes?"

"Should I tell him about Zane? If Wolf knew why I was upset that night, would it help things between you two?"

"Tell him because *you* want to tell him. Don't tell him because you think it will help him and me. It won't."

Lindsay didn't say anything and Andi didn't try to fill the silence right away. It was better to be honest. Better than giving false hope.

"You're not getting back together, are you?" Lindsay said softly.

"No."

"Dang it." Lindsay's voice wobbled. "I can't believe this. You did nothing wrong. You were my friend, and all you ever did was try to help me."

"I will always be your friend, too." The last month had been so hard. She'd cried for hours these past few weeks, but she was done crying. She was ready to move forward. Ready for new dreams. "I love you, and I love Charlie, and that will never change."

"Can we come live with you, then? I don't think I should be here. It doesn't feel right here anymore. Ever since that night I got sick, it hasn't been the same."

Andi's chest tightened. "Give him time. He loves you and Charlie—"

"Why can't I live with you? I'll pay rent, I'll do my part—"

"I don't want your money, sweetheart, and if I wasn't moving, I'd love your company, not that Wolf would like it."

"You're moving?"

Andi hadn't realized until that moment that she'd made her decision. She was no longer on the fence, no longer weighing options. She was ready to go. It was the right move. Literally. "Yes."

"When?"

"I'm not exactly sure. I imagine I'll wait until the end of the school year."

"And when is that?"

"Mid-May."

"Andi."

Andi winced at the break in Lindsay's voice. Lindsay sounded so raw, so bruised; it was the sound of betrayal. "No one knows yet," Andi added gently. "It's the early stages."

"Then there's time to change your mind."

"I won't change my mind. I can't stay here, not after everything that's happened. The good news is that I'm not going that far, just up the coast, north of San Luis Obispo."

"I can't believe you're leaving me."

Andi's nails pressed into her palm, her heart hot with guilt and regret. "I'm not leaving you. I need space from . . ." She couldn't say it. She wasn't going to blame Wolf. It didn't make sense to blame anyone anymore. It just made everything hurt more. "I've lived here for a long time. Kevin and I were here for years. I should probably see something else, try something else before I'm too old to try new things."

"Charlie will miss you, too."

Andi was losing her battle. Salty tears stung her eyes. "I'll come down and visit. Maybe you and Charlie can come see me, stay with me. Cambria is beautiful. We could go to a rodeo and visit Hearst Castle—"

"You're not going to come back. If you're leaving because you need to get away from Wolf, you're not going to come back. Why would you? You have no one here, no family here."

"That's not true. You're my family." Not that Wolf thought so, but right now she didn't care what Wolf thought.

"If that were true, you wouldn't leave us."

HER HOUSE SOLD. FAST. ANDI KNEW SHE'D PRICED IT well, not wanting the sale to drag on and on, but she hadn't expected a cash offer, with a thirty-day closing. Fortunately, she had a place to go—Margot's for now—and a job waiting for her in Cambria. Dr. Nair had accepted her resignation and in just a week she'd be heading north.

Everything was happening quickly now, which was both good and bad.

Last night Paige and Elizabeth had taken her out, wanting to hear all the details. They were excited she'd be working with Margot at Sally's company, and both reminded her that Cambria was close to Paso Robles, their hometown, and they returned to Paso regularly to see family.

They'd offered to help her pack, but the buyers had wanted the house furnished, and Andi had done a hard clean, donating boxes and boxes of clothes and items that she didn't need. There were things she couldn't bear to get rid of, and those went into a storage unit in Laguna Niguel. Now it was just a matter of finishing the week at Orange, packing her car, and driving north.

She heard the motorcycle before she saw the bike. Andi's heart did a free fall. Wolf.

She stepped out of her house, closing the front door behind her, not wanting him to see the boxes and crates, her life dismantled.

He wasn't wearing a helmet, and as he climbed off his bike, wearing just a black T-shirt, jeans, and biker boots, she realized yet again how big he was, and how absolutely different he was from her in every way.

As he approached she fought the urge to run, but she wouldn't run from him. She refused to be a coward. Instead she tipped her chin up and tried to fill space, wanting to be equally imposing.

"I owe you an apology," he said, standing below her. She was on the front step and yet he was still so much taller. His voice was still deep. He still had that rasp in his tone.

Andi steeled herself, determined not to feel anything. "It's fine," she said calmly. "It was a misunderstanding."

"It was more than that. I was rough. I hurt you."

He was more than rough. Wolf was cruel. But she wasn't going to say it. He knew what he said. She did, too. "I forgive you." And she did. She knew long before she'd ever grown close to Wolf who he was. What he was. She had plenty of experience in dealing with him. But just because she forgave him, it didn't mean she'd forget. It had been a brutal month. He'd hurt her badly.

"I'm sure Lindsay has been in touch, but she's already heard from some schools. Chapman has accepted her. They're offering her a scholarship."

No, Lindsay hadn't been in touch. Ever since Andi had told her three and a half weeks ago she intended to move,

Lindsay had pulled away, and even though Andi reached out a couple of times, Lindsay didn't respond. Andi told herself it was for the best. She couldn't come between Wolf and his family anymore. They needed to repair their relationships, and they would do it better without her.

"That's wonderful about Chapman," Andi said. "She must be thrilled. It was one of her top two choices."

"And Orange," Wolf said. "Orange has accepted her." He looked at Andi, shadows in his eyes. "That was her first choice, you know. She wanted to be close to you."

Andi steeled herself. She wasn't going to feel. She wasn't going to be vulnerable and hurt, not anymore. "Lindsay should go to the school with the best program for her. If it's convenience, then yes, Orange, but Chapman is exceptional, and has a wonderful graduate program. I'm sure she's discussed it with you, but she'll need to earn her master's if she wants to be a therapist."

"She wants Orange. She needs to be near you."

"I won't be there. Lindsay knows that."

"Are you retiring?"

"There's an opportunity for me in Cambria. The pay is excellent and it's fewer hours than what I'm working now. I wouldn't mind a thirty-hour workweek. My friend Margot—" She broke off, realizing Wolf knew exactly who Margot was. "Margot works for the same company and has assured me that it's a really positive environment and I've met Sally, the owner of the company. She's a lot of fun. I think it's going to be a good move."

"What about your friends here?"

"I'll still see Paige and Elizabeth. They're both from Paso Robles and they still have parents there."

"I thought you loved this area."

Andi looked away. "It's different now."

"Because I ruined it for you."

She wasn't going to go there. She wasn't going to get personal. She wasn't strong enough to do more than keep things civil. Superficial. "I think I'd feel better in the new place. Energized. It's time for a change." She forced a smile as she looked at him. "And I'm not saying that to be unkind—"

"I know that. You are not an unkind person. If anything, you are far too giving."

She didn't want to hear this, not from him, not now, not after everything he'd said. "Let's just let it go, and move on. We'll both be better when we move on."

"I didn't mean what I said. I was angry—"

"I know. You said things in the moment to hurt me. And Wolf, you succeeded. You're a fighter. You know how to fight. I don't. But I don't want to become hard. I don't want to become good at . . . this. It's not me, and it's just so sad that something lovely became so ugly."

"I hate that I hurt you."

She looked away, tears stinging her eyes. He'd never given her a chance. He hadn't cared about her feelings. He hadn't tried to be understanding or protect her in any way.

"I'm sorry," he said. "You deserved better. If I could go back in time, I would. I'd make different choices—"

"But we can't go back in time, and we can't change what was said. I can't get your words out of my head, and I can still see your face as you said those things . . . you were so cold, so hard. You shredded my heart. It's still not the same."

"I'm sorry."

"I know you are." Her chest ached with emotion. "I believe you, but I don't like fighting with you, and I don't like how you can stay mad for so long. I like to forgive and forget. I prefer to be compassionate." Her voice quavered and she had to stop for a moment and hold her breath, trying to get her pulse to slow. "I loved you so much, but I'm not strong enough to love the hard, angry part of you."

He turned, looked across her front yard, the elegant cobbled driveway lined by flower beds filled with roses and lilies. "I understand."

Her gaze swept his back, the broad shoulders, the narrow waist and long legs. He looked like a Viking. He fought like a Viking. He was dangerous. Too dangerous for her.

But that didn't mean she hated him. She'd never hate him. She still loved him. She just couldn't be near him. It would be way too hard on her heart and head.

"There's no reason for you to move so far, though," he said after a moment. He turned to look at her over his shoulder. "I don't want to chase you away. I can keep my distance, stay out of your way."

"I will feel better in a new environment. There are just too many memories here. It hurts seeing you. Hurts driving down your street. Looking at the coffeehouse. Going to the grocery store. It all just feels bad now and I did this once, after Kevin died, and I can't do this again, not here, not in the same town." She breathed out, a slow stream of air, feeling better for being honest. This conversation needed to be had. They were getting closure they both needed.

"You're the first to know, but Luke has decided to sell the cabin. It will go up for sale right before Memorial Day so it will be new on the market when lots of people will be up there for the long weekend. I hope you'll get a good neighbor this time, someone who won't make your life miserable."

"You never—"

"I meant Kevin." She smiled crookedly. "I was always a good neighbor."

"I will miss you, Andi McDermott."

Her eyes stung, but she kept smiling. "Life is full of change. If I've learned anything these past five years, it's that I have to change, too. I won't survive if I'm not flexible."

HE COULDN'T LOSE HER. IT WAS THAT SIMPLE. WOLF wasn't prepared to let her go, or have her move five hours north.

He'd messed up, big-time, and he needed to make amends, which would be difficult since he hadn't been an ass just once but twice.

He'd shown his true colors, he'd been the person he despised, and he didn't deserve a second chance, but he was going to fight for one. He needed her, and loved her. Andi was worth the fight, and he'd never fought for love before, but it was time.

He called Margot, who was not happy with him. "Yes?" She greeted him tersely.

"I know," he said.

"You screwed up."

"Yes."

"Why?" she demanded. "Why turn on her like that?"

"I was angry."

"You were awful."

"I know."

"She's not a hard person. You really hurt her."

He said nothing, because he had no defense.

Margot wasn't done. "She was like a ghost when she first moved here, so pale, so sad. The first few weeks I could barely get her to talk. She couldn't eat. She didn't sleep. She just worked, and worked, and after a couple weeks, she was doing better, and starting to smile a little bit. She's finally settling in here. She's finally Andi again. Don't you dare contact her, don't you dare stir everything up. You had a chance—twice—and instead of having any compassion, you destroyed her."

He ground his jaw. What she said was true.

"You don't deserve her," Margot added. "She trusted you. She felt safe with you, and you took that away from her."

He couldn't dwell on that. He couldn't change the past. He could only focus on now. "Is she living with you?"

"It's none of your business."

"Where is she working?"

"Again, none of your business."

"I think she's blocked me on her phone."

"Good. I'm glad she listened to me. Stay away from her. She's doing better. She's feeling stronger. Let her be happy."

"I love her."

"You have a funny way of showing it."

Wolf hesitated. "Is she really okay? Because if she is really, truly okay, I can maybe accept that she's better without me. But if she's not really, truly okay, then I'm going to fight to get her back."

"Wolf, you're not good for her."

"That wasn't what I asked."

"She's started a new life here. There are always bumps and hurdles. She's trying to find her footing, and she'll get there. Cambria will be good for her, and she has Sally and me looking out for her. We're going to help introduce her to new friends, and new men."

Margot hung up on him then. Wolf set his phone on his desk, crossed the garage, and punched his dummy as hard as he could.

HE WASN'T DONE. HE WASN'T GOING TO ACCEPT defeat. Not yet. He couldn't.

He was glad she'd sold the house that didn't fit her. He was glad she was taking action, moving forward. He understood that. But she didn't need to leave San Juan forever to start over, she just needed a place here that could be a fresh start. New memories. He wanted to give her a fresh start, too. He needed a fresh start—with her.

Wolf took one of the big sketch pads he kept for client meetings, and thought about all the dream houses she'd shown him. He thought about their mutual love of tall windows and high ceilings, French doors and porches. She needed a room with beautiful morning sunlight, and a space where she could sit with a glass of wine savoring the sunset. She deserved a bedroom that felt like a retreat—not necessarily huge, but full of charm. A window seat. Bookshelves. Maybe a gas fireplace with a beautiful mantel. He'd give her a proper, stylish kitchen that opened to a family room, so she could be cooking and still watch a show, or keep an eye on those she loved. He thought of Charlie. He thought of Lindsay. He thought of himself.

He hoped she still loved him, in some small part of her heart.

But in the end, this house he was drawing, it wasn't for him, it was for her. It was about giving her a place that made her happy, that made her feel loved.

She could buy a place, tear down an old house and build, or maybe she could find an empty lot and build. Her forever house wouldn't happen overnight, but if she liked the plans, she could have the house built in a year. He knew the right people, good people who wouldn't take advantage of her and would deliver the quality home she deserved.

And maybe, just maybe, if she loved the plans, she might find it in her heart to forgive him. Because he needed her forgiveness. He needed her love. Until she forgave him, he wouldn't be able to forgive himself.

ONCE AGAIN WOLF WAS IN HER DRIVEWAY, ONLY IT WAS actually Margot's driveway.

Margot came to Andi's bedroom to tell her Wolf was at the door. "I tried to send him away," she said. "He refuses to go until he sees you."

Andi put down her book. "He's here."

"Yes." Margot hesitated. "I could call the police—"

"No. That's not necessary. I'll go see him."

Andi barely glanced at her reflection. She looked terrible. She was in sweats and her hair was gray at the roots. She needed a color touch-up. She wore no makeup and could use some lipstick, or color in her cheeks, but she wasn't going to bother.

Instead she went to the door, where he was waiting outside on the steps, a paper tube in his hand.

"I have something for you," he said, by way of greeting.

She didn't want to look at him, didn't want to see him, didn't want to feel anything at all.

"I drew these for you. They're house plans."

"I'm not going to build again. I am looking for a place here, and I'm taking my time until I find something I like."

"I remembered the things you mentioned that you liked in a house. I did some research and found those *Southern Living* homes you loved and made a note of everything you wanted."

He held the plans out to her.

She folded her arms across her chest, tucking her hands away so that she couldn't take them. "I'm sorry you wasted your time, but I can't accept them."

"You won't even look at them?"

She felt sick at heart, but she couldn't look at them. She didn't want to be tempted, didn't want to get excited or feel anything. Feelings were bad. Feelings were damaging.

"I'm sorry, but I can't."

"It's a gift, Andi. No strings attached."

"I'm not going to be building a house."

"Maybe not right now, but someday you might find the right piece of land—"

"No. I won't. Building a house is a lot of work. I don't have it in me. I did it once so Kevin could have his dream place, but it was exhausting. It's not for me."

Wolf tucked the tube under his arm. "We miss you," he said quietly. "We all miss you, but no one misses you more than me."

"You have your family, Wolf. They're the most important people in your world. Not me."

He averted his head, jaw jutting. "You're using my words against me."

"It's what you said."

"I was angry."

"I understand, and I forgive you, but I haven't forgotten. I don't want to forget. You hurt me. Your words were like a blow . . . they knocked me down. They knocked me out. I don't think we can recover from this." She hesitated. "I guess what I'm trying to say is, there is no us anymore. It's over."

He left, and it wasn't until after he'd gone that she realized he hadn't taken the house plans with him.

Just seeing them in the house made her eyes burn fresh. She couldn't bear to see them, though, and, drawing a deep, shuddering breath, she hid them at the back of her closet.

She couldn't bear to think of Wolf, either. But she was proud of herself for not getting emotional when he was apologizing. Proud of herself for being calm and in control, even when she wanted to throw herself at him and beg him to hold her, and love her, and never let her go.

She had to remain strong now. She couldn't touch him, couldn't want him; she was the one letting him go. Just as she'd decided with Bruce back in December, if she was going to be in a relationship, it had to be with the right person, and the right person wasn't just attractive and fascinating, but kind, caring, thoughtful. She deserved someone who treated her well, even when things got rough, because life was full of hard times. Life had real problems, serious heartbreaks. If someone couldn't accept an apology, if someone wouldn't listen to her, what hope was there?

But it wouldn't be easy getting over him. She was still wildly in love with him, although the love was tempered with pain. The pain would diminish eventually. Grieving was a process. She'd done this before, she could do it again.

She reminded herself of the things said during those support group meetings. She just had to give herself time to feel all the different feelings. She just had to be kind to herself, and recognize that there would be good days and bad days, but one day, at some point, she wouldn't hurt so much, and she wouldn't miss him so much, and she'd be interested in meeting new men. . . .

Well, at this point that was unlikely, the meeting-new-men part. But the rest of it was true. She just couldn't get weak and think about him, or remember making love with him, or all the fun little moments where it just felt so good being together.

Eating cheesecake on her couch.

Leafing through design magazines.

Watching him at the grill.

Taking a walk through his neighborhood.

Kissing him good night—

She stopped there. This was exactly what she couldn't do.

She'd blocked him on her phone. Now she just needed to block him from her mind.

WEEKS PASSED. ONE MONTH BECAME ANOTHER. THEY were halfway through summer. School would be starting again soon. Staff at Orange would be preparing for the new year. The fall semester was always exciting. New students, new courses, new faces, new plans.

Andi was feeling nostalgic, and more than a little homesick.

Cambria was cold. And windy. And foggy. Not like the coastal fog that drifted inland in Orange County, but damp cold, gray cold, get into your bones and stay cold.

Margot assured her it was unseasonal, that usually this was winter weather, and that it should soon pass, but the two weeks of cold foggy mornings in mid-July were starting to get to her.

Blue, Andi went walking during her lunch hour, but she was struggling. Margot knew Andi was down, but Margot had no idea how much Andi was missing her old job, missing the university staff who'd become friends. She missed Dr. Nair's analytical, rational approach to everything. What were emotions? Who needed them?

She missed the red tile roofs, and the Spanish architecture, not just at the university but in Orange County. She missed downtown San Juan Capistrano, the eucalyptus trees and pepper trees, the roses and bougainvillea, the latte from her favorite coffeehouse, and her favorite cheese enchilada salad at El Adobe Restaurant.

She missed Charlie's hugs. She missed the way he lined up cars across the floor of her house. She missed him demolishing the bad guys. She missed his aggressive painting. She missed the way he ate cookies with such relish, smacking his lips. Laughing.

She missed Lindsay's bright mind and worries, her hopes, her dreams, her need to be valued, and loved. She wanted to be there to see Lindsay start school, and be there to support her and encourage her, to remind her she could do it.

She missed Wolf's gorgeous face, and his big muscular body that filled her with wonder. She missed kissing and being held, she missed talking to him and making love. She missed his tattoos and scars, his fierceness and his sweetness. When he hugged her there was nowhere else she wanted to be but right there, against his chest, in his arms.

She wasn't a young girl anymore. She didn't have time to waste. Didn't have time for tantrums and theatrics. Didn't have time for regrets. And she was full of regret, and longing.

This was a mistake, coming here. This job wasn't a good fit for her. Cambria wasn't where she belonged.

After work she went home, closed the door to her bedroom, and pulled the tube of house plans Wolf had drawn her out from the back of her closet. She unrolled the plans and put books on the corners, weighting them so she could see what he'd made for her.

The front elevation was beautiful. Her favorite tall, multi-paned windows lined the front, two on one side of the front door, two on the other. The windows were framed by shutters, and charming columns supported the roof. The second story had dormer windows, and the windows had flower boxes. The house wasn't big, but it made her heart do a pit-a-pat. It looked like her. It looked like everything she loved.

Her eyes stung and, blinking, she turned the page and studied the main floor with the kitchen and great room combination, as well as the spacious master bedroom suite down a wide hall. The guest bedrooms were all on the second floor, along with a bonus playroom/craftroom, or whatever she wanted it to be.

Andi didn't want to see more. She rolled the plans up and slid them back into the protective tube.

She looked around the room she was in, and then out at the side garden filled with greenery.

This wasn't where she belonged, either.

She blinked again. A tear fell free. She ignored it until it was sliding down her cheek.

Andi didn't want to wait and see if she'd eventually settle in. She didn't want to accept this new life, or adjust. She wanted what she wanted—and that was to find the people she loved and fix this.

Fix things with Wolf.

Apologize to Lindsay.

Hug and kiss Charlie.

That evening during dinner with Margot, Andi couldn't relax. She wanted to talk to Margot but wasn't sure how. There didn't seem an easy or natural way to introduce the subject.

Margot made it easy by muting the music on the surround sound. "You look as if you're about to cry any minute. What's wrong?"

Andi shifted on the dining chair, uncomfortable, anxious, but desperate to get this off her chest. "Margot, I've made a mistake."

Margot said nothing.

Andi pushed on. "I feel terrible because I know this will disappoint you, but I want to go back. I need to talk to Wolf. I don't know that I can do this, without talking to him again."

Margot reached for her wineglass and took a long sip.

"I miss him." Andi's voice deepened. "I really love him, and I don't give up on people. I don't give up easily and I feel like I gave up too early. We had our first real fight and I just walked away. That's not me. I'm not a quitter."

"Andi, he came at you twice. He was an ass, *twice*. And then he finally decides he's wrong, and he made a mistake, but it took him a long time to get there. He was okay being hurtful for weeks. Don't you see the red flags? I do."

"Yes, we've got a problem, and we might not be able to resolve it, but I'd like to try. It's worth trying. Everything I know about him, everything his family says about him, tells me he's loyal and he's protective of his family. Fiercely protective. He was angry because he believed I put Lindsay in danger. In his mind, I hurt her, and that is the ultimate of sins—hurting family. That's why he reacted so badly. But I don't think this is something that would happen with us a lot. I've thought about it. I've thought about it for hours, and days, and everything just blew up."

"That doesn't make it okay."

"No, but I can forgive him for being a jerk."

Margot sighed, shook her head. "I'm worried for you. I'm worried he's going to break your heart again."

"But my heart isn't broken. I'm not broken. I was hurt, and sad, really sad, but people make mistakes. We both made mistakes. He's apologized and I want to apologize, too."

"Your only mistake is going back to him."

"He didn't hit me. He didn't grab me—"

"Harsh words can be worse than a fist or slap."

Andi agreed, but she knew Wolf, and she knew he'd fought dirty because he was in pain. Did it make it okay? No. But she also understood it. "I know you went out on a limb for me. You helped me find a job. You helped me move here. I adore you, and am so thankful you're my friend. Please don't think I'm ungrateful."

"I don't think you're ungrateful. I think you are in love with a really hard man."

"He's not easy, no, but he has so many wonderful qualities, and until this, I've been so happy with him, happier than with anyone."

"Happier than with Kevin?"

"It's hard to compare my feelings for Wolf with my feelings for Kevin—I'm a different person than the girl who married right out of college. But the adult me understands Wolf, and loves him for him. Warts and all."

"You mean, fangs, claws, and all."

Andi smothered a laugh. "He's not a monster, and he's not a bad person. Wolf's an alpha. A special forces veteran. He's not a man of words, he's action. When he doesn't know how to communicate, he roars. He bares his teeth. He snaps, snarls, growls. But underneath all that, he's still Wolf. The man I love."

Andi thought for a moment before adding, "Here's the thing, I'm strong. I don't think I ever understood just how strong I am. Yes, he hurt me, but I want to forgive. I want to see if we can make it work. Margot, I love him. And I love Lindsay. And I love Charlie. I love his family. I understand why he was so protective of Lindsay. He lost Stone, and Lindsay is his connection to Stone. He's vowed to take care of Lindsay and Charlie and so he reacted out of instinct, defending those he loved. This wasn't a fight about money, or sex. It wasn't a fight about me being out late for a girls' night. It wasn't a fight about leaving socks lying around the house, or drinking too much beer. This was a fight about someone he loved, being in danger. He told me, when I forced him to see me, that he wasn't ready to talk to me and he couldn't handle seeing me. And I wouldn't accept it. I pushed things, thinking if he just saw me again, he'd remember how much he loved me. But he wasn't ready and it backfired. Now I know in the future if he's upset I need to give him space, and I need to give him a chance to work through his feelings, and I can do that."

"And I think you need someone more civilized than Wolf Enders," she said, still disgruntled.

Andi smiled, appreciating just how protective Margot was of her. She hadn't had a friend like this since college. She'd never felt close enough with anyone to share how things really were at home, in a marriage, behind closed doors. But Margot was there for her. From the beginning Margot was on Team Andi.

"I was married to Mr. Civilized," Andi said. "Kevin didn't fight dirty. Kevin was a good husband and a great provider, and I loved him. But there was no passion there. He was a nice person, but he was pretty much about Kevin. His career was about Kevin, and his hobbies were about him. He never put his life on the line for anyone else. He never faced danger, nor served our country in any capacity. He knew how much I wanted a child, but it didn't work for him, so we didn't pursue options. I loved him anyway. I was a good wife. But now I love Wolf, and I'm not ready to let him go. I'm not ready to let the love go."

Margot stared at her a long moment and then smiled faintly. "I don't think there is anything I can say to stop you, is there?"

"No." Andi hesitated. "Margot, even if he and I don't get back together, I want to return to San Juan. I'd like to be able to stay close to Lindsay and Charlie. I promised her I would be there for her, and she's starting school in the fall. I loved having them in my life, and my favorite thing was playing with Charlie on weekends. I hope if I return to Orange County Lindsay will let Charlie come over on Saturdays and play again. I miss Wolf, but I also miss them . . . my girl, my boy. They're not mine, but they feel like mine. In my heart, they do."

"Well, I guess we better tell Sally."

"Will she be upset?"

"She'll be fine."

"How much notice do I need to give? Two weeks? More?"

"No notice." Margot hesitated. "She created the job for you. She doesn't really need you."

"What?"

"I told her how worried I was about you. I told her that you were extraordinary and needed a fresh start, and she said let's give your friend a fresh start, and so she created a job, and told me to send you the info and have you apply." Margot's smile was warm, kind. "This is a long way of saying she'll be fine."

"Sally will think I'm ridiculous."

"Sally's been married five times. If anyone believes in love, it's Sally."

Chapter 18

ANDI DIDN'T HAVE THAT MUCH TO PACK SINCE MOST OF her things were still in storage in Laguna Niguel, and so after loading the car with her suitcases and the boxes of pots and pans, wooden spoons, and kitchen utensils, as well as her favorite oils and spices, she gave Margot a huge hug, promised her that she would see her soon, and set off. The first part of the drive was lovely and scenic along the coast-line. The hills were still green, although the farther south she went the greens faded to gold with the heat. California needed rain again soon.

There was traffic as she approached the San Fernando Valley. There was more traffic through L.A. Andi struggled with impatience. She probably shouldn't have taken the 5, but it was too late. She just had to relax. But the five-hour drive turned to six, and then six and a half. It was nearly five o'clock, and traffic was just bumper to bumper all the way to San Juan Capistrano, but finally she reached the Ortega exit, and it was just a matter of a few minutes and she'd be at Wolf's house.

She pulled up in front of his house and parked. A light shone from within the house. The khaki Land Rover was behind the gate in the driveway, and so was the motorcycle. Her chest tightened. Anxiety, anticipation, hope, fear—the emotions warred within her. She should have warned him. She should have told him she was coming. Instead she was just going to burst in and surprise him. Oh, this could go badly.

Maybe she should text him after all. See if he wanted to talk.

But what if he said no?

She pictured their last face-to-face. She'd been the one who'd said goodbye to him. The time before that, he'd said get lost to her. She hoped they both had cooler heads now. She hoped they had some perspective, and the only way she'd know was if she went for it.

Andi pocketed her keys. She released her hair from the ponytail, letting the curls fall loose. Now or never.

She went to the garage first. The light was on in there, too. She knocked lightly, and then opened the door. Wolf was sitting at his big desk.

He dropped his pencil, stunned to see her.

"Hi." She smiled, nervous, shy. "Do you have a minute?"

He rose. "All the minutes in the world."

"I'm sorry—"

"No. No, Andi, there's no reason for you to be sorry. This is on me. It's one hundred percent me. I was wrong. I'm sorry. Forgive me. Please."

MAKING UP WAS WONDERFUL. WOLF COULDN'T REMEM-ber ever wanting to fix things as much as he wanted to fix things with Andi. It helped that they were both sorry, and they both wanted to try again and make it work.

"I want to come back," Andi said later that night when

she was at his side, in his bed. It hadn't been makeup sex. It had been makeup love and he didn't think he'd ever let her out of this room again. She'd been gone so long. Too long. But at least they'd had a good evening with Lindsay and Charlie. Wolf grilled steaks and they ate outside, and he'd even lit the firepit just because he wanted to celebrate.

Her, here, with him.

"I want you to come back," he said, kissing her temple. "I want you to stay."

"I might need to look for a lot so I can build," she said. "Maybe building a house won't be overwhelming if you're there to help me."

"Happy to help you." He wasn't sure if she wanted to use his plans. He didn't care. Whatever would make her happiest. "Happy to drive up to Cambria first thing tomorrow, pack your stuff, and move you wherever you want to be." He paused, before asking, "How would you feel moving into this house?"

"You'd want me to live here?" she asked, turning to look up at him, her warm brown eyes searching his.

He ran his hand over her cheek, and then down her hair. He loved her hair. Thick, wild curls, angelic curls. Beautiful Andi. "Too much, too soon?"

She was quiet, thinking. "No."

"You're sure?"

She looked into his eyes again. "I've already left Cambria. Everything is in my car. I'm not going back."

"That was risky."

"I know, but it was a risk I had to take. I'm here for you. I returned to San Juan so I could be with you. We're in good health now, but I don't want to waste time. I want to live. I want to love. I want you."

"You've got me," he answered, wrapping an arm around her, securing her to his chest, his palm caressing the curve of her butt. She was full of curves and softness, warmth and love. He was so comfortable with her. He hadn't felt this way about anyone in years, if ever. He could be himself with Andi. He could relax. Laugh. Love. Good God, he loved her. "Marry me."

Andi scrambled into a sitting position. "What?"

He sat up, too, and tucked one of her thick curls behind her ear. "I love you. I don't want to lose you, not ever again. Marry me. Let's make the leap. Let's make this real. Legal. Permanent."

"What if we have another fight?"

He leaned forward, kissed her. "I will listen to you. I will not shut you out. I promise."

"I don't play games, Wolf."

He tried to smile but couldn't. "I know. You're not Jessica. You're Andi. And I know you love me. I know you have my back." He hesitated. "And Lindsay's back. And Charlie's. Marry me. Be part of this crazy Enders family."

Andi's eyes shone. Her full bottom lip quivered. "Yes," she said, wrapping her arms around his neck and kissing him. "Yes, yes, forever yes."

THE SUMMER WAS COMING TO A CLOSE. THE WEDDING invitations had been sent out. It would be a small ceremony with an intimate dinner reception at the luxurious hotel across the street from the mission. It had been almost forty years since Andi was a bride and she shouldn't have been excited about planning a wedding, but she was.

She and Lindsay pored over bridal books and looked at ideas online. She and Wolf had invited only fifty people, and doubted even half would make it, as many of the invitations were going to friends who had served with Wolf, and they were scattered around the country.

It was Lindsay who found Andi's wedding gown. It was a gorgeous off-white silk, long-sleeve dress, floor-length, with an elegant deep V neckline and asymmetrical waist with a romantic white silk rose just above her right hip. The flattering cut minimized her waist, and the placement of the rose elongated her frame. In the lovely silk gown Andi felt beautiful. Even without her hair and makeup done, she couldn't stop smiling at herself in the bridal store mirror.

Margot had agreed to be her maid of honor. Maverick and Lincoln would stand up with Wolf. Charlie would be the ring bearer.

Andi knew Wolf would have preferred to get married at the courthouse, or drive to Las Vegas, but he didn't protest when she asked if they could have a real ceremony close to home. Wolf wasn't about to deny Andi anything. They'd already bought a two-and-a-half-acre lot not far from where she'd lived before. The house was a teardown, which was exactly what they wanted, but the landscaping was mature, with tidy rows of orange trees marching down the hillslope.

Everything was coming together.

Lindsay was starting classes at Orange tomorrow. Charlie started a new year of preschool tomorrow as well. Wolf and Andi had met with the contractor today, going over the plans, which the city was reviewing. By this time next year, they'd have a new home, and would be close to celebrating their first anniversary.

But she was jumping ahead of herself. Andi knew she had a tendency to do that. She was also looking for a part-time job, but Wolf liked having her around the house, and he urged her to take her time and make sure it was the right fit for her. He wanted her happy. She deserved to be happy, he said.

"I am," she told him that evening, dozing in his arms, sleepy from making love. "I'm completely happy. There is nothing I want. Nothing I could ask for." She kissed his hard chest, kissing one of the scars running over his heart. "What about you?"

Wolf didn't answer immediately. He just touched her, his hand moving down the length of her spine and then slowly moving up again. He didn't say I love you to her constantly, but he said it at least once a week, and always, he touched her. Held her. Kissed her. Opened doors for her. Carried the groceries for her. Washed her car for her, filled the gas, made sure it was serviced regularly. In short, Wolf showed in actions how much she meant to him, and those actions meant everything to her.

To be safe.

To feel loved.

To have a second chance like this.

"I am happy," he said, breaking the silence. "But of course I always think of Stone. I think how proud he would be of Charlie. He would have been such a good father. He was such a good son."

A lump filled Andi's throat. She pressed another kiss to his chest. She had always wondered how he died, but no one ever talked about it. They made vague references— blown up, Afghanistan—but never anything specific. But tonight she wanted to know. Tonight she summoned up the courage to ask. "How did he die? No one has ever said, but I wonder, and I shouldn't wonder—"

"It shouldn't have happened," Wolf answered. His voice wasn't hard as much as sad. "He died because he saw a little boy running toward the road. The boy was four, Charlie's age now, and Stone jumped out of the vehicle to stop the child from running in front of the tank, and the roadside bomb detonated."

Andi curled her fingers into a fist and closed her eyes. She'd never met Stone and yet the pain washed over her, sharp, brutal. She said nothing because she was afraid if she spoke she'd cry, and she couldn't cry on Wolf's chest.

"It was all a setup," Wolf said. "They sacrificed a little boy to kill American soldiers."

Andi kept her eyes closed and yet her heart hurt. She

pressed her cheek to Wolf's warm chest, but the tears slipped out, she couldn't stop them.

Wolf said nothing, his hand at the back of her head, his touch comforting.

Andi cried, for Stone, and Lindsay and Charlie, for Wolf and Stone's brothers. She cried for Jessica even though she didn't know her. Andi cried for all of them, this family of warrior men and the women they had left behind.

It was impossible.

Who did this? Who survived this?

And while she cried, Wolf held her, and she knew after a bit she wasn't just crying for them, she was also crying for herself, for all the hurt of the past few months; but at least she was back with Wolf, and they were together again, marrying soon, and that was the important thing. Not the fights or the sharp words. Forgiveness mattered. Tomorrow mattered. Hope was everything.

She fell asleep in his arms, her cheek on his chest, and when she woke up just before dawn, he was still there, at her side, his big arm over her, keeping her close.

She put her arm over his. The worst of the pain was behind them. The sun would be up soon. Everything was good.

THE RESPONSES TO THE WEDDING INVITATIONS ARRIVED daily. Every afternoon while Wolf worked in the garage at his desk, she'd take the mail and open the cards and fill up her spreadsheet. Yes. No. The number responding.

The wedding was just three weeks away, a late September wedding with friends from the university coming— Paige, Elizabeth, Dr. Nair, as well as a number of other professors from the math department. Wolf's friends were coming from all over. Margot would of course be there, and even though her friend still had concerns, Andi knew that with time Margot would realize that Wolf was perfect for Andi.

But who would have thought that Andi would become such a rebel?

She didn't want anyone telling her how to do things, much less older men giving her helpful tips or suggestions. She didn't want younger men giving her suggestions, either. The women who were her friends—Margot, Paige, Elizabeth, Lindsay—weren't interested in managing her. She didn't have to do anything to win their approval. They were all grown-ups. Equals. She was lucky to have friends who respected her, friends who trusted her.

Growing up, there had been a lot of pressure to be a certain kind of woman. There had been standards of femininity. Girls were competitive, and judgmental. She'd never felt good enough in high school, never pretty enough or smart enough, but then she met Kevin, and she made him her world and he'd given her focus, and a purpose. But by the time he died, she'd become an adult, and she was ready to be herself. Working at Orange helped build her confidence. Earning her own income gave her a sense of self and independence. Making friends who understood her gave her support.

She looked forward now, not back. She was free to love, free to fail, free to hurt, free to forgive, free to forget. At fifty-eight she could make whatever decisions she wanted to, decisions that were right for her.

And Wolf, despite his edges and toughness, was right for her.

She knew it, believed it, had no doubt about it. And if others doubted? That was their problem, not hers.

Andi slit open the next response card, pulling the small paper from the envelope. "No."

Wolf looked at her. "What's wrong?"

"I can't believe it," Andi said.

"What?" Wolf rose, faced her.

She flashed the RSVP card at him. "He said yes."

"Who?"

"Luke. Luke and Kelsey RSVPed for the wedding." She was breathless. Silly, but she couldn't help it. She was excited. *"They're coming."*

WOLF FORCED THE SMALLEST OF SMILES, EVEN AS HE counted to ten, and then twenty, feeling none of Andi's happiness.

Truth be told, he wanted to strangle Luke for responding with a yes. Luke had let Andi down for years. Wolf didn't trust him one bit, nor did he believe Luke would actually show up for the wedding. Something would come up, he'd have an excuse, and Andi would be hurt. Again.

"I didn't know you'd invited Luke," he said, hiding his anger. "I thought we weren't going to."

"It was a courtesy invite," she said, adding the response card to the yes pile. "I didn't expect him to come. It's a long way from DC—" Andi broke off, shook her head. "But I'm glad," she said, her voice firming. "It makes me happy that he's going to come. I love him, and will always love him—"

"He's going to disappoint you."

"Maybe not. People change, and this is my wedding, our wedding, I'd like him to be there, if he can make it. He was part of my life, a big part of my life, and he represents the years I was married to his dad." She paused, waited. "Don't be upset with me."

"I'm not."

"We promised to be honest. I want you to be honest—"

"I hate him. I'd like to break every bone in his body." Wolf looked her in the eye. "There. That's how I feel. Not upset with you. Just not a fan of Luke's."

"He might surprise us."

"Andi, I don't want you to be sad on our wedding day. You've worked so hard to make it special. I don't want anyone to hurt you."

"Wolf?"

"Yes?"

"Will you be there?"

He slowly smiled. "Yes."

"Then it'll be perfect."

BUT WOLF WAS WRONG.

Luke and Kelsey showed for the wedding, flying in the night before and joining them at the rehearsal dinner at her request. Once there, Andi asked Luke if he'd walk her down the aisle. She told him that it was a symbolic gesture really, but it would mean a lot to her, because Luke represented his dad, and the wonderful years they'd had together. She also wanted Luke to know she'd always be there for him, and she'd always think of him as her son, too.

Luke, who never showed emotion, was visibly moved, and hugged her, and apologized for being distant, aware that he tended to be clinical and detached and he'd never been fair to Andi, who had tried so hard, in so many ways.

Andi didn't need the apology, but she welcomed the hug, and of course, the love.

The next day, when Luke walked Andi down the aisle, Wolf didn't think he'd ever seen Andi look so happy, or so beautiful. She glowed as she walked toward him, she floated and glowed and her joy burrowed into his chest, deep into his heart. She deserved to be that happy every day. He vowed to make her that happy. She had so much faith in people. She always hoped for the best. It was a special gift to always see the good, to forgive, to turn the other cheek.

He'd never met anyone like her, and he knew he was the lucky one. He didn't deserve her, and yet she loved him. Wolf felt her love in every bit of his being.

Luke found Wolf after the ceremony. "Congratulations,"

Luke said, shaking Wolf's hand. "I'm happy for both of you."

"You don't think your dad is rolling in his grave?"

"No." Then Luke smiled. "Okay, maybe. But, so what? And I mean that in the nicest possible way. He's not here, but Andi is, and she needs someone who will love her and take care of her. She's a good person, and I wasn't always a great stepson, but I appreciate all she did for me. She was always there for me."

"And I'm glad I finally got to meet her," Kelsey said, smiling at Wolf. "I'm just sorry it's taken so long."

ANDI COULDN'T STOP SMILING. THEY'D INVITED FIFTY people. Forty-eight came. The reception dinner menu was Wolf's favorite—steaks, shrimp—and for Andi, enchiladas. The olive trees off the dining room shone with white lights, while candles flickered on all the tables, the candles nestled in the red rose and orange and pink dahlia flower arrangements. There was no head table, just six rounds of eight, perfectly accommodating everyone.

Margot was seated at the table with Paige and Elizabeth. She'd brought a date, but Andi didn't think she was into him.

Wolf's sons looked gorgeous in their dress uniforms. Wolf wore a traditional black tuxedo, but he paired it with a black shirt and looked properly dangerous and gorgeous at the same time.

During dinner there were some toasts. Lincoln made the first toast—brief, articulate, but sincere. Everyone cheered and drank.

Margot rose and gave a toast. "To my favorite beauty and her beast, may happiness forever reign in their kingdom."

There was more laughter, more clinking of glasses, more drinking.

And then Maverick rose to make a toast, and the guests quieted again.

"My dad," he said, "is a very private person. He's not what you'd call neighborly. He bought a cabin in Blue Jay, near Lake Arrowhead, after he moved to California, wanting peace. Just wanting to be left alone."

Andi clapped a hand to her mouth. Maverick wasn't . . . oh, he wasn't going to air dirty laundry here?

"Dad always said he didn't start the feud," Maverick continued. "He wasn't interested in fighting with neighbors. He'd been a career soldier, trained for dangerous, lethal missions, not fighting with ordinary people next door."

There were chuckles and snickers and Wolf extended his arm across the back of Andi's chair, his fingertips grazing her shoulder. He glanced at her, smiled, amused.

She shook her head, torn between amusement and horror.

"But when Dad's neighbors began spreading rumors that it was Axel, his beloved shepherd who was in the latter years of his life, who'd attacked the little white fluffy dog down the lane, Dad wasn't okay. If you know my dad, you know he trains his dogs. He likes discipline. His dogs would never attack little fluffy dogs. They attacked the bad guys."

Maverick smiled at Andi now. "Apparently the neighbors didn't like Dad, either. In their minds he was an outlaw. Uncivil. *Savage*." Maverick's voice dropped and he emphasized the last word, making guests laugh again. "But here's what no one else knew. Dad might not have liked Mr. McDermott, but he very much liked Mrs. McDermott. It might have taken Dad a decade plus, but he finally stormed the castle and got the girl."

Maverick held his champagne glass higher. "Andi, welcome to the family. We love you. We need you. And we are never letting you go."

Andi's eyes filled with tears and she smiled and smiled as she looked around the room and realized she was the luckiest woman ever.

The sound of silverware tapping crystal filled the room, the guests clinking their glasses, wanting to see them kiss.

Wolf leaned toward her. "Kiss me, my beautiful bride."

She did. And she'd keep kissing him for the rest of her life.

Epilogue

ANDI STEPPED TO THE CABIN'S KITCHEN DOORWAY, where she could see both the living room and dining room. The mantel of the huge fieldstone fireplace was covered with a fresh, fragrant garland and glowing candles. In the dining room, Wolf's drafting table had been replaced by a solid pine table she and Wolf had found at an estate sale in Riverside.

She'd set the table with the red glazed pottery. The elegant centerpiece of red peonies, red roses, and pine boughs was dramatic without being overpowering. There were more fresh flowers on the coffee table in the living room. Andi might not be able to cook the perfect turkey—*still*— but she knew how to make a house a home.

But the turkey. She was fretting about the turkey, just as she did every year. Turkeys historically were problematic for her, either too dry or too tough or far too undercooked. She didn't know why, as she followed directions exactly. She brined them. She rubbed them. She called the Butterball hotline. One Christmas, years ago, the turkey was so underdone that she'd returned it, and all the sides, to the oven four times. Four times she'd invited Kevin and Luke to the table before excusing them again. That had been the worst.

But she was feeding a different crowd tonight.

The Enderses didn't care. Not one of the guys had expectations, nor did they want a fancy, formal Christmas Eve dinner. Instead they just wanted food, and the chance to sit and talk, laugh and relax. They wanted to enjoy each other, celebrate each other.

Celebrate all the good still in the world, including the men and women who served the country, those who fought for freedom.

Heart full of gratitude, Andi carried her glass of red wine into the living room and admired the tree with all the old-fashioned colored lights. She had added some of the ornaments from her cabin, along with some new ones Wolf had made with Charlie. Wolf's boys had grown up with colored lights, and so she'd had to put colored lights on the cabin tree for them. She'd doubted anyone would notice, but the first thing Maverick said when walking through the door was how much he liked the tree, and how beautiful the lights were.

Wolf entered the living room, a stack of brightly wrapped gifts in his arms. He put the presents beneath the tree and then turned to her, a frown creasing his brow. "What have you done to yourself?" he asked, taking her wineglass away and placing it on the mantel.

She put her hand up, touched her cheek. "Oh, scratched myself. It's nothing."

He tilted her chin to better study her cheek. "How?"

"It was silly. I was trying to take off a couple of the lower branches. Whacked myself."

"With what?"

"The ax."

"You've got to be kidding."

"It's nothing. Wolf, it could have been worse."

"Exactly. You have no business touching an ax, a hatchet, a knife—"

She laughed, interrupting him, and wrapped her arms around his waist. "I know how this goes. I'm a danger to myself and everyone else." She smiled up at him. "Kiss me, my fierce love. You don't scare me anymore."

He did kiss her, and they were still kissing when Maverick and Charlie entered the room, Charlie running straight to the tree to check out the presents, his cheeks still pink from sledding with his uncles. They broke apart, but Wolf kept an arm around her, holding her close to his side.

And then Lindsay walked in, talking to Lincoln and Lincoln's girlfriend. Lincoln was carrying more packages. Charlie was dancing back and forth, excited. What a perfect Christmas Eve.

Emotion flooded Andi. She couldn't remember when she last felt so happy, so content.

A year ago she'd been alone. A year ago she'd craved change . . . wanting new experiences and new memories.

A year later she had a new family, one that needed her. One with little people and big people and love.

So much love.

ACKNOWLEDGMENTS

Living in San Clemente has taught me appreciation and respect for the United States Marine Corps based at Camp Pendleton and across the country. Thank you to all branches of the military, and the service you provide for our country and citizens around the world.

Thank you Crystal, Nick, John, Meghan, and Sean for always answering my many questions about the Marine Corps.

Blue Jay is a real village near Lake Arrowhead, but the gated community in my story is fictional. San Juan Capistrano is every bit as delightful as I portrayed in the novel.

Thank you to my agent, Holly Root, and my editor, Cindy Hwang, for having my back during a challenging year. I am grateful!

Thank you to all readers, writers, and friends for sharing my love of books and stories. Let's keep making life—and reading—fun.

I do what I do because I love happy endings, and thanks to my husband and sons, I have a happy life every day.

We're never too old to fall in love, and never too old to be who we want to be.

Keep reading for an excerpt from

FLIRTING WITH FIRE

Coming soon!

MARGOT HUGHES MANEUVERED THROUGH THE CROWDED private room at the Fog Horn restaurant, trying to reach the exit without getting drawn into another conversation. She'd promised Sally she'd stay for an hour, and she'd stayed ninety minutes. Surely it was safe to slip out now, especially as Sally was engrossed in conversation with the mayor of Cambria.

Sally loved people. She was an introvert to the core, one of Cambria's most successful business owners, a former president of the Chamber of Commerce, and a woman with five ex-husbands. Sixty-seven-year-old Sally certainly didn't need a wingwoman, but when Sally asked Margot to join her tonight, it was virtually impossible for Margot to say no. Margot adored her boss, and Sally was fun, truly good company, provided she didn't try again to persuade Margot to get involved with her theater, the Cambria Playhouse.

The playhouse was Sally's passion project—which was wonderful—but Margot had walked away from the theater world when she left New York two years ago.

"Ditching me, already?" Sally asked, her deep voice husky with laughter. "You're a terrible date."

"Date, employee, friend . . . we do have a complicated relationship," Margot teased, turning to face her boss. "And you were busy talking to Bill. He likes you."

"No, he likes *you*. He wants to be introduced."

"Oh, Sally, no. He must be what? In his sixties?"

"Yes."

"I haven't hit fifty yet . . . don't rush me."

"You'll be fifty in a year, and he owns a big car dealership. He'd be able to take care of you—" Sally broke off seeing Margot's shudder. "But wouldn't it be nice for a change? You were the primary breadwinner with Stephen."

"He was a writer. He had things in play, and we agreed not to discuss him." Margot leaned forward, kissed Sally's soft cheek. "See you tomorrow."

"Why the rush? Let's go get dinner. I'm not a charcuterie kind of girl."

Even though Sally had to be close to seventy—her actual age was a closely held secret—she was more fun than anyone else Margot knew. But at the same time, Margot was tired, and ready for some alone time. "Maybe later this week," Margot suggested. "Right now home is calling. Feet hurt. Must ditch my bra, crash on the couch, watch my show. I have some new episodes—"

"You won't meet a man crashed on your crouch," Sally said sternly.

Sally, with all those ex-husbands, was a big believer in love. Margot, not so much.

"I'm not looking for a man, at least, not man hunting. Should one fall into my lap, that's something else." A year ago Sally had hired Margot to "help organize" her office. The job, and Sally, had turned out to be a lifeline. Margot had been so angry when she arrived in California, and she'd needed time to move through the hurt, and then learn to let go and move on. And when she was finally ready to date again, it would be on her terms. No more writers. No more theater people. No more drama . . . in any form.

"I do need some advice, though, if you can spare five minutes," Sally said.

Margot eyed Sally suspiciously because Sally never needed advice. Sally was usually the font of all wisdom. Margot just hoped this wasn't another tactic to drag her into the troubled summer season at the playhouse but held her tongue.

"Cherry, our director, quit. Just an hour ago." Sally's red lips pursed with disapproval. "Do you want to read the text? She quit through a text, saying that the leads weren't strong enough—"

"Maybe they weren't?"

"But she didn't have to tell them that! Because now they've quit, too. As of tonight, we have no director, no Paul, no Corie, and the show opens in five weeks. What do I do?"

"You refund the tickets, skip the summer season, and concentrate on your September show," Margot answered.

"We can't do that. The show must go on."

"Sally, *Barefoot in the Park* has been nothing but a headache since you announced the summer season. Let it go. Hold the auditions for *Next to Normal* and use the summer so that opening night September 7th will be wonderful."

"People are expecting a summer season."

"This is Cambria, not Ashland."

"You had a successful Broadway career. If anyone can save this show, it's you."

Margot had loved theater ever since she was a little girl. She'd gone to New York after graduating from high school and juggled jobs while auditioning. She'd been on the East Coast nine months when she was cast in her first off-Broadway play. She'd never looked back, working hard, supporting her talented playwright fiancé, until one day he was gone, having found someone more successful, and available, and Margot was forced to confront the fact that she was forty-two and had nothing. It took her another five years to give up on New York itself, but performing had sucked her dry. It had also—along with Stephen—broken her heart. "Sally, no. I can't. I love you, but I *can't*."

Sally wagged a finger at her. "Everyone has a price. I'm sure you have yours. Tell me what you want. I'll pay it. Please just step in for this one production—"

"Sally! You said you wanted advice. This isn't advice. This is bribery." Margot tried to keep her voice light but she hated this topic. It actually hurt to think about acting. It made her feel sick inside. "I can't act."

"What about direct?"

"Sally."

"Just this one play. I'll never ask again."

Margot held her breath and looked from Sally's hopeful expression to the chamber members mingling behind them. She glanced back at Sally, the most fearless person she knew, as well as the hardest working person she'd ever known. "Maybe." Margot drew another breath. "Let me think about it tonight."

"You'll love directing. You're a natural."

"I haven't agreed yet."

"Just remember I need to tell the cast and crew something tomorrow, especially since we'll need to hold new auditions for the lead roles of Corie and Paul."

"How can I forget?" Margot said, placing her empty wineglass on a tray behind her. "When you won't let me?"

Sally laughed and Margot headed out. The evening was cool and cloudy, and the drive home to her rental house took less than five minutes. Sally had turned the former vacation rental—a snug one-bedroom 1930's cottage just steps away from famous Moonstone Beach—into a long-term rental for Margot.

Margot loved her tiny gray shingled cottage with the living room bay window and its extensive window seat. The old stone fireplace was made with the smooth stones typical of Moonstone Beach, and the exterior window trim had been painted a whimsical lilac, which charmed Margot to no end, especially now that she'd tackled the once neglected yard and turned it into a garden filled with plants that called to the butterflies and hummingbirds. After a lifetime in New York City without a yard or greenery, Margot couldn't get enough of her own little garden with its patch of grass, bright red picnic table, and pair of pale blue Adirondack chairs not far from the front door where she had a peekaboo view of the ocean.

She smiled at her cottage as she parked in the gravel driveway. The front porch light was on, casting light and shadows on the gray shingles, making the little house look like something from Hansel and Gretel.

Inside the cottage, she locked the door, and set the alarm—something her dad, a retired sheriff had insisted on—not that there was much crime in sleepy Cambria, but she wasn't about to argue with an eighty-eight-year-old man. Her dad lived half an hour away in her hometown of Paso Robles and she wanted him to sleep well at night, and not worry about her.

In her pajamas, Margot heated up the leftover chicken tikka masala from two nights before, sat down on her couch with a wedge of warm naan and the chicken tikka, and turned on the TV. She watched one episode of her show, and then another, and then a third, unable to resist the cliff-hanger at the end. Margot had nearly finished the third when her phone rang. She glanced at the antique clock of the stone mantle. Almost eleven. Her first thought was of her dad. But as she reached for her phone on the end table, she saw it wasn't Dad, but Sally, and Sally never called late.

Margot answered quickly. "Sally, everything okay?"

"I've called an ambulance and it should be here soon. I haven't felt well for the past couple of hours. Not sure, but I might be having a heart attack."

"I'm on my way—"

"No, the ambulance is already coming and there's nothing for you to do in the ER. I just thought you should know. Tell everyone at work that I'm fine, that I'm going to be fine, and honestly, it might only be heartburn, but I'll feel better knowing."

"Where will they take you?"

"I imagine it'll be Memorial in Paso Robles."

"Please take your cell phone with you to the hospital."

"Of course."

"Call me when you need a ride home. I'll be there as quick as I can."

"I hear the siren. The ambulance is here. I'll call you when I know more."

"Sally?"

"Yes?"

"I love you."

Sally's husky voice deepened. "Nothing's going to happen to me. And I love you, too."

Margo hung up the phone and stared blankly at the TV. Her eyes burned. Her throat squeezed closed. Fighting tears, she dragged a hand through her hair, trying not to panic. Sally was one of the most important people in her life. Yes, she was her boss, but she was also her friend, a mentor, a sounding board. And Sally was tough. Sally was a legend. She'd be fine.

She had to be fine.

MAX RUSSO HADN'T EVEN WOKEN UP PROPERLY WHEN his agent, Howard Levering, called, wanting to get Max's thoughts on upcoming projects.

Yawning, Max poured a cup of coffee and struggled to focus even as Howard bemoaned the fact that Max hadn't read any of the scripts he'd sent him. Howard was still going on when Max carried the coffee into the living room and dropped onto the low leather couch.

"You have a name now," Howard said. "You're a hot commodity. You can't let these opportunities pass. This is what you've been working for your entire career. The best roles, significant money. Respect. This is not the time to—".

"Howard," Max interrupted, patience wearing thin. "I'm going to look at them, I'm just not going to do it today, or probably this week. Give me a week—"

"Everyone's waiting to hear back from you. I can't keep making excuses."

"I only got back a day ago. I've been working nonstop this year."

"Because people want you *now*."

Max bit back his smart-ass response. Howard was a good person, and he'd done a lot for Max's career but Max couldn't even think about another job, not until he got through his mail, caught up with friends, and slept in his own bed for more than a night. "Maybe right now I wouldn't mind missing out on a few things. I have been working hard, steadily, for years. I'm grateful for the work, but I only just got back home and I need a few days not to think, and not to make decisions. But I will look at the scripts. Tell me the ones you like best and I'll move those to the top."

"Feature films with the futuristic drama produced by the Sherridan brothers at the very top. In fact, I thought you'd already looked at that one. That's huge."

"*Space Ranger*? Come on."

"It's what you're doing already, but just in the future."

Being a rancher on *Big Sky* was nothing like playing futuristic law enforcement. "I'm not a sci-fi guy."

"Sigourney Weaver wasn't a sci-fi girl but she made it work and look what it did for her career."

"I thought you just said my career is fine. That I'm at a point in my career where I can pick my projects."

"You could *almost* pick your projects. You still have to be smart. You can't afford to slack off now. It's important you make the right choices, it's important you follow up

Big Sky with something appropriately interesting. Layered and complex. Show more of you. People want to see you."

"When is the *Space Ranger* shoot?"

"They're starting early November but understand you wouldn't be free until later in the month. But you still have to audition. They want you to read with Courtney."

Max groaned inwardly. Courtney Vale was the new bright young thing Hollywood was enamored with. He'd heard she was a bit of a diva, believing all her own press. "I don't know if that's the right role for me," Max said, breaking off to glance at the text vibrating on his phone. Call me, his dad texted. Max ignored the text, concentrating on the conversation with Howard. "Let me have a look at the scripts and we'll talk next week, okay?"

"You can't get comfortable," Howard replied. "Now is the time to be proactive."

"I understand."

Max's phone vibrated again. It's about Sally, his dad texted.

"And you don't have the Remington role yet," Howard added. "They're just interested. Right?"

"Got it."

She's in the hospital, came the next text. Sounds serious.

Max couldn't focus anymore. "Howard, I'll call you Monday."

He ended the call with Howard and immediately phoned his dad. "What's this about Sally?" Max asked, when his dad answered.

"She was hospitalized last night. Had a heart attack. Melinda called just a few minutes ago with the news, and I figured you'd want to know right away."

Melinda Rojas had been his dad's last girlfriend, a sweet hardworking nurse at Memorial Hospital in Paso Robles. Her late husband had been a truck driver and died in an accident, leaving her to raise their five kids. Max's dad liked Melinda and appreciated her cooking, but didn't deal well with kids and broke up with her for Allison, a self-taught horticulturist who grew strawberries and marijuana in Watsonville. His dad had moved up to Watsonville a couple years ago and Max hadn't been back to the Central Coast since.

"I didn't realize Melinda knew you'd been involved with Sally."

"She saw the photo of you and Sally at your Yale graduation, and I filled in the missing pieces. Melinda called me because she felt funny calling you, now that you're a big star and all."

"Not a big star, Dad."

"You must make plenty of money, though, if you can afford a seven-million-dollar condo in New York."

"How did you know?"

"Allison follows you, and then looked it up online. Real estate is a public record."

Max glanced out his living room window at the view of the Hudson River, with skyscrapers framing one side. It was just after nine, still early enough to fly out if he acted soon. He should go. He needed to go. He needed to thank her, properly, for all she'd done for him.

"So Sally's at Memorial?" Max asked.

"Yes."

"You're going to call her?"

"Yeah." Max wasn't about to tell his dad he was going to go visit Sally. His dad would hit him up for money, ask for another loan, the very same things that made Sally walk away from him. From them. "Thanks, Dad. Appreciate the heads-up."